T0323878

LEILANI

LM DEWALT

central
avenue
PUBLISHING

2023

Copyright © 2023 LM DeWalt
Cover and internal design © 2023 Central Avenue Marketing Ltd.
Cover Photography: © CanStockPhoto: Deklofenak

All rights reserved. No part of this book may be used or reproduced in any
manner whatsoever without written permission from the author except in the
case of brief quotations embodied in critical articles and reviews.

This is a work of fiction. Names, characters, places and incidents either
are the product of the author's imagination or are used fictitiously and any
resemblance to actual persons, living or dead, business establishments, events
or locales is entirely coincidental.

Published by Central Avenue, an imprint of
Central Avenue Marketing Ltd.

www.centralavenuepublishing.com

LEILANI

Trade Paperback: 978-1-77168-227-5
EPUB: 978-1-77168-000-4

Published in Canada
Printed in United States of America

1. YOUNG ADULT FICTION / Romance - Paranormal
2. YOUNG ADULT FICTION / Vampires

For my mom, Carla Monteverde, my mother-in-law, Linda DeWalt,
and my father-in-law, James DeWalt, Sr.
For all the love and support you've shown me—thank you.

❧ ONE ❧

Why do I have to take them?" Jose Luis hopped across the wooden floor on one foot and plopped onto the plush sofa. "It's only a movie."

"Because it's not safe, that's why! You can't be wandering the city by yourself," I said as I picked his casted foot up off the coffee table and propped it on a throw pillow. "And where are your crutches?"

Christian laughed as he leaned against the doorway watching us. He exchanged an amused look with Jose Luis. I threw my arms up in defeat. "Fine. Have it your way."

"Thank you," Jose Luis smiled broadly. "I'm going with friends, and I would feel weird, you know."

"Wait a minute," I crossed my arms. "I didn't say you didn't have to take any. You are still taking one. I'll make sure he keeps his distance."

"But…"

"That's final. It's either that, or Christian and I go with you," I said with a smug smile.

"Ok, ok. One bodyguard then. But I don't have to like it." His English was definitely improving.

Christian walked over and wrapped his arms around my waist. "You're doing the right thing," he whispered in my ear.

"He doesn't seem to think so," I said and leaned away to look at his perfect face. *I say we still follow him…*

"Hey! I can hear you, remember?" Jose Luis threw the remote on the coffee table and pouted.

"Oh, right. I forgot," I said with a laugh. I couldn't stay mad at either one of them for more than a few minutes.

With Melinda, her sister Ryanne, and some of the hunters still running around Lima, I wasn't taking any chances. Christian and I could take care of ourselves, but Jose Luis, being human, though he did possess some powers, needed the extra protection. He was still healing from his wounds after being thrown off the top of the cross on the mountain, and I wasn't willing to take any more chances with his life. Before Aaron's great-grandfather, Aloysius, left for Italy with Fiore, he made sure he left us with his apartment, a car, and bodyguards to protect us. I was taking full advantage of it.

The thought of Aaron's name turned my stomach into knots. Attempting to kill Maia, my begrudging sister, was one of the most difficult things I'd ever had to do, and I'd lost my family because of it. Kalia and Aaron had taken her in, after she told them she was terminally ill, turned her, and treated her as their daughter. That never changed for them. I could still picture the crazed look in Kalia's eyes as Aaron held her, keeping her from running at me, after I slashed Maia's throat. The horror of it was that I had meant to cut her head off, but Kalia pushed me aside, causing only a long gash from my sword.

"Please don't do this, Lily," Christian said, leaning his chin on the top of my head. "You didn't have much of a choice in the matter. She tried to kill both of us. I'm sure, in time, we'll be able to get through to Kalia."

"I hope you're right," I took a deep breath and pushed away from him. "Jose Luis, are you hungry?"

He turned worried eyes to Christian before answering. "No, just thirsty. Inca Kola would be good."

Being a vampire for more than ninety years meant I was not exactly a good cook. I understood his concern, but Carmela, Aloysius's housekeeper, had left some meals already prepared in the freezer for Jose Luis. All I had to do was push some buttons on the microwave we had bought. "I'll get it," Christian said and headed to the kitchen.

"And I'll go get your crutches," I narrowed my eyes at Jose Luis. "I don't know why you refuse to use them." He laughed and turned on the television, his way of dismissing me.

Bringing a human boy into our lives had never been something I'd considered in the past, but I wouldn't change our decision for anything. Jose Luis, an orphaned fifteen-year-old, had been sent to kill Christian and me. A group of vampire hunters had taken him in when his parents died in an accident, and with the promise of feeding and supporting him, was using him for his talents. They were also using this newest and youngest member of their pack to do their dirty work while they sat back and kept their manicured nails clean. With Kalia and Aaron not speaking to me, it seemed our best option was to stay in Peru, which was probably best for Jose Luis anyway. As soon as he was well enough, I wanted to hire private tutors so he could finish his schooling.

"What time did he say he's going?" I asked Christian as he walked into Jose Luis's bedroom. I was just pulling the covers over his bed and fluffing his pillows. His crutches lay untouched on the floor by his dresser.

"Since when did you become such a mother?" He smiled, showing he was not trying to be sarcastic. My fuse had been a little short lately.

"I am acting like that, aren't I?" I grabbed the crutches in one hand, a dirty glass in the other.

"Believe me, I like it," He picked up the sneaker in the doorway and tossed it to where its mate lay across the room. "I actually feel like a father myself."

"What if someone decides to claim him? That really scares me. Or what if he's killed because of us?" I leaned on the crutches.

"Neither of us is going to allow that to happen. Anyway, he's going to a nine o'clock show. His friends are meeting him there, so he'll be riding with Giovanni. Is that ok?" he asked.

Giovanni, the leader of the bodyguards Aloysius had loaned us before he left, was the best choice to accompany Jose Luis. Though I hadn't known him for long, I trusted him.

"That's good. Just make sure he's replaced by someone, maybe Margarita. I don't want the front door unattended. Maybe we should have another guard already in place at the theater, just in case."

"Let's not overdo it. We agreed to one. He'll be fine, and besides, that gives us some time alone." He winked at me. I smiled to ease his mind and followed him to the living room.

That was something to look forward to. We hadn't been alone since we were married. The trip to Lima was supposed to be our honeymoon, a gift from Aaron, Kalia, and Fiore. But before we knew it, it had been one problem after another and all our vampire friends were here to help us in yet another battle that had nothing to do with them. That battle had not turned out well. We had managed to get Jose Luis back but lost everything else in the process.

"Your cell phone is charged. Anything at all happens, you call us. What Giovanni says goes, you hear me?" I asked as Jose Luis put his jacket on. He nodded.

"I will be fine. I am sure I'm the only poor kid running around Lima with a bodyguard."

"Believe me, Jose Luis. We don't like it much either but it's for the best. Just as soon as things settle down again, we can live normally," Christian assured him.

"I am sorry to give you this news, but neither one of you is normal." Jose Luis laughed.

"You know what he means," I lightly smacked his back, trying not to knock him over. "Anything at all out of the ordinary, you call."

"Ok, ok. I promise." He kissed my cheek and waved to Christian. He hobbled out the door to meet Giovanni. I saw he'd already been replaced by Margarita, who sat in her chair paging through a magazine. She raised her head and nodded a greeting. I nodded in return and closed the door.

"You're uncomfortable with the whole bodyguard thing, aren't you?" Christian beckoned me to the sofa.

"It's just really weird. I spent so many years alone, talking to people only when I absolutely had to, and now, I'm surrounded. I feel like we have no privacy." I laid my head back and sighed. "I'm married with a child, too."

He laughed and took my hand. "It sure does feel like we have a child, and I like it. He's a good kid."

"I know he is," I turned my head to look at him. "I just hope we can keep him that way. And I wish he would stop thinking of himself as poor."

"That's probably going to take a little time for him to get used to, considering where he came from."

"Yeah, I guess you're right."

A couple of hours later, we lay in each other's arms under the covers and sighed.

"How perfect is this?" Christian said as he snuggled me closer.

"It is, isn't it? I wish it could be like this all the time," I sighed.

"Yeah, but you know," He sat up a bit and pushed me away so that he could look into my eyes. "Our relationship was forbidden in the beginning and no matter what we did to stay away from each other, it never worked. We are magnets attracted to each other, no matter what. I think all the difficulties we face only make our love for each other stronger. It just wouldn't be the same without the chaos."

"Yeah, I guess you're right," I said and climbed on top of him. "I can show you some chaos right now."

He smiled and nibbled my bottom lip. "I'd definitely like to see the kind of chaos you have in mind."

Once we were back in the living room, I was back in the real world and checking my phone every few minutes. Christian kept laughing at me but wasn't doing a great job of masking the worry in his eyes. A little after midnight, the front door was pushed open and Giovanni rushed in, Jose Luis in his arms. Margarita ran in behind him, leaving her post unattended. She carried his crutches under her arm.

"What the hell happened?" I yelled as Giovanni gingerly set Jose Luis down on the sofa.

"I am ok," Jose Luis assured us before Giovanni could answer.

Giovanni took the crutches from Margarita and signaled for her to return to her post outside the door before turning to face us. "When we were coming out of the theater and into the lobby, someone fired a shot. People started running and screaming. It was total chaos. Jose Luis got knocked down to the floor and someone landed on top of him. I searched for whoever fired the shot but didn't see anyone with a gun."

I ran to sit at Jose Luis's side. A black and blue bump was already visible on his forehead. "I am ok, really," he assured me. "A girl tripped and knocked me down. I hit my head on the bar where they sell the food."

"You left him alone?" I turned a furious gaze to Giovanni.

"He was down and covered. I took that opportunity to look for the shooter," Giovanni argued, his shoulders squared, his posture confident. I knew he was the best we had. "Whoever fired that shot must have run back out in all the commotion."

"Could it have been a random robbery?" Christian asked.

"I highly doubt it," Giovanni said. "I think I sensed another vampire in the lobby when we first left the theater, but only for a moment."

"Were the police involved?" Christian asked.

"Of course not, at least not while we were still there. I took Jose Luis back into the theater and exited through the emergency door on the side. There was so much commotion in the lobby, I don't think anyone even noticed," Giovanni explained.

"You honestly don't think it was a robbery?" I was grasping at straws.

"I'm sorry but no. Jose Luis was definitely the target. The bullet hit the wall behind him. Had someone not noticed the gun and screamed, causing chaos before the gun was even fired, it would have hit him."

"Thank God for the girl," I sighed.

⤜ TWO ⤛

"D o you think we do what we do just to ruin your image?" I asked Jose Luis as I set his glass of Inca Kola on the coffee table. He looked at me with no expression on his bruised face.

"Lily, maybe we should just let him rest a while," Christian suggested. His tender look calmed me down, just a bit.

"He just got up," I argued and went to open the living room curtains, letting sunlight flood the white room. Christian shielded his eyes. "I want him to understand that this is not a game. I'm not exactly ecstatic about having extra people around me all the time either but, I'm not arguing about it!"

As hard as they tried to conceal their laughter, they were unsuccessful, and I glared at both of them. "I'm sorry…I'm sorry," Jose Luis managed between laughs. "I will be serious now." But he couldn't stop laughing. I huffed, making him and Christian laugh so hard they held their stomachs.

"Fine," I threw my arms up in defeat again. "Whatever. You think it's funny that I'm all motherly? Go ahead and laugh, suit yourselves. You can take care of yourselves, too. I'm going to take a bodyguard and go shopping. We are almost out of people food."

"People food? As opposed to what?" Christian asked.

The laughter died down only after I slammed the bedroom door. Once alone, I smiled. The truth was that I loved seeing Christian so happy. He'd endured so much confusion, sadness, and actual torture since he met me. He was quickly becoming a father figure to Jose Luis and a protector to me, something I hadn't had since my own father more than ninety years ago.

"Lily?" Christian poked his head into the room. "Why don't you make a list for Carmela, just this once? We can spend some time with Jose Luis; maybe get him to open up a little."

"That might be a good idea. I don't much feel like fighting crowds right now anyway." Aloysius had been kind enough to not only leave us his apartment, but also his housekeeper. Though I had been more than a little reluctant to be in her presence in the past, since she is a human who not only knows about vampires but also works for one, I felt more comfortable with her since she had supplied us with weapons. She never asked questions and she never judged, no matter what she was asked to do. Jose Luis also felt comfortable with her and that was important. I pulled out my cell, dictated a shopping list to Carmela, and then followed Christian out to the living room. We sat on the chairs opposite him and regarded him expectantly.

Jose Luis sat on the sofa paging through a comic book. He threw it onto the coffee table, looking at us through narrowed eyes. "What did I do now?"

Christian laughed and glanced at me. "Nothing. We just want to chat," I said.

"You never just want to chat. You want to know something." He sat up straighter, waiting.

Christian nodded for me to continue. "We just want to know what happened last night. What did you see and hear? Did you recognize anybody?"

He shook his head, his dark hair falling in his eyes. "I did not see anyone I knew, except my friends, of course. We were leaving the cinema, all of us in a line, and people started screaming and running. A girl was pushed into me, and we fell. All I could see was her pretty face. Then there was a very loud boom." He blushed and Christian's eyes lit up with amusement.

"That's it? You don't remember anything else?" I insisted.

"I hit my head on the snack thing. People were really screaming. It was so loud. Then it got quiet, and the girl got off me, stood up. She gave me her hand to help me up. Then Giovanni came and picked me up and took me back into the cinema, to another door, and we went out to the street. When we drove past the front, the police were just getting there," he explained.

"You sensed nothing?"

He folded his arms over his chest and shook his head. "No. I was…" He looked at me and then at Christian. "I was sitting with that girl, the one that fell on me. I was not even watching the movie."

"You were on a date?" I yelled. Christian laughed. I ignored him.

"Yes. And it was not my first date, either."

"You're too young for that." I crossed my arms over my chest.

"Lily, he's fifteen. He's not a child, but that's not the issue here," Christian said noticing my displeasure. "Someone was there to shoot him. That's what we need to focus on." He turned to look at Jose Luis. "I know you don't like this any more than we do, but from now on you will have more than one bodyguard whenever you go out."

"Why? Other kids my age don't run around the city with bodyguards." Jose Luis turned on the sofa and put both feet on the floor.

"Other kids your age aren't constant targets, either. It's only for your own safety," I said. "I don't think the hunters want you back. I think they want you dead. You don't want to die, do you?"

He looked at both us, his face still expressionless. "No. So why can't we leave here, go to America?"

A lump formed in my throat at the thought of no longer having a home with Kalia and Aaron. Christian took my hand and squeezed it. I couldn't speak and he knew it.

"That's not an option right now. We don't have a home there anymore," he explained.

"So, we can get a new one," Jose Luis offered.

"It's not that simple. We have things to finish here. If we don't end this here and now, they will only follow us and find us no matter where we go. When we know we're safe, and only then, we can think about where we want to settle down more permanently. So, for now, this is home." Christian looked at me and I nodded, assuring him I was fine.

"Right now, I would like to talk about what you want," I sat at the foot of the sofa and placed his casted foot on my lap. Focusing only on his recovery, the question of whether or not he wanted to stay with us had been left un-asked. "We want to know what you want to happen."

"I don't understand what you are asking." He looked at Christian.

"I think what she's trying to say is that we want to know if you want to stay with us from now on or if there someone else you want to live with, maybe a relative somewhere? Maybe a family friend you'd rather live with?"

Jose Luis's eyes grew wide. He pushed the hair out of his eyes and looked at me with sadness. "No. There is no one. I thought you knew what I wanted."

"We hoped but we didn't know for sure. I'd feel better if you told us." I held my breath, nervous about his response.

"I want to stay with you. There is no one else, but if there was, I would still want to stay with you." His eyes watered and he blinked against the coming tears.

"We are very happy to hear that. That's what Christian and I wanted," I looked at Christian who looked as confused as I felt over Jose Luis's tears. I turned back to Jose Luis as he wiped his eyes with the corner of his blanket. "If that's what you want, then why are you crying?"

"I am sorry, it's just that…" he looked away and focused on the blanket on his lap, pulling at a loose thread. "I feel very lucky but also very sad."

"Why sad?" Christian asked, moving to kneel in front of us.

"Because my sister was not as lucky as me."

"I'm sorry, what?"

"My sister." He raised his face and met my eyes. "My sister is lost."

With my mouth hanging open, I looked at Christian. He shrugged.

"What sister?" I asked, taking Jose Luis's hand so he would not unravel the blanket.

"Her name is Leilani. She would be nine now, if she is alive."

"When is the last time you saw her?" Christian asked.

"She was four, I think. She walked to the store to buy a candy because she had a coin from the mouse, Pepe…she lost a tooth. Anyway, she did not come back." Jose Luis wiped his eyes again.

"So, you were both living with the hunters?" I asked. He nodded. "What did the police say?"

"They did not want to talk to the police. Arturo, the man we lived with, said they could not help. He said they would take us away from him if they knew he was not our father, so we looked for her in groups, for days. I made signs with her picture and put them on trees. It did not help."

I looked at Christian. He folded his arms over his chest, his anger obvious. I thought asking about the police would have been a stupid question, since that is what most people would have done in that situation, but I should've known better. These were the hunters we were talking about. Arturo, the human leader of the so-called vampire hunters, from what I had witnessed so far, was not especially caring. Why would he do the logical thing?

"Maybe they were trying to hide something?" Christian answered my thought.

"Like what? She was just a little girl." I turned to face Jose Luis again. "Can you tell us about her? What was Leilani like?"

Jose Luis's skin changed from deep golden tan to something with a sickly grayish hue within seconds. His fingers pulled at the thread on the blanket again before shoving it off his lap and onto the floor. He raised his watery eyes to me as he stood. "I'm going to get sick," he said before hopping on one foot down the hall toward the bathroom.

∽ THREE ∽

Jose Luis?" I knocked on the bathroom door a few minutes later. "Are you ok?" The door opened and I jumped back.

"I am sorry. I don't know what happened," Jose Luis explained, still holding a hand towel. His face lost all signs of his deep tan and his bottom lip shook.

"It's ok. You don't have to talk about Leilani if you're not ready. We'll have plenty of time for that later."

"But I am ready. I have to talk about her. What if she is still alive?" He threw the towel onto the sink and started down the hall. I followed without saying anything else.

When we reached the living room, Christian looked at me. I nodded, smiling to let him know Jose Luis was ok, at least for the moment. We stood until Jose Luis sat on the sofa and wrapped the blanket around his legs. He looked ready to talk.

"Leilani was such a smart little girl. She was born smart. She did everything early, got her first tooth when she was only four months, said *mamá* when she was six months old. She never crawled, just walked and ran. My mother was so proud of her, her little angel. We were all proud.

"She got to start school a year early too. She got the best grades in her class, but she was always in trouble. Her teacher sent letters to our house almost every day."

"How was she always in trouble? She sounds perfect," Christian said, leaning forward, elbows on his knees.

"Something was not right with Leilani since the beginning. My father knew it. My mother knew it and tried to hide it." He took a sip of his soda, looking into the glass as if it held the answers he needed.

"Why would your mother try to hide it?" I asked.

"My mother was the witch in our family. My father knew when he married her, of course, but he didn't want anybody else to know. He was afraid of how people would act around her, of how people would treat her. I got some of her powers. We could only use our powers only in the house, never in public. We started to notice things with Leilani when she was still a baby.

"One day, when she was about six months old, she was crying in her crib. My father was gone to work already and my mother was helping me finish my math lesson before I went to school.

"The baby is crying," I said.

"I know. I hear her. She will be ok until we are finished. She is probably just hungry," my mother said. We went back to the lesson and Leilani cried harder for a few more minutes. I was putting my books in my bag when it got very quiet. My mother and I looked at each other. I thought maybe she went back to sleep but then I smelled it, the smoke. So did my mother because she ran to her bedroom. I was right behind her. The curtain on the window by Leilani's crib was on fire. My mother pulled her out of the crib, and I ran to the kitchen for a pot of water. Leilani had a big smile on her face, like it amused her, and maybe it did. She was too young to know fire as a dangerous thing that could have hurt her, all of us. That was the first time. More fires started after that and it got hard to hide them from my father. It was hard to replace the things Leilani destroyed. We did not have much money and the fires happened every time Leilani was angry."

"You think she was starting the fires?" I asked.

"I knew she was doing it. When she wanted something and did not get it, she would cry. Every time she cried, something burned. She accidentally burned her favorite doll one time, so she cried even harder. More toys burned. When she was like that, whatever she looked at burned. I was afraid she would look at me, or my mother, or my father. I think she knew she was doing it and refused to look at any of us. Because of the fires, my mother always tried to make her happy. She let her do whatever she wanted. Anything was better than having things burning all the time and it was easier to keep my father from worrying."

"Did your father ever find out?"

"Yes. I heard him and my mother talking about it one time when they thought I was sleeping. My mother could not replace the more expensive things Leilani burned. She made excuses at first but then she didn't know what else to say. That was the only time they talked about it, though. My father loved my mother very much, but he did not love the magic. I think it was easier for him to pretend it did not happen, that it wasn't real. He knew I could do things and I think he thought, or hoped, that it would skip Leilani." He looked at our faces for a reaction. We both stayed calm, or at least, we tried. I just wanted to keep him talking, now that he was finally opening up.

"You've spent a lot of time with the witches and hunters. Did you ever see any of them do something like that?" I asked.

"No. They have to do spells they get from a book. None of them can start fire like that."

"Was Leilani ever able to control it?" Christian asked.

Jose Luis shook his head. "She was not allowed to practice. It was too dangerous. It would just happen when she was angry and she would destroy whatever was near her, even her own things. She hated it. When she did it at school, the teachers told my mother that she was playing with matches. My mother did not argue with them. After a while, when she got angry at school, she would just leave the school and run home. She got in trouble a lot for that too."

"Is it possible that someone else knew about it? Is it possible she was taken for that reason?" I looked from Jose Luis to Christian. Christian raised his eyebrows.

"I never thought of that," Jose Luis said and stared into his glass again. "Do you think that could be it?"

"We shouldn't rule anything out when it comes to the hunters. If they have her, they wanted her for a reason."

"Maybe. But why separate us if they have both of us? She is my sister. I should be the one taking care of her."

"That part I don't know," I stood and walked to the window, looking out at the familiar cloud of smog covering the upper floors of the skyscrapers. "We need to start looking for her."

"Do you have a picture of her?" Christian asked.

"I have some pictures, but they are with my things, at Arturo's house."

"Right," I returned to the sofa. "I forgot about your things. Since we bought you clothes, I forgot you still have other things you might want. We'll have to figure out a way to get them."

"I could go," Christian volunteered.

"That is out of the question," I snapped, wishing I could take the words back as soon as they left my mouth. I had to stop treating Christian like a human.

"Arturo does go to work. He is out of the house every morning and comes back late in the afternoon," Jose Luis said before Christian had a chance to argue with me.

"That helps a lot. But what about the others?" I asked.

"Some of them work but some are there all day. Maybe we can get them to leave somehow."

"Like create a distraction?" Christian asked.

"That sounds like a good idea. We will have to think of something." Getting them all off the mountain long enough to get his things and get out of there was going to take some careful planning.

"I will have to go too. Christian will not know what is mine," Jose Luis said.

"I was afraid of that," I looked at Christian. He nodded in agreement. "Then that means we have to wait until your cast comes off."

"Too bad Aloysius isn't here. He could just materialize there and get right out." Christian smiled, no doubt remembering the experience of traveling that way with Aloysius the night of the battle on the mountain.

The landline in the apartment rang making us jump. That phone never rang. "I'll get it." I jumped up and ran to the kitchen. Christian was picking up a lot of Spanish but not enough to answer the telephone quite yet.

"*Aló*," I said into the receiver. A welcome voice greeted me in English on the other end. The anxiety I felt disappeared. "Fiore! It's so good to hear your voice."

"What did she say?" Christian asked as I walked back into the living room and sat down next to Jose Luis. He looked calmer now and I wanted to keep it that way for as long as possible.

"She said that they will be home tomorrow night. She also said that you and I are going away for a few days and that Aloysius won't take no for an answer," I explained trying to gauge Jose Luis's reaction.

"Yes, go. I am better now. You need some time alone," Jose Luis volunteered before Christian could say anything.

"I don't think this is the time to go on any kind of a trip. We have too much to do yet," I protested.

"That may be so but, like you said, we will have to wait until his cast comes off before we can get his things. That will be another couple of weeks yet," Christian explained. "Besides, Aloysius and Fiore will be here, plus all the bodyguards. No one will dare come near him while they are all with him."

"I understand that, but it just doesn't feel right. They will all be stuck here while we are out having fun. It just doesn't seem fair."

"Two or three days are nothing. Besides, your honeymoon was ruined. I will be fine here. I will be surrounded by lots of protection." Jose Luis pushed the blanket off his lap and stood. "I am going to take a nap. Please say you will go."

I looked at his pleading eyes, the usual strands of his hair hanging in front of the right eye. How could I ever say no to that face? I nodded. "As long as you promise to call us every night before you go to sleep and to listen to Aloysius and Fiore."

"I promise," He threw his arms around my neck, and I squeezed him gently against me. "Good. Now go pack."

"Yes, sir," Christian answered with a laugh.

✥ FOUR ✥

"A re you sure that's all you need?" Christian asked as we left our room with two suitcases in tow.

"It will be less than a week. I think I'm all set." I turned the light off and closed the door. Fiore and Aloysius met us in the living room a moment later. Jose Luis was just joining them with a glass of soda in his hand.

"Is that all you're taking?" Fiore raised her brows at me.

"Shorts, pants, shirts, underwear, and a bathing suit. What else is there?"

"Yeah, I have all the toiletries and the hairdryer in my suitcase," Christian added with a smile.

"Did you remember your camera?" Aloysius asked with his arm firmly around Fiore's waist as her face glowed with her smile.

"Yes, I did. I wish you would let us take a less conspicuous vehicle," I reminded him again.

"Nonsense. It's a three-hour drive. I want you to be comfortable." Aloysius grabbed my suitcase and headed toward the door with Fiore and Jose Luis following. As soon as we went through the door, Margarita, the guard stationed there, picked Jose Luis up in her arms and propped his crutches against the wall. Instead of protesting as I expected, he wrapped his arms around her neck and relaxed, letting her carry him.

"We'll see you down," Fiore summoned the elevator. "Trust me; you're going to love this."

"I do love what you're doing for us, believe me. I just don't think we need a limo. Any car would have been enough," I protested as we set our suitcases in the trunk.

"I understand how you feel but you will be more comfortable this way. Besides, the limo has bullet proof windows. The thing sits in a garage all the time. It was begging to be driven," Aloysius said. "There will be a car in front of you, and a car behind. You'll have five bodyguards with you. They won't bother you."

"You're too much, Aloysius, but thank you. For everything," Christian said as he patted Aloysius's back. He hugged Fiore and Jose Luis and then stepped into the car. I said my goodbyes as quickly as I could and got into the car. The last thing I wanted was to start crying in front of Jose Luis. Seeing blood running down my face would probably scare him even though he was fully aware of what we were.

"It's a really nice thing they're doing for us. Let's try to enjoy it," Christian wrapped his arms around me and leaned his face into my hair, inhaling deeply. "For the next few days, let's pretend this is our real honeymoon."

"That sounds like a great plan to me." I leaned into him and tried to erase my mind of all the trouble and the losses we'd experienced lately. They were right—we deserved a honeymoon. We had fought so hard to be together, met so many obstacles, and for every one we overcame, it seemed more were thrown our way. Since we had arrived in Peru, we had not spent more than an hour or two alone. A few days would do us good and would not cause any harm, at least not as far as Jose Luis was concerned. He would be safe in the hands of Fiore and Aloysius.

"You are very right. He couldn't be in better hands," Christian responded to my thoughts. "From this moment on, we will worry about nothing except each other, until we get back, at least."

"Agreed," I said and leaned to kiss his lips. "It's going to be gorgeous. Churín is perfect for us. We can relax in the hot springs all day if we want."

We settled into the ride and watched the scenery whiz past. The driver kept the tinted divider window up the whole time and gave us the privacy we craved but never voiced. For a while, I rested my head against Christian's shoulder and closed my eyes, getting as close to sleep as my vampire mind allowed, and daydreamed of the next few days we would spend alone, with the exception of the guards, of course. Every time I pictured something intimate, Christian sighed as if he was living the fantasies with me. And knowing his mind, he probably was.

"Stop that or you'll get yourself into trouble, driver or no driver," he warned with laughter in his voice.

"It doesn't matter," I said, lifting my head and gazing out the window. "I think we just arrived."

The limousine came to a complete stop on a dirt path in front of Aloysius's bungalow. The setting sun reflected off the windows, bouncing oranges and yellows off the shiny black vehicle. Before we could look around, the door to my side opened and a hand reached in to take mine and help me out of the car. The bodyguards who parked behind us already had our luggage on the small front porch that only fit two chairs and a little round table. The metal table contained a weathered, old-fashioned storm lamp.

"*Por aquí*," the vampire who helped me out of the car instructed. Christian and I followed him to the front door as he opened it and flipped on a light.

The little bungalow took my breath away. It was just one room, with a small bathroom off to the left, but it was cozy, warm, and clean. The fresh scent of orange cleaner filled my lungs. The main living area was decorated with country-style sofas surrounding a round, glass coffee table stacked with magazines. The windows were already opened, and the cream and maroon curtains blew gently in the breeze. The stone fireplace was the focal point of the room and was ready for use. Someone had stacked logs on either side and a box of matches lay on the mantle. A large mirror with an intricately sculpted silver frame hung above the mantle.

"If you move the table aside, the big sofa pulls out into a bed," Carlos, the guard who had escorted us in, informed us.

"Where will you be staying?" I asked, curious as to where the bodyguards were going to stay.

"There is another bungalow like this one just behind those trees," he said as he drew the curtains aside and pointed. The setting sun turned the trees to a golden color. "That's where we'll bathe and change our clothes. So, what would you like to do first?"

I looked at Christian and he shrugged. "Well, I don't know. It was a long ride. I wouldn't mind going to one of the baths," I said, hoping they weren't all going in with us.

"Don't worry. We will be outside the water," Carlos answered my thought with a smile.

"Great. Can you give us a moment to change please?" I started toward my suitcase that was already on the bench in the corner of the room, neatly placed next to Christian's. Carlos nodded and left without another word.

"Are they seriously going to be watching our every move the whole time we're here?" Christian asked, already pulling his trunks up and tying the drawstring.

"I sure hope not. I'm sure we can convince them to leave us alone, some-how." I slipped into my bikini bottom and held the top up to my chest. "Can you help me with this?"

"Do I really have to fasten it? You look great in just the bottom." He slipped the hook into the opening anyway, kissing my shoulder before closing the strap across my back.

"You wouldn't want *them* to get an eyeful, would you?" I grabbed the beach towels and threw one to him. He caught it without taking his eyes off me.

"I guess you're right. You look absolutely gorgeous in black. It makes your skin look like porcelain." He grabbed my hand, and we walked out the door.

The spring we would be enjoying tonight was located behind the bungalow. Lush trees and shrubs surrounded the whole property, so I was not worried about strangers finding us. As we neared the spring, which was circular in shape and had cement steps leading into it, I saw that the four guards had already positioned themselves, one on each side, facing the tree line. At least they wouldn't be watching.

Christian stepped in first, taking my hand to help me down. The steps were slicker than I had anticipated, and I was grateful he had a hold of my hand. The temperature of the water made steam float across the surface, moving as if it had a life of its own. My skin tingled and I sighed, finally starting to feel relaxed. I didn't like the fact that we needed guards surrounding us, but I knew we had no choice at the moment. At least now I knew how Jose Luis felt.

We made our way into the middle going deeper with each step until the steamy water covered our shoulders. Christian pointed to the bench carved out in the stone interior and we waded over to it and sat down, leaning against the warm rock, our legs floating in front of us. "This is wonderful."

"It is. Wouldn't it be great if we lived here?" Christian asked. "It feels like we're the only ones here, even with them standing there." One of the guards chuckled. Which one, I couldn't tell since I couldn't see their faces. It was definitely one of the four men.

"We have plenty more to see yet. We can leave the bungalow tomorrow and explore. I've heard there are some thermal baths that are actually inside caves." I pushed off the bench and dunked my head under water, pushing my hair back as I came up. Christian followed me to the center, standing in front of me and wrapping his arms around my waist.

"When is the last time I told you that I love you with all my heart and soul?" he asked as he planted nibbling kisses down my wet neck.

"Just this morning, I think," I whispered a bit out of breath already. I wrapped my arms around his neck and circled his waist with my legs. "You can say that as many times as you want though. I can never get enough of it."

His moist lips moved across my chin, inching their way to my parted lips. As soon as they touched, a chill ran through my body despite the warmth of the water. My breath came faster as he parted my lips with his tongue. I closed my eyes but opened them again, looking outside the bath at the four figures surrounding us. I pulled away from Christian's eager mouth. "Um, guys?"

"Yes?" Mariana, the only female guard who came on the trip, answered. I think that's the first time I'd heard her voice. Though she was very beautiful, with long dark hair and an olive complexion that hadn't changed when she was turned, she was very quiet. She just did as she was told. From what we'd heard, she had been working for Aloysius almost as long as he'd been a vampire.

"Would you mind moving a few more feet away from us?" I asked. Christian's eyes beamed.

"Uh, sure." All four moved forward toward the trees, never turning to look at us.

"Now where were we?" I said as I turned back to Christian.

"Right about here," he said in a breathless voice as his lips connected to mine again. His hands traveled up my spine, grasping with more roughness than he had ever shown my body. I clung to his body, tightening my legs around him. His mouth left mine and I grabbed the back of his head and pulled him back.

"Oh, God. It's been way too long," I panted as I parted his lips with my tongue this time, tasting the warmth and sweetness of his mouth. His hands made their way up my spine again, this time settling on the back of my neck as he pushed his body against me even harder, making it impossible to think, let alone breathe.

He pulled away from my mouth, much to my disappointment, at least until I felt his lips on my neck again, his teeth nipping at the tender flesh. His fingers undid the clasps on my top, and he moved his mouth down the front, tossing the top out of sight. I threw my head back and a moan escaped my parted lips. Christian laughed but never took his mouth from my sensitive flesh. "Now. Please, Christian?" I begged in ragged gasps.

He lifted his face to look into my eyes, starting the frenzy of butterfly wings in my stomach. "What about them?" He motioned with his head toward the guards.

"Who cares about them? I want you now." I pushed his head back down. He moaned before continuing to bring me pleasure like only he could.

✦ Five ✦

Christian carried me, cradled in his arms, from the bath to the bungalow with Mariana, the only female guard, following and carrying my discarded bathing suit. She dropped it at the front door before she signaled for the other guards to follow and position themselves around the building. I was pleased that they had the respect to keep their distance while I was in this state. We started in the bath continued in the bungalow. As minutes turned into hours, all the grief and desperation from the past months melted away with each caress, with each kiss, with each moan, and gasp escaping our lips.

It wasn't until early afternoon the next day that we emerged fully dressed and ready to explore our surroundings. Neither of us could wipe the smiles off our faces, but the guards pretended not to notice. They nodded to us and continued on their way toward the road. I was feeling more comfortable with their presence, until Mariana appeared alone. "Where to?" she asked. She had braided her long dark hair and dressed in cargo pants and hiking boots. A walkie-talkie hung from her belt, as did her pistol.

"Where are the others going?" Christian asked, grasping my hand a little tighter as if protecting me from her narrowed stare.

"I sent them to survey the area. We need to make sure no one suspicious is in the town. They will meet us wherever you want to go," she advised, motioning for us to follow her to the edge of the property and toward the dirt road.

"I thought they were supposed to stay with us." We walked slowly behind her, looking around for any signs of their return.

"Aloysius said we should make sure the town is clear first. We didn't have a chance to do that when we first arrived, so they are going there now. I thought you would be in there longer." She motioned to the bungalow with her head.

My eyes dropped to the ground but a smile at the memory of the hours we spent lost in our love spread across my face. "We were just resting," I lied, not sure why.

"Oh, ok," Her face betrayed no emotion. "I will call them when we get there. You still have me to protect you."

I nodded as we followed her onto the path that wound around the mountain just above the town of Churín. As we descended, Mariana leading and Christian still tightly grasping my hand, we looked around. A valley spread out below, intersected by a river. Houses dotted the river's shore here and there. Though the scenery was breathtaking, uneasiness settled in the pit of my stomach. I wanted to communicate my feelings to Christian, but Mariana would most likely hear my thoughts. Christian looked at me and nodded. I had no need to tell him how I felt. He knew and he felt it too.

Once we reached the bottom of the mountain, we followed another path for a short distance into the town. The main road through it was paved but narrow. Small businesses lined both sides of the street and people carried baskets loaded with fresh bread, fruit, and vegetables as they strolled past us. No one seemed to be in a hurry. They looked at us as we passed and some pointed, but I heard no incriminating comments from either lips or minds. Mariana scanned the area as we walked with her now behind us, but her calm face showed no concern.

"Are you calling the others?" I paused to look at her. She reached for her walkie-talkie but stopped with her hand in midair.

"No need. Carlos is right there." She pointed to the vampire walking out of the *panadería* with a bundle in his arms.

"What is he doing buying food?" Christian asked.

"For Tomas, your driver. He's human." Mariana answered.

"Really? How did I not notice that?" I asked, pausing with the rest to wait for Carlos to join us.

"You have a soundproof barrier in the limo, along with bulletproof windows," she informed us. She took the bundle from Carlos as he neared then gave him instructions. "Go with them. I have something I have to do. I'll find you." Carlos nodded and took his place behind us.

"Where are the other two?" I asked, watching Mariana walk away toward the road leading back up the mountain. I wondered what she could possibly have to do but didn't voice it. Aloysius must have given her instructions and I had to try not to question them.

"They are making sure the cave is safe and clear of people. We knew you wanted to go there today." He pointed to the end of the block. "It's that way, if you're ready."

We both nodded and walked in the direction he signaled. The afternoon was warm but cloudy. A gentle breeze blew my hair around my face and caressed the bare skin on my legs as gently as the touch of Christian's fingers.

People walked around town shopping, smiling, and deep in conversation. There was no way not to relax in their presence. They all looked happy. It was going to be difficult to feed and I knew we would need to do that soon. Christian had not fed in days and, being a newborn still, he could not go much longer without blood.

"It's right through there." Carlos pointed to a hill with an opening dark enough to look like it was painted in black. A sign that read, "Closed for Cleaning", hung on a post just next to Mauricio, one of the guards. Vicente, the other guard Aloysius sent, stood on the other side of the opening.

"We checked it already. It's safe to enter," Mauricio announced as we approached.

"Is that your sign?" I asked, surprised at the simplicity of their evacuation plan. Both vampires nodded with satisfied smiles.

"Go on in. I will stay out here too," Carlos said as he walked a few paces away from the opening to face the dirt path. I nodded a thank you and grabbed Christian's hand, leading him into the cave.

It was dark, except for the soft orange glow of the wall sconces someone had already lit. Despite the glowing light, the water looked black beneath the ghostly cloud of steam dancing on the surface. Christian didn't seem to mind and was busy stripping out of his shorts and t-shirt, letting them drop to the floor as I regarded the perfection that was his body. A wave of heat seared my face as his gaze scanned my half-naked body. I let my shorts and panties drop, taking a step away from them.

Christian stepped into the water and turned around. Without a word, he reached up to take my hands and guided me to sit at the water's edge with my feet in the warmth. He ran his hands along my thighs, squeezing them as he looked into my eyes. He lowered his lips to my knee, never taking his eyes from mine. As he kissed my knee, his hands parted my legs and then he motioned for me to lie back. Instant heat ran through my body as he awakened every inch of my thighs with his wet mouth. He placed his hands under my bottom and gently pulled me forward. A moan escaped my mouth before his even made contact with what it sought.

Lost in his kisses and caresses, I didn't even notice the noises coming from the entrance to the cave until he pulled away from me. "Excuse me," a deep voice interrupted my pleasure.

I sat up and jumped into the water, bending my knees enough to hide my bare chest under the steam. "What is it?" I managed to say though I was out of breath.

"Mariana called. She says we need to return to the bungalow right away."

"Is there a problem?" Christian asked as he pulled me against him, my back against his wet chest, his hands still groping at my body. I sighed, not caring if our guard heard.

"I am not sure. She didn't say but she sounded like she was struggling. I am sorry but we should go. Dress quickly, please." He left the cave.

"Lovely, just lovely! Couldn't it wait just another few minutes?" I complained as I pushed my body against Christian.

"I guess not but we will continue this later. That's a promise." He kissed my neck before separating from me and leading the way out of the water.

As we followed one guard, with the other two bringing up the rear, we kept conversation to a minimum. I was trying not to take my frustration out on them. It wasn't their fault any of this was happening and their only objective was to protect us. That is exactly what they were trying to do; at least, that is what I was trying to convince myself of, though something tugged at my gut.

When we reached the bungalow, the front door stood wide open, just like all the doors on the limousine. It was quiet except for our footsteps. "Mariana, are you here?" I called. One of the guards raised his hand, motioning for Christian and me to stay outside. I nodded and he entered without hesitation. A few seconds later, he reappeared alone.

"No one in there."

"What do you mean no one in there? She just called us." I pushed him aside and stepped into the front room, Christian close behind. The table was overturned, the maps and papers scattered about. One chair lay upside down in the entrance to the bathroom and another lay against the wall by the window. Somehow, they had missed breaking anything. "What the hell happened here?"

"It looks like there was some kind of struggle. Try Mariana on your radio," Christian said turning to the guard. He nodded and stepped out onto the porch.

"Do you think Melinda found us already?" I asked as I straightened the chair closest to me. Melinda, in her need to avenge the death of her sister Ryanne's mate, Fergus, had taken it upon herself to create nothing but havoc when we arrived in Lima for our honeymoon. She also managed to use Maia against us. It hurt to even think of Maia, not because of her, but because of Aaron and Kalia. They considered Maia their daughter, and for a short while, they considered me their daughter, until Maia messed with their heads and turned them against me.

"Lily, please don't do this to yourself. I told you, give them some time and they will realize their mistake. Maia can't keep up the good-girl charade forever," Christian reassured me.

"Excuse me," Carlos started as he entered. "Mariana is not answering. I tried the driver, Tomas, and neither is he. Should I contact Aloysius?"

I shook my head. "Not yet. Let's give it a little time. Maybe it was just a robbery attempt and Mariana went after them." That didn't explain Tomas's absence or the fact that the limo doors were left open, but I wanted to keep Aloysius out of it as long as possible. He had done enough. Besides, when we inspected the limo, we found nothing out of the ordinary, except that the keys were left in the ignition.

"I am going to call Mauricio back from his break. He can stay here and wait while Vicente and I stay with you. My orders were to make sure you have a good time and that is what we are going to do for now." Carlos's voice was so full of authority that Christian and I just nodded, as much as I wanted to argue.

"So, what's next on the itinerary?" Christian asked.

"Why don't you go change and we can go to town, do some shopping, maybe go to a *peña* later," Carlos suggested.

"That actually sounds wonderful. What's a *peña*?" Christian asked as we started getting out of our clothes.

"You'll see when we get there," I teased.

"Does it involve dancing?"

"Of course, it does." I laughed at the shock in his eyes. He didn't consider himself a good salsa dancer, but I didn't mind at all. It wouldn't matter to me if he just stood there as long as he was close. His smile and the squeeze of his fingers around mine told me he heard my thought.

As we browsed the little shops in the center of town, it was difficult not to think of Kalia and Aaron. I saw many things I thought Kalia would love to display in her beautiful house. Tears welled in my eyes as I held a hand carved wooden container that would have been perfect to hold her paintbrushes. Carlos looked at me with pity in his eyes. I smiled to reassure him though I knew he could also read my mind.

We managed to find some gifts for Aloysius, Fiore, and Jose Luis. I even found a little cloth doll I thought Leilani would like, if and when we found her. Two hours later, we still hadn't heard a word from the driver or Mariana. Carlos assured us he would keep trying throughout the night, that it was possible her phone went dead, or she had no signal wherever she was. We agreed with him and decided it was best to try to have fun, at least for Aloysius's sake.

As we made our way to an empty table in the back of the adobe building that housed a restaurant and bar, Carlos went back outside to try calling Mariana again. Mauricio stayed with us, pulling a chair out for me before taking his position by the front door.

"Lily, Christian, there you are," Aloysius walked toward us with a quick stride. "Glad I found you."

"What are you doing here?" I asked as I stood from the chair I had just taken. My stomach tightened with fear.

"We have to go back to Lima." He took a seat and motioned for me to do the same.

"Did they find Jose Luis? Do they have him?" I took Christian's hand without looking, hoping for the strength it always gave me.

"No. It's not that," he cleared his throat. "It's worse than that."

⤫ SIX ⤫

Talking while disappearing and materializing somewhere else was not possible. The speed with which we swirled through a black tunnel as we clung to each other's hands was even faster than flying through a hurricane might be. The whole trip home, which couldn't have been more than seconds, my stomach felt like it was sinking into nothingness. I couldn't image what could be worse than the hunters or Melinda kidnapping Jose Luis, except maybe...no, I refused to even think it.

Instead of landing in the apartment like I expected, we landed in a very bright and noisy room. Phones rang without pause, machines I didn't recognize beeped, and people dressed in white ran from one place to another. "What are we doing in a hospital?" I asked as soon as my head stopped spinning from the trip. Christian still leaned with a hand against a counter to steady himself.

Aloysius swallowed hard before answering. "Jose Luis is here. He wasn't feeling too well this morning, complaining of headaches. Fiore made sure he rested all day. He just watched TV and read his comics. After we made him eat some dinner, though he complained about nausea and no appetite, he got up to go to his room for the night. He passed out in the hallway. He's been out since."

Christian caught me in his arms as I stumbled backward. He led me to a chair against a long white wall with no end. My head spun and my hands shook. Jose Luis had a broken leg, but he was otherwise ok. The tests after the accident confirmed that. Most of his wounds had been superficial and he was given a clean bill of health and released with just the cast. This made no sense.

Aloysius turned to Christian. "The doctors are doing a series of tests on him. We will, hopefully, have answers soon. In the meantime, all we can do is pray and wait." He sat in the chair next to me and took my hand.

"You believe in God?" was all I could think to say.

"Don't you?" he asked.

"I guess so. I haven't given it much thought since I died."

"God is not only for the living, Lily. I believe we are his creatures too and we really need him right now," Aloysius explained as he offered his chair to Christian.

The idea that God looked after us, the walking dead, the monsters that preyed on the living, puzzled me, but he was right. We needed to believe now more than ever. My mind snapped back to the present. "Where is he now?"

"Like I said, they are running tests. They have a room ready for him on this floor. I was told to wait here, though it could be hours," Aloysius told us.

"Where is Fiore?" Christian asked.

"I sent her home to get some things for you. I figured you would want to change your clothes at least. I'm going to go find a pay phone and see what's keeping her." He turned and walked down the hall without a backward glance.

"What is going on?" I moaned as I leaned against Christian's shoulder. Jose Luis was just an innocent boy. He had already experienced so much pain in his few years on this earth. Why did it seem like he was being punished along with us?

"I don't know." Christian tightened his grip on my hand. "Maybe it has something to do with his fall."

Melinda, in her desire to destroy me, had used anybody she could in her madness. She had thrown, or actually willed Jose Luis to jump off the top of a tower. Our efforts to stop his fall had failed because one of the witches had created a tornado that threw him through the air and out of our reach. We all expected him to fully recover. The doctors had assured us he suffered no internal injuries, just some broken bones. "I don't understand. He seemed fine. His last checkup went well, and his cast was due to come off soon, and now this."

"He was getting headaches before his fall, remember? We thought Maia was causing them. I doubt Maia is here now, not since she's back with Aaron and Kalia."

The mention of their names felt like a knife through my heart. "You're right. We were quick to blame Maia, because of what she did to me, but what if there is something more going on with him?"

"Then we deal with it," he stood and pulled me out of my seat. "Let's go get some fresh air. I can't sit still right now. Unfortunately, all we can do is wait for the test results."

I agreed and let him lead me down the sterile, white corridors. Nurses walked by and nodded or smiled in greeting as they passed. The smell of chemicals invaded my lungs. The fluorescent lights were blinding, and their humming almost maddening. Fresh air would be better than sitting here while the minutes from the clocks all over the hospital ticked in my ears. "I know this is silly but, I kind of wish I had a cup of coffee."

"Why is that silly?" Christian asked as we neared the elevators. "I know how soothing it is to feel its warmth in your hands."

"I mean I'd like to drink one. It's been so long since I tasted it." I pushed the button to the lobby and the doors closed. Leaning against the wall, I rested my head against it and closed my eyes.

"We could right? Drink one, I mean?" he said as he put his arm around me and kissed the top of my head. He always knew what to do to calm me down.

"We could, I think. After all, what could happen? Let's go find some." The thought of actually tasting the coffee, not just smelling its rich aroma, or feeling its warmth on my fingertips, made me smile despite the circumstances we were facing. Christian, seeing my smile, however brief it was, smiled too, and as we got off the elevator, I almost forgot where we were.

"There you are," Aloysius said as he walked toward us, his dark hair out of its usual rubber band and flowing around his face with each stride. "Any word yet?"

"No, nothing. Did you talk to Fiore?" I asked.

"Yes. She was already in a cab when I reached her. Where are you going?" he asked as we stepped away from the elevator.

"We actually wanted to find some coffee," I admitted, thinking it sounded way too human.

"Coffee, hmm, now that's different." His eyebrows arched as he thought about it. "Is it ok if I join you?"

"Of course. We would love it," Christian answered.

Aloysius pointed down the hall to the left and we followed without speaking. After walking down the first hall and turning left again, we found a small cafeteria. We chose a table by the window and Aloysius offered to order for us. He came back with three *cafés con leche*. They were not in Styrofoam cups but in china cups complete with saucers. He picked up the sugar bowl he carried on the tray with the cups and placed it on the table. The sugar was not white, nor was it brown; it was more of a yellowish gold color with large crystals and a bit of a shine. "They call it blond sugar," he offered as I eyed it.

Dumping two heaping teaspoons of it into my cup, I stirred it and put the spoon on the empty tray. Aloysius and Christian both watched me closely. I smiled and raised the cup to my lips, feeling the steam seeping into my pores. "Umm…So good."

Christian smiled and picked up his cup, swishing the coffee in his mouth before swallowing. "I guess we really can drink. We can actually enjoy it when we go out and not just pretend."

"Since our bodies don't really need it, I never bothered. It was good enough just to hold it and enjoy the heat," I said as I prepared for another delicious sip.

"Oh, there you are," a young man with a white coat walked toward us, his black hair neatly trimmed around his ears, his glasses in his right hand, a clipboard in his left.

I set the cup down on the saucer with a shaking hand, making it clank against the china. "Doctor, please have a seat," I indicated toward the empty chair.

"How is he?" Aloysius asked as he stood. "Would you like a cup?"

"No, thank you. Please, sit," the doctor said. "He is resting comfortably. We ran some tests, as I said. We are still waiting for the results of his blood work, but I have the results of some of his other tests." He smiled at us before looking at his clipboard.

"Please tell us the truth. We will do whatever is necessary to take care of the boy," Aloysius offered. I swallowed hard and clasped Christian's hand under the table.

"We did an MRI and an EEG. He had an accident recently, correct?" Dr. Vega asked.

"Yes. He was pretty banged up but suffered some broken bones, nothing else. The cast on his leg comes off next week," Christian answered and squeezed my hand.

"Well, there is some swelling in his brain. It's only a small area, but," He flipped the page on his clipboard before continuing. "There is also a tumor. It's located in the lower part of his brain at the stem. That one is of significant size. There are smaller ones scattered throughout."

"What does this mean?" Aloysius asked the question I could not bring myself to voice. Somehow, I already knew.

"He has a grade IV primary brain tumor. That's the reason for the headaches and the loss of consciousness." He stopped as if allowing the information to sink into our brains.

"So, you can get rid of it, right?" I asked as I pushed my chair back and stood, my hands clenched at my sides. "Right?"

"We can try, but the chance of removing all the tumors is slim. It's spreading quickly. This is an aggressive tumor. The possibility of it having infiltrated into the healthy tissue is high. This is not something that occurred overnight. He's had them for a while." Dr. Vega stood and placed a hand on my shoulder. Looking into my eyes he said, "I would like to keep him for at least a few days, make sure he's not in pain and he is comfortable. If you would like me to go ahead with surgery, I want to make sure you have all the facts. You can take some time to decide then." He looked at Aloysius and Christian, both standing now and looking at me.

"Thank you, Doctor," Christian wrapped his arms around my waist from behind.

"Now if you'll excuse me, I need to check on his blood work results. He is in his room now if you'd like to see him. I will have a nurse come get you when I'm ready so we can talk in my office before you leave." He shook Aloysius's hand before nodding to me. "I'm sorry I didn't have better news for you." He turned and walked out of the cafeteria.

"I want to go see him," I said as I pulled away from Christian.

"Wait, Lily," Christian grabbed my hand, stopping my progress toward the door. "We should talk about this first. It's not a good idea to let him see us like this."

"He's right," Aloysius said and helped Christian lead me back to my seat. I let them push me onto the chair. "We need to calm down. He needs the rest and seeing everyone upset is just going to upset him."

I nodded but stared into my half empty cup. "Why him? He's so young. What did he do to deserve this?"

"Let's not jump to conclusions. We don't know all the facts yet. We have to be optimistic, at least in front of him," Christian stated with a steady voice.

"Fiore is here," Aloysius announced as he placed the coffee cups on the tray.

"How do you know?" Christian looked at the entrance. She was not there.

"I can sense her. Let's go." He turned and carried the tray back to the counter. We stood and followed without a word.

We found her just outside Jose Luis's room, pacing back and forth with a small suitcase in her hand. She smiled when she saw us approaching but one look at our faces and her smile faded. She nodded at Aloysius and confirmed what I thought. He wordlessly told her what the doctor told us.

"Ready?" Aloysius asked, grasping the knob to Jose Luis's door. I took a deep breath and nodded.

Jose Luis sat propped up on pillows, the TV remote in one hand, a cup of water in the other. He smiled apologetically as we entered and surrounded his bed. I leaned and kissed his forehead, closing my eyes as my lips touched the warm skin of his head. This was the most unfair thing I had ever witnessed.

I backed away and looked down at him. He looked like he always did, with the exception of the bags under his eyes and the IV tube coming out of his hand. He looked like an ordinary fifteen-year-old boy. A boy that would fall in love, get married, and have children who would adore him one day. "I am so sorry that I scared you," he said looking at all our faces.

"No need to apologize. It's not your fault," Christian answered smiling at him. "You'll be out of here in no time. You'll be fine."

Jose Luis shook his head. "Thank you for saying that but I don't think so. I..." His eyes welled with tears. I took his cup and set it on the table, grasping his hand in mine. "I'm going to die. I can feel it."

⮜⮞ SEVEN ⮜⮞

"You're not going to die," I insisted. "Why would you even say that?"

Jose Luis looked up at me and his eyes filled with sadness. "I have cancer. I know I do."

"Who told you that?" Christian asked as he sat on the other side of his bed.

"I heard Aloysius when he told Fiore just outside the door," he explained. I looked at Aloysius and he averted my eyes.

"Is that what you told her?" I asked. Fiore nodded before Aloysius could answer. "Are we sure of this? There might be some other explanation."

"Lily, did you hear what the doctor said?" Aloysius moved to stand in front of me. "Even Jose Luis understands."

"I know. But, there must be something that can be done. He's too young for this."

"We can get all the facts from the doctor when we see him. Until then, let's visit with Jose Luis before the nurses kick us out for the night," Aloysius said with a smile, trying to calm me.

"You're right," I answered and turned back to Jose Luis. "Is there anything from home you want us to bring?"

"Oh, that reminds me," Fiore said coming closer to the bed and opening the front pocket of the suitcase. "I brought some of your comic books."

"Thank you, Fiore," Jose Luis smiled sincerely. "Now I have something besides TV."

"Yeah, but how about you just stay out of the hospital? We've only known you for a short time and here you are again," Fiore joked.

The prevailing sadness was overwhelming, but we tried to keep the mood light for him. We spent another hour in his room, trying to seem interested in the TV as he flipped through the channels and making idle conversation. At eight sharp, a nurse came to tell us visiting hours were over. We said goodnight to Jose Luis and left him.

As the four of us sat in the living room, the mood was glum. No one spoke for what seemed like an eternity and I felt as if I would jump right out of my skin. Finally, not being able to look at the sad faces surrounding me, I stood and did what I do in these situations: I paced back and forth between the window and the coffee table.

"Lily, what are you thinking? I can't hear your thoughts at all." Fiore broke the silence.

Taken by surprise, I stopped. I wasn't trying to conceal my thoughts. "Really? You can't hear anything?" I asked and looked at the others. They shook their heads. "If my heart beat and you could hear it, you'd know it's breaking. How is that possible, to feel it breaking right inside my chest when it's been dead and rotting for ninety years?"

Aloysius stood and came to my side. "Just because we are technically dead doesn't mean we can't feel. We definitely feel love and I believe it's a hundred times stronger than the way any mortal feels it." He looked toward Fiore before turning back to me, taking my hands in his. "We will do whatever you wish."

I turned to look at Christian's face. His eyes glistened with the tears he tried to fight back. "You heard what the doctor said. The surgery could be more harmful than not. He could end up paralyzed, or worse, a vegetable. How could anyone let this go on for so long? Didn't anyone realize he was sick?"

"To tell you the truth, I doubt anyone cared. They were using him for his abilities and nothing more," Aloysius led me back to the sofa beside Christian. "What do you wish to do?"

"Why are you asking us?" I asked and allowed myself to settle into Christian's comforting arms. Not long ago I would have continued my pacing with my nails digging into my clenched palms. Now, I couldn't stay out of my husband's arms when he offered them.

"You two are his true parents now. I will respect your decision, no matter what it is," Aloysius smiled and sat next to Fiore, taking her hand. "I know you have his best interest in mind. Fiore, will you accompany me to feed? They need some time alone to discuss things."

"Certainly." She stood and straightened her skirt. "I am with Aloysius on this one. We will back you in whatever you decide." She leaned to kiss me on the forehead and smiled at Christian before placing her hand in Aloysius's and disappearing from the room.

Sliding down on the sofa, I laid my head back and rested my feet on the coffee table. Christian stayed silent, giving me a moment. "What if we go ahead with the surgery? At least give it a chance?"

"We could do that. It is only a chance that the outcome will be negative. I think we should focus on the positive," he said, laying his head back and turning to look at me.

"Right. He's a strong kid. What if he does beat it? He's a fighter, I think."

"Yeah. If anybody can beat this, it's him." He said it, but I heard no conviction in his voice.

"You have doubts, don't you?" I sat up again so I could see his face.

"I have no doubts about his will to live. That seems pretty damn strong. But you heard what the doctor said. This tumor is large. It's spreading quickly. If they had caught it sooner, his chances would have been much higher," he explained.

I nodded and sighed. I knew the hunters cared nothing about him. They took care of his material needs so they could continue to use him. Nothing more. "If we go ahead with the surgery and the outcome is bad, can we do anything to save him? I mean, can we reverse the paralysis if it happens?"

Christian sat up and looked at me with raised eyebrows. "I truly don't know. What are you thinking?"

"I'm not going to let him die. How can you even think that?" I stood and walked to the window. He followed.

"Lily, you can't be serious. He's just a kid."

"That's exactly why I'm thinking it. He's too young to die and he's too young to live the rest of his life paralyzed, unable to do anything for himself, to enjoy anything. That's not a life. Either way, he's doomed."

"Think about what Aaron would say."

"Who cares what Aaron would say? I don't give a damn. Do you see him here? Do you see Kalia by our side while we're dealing with this? No! They don't care. They turned their backs on me, on us. I don't give a rat's ass what they think!"

Christian laughed despite the anger in my voice. "I understand how you feel about them right now. I also know that in time, you'll forgive them and remember how much you love them. Maia may have been with them longer than you, but I honestly believe someone as cold-hearted as her can't keep up the charade too much longer. She will show her true colors to them eventually and your relationship with them will be mended. What then? You know how Aaron feels about making more vampires."

"As much as I want to believe what you're saying, the point still is that they love Maia. If they end up finding out the truth and she pleads hard enough, they will most likely forgive her. Where does that leave me? Still out of their lives. She didn't want me there from the start and she will make sure I stay away. I have to forget about them. Aaron's opinion no longer matters in any decision I make." I turned away from the window and went back to the sofa. Even though I was looking down at the street, I could not remember anything I saw. My anger started to boil again at the mere mention of Aaron's name. How could the love I felt for him cause so much pain and anger now?

"So you're really considering turning Jose Luis?"

"I haven't really given it too much thought yet. I just know I can't let him die. I'm sick of losing the people I love." My eyes burned with the start of tears. "I can't handle anymore."

Christian kneeled in front of me and took my hands in his, his eyes softening as my tears finally spilled over. "Is this about you or him?"

"How dare you insinuate that I could be that selfish?" I tore my hands away and stood.

"I'm sorry. I didn't mean it as harshly as it sounded. I understand how much you're hurting after all the loss, even Ian's, but do you think Jose Luis would be better off like us?"

"I don't know. I would just rather he be like us than not be at all. Does that make sense?"

"It makes perfect sense."

"But why would you think I feel anything for Ian after all he did?"

Christian opened his mouth but a knock at the door interrupted his response. Fiore and Aloysius would not be knocking, and we weren't expecting anyone else. Christian rose to answer the door but it opened before he could reach it. Mariana entered alone.

"What are you doing here?" I snapped before she could say anything.

"Let me explain," she looked at my angry face with fear. "The driver, Tomas, he was in the car as soon as you left to go to town. I watched him from the window, and he was dialing his cell phone. I wouldn't have given it much thought, since he was free at the moment, but he looked nervous. He kept watching me as I watched him, his hand covering his mouth as he talked. I got suspicious so I went outside."

"And? What did you hear?" I asked standing in front of her, hands on my hips.

"Nothing, that's the problem. As soon as I stepped out the door he shut his phone, dove to the passenger side, and ran out the door. I searched the car since I thought I saw him throw something toward the back, but he must have taken the phone with him. I was only a few minutes behind him but, somehow, I lost him. His footprints disappeared suddenly."

"What do you mean *suddenly*?" I didn't try to hide my annoyance.

"I followed them for a couple of miles, just before town, and the tracks stopped at a tree. I figured maybe he climbed up but when I looked, he wasn't there. I even climbed it myself. He just disappeared." Mariana stepped back a few paces and tried to smile, faltering when I glared.

"That doesn't even make sense!"

"Lily, do you think maybe...Melinda?" Christian suggested.

"Why would she do that? If she was there, she would have been after us, not the driver. And besides, wouldn't they have taken the opportunity of us being in Churín to go get Jose Luis?"

"That does make more sense," Christian crossed his arms and frowned. "We need to find the driver and clear this up. Why would he run? Why would he risk his own life? He was surrounded by vampires, totally defenseless."

"I will find him," Mariana said with authority. "I know where he lives. I know his family. I recommended him for this job."

"Please tell me you checked him out before you hired him," I stood eye to eye with Mariana and she didn't back away this time.

"Of course, I did. He has a wife and two children. He drives a taxi but is barely surviving trying to pay for his kids' school. He used to drive for Aloysius whenever he came to Peru, but Aloysius would rather take taxis or just appear where he wants. He's too private. I figured this was a good opportunity for Tomas to make some extra money."

"And why didn't you stay in contact with us?"

"It was kind of hard to talk while running. Besides, I had no signal most of the time," Mariana explained and looked at her watch. "I'm going to go pay a visit to his wife. He might be there."

"No, that will be all for now. Giovanni is in charge. I will send him. You can take the rest of the night off," I put a hand up when she tried to speak. "That will be all, Mariana."

"But, ma'am, you're not in charge here. Aloysius..."

"He may have hired you for this job but it's us you're guarding. I will decide what happens when he is absent." I opened the front door and ushered her out. Margarita was just relinquishing her seat outside the door to Vicente, her replacement for the night. I stopped her before she could walk down the hall. "Margarita, can you get a message to Giovanni for me?"

"Of course," she answered. I told her what I needed and gave her the address I got from Mariana. "Please make sure Giovanni goes personally. He can call my cell when he has something to report."

"Very well. I will go to him right away." She rushed down the hall toward the elevator with Mariana following. Mariana left without saying goodbye. She was angry that I wasn't buying her story, but I didn't care. I was tired of letting others take the lead in my life.

"You don't believe her, do you?" Christian asked as he bolted the front door.

"Was it that obvious?" I asked and rolled my eyes. "There's something about her...I'm not exactly sure why but I don't like her."

"Remind me to never get on your bad side," he replied as he took my hand and led me toward the spiral stairs.

"Where are we going?"

He smiled and looked at my eyes as he pulled me by the hand. "I liked the way you took charge. Think you can do that again upstairs?"

I laughed but quickened my step. A few hours alone with Christian was just what I needed to help me decompress. The rest could wait until morning.

⤳ EIGHT ⤳

"You are truly amazing, Mrs. Rexer," Christian whispered as my lips trailed down his chest and over his perfect stomach. He jumped when my tongue reached the top of his jeans and his fingers wound in my hair at the top of my head.

I raised my head enough to gaze into his eyes as my fingers fumbled with the button of his pants. As I slid the zipper down, my stomach turned and jumped, and my fingers started trembling as I pushed his pants down his muscular legs. I never thought a man could make me feel as if every time with him was the first. It had been different with Ian, not because I hadn't wanted him that way, but because his passion seemed more like an act than true desire. Had I felt that then and was just blinded by what I thought we had? Christian kicked his pants off the bottom of the bed and sat up. "Lily, what's wrong? Why are you thinking about him?"

Guilt turned the fluttering in my stomach into a tight knot. "I don't know. Believe me; the last thing I wanted was for him to pop into my head."

He took my arms and gently guided me to sit by his side, taking my face in his gentle hands, so unlike Ian's. "Do you still love him?"

"What are you talking about? How could you ask me such a question?" I grabbed his wrists and pulled his hands off my face.

"Please don't be angry, it's just that…Well, he was your first love. It's only natural that you should still feel something for him, and…"

"And what?" I said though gritted teeth.

"Lily, I love you and I know you love me. That is not even an issue. But Ian was a huge part of your life, of who you are and how you became what you are. I would totally understand if you still did feel something for him." He touched the back of my hand with his fingertips, asking my permission to hold it in his. I looked at his calm face and relented, entwining my fingers with his.

I swallowed hard before I answered. "I'm honestly not sure what I feel for him. I know I should hate him. I want to hate him for everything he did, for all the losses we suffered because of him, but something inside me won't let me."

He nodded and stayed silent, waiting for me to continue. If I were in his shoes, I don't think I could listen to any of this. The man should be sainted. "I know the connection between a vampire and a maker is supposed to be stronger than any other, but he's dead. He caused so much pain and anguish. I should hate him. Instead, I feel sorry for him. I pity him for his past and for what he became. I pity him for his loneliness and selfishness. He died because of his selfishness."

"You have to remember one thing," He turned my face to look into my eyes. "He only wanted you back when you fell in love with me. It was like a game to him, a challenge. Before that, he stayed away for years. He left you, remember, not the other way around."

"I know. If I can figure out why he left me in the first place, maybe then I can finally hate him," I suggested, still feeling guilty for my feelings, whatever they were.

"If that's what you need to get some closure on this, I will do whatever I can to help you," he smiled before continuing. "But, Lily, I still don't think you could hate him. Regardless of what he did, your heart is too full of love to fit hate in it, no matter who it's for. That is just one of the many things I love about you."

"I do love you. I never loved him the way I love you. I feel like my love for you could consume me, all of me. It was different with him. I think I just felt like I needed him. I was young and inexperienced and needed him to take care of me. I think I thought that if he didn't love me, I was nothing. I don't feel that way now. I know who I am, but I *want* you to love me, not *need* you to. Does that make any sense?"

"It makes perfect sense, and you don't have to worry. I will love you for the rest of eternity. That's not even a question in my mind. You are the air I breathe, but our first loves often feel like the true thing, no matter how real they truly are or aren't. Ian was your first love. Let me be your last."

My stomach welcomed the butterflies back in full force and I reacted without speaking. I moved to straddle his legs and pulled his face toward mine with more force than I intended. My mouth crushed his as my legs pulled me up and positioned me where I needed to be to be one with him. As he kissed me back with as much force as I kissed him, I saw Ian's face as he smiled and winked at me, and then it rippled and wavered before disappearing from my mind.

Let me go, please...

For now…For now, my love… his voice echoed in my ears as I made love to my husband like I never had before, without holding anything back, without an ounce of guilt.

The front door crashed against the wall and footsteps echoed on the metal stairs. I jumped out of bed and grabbed my robe from the back of the door, locking the door as I slipped it on with one hand. "What is it?" Christian asked, sitting up and pulling the sheet up to his chest.

"Smells like Aloysius, but something's wrong," my answer was cut short by the knock on the locked door. I unlocked it and pulled it open a crack. "What is it? Is it Jose Luis?" I asked and moved aside so he could enter.

"No. I called the hospital a few minutes ago. He's sleeping peacefully. It's…I think we might have seen Leilani tonight," He placed his hand on the doorknob. "May I come in?"

I turned to make sure Christian was covered before pulling it open. "Where? How?" Christian asked but didn't meet Aloysius's amused gaze.

Aloysius looked between Christian me and smiled before continuing. "Fiore and I decided to go to a café after we fed. We liked the taste of coffee and decided to enjoy a cup while we talked. Anyway, as we were sitting there waiting for a second cup, we happened to glance across the street. Do you remember the witch I followed one night, the one I bit?" I nodded, remembering the night he came home with his shirt covered in someone else's blood. "She was walking across the park and toward the sidewalk, holding a little girl by the hand. She didn't notice us watching her until I stood. That's when she panicked and ran, dragging the girl with her."

"It could've been anybody. Maybe she has a kid," I suggested, trying not to get my hopes up.

Aloysius shook his head. "I thought about that too, but why run?"

"I'm sure she didn't forget what you did. After all, you cornered her in a dark alley and bit her. She was probably afraid of you," Christian said. He stood with the sheet wrapped low around his waist. The butterflies invaded again as soon as I glanced at him.

"We weren't close enough to them to do anything. Besides, there were a lot of people around, too risky. She has powers she could have easily used from that distance." He shook his head again. "She was more concerned about protecting the girl."

"So, what did you do?" I asked.

"There was a glass wall separating us from them. We had to go through the restaurant to get back out onto the street. By the time we got outside, they were gone, probably jumped into a taxi."

"Shit!" I balled my hands into fists as I walked toward the closet.

"What is it, Lily?" Christian asked.

"Well, now at least we know she's alive," I walked into the closet and threw on the first outfit I found, not caring whether or not it matched. "The problem is we don't know where she is. If they know we know, and by the woman's reaction I'm almost positive they do, then they will be moving her off the mountain tonight."

"If she was being kept on the mountain, we don't know exactly where. It could take hours, if not days, to find the right house and, by that time, they'll be gone," Christian still stood with the sheet wrapped around his waist and turned to me. "Are you going someplace?"

"Um, no. I figured some clothes would be good considering Aloysius is in our room. Actually, think they'd let us into the hospital to talk to Jose Luis?" I knew it was a long shot, but I needed to know more about Leilani.

"Those nurses are stricter than nuns on Sunday. I would venture to say no," Aloysius backed toward the door resting his hand on the frame. "We will find a way to get to her. I think our first priority right now is Jose Luis. Have you made any decisions yet?"

I looked at Christian, but he remained silent. "I want to turn him," There was no hesitation in my voice.

"Very well. If that is your decision, I will support it." Aloysius turned to leave then stuck his head back into the room. "Have you ever done it before?"

"No, not on purpose, anyway," I thought of how I accidentally turned Christian. "Do I have to do it myself?" I asked with a bit of doubt.

"No, but if you want his attachment to be to someone else, then it should be you. When the time comes, I can guide you. There is nothing to be afraid of."

"But…What if it doesn't work? I mean, what if I mess it up?" I suddenly panicked at the idea.

"Believe in yourself, Lily. If you only believed in yourself half as much as the rest of us do, your life could be very different." He hurried down the hall without another word.

"What was that supposed to mean?" I turned to Christian, who had finally dropped the sheet and was picking his clothes up off the floor.

"I have no idea. But then again, that man is always cryptic," he said with a smile that betrayed his frustration.

"I was wondering," I paused on my way out the door and turned to Christian. "Ian drained your blood, and I gave you mine, unknowingly, of course." Christian nodded. "Technically, we both made you."

"Yes. I suppose that is true," he smiled as he understood what I was hinting at. "Do you really think we could?"

"I don't see why not. It worked for you."

"True. But if in fact you both did make me, shouldn't I feel some kind of a connection to Ian too?" He leaned against the dresser and ran his free hand through his hair.

"I didn't think of that," I walked back into the room and sat on the edge of the bed. Thinking about Ian was something that required me to sit so I couldn't wear circles into the floor. "Are you sure you don't?"

"I'm sure. I feel nothing for him, well, besides disgust. It's your blood that made me what I am," he explained with a sudden look of disappointment.

"Maybe it's because you didn't spend any time with him afterward. Maybe it's because…"

"Lily, I think it was just you that made me. He killed me and that was his only role. There was no blood exchange between us. Even when he was drinking from me in Ireland, I never tasted his blood."

As much as I wanted to analyze what he said further, though I was happy he felt no attachment to Ian, I had to agree with him. Ian took his life and planned for that action to be permanent. "So basically, only one of us can transform Jose Luis?"

"I think so," He moved to stand in front of me and take my hands. "It doesn't matter. If you want it to be both of us, then it will be. We'll figure out how. I don't care who he has the greater attachment to anyway. We are a family, and we will both play a part in his transformation."

The phone rang as I waited for Christian to dress so we could join Aloysius in the living room. Aloysius's voice boomed up the stairs as he yelled at whoever was on the other end. He spoke so fast I could make no sense of what he was saying. My stomach dropped as we ran down the spiral stairs, dread filling the silence as Aloysius slammed the receiver down hard, shattering the base unit.

∽ NINE ∾

Aloysius was already wearing his own circles in the carpet as we reached him. His usually calm features turned into those of an angry old man. "What's going on?" I asked.

"That was the hospital calling to ask why we took Jose Luis home without their permission."

"What?" I yelled as Christian wrapped a concerned arm around my waist.

"Obviously it wasn't us." Aloysius sat on the edge of the sofa and ran his fingers nervously through his hair. "Someone snuck in and took him without anyone noticing."

My knees unlocked and Christian tightened his grip, keeping me from hitting the floor. "I don't understand this. Why? Why an innocent child?"

Aloysius shook his head, his eyes not meeting mine. "How did they even know where he was? We were so careful."

"Do you think we're being watched?" Christian led me to the sofa before going to the window and pulling the curtain aside. He opened the window and stuck his head out, scanning the street below.

"Do you see anyone?" I asked.

"Nothing unusual, just walkers who look like they have a destination and a few cars here and there." He stepped away from the window but left it open. "Can either of you hear any thoughts?"

I looked at Aloysius before answering. "It's worth a shot."

The three of us remained silent while we focused our thoughts on the street. Even Christian looked frozen in concentration. After a few minutes, I threw my arms in the air, defeated. "I hear all kinds of stuff but nothing we need."

"Same here," Aloysius replied. "I was thinking, if they already have him, then they are probably not watching us anymore. They got what they were after."

"You have a point there," Christian answered. "So, what now?"

"We need to get to the hospital. Maybe we can find out more there," Aloysius said as the front door opened. Fiore walked in with a few shopping bags in her hands.

Before we could say anything, she said, "I heard your conversation as I came up the hall. Let me throw these in my room and I'll join you." She disappeared up the stairs.

We arrived in Jose Luis's ward about a half hour later. As soon as we turned the corner within view of the nurses' station, we saw them. "Shit!" I said before I could stop myself. Everyone stopped short.

"What's wrong?" Fiore asked as all raised their eyebrows at me.

"I don't know that we should talk to the police."

"Why not?"

"Well, remember what I did at the beach?"

"Oh, right," Fiore said. "What you did was warranted, remember? Those guys were going to rape you and God knows what else. You had no choice but to kill them."

"I have a feeling that wasn't even reported. Those men weren't exactly law-abiding citizens," Aloysius replied. The three of us nodded and I felt a bit more relaxed.

"You're right. This is about Jose Luis," I answered as we started walking toward the three officers who were talking with a doctor and two nurses at the counter. A bouquet of flowers with a birthday balloon tied to it sat on the counter.

Aloysius walked up to one of the officers and introduced himself in flaw-less Spanish. After speaking for a few moments, he turned to us. "The doctor said we can use his office to talk." He led the way as we, the doctor, and two of the officers followed. As we walked, I couldn't help but notice that the two nurses standing at the counter with the remaining officer avoided us. They averted their eyes every time we glanced their way.

The doctor opened the door and led us to a round table at the corner of his office. Once we were seated, the conversation began, in English for Christian and Fiore's sake. "I am in charge of this case. My name is Lucas," the officer said with absolutely no Spanish accent. It wasn't until that moment that I noticed he was blond with blue eyes, his skin as pale as mine. As I looked at him, something in him stirred a memory in the back of my mind, too far back to reach.

"How did this happen?" Aloysius asked interrupting my thought.

"It's one of the nurse's birthdays today. They checked on all the patients before moving to the conference room to sing to her and have some cake," he paused, staring at me for a moment before continuing, obvious confusion on his face. "They left the nurses' station unattended."

Christian looked from my face to Lucas's, making me aware that I was staring. I looked at the floor, trying to ignore the foggy memory that was trying to make its way to the front of my mind. "So, in the time that they were singing and eating cake, someone came in, unhooked Jose Luis's machines, took out his IV, and carried him out of the hospital with no one noticing?"

The doctor's face suddenly flushed, the warmth of his blood obvious in his cheeks. Christian gasped and I wrapped my arm around his shoulder, sliding my chair closer to his. *I'm ok…*Christian thought. Lucas turned toward Christian as if he heard his thought.

"I am so sorry that this happened. I do not know how nobody saw them going out of the hospital. We were only gone for about fifteen minutes, maybe twenty," the doctor explained.

"Are there cameras in the hallways?" Aloysius asked.

"Sorry but no. They are only at the exits, and we already checked those. We found nothing. Whoever took him went out another way," Lucas explained.

"Is there another way in and out of here?" I asked, trying to focus on Jose Luis and not on the confusing signals I was getting from the officer.

"There are service entrances. They are used mostly for deliveries," the doctor offered. "But no cameras there."

"One moment, please. I'll be right back." Lucas left the room.

"What's going on, Lily?" Christian whispered as soon as the door closed behind Lucas. The others were talking to the doctor and the other officer, paying no attention to us.

"I don't know. I feel like something is off with that cop. I get the feeling I know him but don't know how. It's weird."

"Hmm… And did you notice he looked right at me when I sent you that thought?"

"Yeah, that's another thing. Do you think he's one of us?" I asked.

"I thought so for about a second, but then I heard his heart." Before we could say more, Lucas entered the room.

"I sent the officers to the service doors. They will check that out and talk to anyone who was working at the time the boy was taken." He still focused only on me while he explained. Annoyed that I still couldn't place him, I turned to Aloysius.

"I need to go see his room."

"Why?" the doctor asked. "We've already looked and there are no clues. The police also looked."

"It doesn't matter. I want to see for myself. And besides, I want to take his things home." I explained.

"Do you want me to go with you?" Christian asked.

"Of course. We won't be long," I said to the others and left before they had a chance to protest. I was not exactly sure what I was trying to gain from examining his room, but it was worth a shot.

"Why would he take his comic books?" I asked as I opened and closed his nightstand drawers.

"What? Are you sure about that?"

"They're not here, or anywhere. Someone also took the time to put his sneaker on." I held its mate up in the air.

"That seems more like he left on his own. Do you think he was really taken?"

"Unless that's what somebody wants us to believe. I can't think of a reason why he would leave on his own. Where would he even go? He wasn't happy with Arturo, and he has no family." I sat on the edge of his bed and ran my hands through my hair, thinking.

"What is that?" Christian asked approaching the head of the bed. The corner of a piece of paper stuck out from beneath the white blanket.

"Open it," I said when Christian pulled it out and I saw it was a folded piece of lined paper.

"It's a note from him," Christian sat on the chair next to the bed and started reading. "According to this, he left. He thought it was best that he dies alone and not burden all of us. He apologizes and thanks us for everything we've done for him. He doesn't want us to look for him."

"That's ridiculous! Why would he do such a thing?" I grabbed the paper from his hands and read it myself, as if the words would change in front of my eyes.

"Is that even his handwriting?" Christian asked.

"I don't know. I don't think he's ever written anything that I've seen." I turned the paper over and held it to my nose. I inhaled, hoping.

"Well?"

"Nothing, just him. He is the only one besides us who touched this paper." As I realized what that meant, my stomach dropped. "He really did leave."

"We need to take the letter to Lucas and the rest. They will want to examine it themselves, I'm sure." He stood and walked toward the door.

"You go ahead. I need another minute here, I want to gather the rest of his things," I waved him away as I went to open the cabinet door. The only thing left in there was his windbreaker. That's odd. Why would he leave in the middle of the night, when it's coldest, without his jacket? Deciding that question could wait until later, I grabbed the bag and left the room.

Turning the corner in the hallway stopped me short as I slammed into someone's hard chest. "Lucas, sorry I didn't hear you."

"That is the one thing I remember best about you, Lily. You were always so distracted."

TEN

"What does that mean?" I stepped away from him and looked at his face. "How do you know me?" Did he live in my building in Washington? Was he in one of my many college classes?

Lucas smiled and took a deep breath. "I've known you since…"

"What is this all about?" Aloysius asked as he and Fiore hurried down the hall. He held the note in his hand.

Lucas smiled at me once more and turned toward the others. "May I please see that?"

Aloysius handed the folded paper to him and moved to stand by Fiore, wrapping an arm around her waist. They were definitely a couple.

"The note says he left on his own but I'm not sure I believe it. It just doesn't make sense," I explained what Christian and I had discussed. "He really has no place to go, no family. Why would he want to die alone on the streets?" What I didn't voice was why would he even be willing to give up? He was a fighter. None of it made sense.

"Do you have any other writing samples of his at home?" Lucas asked. "It would help if we could compare the handwriting."

"I'm sorry but we don't. He hasn't been with us very long." I regretted what I said as soon as the words left my mouth. How could we explain how we met him without revealing our identities and the chaos that brought us to Jose Luis?

Lucas looked from me to Christian and nodded, as if he already knew something we hadn't said. "I'd like to take this to the station. I'm going to go find the other officers and head over there. We will be in touch as soon as we know something. In the meantime, stay close to the apartment and to a phone. If he really did leave on his own, he may have a change of heart and return. Here is my card." He handed the card to me and as I took it from his fingers, I noticed his skin was the same temperature as mine. Christian was right though; his heart did beat.

"Thank you. If we think of anything new, we will be in touch," Aloysius said as Lucas turned and started down the hall.

As the taxi headed toward the apartment building, our discussion remained on Lucas. "So, he looks like a vampire, he seems to know what we're thinking, yet his heart beats. Isn't that impossible?" I asked.

"Not necessarily," Aloysius explained. "He may be what we call a half-breed."

"But the term half-breed insinuates that he was born half vampire, half human. Vampires can't be born, can they?" Christian asked.

"No, of course not. What he means is that he may be only part vampire, as in the process of his transformation was not completed," Fiore answered, looking at Aloysius to confirm his suspicion.

"Is that even possible? And if so, why would anyone do that?" I asked.

"It is possible, and it is usually done for selfish reasons," Aloysius said. "It is possible that whoever is keeping him a half-breed is afraid that he will leave if he is turned completely. That may be the only way this vampire can keep him by his or her side, whatever the case may be."

"Hmmm… It still makes no sense to me, but I know one thing for sure. Lucas is definitely not a Peruvian. Luke, I think, is a better name for him," I added.

"Yes, I think you're right there. He is definitely a native English speaker. Which leads to another question…What the hell is he doing in Peru?" Aloysius said as the car pulled up to the curb in front of the building.

By the time we entered the apartment, we had stopped worrying about Lucas. Finding Jose Luis was our first priority, regardless of whether or not he wanted to be found. I refused to believe he had walked out of that hospital on his own. Why would he want to die alone when he finally had what we thought he desired most: a family who loved him and cared for him?

"We will find him, Lily. I promise you that," Aloysius said interrupting my quiet contemplation.

"I know, and I believe you. You have never broken a promise yet and I don't think you are the type who would. I'm just worried about him being all alone, if he really is. What if it's too late?" I imagined the worst.

"Don't think like that. Keep all positive thoughts in your mind and the love you feel for him in your heart." Aloysius stood and went to the cabinet in the corner of the living room. He opened the door and shuffled some things, finally pulling out what looked like a thin book.

"It's time we search the mountain, house by house," Fiore announced.

"I totally agree, but that will take a lot of time. And I have a feeling they are no longer there," Christian said and motioned for me to sit next to him. I paced a few steps more and decided to join him.

"This is a map of the mountain, or some of it, anyway," Aloysius said as he held it up for us to see. It was open to a page somewhere in the middle. "Not everything up there will be on here. Most of the people who live up there are not even supposed to be there. The majority are squatters."

"Squatters?" I held out my hand and he handed me the book.

"Squatters are what they call the people who make their homes anywhere they want. They either take an abandoned house and claim it as their own or build their dwellings out of whatever they find to make a shelter on someone else's property."

"That's sad," Christian said as he looked at the map that lay open on my lap.

"I wonder… Do you think the police would be willing to search with us, since they're already involved anyway?" I asked. More manpower would help us save time.

"That is a possibility, but it would be difficult to hide what we are," Aloysius explained. "I would not want to go up there unarmed."

"You have a point there. So, what do we do?" I passed the book to Fiore.

Aloysius ran his hand through his hair. "I say we wait for a call from Lucas and see what they find. If they find nothing, then we go to the mountain on our own. All the bodyguards can go with us and help out. We start at the bottom and work our way up, that way no one can get past us if they are warned of our presence."

"How long do we wait? We don't know for sure how long Jose Luis has, and how much worse he feels since he's not on the pain meds," I said.

"If he had such a short time to live, the doctor would have told us that. He was kept in the hospital for his comfort. Dr. Vega was waiting for our decision on the surgery," Aloysius said as he took the map from Fiore. "Maybe we should give it a couple of days."

The next morning, while we sat discussing how the search of the mountain would proceed, a knock on the door interrupted us. Aloysius opened the door and Margarita entered with a couple boxes stacked in her arms.

"What is that?" Aloysius asked.

"Pepe brought these up. He said they arrived yesterday afternoon. They are addressed to Mrs. Rexer." She set them down side by side on the floor and went back to her post by the door.

"What could they be? I wasn't expecting anything," I stood and went to look at the boxes. There was no return address on them.

Christian went to the kitchen and returned with a knife. He sliced the tape across the seam of each box. My stomach sank and my eyes teared as I pulled the flap on the first box and realized what the contents were. Christian dropped to his knees and wrapped his arms around my shoulders.

"What is it?" Fiore asked from the sofa.

"Some of our things from the house in Oregon," Christian answered as he stroked my head.

Hope returned as I started looking through the contents. One by one I searched the articles of clothing as I pulled them out and folded them, making a pile on the floor next to me.

"What are you looking for, Lily?" Aloysius asked as he approached.

"A letter, a note, something, anything personal," I grabbed the piles I made and shoved them back into the boxes, standing to grab both. "I'll take these upstairs." Before anyone could reply, I hurried up the stairs with both boxes in my arms.

"Give her a minute," I heard Aloysius say as Christian tried to follow me.

I pushed the door open with my foot and dumped the contents of both boxes on our bed. Searching through each article a second time, I succumbed to the tears that threatened downstairs, my body shaking with my sobs. As hard as I had tried to keep Aaron and Kalia from my mind lately, the inevitable was happening. Since we had not been there to claim our things from the house personally, they had taken it upon themselves to erase us from their lives, one box at a time.

"Can I come in?" Christian called from the other side of the cracked door.

"Of course," I wiped my tears with the back of my hand. "I'm just putting these away." I walked to the closet and yanked a handful of hangers from the rod, a piece of plastic landing on my foot as one of the hangers snapped.

Christian placed a tentative hand on my shoulder. "Please put those down. Come, sit." He guided me to the edge of the bed, taking the hangers from my tight grasp.

"What for? I'm fine," I said through clenched teeth.

"Lily, I know better than that. It's ok to let it out. It's ok to talk about it. It would probably make you feel better."

"I could talk about it every minute of every day and it would change nothing." I reached behind me for the hangers, determined to put the pain out of my mind.

"Stop, please. Why are you so damned stubborn? Why do you refuse to let anyone in?" He wrapped me up in his arms. "I wish you would understand you are not alone in this. I lost them too."

He was right. He had only been with us for a short time, but he had so easily let them into his heart. It was his loss too. "I know. I'm sorry," I wrapped my arms around him. "It just hurts so much."

"We will get them back. I don't know when and I don't know how but I know we will. We both want it badly enough." He sounded so determined and I wanted to believe him.

"I wish I were more like you," I tightened my grip.

"What do you mean?" He pushed me away enough to look at my face.

"You love and trust so easily. All I do is run when anyone tries to get close. Even if someone manages to get close enough, I manage to push them away somehow. I know it's wrong," I explained.

"It's only natural, Lily. You trusted and loved Ian so fully and look what he did. It will take some time but you're already getting better."

"How can you say that?"

"You love me, right? Aaron, Kalia, Fiore, Aloysius, Jose Luis?" He smiled.

"I hadn't thought of it like that."

"It didn't take you long to fall in love with me, remember?" He looked into my eyes.

"I guess you're right, but I did try to push you away," I reminded him.

"That you did, but not because you didn't love me. It was because you were trying to protect me."

"It all seems so pointless now. Here you are, a married vampire," I laughed.

"And totally worth all the problems that led us to this," He kissed the top of my head. "I would die for you all over again."

A knock on the door interrupted my response. "Come in," I called and stepped away from Christian.

"Lucas just called," Fiore said.

"Does he have something?" I asked, already trying to leave the room but unable to get past Fiore.

"No, not yet, but he wants you to meet him, Lily. He says he needs to talk to you alone," she said and shrugged her shoulders.

"I'm going with you," Christian replied.

"No. I can handle this on my own," I turned to him and took his hand. "I'm not sure what he is, or even how he knows me but, I feel he's harmless." Or at least, that's what I told myself.

ELEVEN

The setting sun shot forth bright oranges and purples as I glanced toward the street. People hurried past the street side tables, some alone, some laughing with their companions. I picked up my cup and inhaled the nutty aroma of the steaming coffee before taking a gulp, swishing it around in my mouth and enjoying every drop.

"I'm so sorry I'm late," Lucas said pulling a chair out and taking a seat.

"It's no big deal. You're only five minutes late," I said looking at the time on my cell phone, surprised Christian had not tried to call. He was worried about this meeting, but I assured him I would leave if I sensed anything wrong. So far, I did not.

"Lucas picked up a menu and opened it. "You don't mind if I order something to eat, do you? I'm starved."

There went that theory. He was starved. Not for blood but for food, regular human food. He smiled as he continued to scan the menu. The waitress came over and he ordered a sandwich and a cup of coffee. "Would you like another cup?" he asked me. I nodded.

"Thank you," I said and straightened in my seat. "What did you want to talk to me about?"

"I think you already know something. I can tell you remember me." He stirred the sugar in his cup and banged the spoon off the side before placing it on his napkin.

"I do get the feeling I know you, but I have no idea how," I admitted. "I can't place you, no matter how hard I think."

"Elementary school. You were friends with Elizabeth. The two of you were inseparable as I recall," he laughed as he recalled. "You used to write those stories."

That was impossible. His heart beat like a human's. He needed food to survive. This made no sense at all.

"In case you were wondering, I can read your thoughts," he thanked the waitress when she brought his sandwich.

"So, what are you? How is this even possible that you sit here looking like you do?" I asked. He should be much older than he was, if not already gone and buried.

"I have a feeling you didn't know this, but I read some of your stories in school. I sat behind you. I used to read over your shoulder as you wrote."

"What does that have to do with anything?" I asked, frustrated, not because he had read my stories without my permission, but because he avoided answering my question.

"Because of your stories. You started writing about vampires when we were in secondary, I think. That's when I became fascinated with vampires, too. The more I read, the more real they became to me," he stopped to take a bite of his sandwich.

"That still doesn't answer my question. How is it that you look so young?"

He held a hand up and chewed a bit more before swallowing. "The point is I wanted to be one. I wanted to be like the powerful beings you described in your stories. When I graduated from high school, I left home. I traveled around for years, looking for anyone that resembled what you described." He sipped his coffee.

"You believed my writing was truth?" I sipped my coffee just to keep my hands busy.

"Not exactly. What I believed is that there must be some truth to the whole thing. Vampires were so popular then. So many stories and movies portrayed them in the same way that I thought, somewhere along the way, they must have existed, at least in some form."

"Did you ever find what you were looking for?" I was intrigued now.

"Not really. I finally got tired of wandering and gave up. I settled in a small town in California and decided I needed a career, so I became a cop. It was shortly after I graduated from the academy that a vampire found me." He took another bite.

"I do remember you now. You came to our school in, what? Fourth grade?" He nodded. "I remember all the girls liked you, including Elizabeth, but you paid no attention to any of them." He laughed and swallowed. "So, what happened when this vampire found you?"

"I didn't know she was a vampire for quite a while. I suspected something, but I was too chicken to say anything. I thought she'd run away from me. I fell hard for her and the last thing I wanted was for her to think I was crazy. We dated for about a year and one night, we had a big fight. I tried to break if off with her."

"I thought you loved her?" I asked.

"That's just the thing. I loved her and I kept telling her so, but she never said it back to me. I got sick of it. The relationship was becoming too one-sided for me. I felt like I was wasting my time so I did the only thing I could. I told her I wanted a family and if she didn't want the same thing, she should just tell me and let me go. It didn't quite go the way I planned."

I had an idea where this was going but I needed to hear it from him. "She didn't let you go, did she?"

"No," he sipped again and pointed to his cup. The waitress hurried to take the cup and return with another. "She finally admitted what she was to me and made sure I knew a family was impossible with her."

"Didn't you love her enough to become a vampire?"

"I thought I did, however, she thought differently. She wanted me to take my time to decide, considering I had just told her I wanted a family. It was that same night that we exchanged blood for the first time. It was the most…"

I held a hand up to stop him. "Trust me, I know how it is. If you exchanged blood, how is it that your heart still beats?"

"Like I said, we exchanged blood, from that day on. It became a daily ritual between us. She never took enough to drain and kill me, just enough to keep me half-vampire."

"Half-vampire? What does that even mean?" I picked up my cup, realizing it was empty.

"I stopped aging when the exchanges started. I acquired a few gifts, as you know from my mindreading. Regardless, I am still mostly human."

"Why would someone do that?"

"She says likes the human side of me."

"It still makes no sense to me. What happens when the exchanges stop?"

"I start aging again and the vampire part of me starts fading until it eventually dies."

"But are there many vampire parts? You still eat."

"That's true. I do eat, but I also crave blood," he explained.

"I didn't know that." I raised my empty cup toward the waitress. She rushed over and replaced it with a full cup.

"We share people sometimes but mostly, I eat food. I crave blood but I don't need it. My own blood still flows through my veins."

"What happens if she leaves you?" I asked.

"I would be without her blood. I don't know if the aging process would be slow or if it would be speeded, kind of like catching up, but I will age and I will die, just like any other human."

"So basically, neither of you can leave."

"Not exactly," He suddenly looked sad. "She can leave anytime she wants. I'm the one who is dependent on her, not the other way around. I'm the one who is stuck."

"Wouldn't it be easier to just turn you completely?"

"I've asked her that but the subject angers her so much I stopped asking years ago."

It seemed selfish to me. She was keeping him totally dependent on her. If he left her, he would die. He just didn't know how quickly or slowly. He had no other alternative.

"Maybe it is selfish of her but, I love her. I have no intention of leaving her, ever."

"Do you still want to be a vampire?" I asked, though it was none of my business.

"I do and she said that, in time, it could happen. For now, I'm just happy to be by her side," he explained, smiling again.

"How is it that you are working here, in Lima?" I asked. I was more curious about that than how he knew me from the beginning.

"She was in California temporarily. Mariana is Peruvian."

"Did you say, Mariana?" It couldn't be. Mariana was a popular name in Peru. It had to be a coincidence.

He nodded. "I did. She works for some other vampires, here in the city."

"Did she happen to say who?" I straightened in my seat again, my back stiff against the cold metal.

"No, and I don't ask either. I know better."

"When is the last time you saw her?"

"Yesterday. But she should be back sometime tonight, or by morning. She won't leave me more than a day without her blood," he explained. "She has to come back."

"And if she doesn't?"

"She will." He seemed so sure. It broke my heart. "Do you know something I don't?"

"Uhh, no, of course not," I made sure my mind stayed off Mariana. "I need to get back. Please call as soon as you find out something. Jose Luis needs to be found. He's dying."

"I know. We will find him, I promise, and Lily…"

"Yeah?" I stood and pushed my chair in.

"Thank you for listening to me. It was good to talk to someone familiar."

"No problem. If you need anything, anything at all, just let me know," I added before turning to walk up the street. I didn't know what I could do for him but, if it was the same Mariana we were dealing with, she may not be returning any time soon. What Mariana was or wasn't doing was not his fault, after all.

As I hurried down the street, I reached into my front pocket to retrieve my phone and call home. No doubt they would be worried about Lucas's intentions. I wanted to stop at a store and buy some coffee to make at home. I was enjoying the taste and it seemed to have a calming effect I needed more than anything right now. As I hit the button programmed to dial Christian, there was a sudden pressure on my neck. An arm grasped tightly around my waist as another hand clamped over my mouth. I kicked my legs as I was dragged backward into darkness. The smell of smoke filled my lungs as the phone fell from my fingers.

Before my eyes could adjust to the darkness and distinguish anything, a cloth that smelled of old rotted potatoes was slid over my head. While someone held me around my waist, someone else tightened a string around my neck, pulling so tightly that I could not breathe. Good thing I didn't really need to. I kicked again but made no contact. My legs slid across what felt like a dirt floor as my body was turned and flung, leaving me upside down over what I assumed was someone's shoulder.

"Put me down," I gasped through the tightness around my neck. "What the hell are you doing?"

"Relax, my pretty. We are going for a little ride." With that, I was thrown against something hard and cold, my legs shoved in at an awkward bent angle, pain shooting through my knees. A door slammed and the darkness became as dark as a black hole, the smoky odor disappeared. I kicked and thrashed but to no avail. The space was so small I had no room to bend and straighten my knees. My stomach sank as the realization of my predicament hit me full force. I was in the trunk of a car, my cell phone on the dirt floor of whatever building they had dragged me into. I was being kidnapped and no one knew where I was. No one knew where I had met Lucas or even that our meeting had ended. I was totally and completely alone.

⟶ TWELVE ⟵

"Can you hear me?" I called from the trunk. "Hello? Can anyone hear me?" The motor roared to life, drowning out my pleas. No one had said a word as they tied me up and shoved me into a trunk. I don't know what made me think someone would answer me now.

As the car started moving, I lay still. If I couldn't get anyone's attention, I could at least try to learn something from my captors. I listened until they finally started speaking.

"Where are we going?" A male voice asked in Spanish.

"We already told you, stupid. Just drive," a female commanded.

"Where the boy is?" the male asked.

"Shut up, you imbecile! Say that again and I will have you killed. You're useless!"

"Sorry. Of course, not where the boy is. That would be a stupid move," he said. A thump. "Damn you! Hit me again and I will stop the car!"

"And do what?" The woman chastised. "Keep driving and shut your mouth."

Great, just what I needed. It appeared as though I was being kidnapped by a couple of morons, strong morons, but morons none the less. I moved my arms, testing the restraints binding my wrists. They were solid, probably plastic, and I had no room to move or maneuver a possible escape as I lay in the fetal position with my ankles bound by the same material. The cloth over my head stank and I was grateful my lungs didn't need air.

"There's a cop. What do I do?" the man said with a shaky voice. He was obviously not happy with his current task.

"What do you mean? Are we doing something wrong? No. Just keep driving and don't look at him," the woman barked.

Not sure how far we had actually driven at that point, I tried to call for help. *Christian, Fiore, Aloysius, can anyone hear me?* I waited for a response. When nothing came, I tried again. *If anyone can hear me, I've been kidnapped. I was last at the café at the corner of the park in Miraflores. I was walking up the street after my meeting when someone grabbed me from behind. I'm in the trunk of a car.* Well, that told them absolutely nothing useful; still, I had to try.

"He's looking at us," the driver said as the car slowed. Could it be Lucas? *Lucas, can you hear me? I'm in here... Stop the car... Stop them...*

"See? I told you we were fine. He looked away. Just keep driving. We're almost there," the woman said.

The sounds of the city, the beeping car horns, and the sound of voices faded as I rolled to the back of the car. By the feel of it, we were climbing. Hopeful that we were going to the mountain where Jose Luis and Leilani most likely were hidden, I kept silent and waited. They would be taking me out of the car soon enough and I would be close to them, or at least I hoped.

"You just passed it, you ass. Back up," the woman commanded.

"Oh, right. I just thought since the boy..."

"Shut your mouth! Nothing about the boy. Right here is good," she said.

"Should I pop the trunk?" the man asked.

"Now think about it a moment... Pop the trunk from in here and what happens to the vampire? I'm waiting," the woman spoke as if to a five-year-old.

"Uhh, ha, ha, you're right. Never mind," the man said and opened his door.

The trunk popped open with a groan, and a pair of hands grabbed me, one behind my neck and one behind my bent knees. After a few steps, the smell of urine and dirt filled my lungs. I could almost taste them. "Put me down," I commanded.

"Soon enough," the woman answered in Spanish though I had said it in English. "Right there," she said to the man.

He dropped me on the ground, my head bouncing off cement. "Damn it!" I yelled.

"Shut up!" the woman yelled back. "Undo her arms," she commanded. He roughly undid the binds holding my wrists. I immediately rubbed them, feeling blood where the binds had rubbed my skin raw. Then, I felt his hands on my legs. "I said her arms!"

"Right," he said and moved away. "Now?" he asked.

"Of course, now. You should have stayed in school." The woman grabbed my arms and held them up above my head. She dug her nails into the already raw flesh, making me bite my lip to stop from screaming. Cold metal replaced her warm hands. A click on each side and my hands were released. They now hung above my head, bound by some kind of cuffs. I wiggled them. Chains rattled.

"Are you kidding me?" I barked when I realized I was bound to the damp wall behind me. "Who the hell are you?"

"We are your new family so be nice to us. We will be the ones taking care of you, the ones feeding you. If I were you, I would be especially nice," the woman said right into my ear, her cheap perfume mixing with the dirt and urine, making me gag.

"What makes you think I would eat anything, or anyone, you offered? It smells like a urinal in here," I complained.

"When you are starved for blood, you will. It is in your nature, that is your way, vam-pire," she pronounced vampire as if it were the dirtiest of words.

"I will take nothing from you," I answered through clenched teeth. "Take this thing off my head."

"Oh, no you don't. You don't tell me what to do." The woman said. The man laughed from somewhere in the room.

"You're nothing but cowards. Show yourselves."

"Not yet, my dear. Maybe later, if you behave," she said and moved away from me. "Let's go, and make sure the door is locked."

"But she can't move," the man argued.

"She's still a vampire and I'm not taking any chances." Heavy metal slammed and a key turned in a lock. They were gone. I was alone in this dark, cold, stinking room, the dampness of the ground and wall seeping through my clothes and into my skin.

Please, if anyone can hear me, I'm here... The only problem was I didn't know where here was. The car had climbed for a while before coming to a stop. We were somewhere high, but it could be anywhere. The Andes surrounded us. It was hopeless. My pleas would reach no one from this distance. No one knew where I was. No one could come for me.

I rested my head against the cold wall, my hair caught in something, probably a loose rock. Tears filled my eyes as I realized just how bad my situation really was. At that moment, I regretted going to meet Lucas alone. Had Christian been with me, this would not have happened. Or maybe it would have. Maybe he'd be locked in here with me, or worse, dead. Someone had been watching us. They knew when I was alone and knew exactly when to strike. Though we had listened, we had heard no thoughts about us near our building. We had become too comfortable, too complacent. We were worried about finding Jose Luis and nothing more. We stopped worrying about Melinda, and Maia, and anything else that had led to this in the first place.

I wished I had my cell phone, but even if I did, it wouldn't do any good.

My hands were shackled above my head in a most uncomfortable position. It was metal in stone, or at least that's what it felt like against my back. How hard could it be to pull them out of the wall? I pushed against the wall and sat up straighter. I wiggled my arms and confirmed by the sound that it was some kind of metal. Pulling my head and torso away from the wall as hard as I could, I clenched my teeth and withstood the pain in my already tender wrists. Nothing happened. I took a deep breath and tried pulling just my wrists away from the wall over and over, the chains banging against the wall, grunts escaping my mouth. "Come on!" I screamed.

The door hitting the wall behind it stopped my furious attempts. "What are you doing? You will wake up the whole mountain," the woman yelled.

"Nothing."

"It does not sound like nothing from out there. Here, let me have it," she commanded to someone else.

"Do you have to? Maybe we can make her be quiet another way?" the same man from earlier asked.

"You think you can reason with a vampire? She's no different than an animal. Shut up and give it to me."

"Take it. Can I go?" the man asked in a whisper.

"You are such a coward. You can't watch me shoot a vampire? It won't kill it," the woman answered.

"Wait, what? Shoot me?" I tried to sit up straighter. At that moment, I really wished I had Aloysius's power to vanish. "I promise I won't try to escape." I brought my knees close to my chest, as if that would stop her from shooting me, as if making myself into a ball made me invisible.

"Don't worry. It will only hurt for a little while. I just need to keep you weak," she said and took a deep breath. What came next was searing pain and burning fire in my left thigh. The instant wetness ran down my thigh. I tried to straighten my leg but cringed from the effort. It was already going numb.

"Shit!" I screamed. "You really shot me!"

"Take it easy, lady. It was only your leg. Wooden bullet. Should keep you down until we remove it, or until she kills you, whichever comes first," she bent down and fussed with the sack on my head, making sure it was still tight around my neck. "It's a shame you do not need to breathe. It would save a lot of time. You would already be dead. Come on, idiot. Let's go."

Oh, God! The pain was unbearable. I wanted to see the wound, dig the wooden bullet out of my leg myself but I was completely helpless. All I could do was sit here and await my fate.

I don't know how many hours passed since they dumped me in this stinking room, but no one came back for what seemed like an eternity. The wound in my leg had stopped burning, but I could feel in every muscle of my body that I was much weaker. Maybe it was more from hunger than the bullet, but regardless, I could do nothing but hang my head, close my eyes, and wait. I would have welcomed sleep to pass away the hours, to take me from the dread consuming me, but no. No such escape would ever come.

The key turning in the old lock made me sit up. "Who's here?"

"Are you ready to eat yet?" the woman asked. "I am sure you are hungry by now." Her voice was close to me now. I jumped when her hands touched my neck. "I am taking this off. Try anything and I will shoot you again, and this time it won't be your leg."

She undid the tie around my neck and slowly pulled the smelly cloth off my head. A flash of white hit my eyes and I blinked to stop the burning and watering. Eager to see who my captor was, I blinked a few more times to clear my vision since I could not wipe the wetness away. Black dusty boots greeted me first. Somehow, I had pictured my captor as older, a woman slumped over from age and wearing rags. That was far from the truth as I looked at her slim jean-clad legs. As I raised my head, she placed both hands on her hips and tapped one dusty boot on the ground. Her black sweater was also dusty but far from a rag. It hung off her bare shoulders without falling and revealing too much. Her long black hair lay in a thick braid against her left breast. She smiled at me, her dark eyes amused. "Not what you were expecting, huh?"

"Who are you?" I asked as I looked into her almond shaped brown eyes.

"That's not important right now. Are you ready to eat?" she asked again.

"What? From you?" I shuddered at the thought.

"I would love nothing more than that but unfortunately, I have my orders. I'm being watched too so I can't do what I truly want, at least not right now. But we do have someone for you, someone who may be more appetizing than me." She walked to the door.

The room was small, illuminated by a single uncovered light bulb that hung low from the ceiling. Graffiti covered most of the stone walls. On the far side sat a table with some wrapped bundles on it. As I suspected, the floor was dirt, muddy in some spots and I shuddered to think of how those spots got wet. I looked above and saw my wrists hanging from steel cuffs, dried blood on my skin from the already healed wounds. Upon closer examination, I noticed three more pairs of cuffs hung from chains. Who the hell were these people? Did they make it a habit to keep prisoners in this disgusting room?

"He is coming with your meal. You best show your appreciation by eating what we are offering," she advised as she knelt beside me.

"And if I don't?"

She stroked my cheek with the back of her warm hand. Before she could answer, a man walked in holding someone's hand. The small hand belonged to someone who hid behind his legs. My stomach flipped when I realized the hand had to belong to a child. The woman's smile broadened as she stood and walked over to the man. She reached behind him and took the child's hand, pulling her from the safety of the man's legs.

"This is dinner," she announced as a wide-eyed little girl stared at me, her bottom lip quivering as her eyes locked on mine. She lifted a shaky hand and pulled her dirty collar to the side, revealing small scabs.

"Are you crazy? I will not do this!"

"Either you eat from her, or she dies. You get the power to decide her fate," the woman placed her hands on the child's shoulders and nudged her forward. "You don't want little Leilani to die, do you?"

Leilani! It couldn't be, could it? "I cannot drink from a child. I will not!"

"You can and you will. This is what we are offering, take it or leave it. You choose, but you know what the consequences are." She shoved the child closer to me.

"I will not, and besides, I'm not even hungry," I argued. "Where did you get this child?"

"That is none of your business. You don't get to ask questions. You are to do as you are told and nothing more," she said as she stroked the girl's neck. "She is delicious, or so I've been told."

"You people are sick! How dare you take advantage of an innocent child," I shook my head, never taking my eyes from the child's. "You cannot make me do this!"

"Please, *señorita*, drink from me," the child's timid voice was barely audible. She tilted her head, her dark tangled hair falling to the side. "It does not hurt... Much."

What could I possibly do? If I didn't obey, the child would die. That would be just as much my fault as if I made her my meal. "Come here, please," I said as I looked at the girl's face with a smile. As the woman approached with the girl, I looked at her. "Just the girl. Back away if you want me to do this."

"I don't think so," the woman said and continued forward. "I cannot trust you."

"What exactly do you think I'm going to do? I'm chained to a wall. I'm

63

weakened from your damned wooden bullet. I'm helpless and completely at your mercy."

The woman hesitated for a moment, thinking about my words. She nudged the girl forward again, but she did not move. "Fine, have it your way. I will be right here so don't try anything stupid." She walked toward the entrance and stopped, leaning against the wall.

The child took small steps and closed the distance between us. She sat on my lap, taking a handful of her hair and placing it to the other side, revealing her already abused neck. *Listen, I really do not want to do this. Blink two times if you can hear me...* The girl's eyes widened before she blinked. I looked at the woman to make sure she had not heard. She stood against the wall, chewing on her fingernails.

I am going to bite; making a wound... I will not drink but pretend that I am... Please... For your own good...

Leilani blinked twice and leaned into me, placing her neck against my lips. Could I really bite without indulging in her warm blood? I had to. I wrapped my lips around her warm neck and positioned my fangs, biting down to pierce her tender skin. Blood flowed instantly and I lapped it with my tongue allowing a few drops to reach her shirt. As I kept my mouth against her neck, my fangs withdrawn, she moaned and fell against me. It was obvious she had been a source of blood many times before, as she knew exactly what to do. The burning in my throat added to my anger, but I had to keep my cool. I had to make these people believe that I was feasting on this girl.

After a few minutes, I pulled my mouth aside, turning my head to the side. "Take her," I panted. "I've had enough."

The woman rushed over to lift the limp girl from my lap. She flopped in her arms. "Did you kill her?" she asked.

"No, just weakened her. She will need some red meat now and plenty of rest," I licked my lips as if licking the last drop off.

"You don't need to tell me how to take care of a feeder. I already know," she said as she stood with Leilani in her arms.

"A feeder? How often do you do this? How many vampires are up here?" I asked.

"It doesn't matter how many there are. There are some who pass through here and will pay top dollar for one of our feeders. It's what needs to be done to keep travelers from killing the population. Believe me, not one of the feeders ever complains. They enjoy it," she turned to leave. "Oh, and by the way, this one is completely yours. She will be your only meal from now on."

⤳ THIRTEEN ⤳

If only I had been able to feed, I would have gained back some strength. Unfortunately, it would not be until the wooden bullet was out of my leg that I could hope to have enough strength to break the chains holding me here. But feeding from Leilani, especially if it was the Leilani we were looking for, was not an option. The problem was, would I be able to resist her blood the next time she was brought to me? I was hungry this time but not to the point my hunger would have forced me to feed from a child, at least not yet.

The key turning in the lock snapped me from my thoughts. The woman entered carrying a bucket. "It's time to wash you up," she said as she turned the light on, shedding a yellow glow on the dingy room.

"What for?" I asked and sat up straighter. My leg was dead weight as I dragged myself back on the dirt.

"You can't meet my boss looking like this, now, can you? You're a mess." She knelt next to the bucket and rung out a cloth. She brought it to my face. I tried to turn away. "Sit still."

"Unchain me and I can wash myself." It was worth a try.

She laughed. "That's funny. You're funny. But do you think I'm crazy?" She wiped my forehead with flower scented water.

"Who is your boss? Is it Melinda?" I asked as she wiped my cheeks roughly.

"I can't tell you that. You will be meeting, um, my boss...very soon." She dunked the cloth in the bucket and continued.

"They will find me, you know. Aloysius has connections all over the city and they will come for me," I said as she dragged the cloth from my chin to my neck.

"I wouldn't put too much trust in Aloysius if I were you."

"Why not? You don't even know him. You're just someone's human servant," I answered as she unbuttoned my shirt. I tried to push myself into the wall, trying to fade onto it.

She looked up at me without an ounce of emotion in her eyes. She wrung out the cloth again and started wiping my chest above my bra. "I may be only a human servant, for now, but I do know some things. Let's just say you're putting your trust in the wrong vampires." As her fingers reached for the button on my jeans, I stiffened.

"That is enough. I don't need a bath. I don't even sweat," I said. She looked up at me and threw the cloth into the bucket, splashing some water on both of us. She sat back on her heels and put her hands on her knees. "What do you mean you're human for now?"

"I won't be human much longer. Can I fix your hair?" She reached toward my head with a tentative hand. I nodded. It couldn't hurt to get on her good side.

"Did they promise to turn you?" She nodded and pulled a comb out from her back pocket. I hung my head forward so she could reach the back. "They'll say anything to get what they want from you; you know that don't you?"

"But they really will. They promised. I stink at everything else. I'm a terrible hunter, I have too much compassion for your kind, they say. I have no witch powers, no job training, no family. I would make a great vampire." She seemed so sure of herself. I hated to tell her they would most likely use her up, chew her up, and spit her out.

"What is your name?" I asked. "I'd like to be able to call you something."

"I'm not supposed to tell you."

"I could just dig around in your head, but I'd rather not." I didn't think she knew that it wouldn't be an easy task in my weakened state.

She fixed a few strands of my hair with her fingers and moved back. "Fine. Maria. Just call me Maria."

"Maria," I repeated. "You said vampires are no different than animals. If you have too much compassion for vampires, why are you doing this?"

"Because I have my orders. If I don't do what they want, I don't get what I want. I only said that because I'm jealous. I didn't mean it."

"So, what you want is to become a vampire. Have you thought about what that really means?"

"Of course, I've thought about it. It's all I think about," her eyes suddenly teared. "It's what I've wanted for years but they say I'm not ready."

"Have they said why you're not ready?"

"They say I'm too soft. I have to toughen up and stop caring about people's feelings. They said I couldn't kidnap you, that I couldn't force you to drink from a child, but I did all that. I proved myself to them."

"Yes, I suppose you did. What about the man? Who is he to them?" If she only knew I hadn't actually fed from the child.

"He's just an old hunter, no longer able to fight. They keep him around to do all the work they don't want to do. He's pretty much useless."

"Is he looking to be turned too?"

"Are you kidding me? Can you imagine him as an immortal?" She laughed.

"I guess you're right. And what about you? What will you do once you get what you want? Will you go off on your own?"

She stood and took a few steps back. "Of course not. Being an immortal will give me strength. It will give me the powers I never had as a witch. I was never one, only my mom, but they never knew that, they just assumed. Anyway, can you imagine the hunter I could be with all the powers?"

I couldn't believe what I was hearing. "You would continue hunting, killing your own kind?"

She backed away a few more steps, nearing the door as if trying to run from me. "It's the only way they'll do it. I promised them. We only rid the city of danger."

"But Maria, you'll be a vampire then, able to take care of yourself, able to leave whenever you want. They cannot keep you their prisoner," I explained. "What I still don't understand is how a vampire can be giving commands to hunters. How can Melinda have that much power over people who supposedly rid the city of vampires?"

She looked behind her and then back at me, her mouth opening to speak.

"That will be quite enough!" Melinda commanded as she stepped into the room, Ryanne, her sister, right behind her. Melinda's hair was different again, long, dark, and covering half her face. But there was no mistaking her voice and the icy look of her visible eye. Ryanne's eyes froze on my face, sending chills down my spine. It was obvious she did not forget Fergus's death and never would.

"What the hell do you want from me?" I snapped. I tried to mask my fear with anger, not sure if it was working.

"Well, it's nice to see you again, too," Melinda mocked. "It's been way too long."

"Trust me, it has not been long enough." I yelled. I pulled at the chains in the wall with all my might, but it was getting me nowhere.

"You're going to hurt yourself. You don't have enough strength to do anything. I must say I like seeing you so helpless and alone. Ryanne, what do you think we should do with her now?" She turned to her partner in crime with a smirk on her face.

Ryanne put her index finger to her chin. "Oh, I know! Now that she's here and all tied up and all, we should go find her husband. Without her to protect him, he is totally at my mercy. I can do with him what I like… Perhaps torture him a little and then end his miserable existence."

"No! You leave him alone," I struggled to free my arms again though I knew it was pointless. "He had nothing to do with what happened at that cabin. He was not the one who killed Fergus. It was my fault. Kill me!"

Both Ryanne and Melinda laughed. I looked at Maria who stood by the entrance, panic in her eyes. She looked away from me and lowered her gaze to the ground. I concentrated on her nonetheless. *Maria, please. Do something. Warn Christian, please.* She raised her head. She was listening. *They'll never give you what you want. You're wasting your time. If you do this for me, I'll make sure…*

"Stop!" Melinda barked. "Just because I can't hear you does not mean I don't know what you're doing," She turned to Maria. "Leave us!" Maria backed out of the room, running as soon as she crossed the threshold. Melinda turned to me again. "That's some pretty good control you have, if that is in fact what you were doing, sending your thoughts only to her."

"I wasn't doing anything."

"It doesn't matter anyway. Maria won't do anything to defy us, not when her fate is in our hands," She turned to Ryanne. "What do you think we should do with her now?"

Ryanne's face lit up. "Kill her."

"Just like that? That's not much fun. I thought maybe you'd want her to suffer a bit first, the way you've been suffering since she took your love from you."

"I did not kill Fergus myself. It was a battle. He was killed because he wasn't strong enough to fight. It was nothing personal against him. It was self-defense." *It was nothing personal?* Even I knew that sounded pathetic.

"But he was killed because of you. Everything is because of you," Ryanne's stare sent chills through my body. "I have an idea." She turned to Melinda who stood with her arms crossed, waiting.

"Anything you wish shall be yours. After all, you deserve it." She nodded for Ryanne to continue.

Ryanne smiled and her eyes glowed like a child spotting the presents on Christmas morning. "I think Christian should be our next guest."

"No! You stay away from him. If you want your revenge, then kill me. I'm here, totally helpless. Kill me and get it over with," my voice shook even though I tried to sound determined.

Melinda ignored me. "I must say I like your idea, Ryanne. We should bring Christian here. There's plenty of room for one more. Besides, I'm sure he's worried sick about Lily. He'll want to be with her while she dies." Melinda took a few steps closer to me. "What do you say, Lily? Want some company? We could torture him first so you can watch, then torture you, let him watch, it's only fair, and then kill you both."

"Please, I'll do anything you want, just leave Christian out of this," I begged though I knew it was useless. Neither woman had a heart. Or a soul.

"Can we have Arturo and the boys go get him?" Ryanne asked.

"We could but, I think I have a better way," Melinda went to the entrance again and stuck her head out the door. "Maria, bring Leilani," she yelled.

"Why are you bringing her? I'm not feeding again," I protested, horrified of where this might be going.

"Oh, that's not what I want her here for. She…" Melinda stopped as Maria came to the door holding Leilani's hand. Leilani rubbed sleep out of her eyes with her free hand, her hair tousled.

"Yeah, Melinda, I'd like to know what you intend too," Ryanne said.

Melinda took Leilani and waved Maria out of the room. Maria left without a backward glance. "I am going to dial Christian from my phone, and you are going to invite him here, alone."

"I will do no such thing. What makes you—"

"That's just the thing. I know you will do this because if you don't, the girl dies, and you get to watch."

Ryanne clapped her hands in excitement. If it were possible for a vampire to throw up, now would have been the time. "Are you really that heartless, that crazy?"

"Apparently, I am. So, what is it going to be? Your husband or this innocent, helpless little girl?" She wrapped an arm around Leilani's neck. Leilani's eyes grew wide, and a tear rolled down, leaving a trail on her dirty cheek.

I had to buy more time, keep her talking. "Who is this girl to me anyway? Why should I really care whether she lives or dies?"

Melinda laughed. "I know you better than that, Lily. Of course you care. You care about everybody, no matter how much you try to deny it. You care about the boy you took in, the one who held a gun to your husband's head. You even care about your lovely sister, Maia. So don't try that tactic now."

"But I thought you wanted this girl. I thought she was one of your so-called feeders. Why would you give that up just for me?" I looked at Ryanne who stood mute watching the whole exchange.

"Though I must admit the little girl is quite tasty, she is otherwise useless," she held Leilani even tighter. Leilani's eyes looked close to rolling back in her head and her skin took on a sick bluish hue. I was running out of time. She was going to kill her before I could decide anything.

"What do you mean by useless? She's just a little girl," I pleaded.

"A little girl with a very powerful talent. The only problem is, she doesn't know how to control it. She has no concentration, no aim, just fire everywhere."

I balled my hands into fists. My fangs poked through my gums as my anger surfaced. She really was Jose Luis's sister.

"I truly thought she would have made a powerful weapon but, no matter how much training has been offered to her, she has learned nothing. She has absolutely no control of her fire," Melinda explained. "We really don't need her so it's no loss. She's more of a liability to us than an asset."

"So, what will it be?" Ryanne finally lost her patience. She was enjoying this way too much.

I swallowed and took a deep breath. "Dial the phone."

⌬ FOURTEEN ⌬

As soon as I finished talking to Christian, Melinda took the phone from my ear and put it back in her back in her pocket. I tried to keep my tone as even as possible as I invited Christian to join me, telling him I had a surprise for him. I didn't want him to hear my fear. I didn't want to give Melinda the satisfaction of knowing I'd lured my husband into her trap. Though I told him to come alone and say nothing, I knew Fiore or Aloysius would be able to read his mind anyway.

"You're doing the right thing, you'll see." Melinda said and turned to Ryanne. "Take the girl back to her room. She needs rest now that she'll be dinner for two."

Ryanne nodded, a wide smile on her face, and dragged Leilani out of the room without another word. I raised my eyes to Melinda. "Why are you so hell bent on revenge? Are you really that protective of your sister; did Ian mean that much to you, or is there something more?"

"Not that it's any of your business but, yes, there is more. Maybe in time, if we let you live that long, you will get your answers. For now, just sit here and wait for the love of your life to join you in your prison." Without another look, she turned and left the room, slamming the metal door behind her, making me jump.

The minutes ticked in my head as I sat, weakened by my rising hunger and the wooden bullet in my leg. What were they going to do to him? Was he strong enough yet to protect himself, to fight back? I hoped he had fed recently though I knew he had never fed alone. Maybe Aloysius or Fiore had taken him to hunt. Hope rose in my gut as a thought hit me. Hopefully Aloysius and Fiore were home when before Christian left. Maybe they would stay close behind him, ready to rescue us. Maybe they had a plan. Maybe…

Faint laughter interrupted my thoughts as the key turned in the lock. I blinked fiercely against the sunlight entering through the door. The shapes were darkened and hard to make out as the sun blinded me. Two shapes, no, three, four, maybe five? I blinked again and again.

"Put him over there," Melinda commanded as two men dragged a third between them. What? Who?

"Christian!" I pulled as hard as I could away from the wall. "Let me out of here. Let me go to him."

"Yes, put him over there where she can see him," Melinda pointed to the cuffs across from me, next to the door. "Leave his ankles tied."

The men obeyed, one of which I recognized as Arturo, the leader of the hunters. They dropped Christian on the ground as if he were an object. He moaned and tried to look around the room, but Arturo blocked his view. He knelt in front of him, his hands on Christian's chest keeping him against the wall, while the other man pulled his arms up and fastened the cuffs around his wrists, the chains clanging and echoing. I still couldn't see Christian's face. How had they subdued him? Why wasn't he fighting?

"Thank you, gentlemen," Melinda said. "Now leave us."

The men made sure Christian was secure before standing to make their exit but not before Arturo smiled at me. Christian lifted his head and blinked; his left eye swollen almost shut. His right eye grew wide as he laid it on me. "Lily? Are you ok? What's happening?"

"What did you do to him?" I snarled looking at Melinda and Ryanne who both smiled with satisfaction.

"Nothing that won't heal within minutes, after all, he's not human anymore. However," She turned to Ryanne and handed her something I couldn't see. "We still need to keep him calm, don't we?"

"Of course we do, Melinda. We wouldn't want him to escape after we went through all this trouble to get him here. I am so glad I get to do this, thank you," Ryanne smiled at Melinda.

"What? What are you—" I followed Ryanne's arm as it rose. "Oh, God! Please don't."

Ryanne aimed at Christian's torso, her hand shaking slightly. Christian's good eye grew wide again.

"Not at his heart, my dear," Melinda said as she placed a hand on Ryanne's arm and pushed it down gently. "We don't want to kill him quite yet."

"Oh, right," she aimed toward his thigh. "That wouldn't be as much fun." She pulled the trigger. Christian's scream shook my whole body. I pulled my legs up the way he did, feeling every bit of his pain with him. Was I imagining that?

"Good. They should both be good and helpless now," Melinda said as she took the gun from Ryanne's still outstretched hand. "Let's leave them for a while now. Let them catch up a bit, say their goodbyes before we end them."

Ryanne smiled and nodded, never taking her eyes away from Christian. Her fangs glowed in her mouth as her hunger boiled to the surface. Melinda put an arm around her shoulder as she led her out of the room. Before she slammed the door behind them, I heard, "His blood will flow through your veins soon enough. Just hang in there a bit longer."

As soon as the door was secured, I turned back to Christian. "Are you ok? What did they do to you?"

He lifted his head and looked above him, giving the chains a yank. "I guess that's not gonna work, huh?" He dropped his gaze back to me.

"Not with the wooden bullet in your body. Believe me, I tried. What did they do to you?" I asked again.

"A taxi dropped me off about halfway up the mountain. I walked a bit and then as soon as I rounded a corner, someone dropped on me and knocked me to the ground. There were hands all over me as they tied my ankles and hands, and then put some disgusting cloth over my head. Next thing I know, I'm hanging over someone's shoulder in front of this metal door."

"How did they do that to your eye? Did someone hit you?"

He laughed. "Someone's knee landed on my face when they knocked me down. How did you get here?"

"After I left Lucas, I was walking up the street. I was trying to call you when someone grabbed me. I dropped my phone. They did the same thing to me, only they threw me into the trunk of a car. I know we're on a mountain by the way I rolled around in the trunk. I think Jose Luis is up here too."

"Did they say anything about him?"

"No, but I met Leilani."

"Our Leilani?" he asked, pushing himself up as best he could against the wall.

"Yes. They were trying to train her. I think they intended to use her as a weapon but she's not advancing enough for their liking. They threatened to kill her if I didn't get you up here."

"You did the right thing, Lily."

"I had no other choice. With this bullet in my leg I'm pretty much useless. I don't know how we're going to get out of here. Does anyone know where you are?"

"You said I had to come alone so I didn't say anything," he answered.

My hope deflated. "Oh, well, you did the right thing too."

"Yeah but… That didn't stop me from *thinking* about where I was going."

"Hopefully that will work. What do we do in the meantime?"

"I have no idea. They plan on torturing us and then killing us both. I won't let them touch you. I won't let…"

"Lily, have you forgotten I am also a vampire? I'm not totally helpless. We'll think of something. I just hope they don't come back too soon."

"Can you use your power at all?" It was worth a shot.

"I don't know. I can try…" He looked around the room. His swollen eye already opening more and more as the minutes passed. He focused on the wrapped bundles on the table and his face scrunched in concentration as I watched. The bundles did not move. "Ugh! I don't think I can."

"When is the last time you fed?" I asked.

"Yesterday morning. Fiore took me," he answered and turned back to the table. I kept quiet so he could focus. This time, one of the bundles rose a few centimeters and shook before falling back down. "I did it!" he yelled with excitement.

"Shh," I cautioned. "We don't want them here any sooner than they plan. Think you can focus on the bullet in my thigh, maybe lift it out?"

"What if I hurt you?" His face showed his panic.

"You can't. It doesn't even hurt anymore and since the bullet didn't completely enter my leg, the skin didn't heal around it. There's a little piece sticking out." I figured that might give him an advantage.

"I can try but if I hurt you…" His sentence was cut off by someone talking outside the door. We both froze. After a few seconds, the talking faded as if someone was walking away. "Thank God," he said. "Not ready for that yet."

As he concentrated on my thigh, tingling sensations ran throughout my leg. It was hard to stay still since it was almost a tickle, but I bit my lip and resisted giving in to the laughter I felt coming. My leg rose without my control. "Oops. That's not right," he said with a faint smile. "Let me try again. Ready?"

I nodded and gritted my teeth. It had to work. As soon as he had the bullet out of my leg, he could work on his own while I worked on freeing my arms.

This time, he focused on just the hole and not my entire leg. "Am I hurting you?" he asked, looking at my face again.

"No. It actually tickles, just keep going," I demanded. Even if they came back for us before I could break free of the chains, being free of the bullet would give me back some strength.

He focused on my leg once again. The bullet slowly rose through my skin and fell to the dirt floor. "There, that should do it," he said as he rested his head against the wall with exhaustion. My whole body began to tingle and the burning in my throat grew stronger.

"Wow, that's so much better. I'm glad you fed so recently. That gave you some strength despite the bullet." My gratitude was interrupted by the lock turning on the door. Too late. I sat up straight. The bloody bullet still lay on the ground next to my leg. I moved my leg on top of it.

"So, how are our guests doing?" Melinda asked as she led a smiling Ryanne into the room by the hand.

"Lovely, just lovely," I sneered. "What does a person have to do to get room service around here?"

"Glad to see you still have a sense of humor," Melinda said. "You're going to need it."

⤜ FIFTEEN ⤛

W hat are you going to do to us?" Christian asked. Melinda smiled but said nothing. "If what you want is revenge for the death of Fergus, then kill me. I'm Lily's mate. Fergus was Ryanne's. An eye for an eye, right?"

"No! Don't listen to him. Kill me. I'm the one responsible for all of it."

"Aww, such love, such devotion. You two make me sick," Melinda spat as she neared Christian, pushing Ryanne along. "Just to make your decision easier, you both get to die. No need to argue about it." Ryanne laughed like a demented hyena. I didn't know if it was the thought of revenge or her thirst, but something was making her crazy.

"Now, Melinda? Now can I feed?" She sounded like a five-year-old child.

"Yes, my dear. Now you may feast," Melinda answered as they stood over Christian.

"Don't do this," I pleaded. "My blood is much older than his. Take mine, I'm begging."

"Nonsense," Melinda snapped. "We're not after strength. We are both way older and more powerful than either of you. Ryanne is just hungry, and he looks quite tasty." The nail of her index finger grazed Christian's jaw line.

"Get your hands off him!"

Melinda laughed, looking back at me for a second before she turned to Ryanne. "He is all yours, my dear sister."

Ryanne turned to me with a crazed and vacant look in her eyes before planting both feet on either side of Christian's outstretched legs. She clapped her hands before she sat straddling him, taking his face in her hands. "You do look delicious. I can't believe you're all mine."

"Get your disgusting hands off him!" I screamed and pulled at the chains in the wall with all the might I could muster. One hand broke free.

"Stop that!" Melinda ordered approaching me. She bent over me and raised her hand, her slap burning my face. "You do anything else, and he will no longer be Ryanne's dinner. He will be killed immediately."

I grabbed a handful of her hair with my free hand. "I'm the one you want, not him! Deal with me, you coward!"

She pulled out of my grasp and jumped away, her mouth in a scowl. "Do it already, Ryanne. Your audience is ready."

Ryanne squealed with excitement before squeezing Christian's face in her hands, tilting his head back. Her face covered his, but it wasn't hard to guess what she intended. Moans escaped her mouth as she kissed my husband, her legs clamping around his thighs possessively. Her display of lust turned my stomach. Her hands kept his face against hers, though by the looks of it, he was trying to turn away. A few more moments of that and her hands left his face and moved out of sight.

Christian's shoulders were bared as she inched his shirt down his back with her lips still locked on his. She moved aside just enough to let me see her fingers tangled in the hair on his chest. Her moans grew louder, mixing with Melinda's laughter. "Are you liking what you're seeing, Lily?" She smiled at me. I turned away from her.

Christian groaned as Ryanne's mouth made contact with his neck, her hands still on his chest, her gulps so loud I knew even from where I sat that she was already indulging in his blood. His feet scraped along the dirt floor as he struggled in vain to get some distance from her devouring mouth.

"You are really sick; do you know that?" I yelled at Melinda.

She rolled her eyes like a teenager. "You killed her mate. It's only fair she enjoys yours for a while."

"Oh, please," I rolled my eyes, mimicking her sarcasm. "Like either of you know how to even love someone. She was only with Fergus out of convenience. It was very obvious she didn't love him."

"Shut up!" Ryanne turned away to yell at me, Christian's blood all over her chin. "You know nothing! I did love him!"

"Look at you," I sneered. "You can't even eat without making a mess of yourself. You need a bib?"

She jumped off Christian and ran at me, dropping to her knees in front of me. I grabbed her by the throat with my free hand. Since I had ripped the cuff out of the wall, Melinda had not been able to secure my arm again. I squeezed, my fingers positioned around her trachea, her eyes bulging. Her hands wrapped around my wrist as she tried to pry it from her neck. "I did not kill Fergus. He died because he was weak. He was useless and powerless. Don't you get that?"

Melinda pulled Ryanne's hands off my wrist. She wrapped her hands around my arm and tried to pull it off Ryanne. I held on as hard as I could with my diminishing strength. I really should have fed. Suddenly, Melinda's body was thrown across the room, bouncing off the stone wall and landing in a heap on the ground before she jumped again to her feet. In the blur of confusion, hands wrapped around Ryanne's waist as she tried to run at me a second time. She too was thrown across the room.

"Lily, we're getting you out of here," Fiore yelled as she grabbed the chain keeping me immobile and yanked it from the wall. My eyes landed on Christian just as Aloysius was pulling his chains out of the wall. Melinda jumped on his back, and he shook her off as if she were nothing more than a pesky bug.

"Let's go!" Aloysius yelled. He held Christian up with an arm around his waist.

"Leilani!" I yelled. "They have Leilani. Jose Luis might be here too!" I tried running toward the door, but Fiore grabbed my hand.

"There's no time for that," Aloysius said. "We'll come back for them."

Fiore pulled me to where Aloysius stood with Christian. "Take my hand," she instructed as she held Aloysius's free hand. We formed a circle. As Ryanne and Melinda ran toward us, the room began to spin and then blurred. We were thrown into what seemed like a black whirlwind and I couldn't even see Fiore's face, though I felt her hand in mine. A few moments later, we landed on something hard, or at least, Christian and I landed on something hard while Fiore and Aloysius stood. "Ouch!" I complained, rubbing my rear end as I stood. Christian sat on the living room floor looking lost, his shirt hanging around the wrist of one arm.

"Well, that was fun," he shook his head and looked around the room. "Let's not do that again anytime soon."

Aloysius walked over and extended his hand. Christian took it and he pulled him to his feet. "You've done it before," Aloysius said.

"Yeah, but that was just with you, and we landed on our feet. This one hurt." Christian rubbed his butt in an exaggerated manner and looked at me.

"Yup! Blame that one on me. Apparently, I can't land whether I fly or materialize," I went to Christian and tenderly wrapped my arms around his neck. "You ok?"

"I think so," he touched his fingers to the puncture wound on his neck. I instantly felt sick, and I shook the image of Ryanne's lips all over him out of my head. "Here, let me." I bit the tip of my tongue and rubbed my blood over the marks. They closed within seconds.

"Thanks," Christian kissed me lightly before turning to Fiore and Aloysius. "How did you find us?"

"It wasn't hard after we listened in on your phone conversation and your thoughts," Aloysius explained. "How did they get to you, Lily?"

I explained it to them like I had explained it to Christian. I also told them about my conversation with Lucas and what I learned about Mariana. "That reminds me, have you heard anything from the police yet?"

"They are still questioning all the staff at the hospital. They also suggested that you or Christian, or both, make an appearance on the news, maybe plead with the public. They think some tears would help, though I know that's not possible," he laughed. "If you let the public know he is gravely ill, maybe someone will step up and call with some information. Someone had to have seen him in a city this populated."

I looked at Christian. He nodded. "We're willing to do anything to get him back safely," I agreed. "When do they want us?"

"Lucas will be in touch. He's setting it all up," Aloysius said and sat on the sofa. "You probably want to at least wash up and change your clothes before we go anywhere. I imagine you're also hungry, Lily?"

"You're right, I am. We'll go get cleaned up and be right back," I said taking Christian's hand and leading him to the stairs.

Once in our room, I threw myself into his arms and held him as tightly as my arms allowed. "You have no idea how happy I am right now. I really thought it was the end."

He hugged me back and kissed my head. "There will never be an end. We could've handled them."

"Them maybe, but you know they don't operate alone. I'm sure they had an army waiting just outside the door."

"You're probably right, regardless; we're home safe and sound. I believe in you and me. I believe in us. We would have defeated them one way or an-other," he loosened his grip and leaned back to look into my eyes. "Regardless, we are together for eternity, no matter where or how that eternity takes place."

After we washed and changed out of our torn and dirty clothes, we went back to the living room to join the others. They were sitting on the sofa, both with their cell phones in their hands waiting for them to ring with some kind of news.

"You said they have Leilani?"

"Oh, yes. Melinda brought her to me as a gift. They have humans there to be used for the sole purpose of feeding vampires. Leilani is one of them. She was supposed to be my dinner but…" I started to tell them, but the door opened and Giovanni rushed in.

"I found Tomas's family," he announced. "It's not good."

∽ SIXTEEN ∾

What do you mean it's not good?" Aloysius stood and offered a seat to Giovanni. In all the months we'd been here, I'd never seen Giovanni sit anywhere but by the front door. He was always on the go, vigilant, and ready for any request from us.

He nodded to Aloysius and took a seat. "They went up north, Lucia and the kids. They're staying in some rundown hotel that doesn't even have plumbing."

"What are they doing there? Does Lucia have family up there?" I asked.

"No," Giovanni turned to me. "That's the weird thing. Her family all lives in Arequipa, south of Lima. I found where they are and went there. I knocked repeatedly but she wouldn't answer the door. In fact, I saw the light go out and then all was quiet, as if they were trying to hide."

"Is Tomas with them?" I asked impatiently.

"She finally opened the door after I begged and assured her I was alone and just worried about her and the kids. She looked terrified. Her eyes were swollen like she'd been crying. The kids huddled together on the floor in a dark corner of the room."

"What the hell? Something really scared them," Aloysius said.

"Something or someone… Anyway, I wasn't able to get much out of her and I didn't want to scare the kids any further by insisting. She did say she hadn't seen Tomas since he went to Churín with you," he looked at Christian and me. "She doesn't even know if he's alive. That started her crying again so I thanked her and left."

"Do you think someone threatened them?" Christian asked.

"It is a possibility. Even if she hadn't started crying again, it's doubtful she would have said anything more," he explained.

"Why would anyone want Tomas?" I asked.

Aloysius turned to me. "Though Tomas is human, he's worked for me for quite a few years. He never asked what my guards and I are, and if he knows, he said nothing. That won't stop whoever took him, however. They must assume he knows something, some information they are after."

"I guess so. Do you think his family is safe where they are?" I asked, turning to Giovanni.

"I don't know. The place is out of the way, however, I found them," Giovanni answered.

"Yes," Aloysius stood and began pacing. I wondered if he was thinking the same as me. He smiled at me and continued. "We need to get them here. They will be better protected here with all of us. That hotel is no place for the children."

"I agree, sir, but how do we get them here? They were terrified of me," Giovanni said.

Aloysius smiled at me again. "Take Lily with you. She's good with kids. She'll convince them," Aloysius explained.

"What?" I sat up straighter. "Since when am I good with kids?"

Christian laughed. "Since you turned Jose Luis's life around."

"Yeah, but you see what good that did," I protested.

"It did a lot of good. I honestly don't think Jose Luis left the hospital on his own. He wanted to stay with us, remember?" Christian explained.

"I guess. I'm just a little nervous about this. They've never met me and besides, it's my fault their daddy's gone."

"Nonsense! They will love you and it's not your fault he's gone. Melinda is behind all of this. Lucia will understand that, I'm sure," he turned to Giovanni. "You and Lily will take a flight out there; bring them back the same way. It'll be much faster that way." Giovanni nodded and stood, looking at me to do the same.

"What about Christian?" I asked.

"He will stay with us, and we'll go to the television studio when Lucas calls," Aloysius replied. "Charge all the plane tickets to me," he said to Giovanni and nodded for him to leave.

"I'll wait for you right outside, Miss Lily." He nodded to Christian and Fiore before departing.

"I guess I'm going," I looked at Aloysius for confirmation. He nodded with a smile. "I was afraid of that."

Christian stood and wrapped me in his arms. "Be careful," he kissed my forehead. "I'll be fine here. I can handle the news." I looked at Aloysius.

"He will have an interpreter, I assure you," he said. "You won't be gone long. The flight is only one hour."

Christian let me go and kissed my lips. "I'll be waiting for you. I know you'll convince them to come and stay with us."

"I'm glad you all have so much faith in me. Guess I'll see you soon." With one last look at Christian, I headed out the door.

SETTLING INTO MY seat on the plane, I turned to Giovanni. "So where exactly are we going?"

"We'll be landing in Chiclayo. I'll rent a car when we get there, and we'll drive the rest of the way. They're in a small village on the outskirts," he said and picked up the map he had purchased at the airport.

"I thought you knew where you were going?" I asked feeling a bit nervous.

"Oh, I do. I just want to make sure there are alternate routes in case we need them."

"Are you anticipating problems?" I really did not like this one bit. I would rather have stayed with Christian. Aloysius or Fiore could have convinced Tomas's family just as well.

"You never know. Melinda causes problems no matter where she goes," he explained.

"Why do I get the feeling this is not the first time you've dealt with Melinda."

He refolded the map and fastened his seat belt. "You better do the same, Miss. We'll be taking off soon and the flight attendants will be checking."

"First of all, you don't have to call me Miss. Lily would be fine," I fastened my seat belt. "And second, don't change the subject on me. Have you dealt with Melinda before?"

He smiled briefly and then his eyes grew serious. "You could say that. I—I mean we, the other vampires in the city—have been dealing with her for a very long time. She comes recruiting about every two years or so, wants as many vampires as she can get."

"For what? What can she possibly get from here that she can't find in Ireland?" I asked.

"I don't know. I've never actually talked to her." He stuffed the map in the pocket of the seat in front of him and relaxed in his seat.

"Has she ever gotten anyone to go with her?"

"She has gotten a few throughout the years. She was here just recently, which is why I'm surprised to see her back so soon. Anyway, I think if she does not get them to go with her, she makes new ones."

"Oh, my God," I whispered. Giovanni turned to me. "I know why she was here recently. She was getting vampires to fight my family and me."

"Why would she do that?" Giovanni asked. The plane gained speed down the runway, bouncing slightly.

"Ian, my maker, had been causing all kinds of problems. He left me years ago, but when I met Christian, he decided he had to have me back. He kidnapped Christian and had him hidden in the basement of a cottage in Ireland though he had promised to let him be if I just joined him. He lied. I found Christian and took him. That's when Ian and his goons came after us, all the way to America," I explained. Could Melinda really have had something to do with all that? What was she to Ian? "Did you ever meet Ian?" I asked.

Giovanni thought for a while and then shook his head. "Never heard of him."

There went that theory. Why, of all the places in the world, would Melinda be coming to Peru to do her recruiting, and for what? Ian had been forming an army before I killed him. Melinda seemed to be doing the same thing. I turned to Giovanni again. "Any idea how many vampires actually reside in Lima?"

"Not really," he leaned his head back in his seat and turned to face me. "I'm sure that's something Mr. Aloysius would know though. Do you think Melinda knew Ian, that she was maybe working for him all along?"

"I don't know what to think. I just find it odd that they would both come here to look for more vampires." Before I could say anything more, the announcement was made that we would be landing in Chiclayo. Giovanni grabbed his map and stuck it in the inside pocket of his jacket. I turned to look out the window as the plane made its descent over the fog-covered runway.

Later, Giovanni settled into the seat of the rental car, adjusting his mirrors. It was as badly maintained as most of the taxis on the roads of Lima, but it would serve its purpose as long as we were not chased. Giovanni laughed at my thought as he coaxed the little car onto the road out of the lot.

"How far from here?" I asked, anxious to get this over with.

"Less than twenty minutes," He reached to turn the knob on the radio before he noticed it was broken off. "That figures."

"There's a pair of pliers right there. Could that be what they're for?" I asked, picking them up. I attached the end to the metal and turned. Static greeted us. "Guess so." I pushed all the buttons for the stations that were preprogrammed. Nothing but static. I turned it off and threw the pliers back down.

"It is good that this car was cheap to rent," Giovanni added with a smile. "Look." He motioned to his window with his head. A group of people were knee deep in water.

"What are they doing?" I asked as I watched another person rolling up his pants legs on the side of the road, preparing to join the others.

"It's a rice paddy. They grow a lot of it in this area. The weather is ideal for it," Giovanni said.

"In all of my travels, I've never seen one of those," I admitted. As we passed, I saw more rice paddies on either side of the narrow road. The workers paused to look as we passed, some of the children waving to us.

"That's it, up ahead," Giovanni pointed to a squat building that looked like it was never finished. Spray painted on the wall was a sign with the name of the hotel. "Sad, isn't it?"

"People pay to stay there?" I asked, amazed. He nodded. "It should be against the law."

He stopped the car on the side of the building and turned off the engine. "They're in number three. We will go together since they've seen me before."

We got out of the car and he led the way to the door. He knocked and stood back. "What if it doesn't work?" I asked.

"It has to work."

The door opened a crack. "*Quien?*" A small male voice asked. Giovanni announced us.

The boy answered in Spanish. "My mother is not here. I cannot let you in."

"Let me take over," I whispered to Giovanni before turning back to the door. "My name is Lily. I am here with Giovanni, your dad's friend. Can we come in and wait for your mom?"

The boy hesitated a moment. "She will get mad at me. I am not supposed to let anyone in while she is gone."

"Do you know where she went?" I asked not liking that she left her children alone.

"She went to the river to get water."

"Paco, who is it?" a little girl asked.

"*Papá's* friends," Paco answered. Much to Paco's surprise, the little girl pulled the door open.

"Hello. I am Alegría," she looked from me to Giovanni. "I know you. Do you have it?"

I looked at Giovanni with surprise. "No. I am sorry, but I did not have time to get it. I will get you one later, I promise." He turned to me. "I usually bring her a lollypop when I see her."

"Can we please come in and wait for your mother?" I asked Alegría. She looked me up and down before answering.

"Come in," she said and turned to her brother. "They are daddy's friends. They are not strangers. *Mamá* said no strangers." She stood with her back straight as if trying to appear taller than she was. A diminutive girl with long dark braids, she was all manners as she pointed to the bed. "Please sit. *Mamá* will be back soon."

"You're going to get in trouble," Paco said as he passed her. She stuck her tongue out at him before she sat on the other bed. Both beds were neatly made. A rag doll lay against the pillow on the center of one.

"That is Lulu. Isn't she pretty?" Alegría picked her up, straightened her dress, and handed her to me.

"She is very pretty. She looks just like you," I said as I stroked the doll's long yarn braids.

"My *abuelita* made her. She is me," Alegría smiled as I admired her doll. "Do you know where *Papá* is? Did you come to take us to him?" She asked. That got Paco's attention and he joined his sister on the bed. I looked at Giovanni for help.

"We don't know where he is right now, but he will be with us soon," Giovanni explained. "He wanted us to take you and your mother to Lima to wait for him."

Alegría clapped her little hands. "I'm so happy. I want to go back home to my other dolls. They are all alone."

Though I knew their apartment was empty, I tried to make her feel better. "We will take you back to them, do not worry." I was interrupted by the door opening. A woman of no more than twenty-five walked in carrying a blue bucket. She dropped it when she saw us, spilling its contents all over the floor, turning the firmly packed dirt to mud.

"Who are you?" she screamed as she gathered her children in her arms. "Please leave my babies alone."

"It's ok, *Mamá*. They are Daddy's friends. That's the one that gives me lollypops, remember? They are going to take us to Daddy," Alegría explained. The woman looked at Giovanni with recognition in her deep brown eyes.

"Is this true?" she asked, still hugging her children closely. Paco tried to pry her arms apart with no success.

"Not exactly," I started and stood from the bed. "We are trying to find your husband. Until we do, Aloysius, his employer, thought it best to have you with us. You will be much more comfortable in Lima than in this place."

"Why would we go with you? We are not safe in Lima," she explained.

"*Mamá*, please let me go," Alegría pleaded. "They are nice people."

The woman looked at Giovanni and me before loosening her hold on the children. The children straightened their clothes before sitting back down on their bed.

"Look, ma'am, I understand you don't know us, or trust us, but you will all be more comfortable with us. In Lima, we can protect you while we find Tomas. We cannot do that here," I explained. "The children will be happier there. Aloysius and Fiore are fixing a room up for you."

"Why should I believe you?" she asked as she sat down next to her children, close to Alegría's side. "You are one of them."

"Look, ma'am," I sat on the other bed. "I know you've never seen me before and I understand your hesitation, but you are all in danger. If you stay here, they will find you. We cannot protect you here and we can't stay."

She looked at her children. They both smiled at her. "But you are one of them, right?"

"If by one of them you mean…Immortal," I whispered hoping the children didn't hear. "Then, yes. But we are the good ones. We are the ones who can keep you all safe."

"I don't know," she started and stood. "Why would someone harm us? Why would they threaten to kill us?"

Giovanni cleared his throat. "We can talk about that on the way to the airport. We need to leave as soon as possible. It is a possibility we were being watched, might have been followed."

The little girl stood and took her mother's hand, turning her around to face her. "*Mamá*, they are very nice. I want to go with them. I want to go on the airplane."

The woman laughed and turned to me. "They have never been on an airplane. I don't know…"

Giovanni moved to the window and pulled the tattered curtain aside. "We need to go, now. Something is not right." He looked at me. *They are close. I sense them…*

"Please, *Mamá*," Alegría begged pulling on her mother's hand.

"Yes, please let's go," Paco echoed.

The woman looked from Giovanni to me, her eyes widening with terror. "Okay. We will go with you, but we have to get our things," She walked to the corner of the room and picked up a duffle bag. "Alegría, Paco, get your things."

"Too late," Giovanni moved to stand with his back against the door. "They are here."

⤜ SEVENTEEN ⤛

"W ho's here?" I ran to help Paco shove things into the empty bag. "How many?"

Giovanni looked out the window, making sure to stay out of sight. "Three, no four, all human. They're going into the office...maybe that's enough time."

"Why would they just send humans?" I asked as I continued working.

Giovanni thought for a moment. "I don't think they know we're here. They were sent to collect a woman and two children, all human."

"That makes sense. But, we'll never make it, not with the children," I said and zipped Paco's bag. Alegría stood in the corner of the room, her doll grasped in her arms, her face hidden behind it.

Lucia ran to the corner and took Alegría in her arms. "What do they want from us?"

"I'm not sure but we'll get you out of here. I promise." I looked at Giovanni whose face remained calm.

What can you do? I asked.

Besides what we're doing now? Nothing. I'm just smart, strong, and dependable. He shrugged.

Great, that would do a lot of good in this situation.

What can you do? he asked as he walked over to where Paco stood as if cemented to the floor, his eyes wide and his hands shaking.

I can fly but not from the ground. I would need some place high...Oh, wait, that won't help all of us. Oh, I can kind of mess with people's minds.

What do you mean "kind of mess with their minds?

Well, I can make them see what I want them to see...

"That just might work," he said aloud.

"What might work? Please, someone say something before they get here," Lucia pleaded with us.

"We are planning something," Giovanni explained and turned back to me. "Think you can make us invisible right now?"

"I don't know," I held Paco against me.

"Ouch!" he complained.

"I am so sorry. I didn't mean to hurt you," I backed away from him and he ran for his mother and sister but smiled at me, assuring me he wasn't angry.

"Lily, now please, an answer. They are leaving the office."

Taking a deep breath, I tried to ground myself. I had to try. I had to get these innocent people out of here safe and sound. I had to. "I think I can. Let's try. If it doesn't work, take them and leave the rest to me."

"No. We go together." Giovanni announced. "I am going to take my gun out, just in case. I will not use it unless I have to protect you," he explained to the three cowering in the corner. "We are going to walk outside, close together, and get into the car. Please do not make a sound."

"This is crazy. They are going to see us," Lucia protested.

"If this plan works, they will not see us and we don't want them to hear us either, so please, be as quiet as you can," he explained with such authority I found myself nodding.

"*Mamá*, carry me," Alegría asked already holding her arms up. Lucia looked at me and I nodded. The less footsteps, the better. Giovanni answered my thought by scooping Paco into his arms, gun ready in one hand.

"Whatever happens, we stay together," I whispered to them, their eyes full of fear. "Ok, here we go."

I took a deep breath and concentrated on the figures in front of me, picturing them as nothing but air. Giovanni, arms full, motioned with his head for Lucia to open the door. She turned wide eyes to me, and I realized I had to concentrate harder. Her image wavered before my eyes before disappearing completely, just as I needed it to. Hopefully, it would last.

To our right, the four humans, three men and one woman, kicked doors open and searched rooms. I counted doors as we took tentative steps and felt panic when I saw they only had three more rooms to check before coming our way. As we inched our way toward the car, the images of Lucia, Paco, Alegría, and Giovanni wavered and swayed in front of me, coming in and out of focus as if a camera tried to zoom in on them. This would never work. I had to make them invisible before the others left the next room.

As we made slow progress on our path, a light breeze picked up the dust of the unpaved parking lot, blowing it in our faces. Alegría sneezed. We froze.

"She has allergies," Lucia whispered.

"What was that?" The woman poked her head out of a room. A man stepped up behind her and stuck his head out, looking around the parking lot.

My eyes stayed in place, glued on the figures in front of me, picturing nothing but the ground, the trees in the distance, the few cars parked along the outer edge of the lot.

"Someone's out here," the woman said from the doorway. "Jorge, go look around."

"It was nothing. It was just the wind, or a car, or something," he argued.

"I said go look," the woman commanded. "You two, next room." The other two men walked out, following her orders. She stood outside the room, hands on her hips, as she looked in our direction.

Keep going...We're almost there... I communicated to Giovanni.

She senses something...

I know...I'm working on it...Keep going...

While I concentrated on the scenery in front of me, I heard the woman's footsteps as she left the room and slowly walked toward us. Lucia stopped breathing. Paco took a deep breath.

"Hello?" the woman called. "Who's there?"

I looked back just long enough to see her arm stretch in front of her as if grasping for something. She just missed me. I nudged Lucia to walk faster. I concentrated harder, picturing a dog, his brown fur dirty and matted to his thin frame, his tongue hanging out the side of his mouth from thirst. Stray dogs were nothing new in these parts.

"I see no one. I looked all around the building," Jorge said as he walked up to her. "Oh, look, it's just a dog."

"I could have sworn...Ok, back to work," she said as she looked down. The dog was lying on the ground, scratching savagely at its neck. With a disgusted look on her face, the woman looked around one more time before following Jorge back to the row of doors.

She had come so close to discovering us, but my concentration remained solid.

Open the driver-side door, Giovanni. We can all get in that way and climb into our seats. I instructed.

Once we were seated, Giovanni pulled his door shut as quietly as possible. *How do we get out of here without starting the car?*

I hadn't thought of that...What if I put in into neutral and you push, at least until we are a safe distance away?

We could do that, but they may notice a car moving with no driver.

That's a chance we'll have to take...

Before moving to the driver's seat, I whispered, "Giovanni is going to push us until we are far enough to start the engine. Please stay down just in case."

I needed to focus on keeping Giovanni and I invisible while steering the car. I wasn't sure my concentration would last long enough so I mentally let go of Lucia and her children for the time being. They ducked down in the seat, huddled together, as Giovanni started pushing. We rolled along the dirt path of the parking lot in the direction of the paved road leading out of town. So far so good. They were still busy searching rooms.

Lily, how far do you think before we start it?

Just a little more…Oh, no! They are coming out of Lucia's room. Stop pushing for a moment.

Giovanni stopped pushing just as the woman's head slowly turned, scanning the parking lot. I held my breath. She shook her head and walked into the open door to the next room. I exhaled. Giovanni resumed pushing the car.

We should be good. Get in… I instructed Giovanni. He ran to the passenger side and jumped in. I looked at him and sighed, turning the key.

"Step on it, Lily," he looked back. "I'm sure they heard me closing the door."

The three huddled on the back seat stopped breathing; their heart beats speeding in my ears.

"Can you do something, disguise us, make us invisible again?" Giovanni asked as he signaled for the others to stay down.

"I'm trying," I accelerated as soon as the road allowed, the tires kicking up stones and hitting the sides of the car. Alegría screamed. "I have to concentrate on keeping us on the road."

Up ahead, the road began to curve uphill. I gripped the steering wheel tighter. Though I couldn't see them in the rearview mirror yet, I heard their tires screeching as their car made its way out of the dirt lot.

"They are coming, *mamá*," Paco yelled behind me.

"Get down, Paco. We'll lose them," I tried to assure him though I wasn't sure I believed it myself.

"Lily, watch out!" Giovanni yelled as we approached the first turn in the narrow road. I jerked the wheel to the right, the car balancing on two wheels before landing on all four with a bang. Screams turned to squeals of pleasure from the children in the back seat. "I can see them now. They're catching up!" Giovanni warned as the road straightened again. In the rearview mirror, their vehicle made an appearance in a cloud of dust. I stepped on the gas, hoping the little piece of junk we rented would cooperate.

"Seat belts everyone," I yelled behind me. "But keep your heads down." The rustle of clothing and the acceleration of hearts and breath in the back seat told me they were doing as I said. As seat belts clicked into place, I coaxed the car to an impossible speed on such a narrow curving road.

"They're getting close. Can't this thing go any faster?" Giovanni yelled.

I pushed the accelerator to the floor. The car rattled and shook. "Doesn't look like it. Take the wheel," I yelled to Giovanni as the wind hissed in my ears.

"What are you going to do?"

I took a deep breath and gripped the door handle. "I'm going after them."

"Are you crazy?" he yelled.

"Lily, don't," Lucia pleaded from the back seat, her eyes in the rear-view mirror wide and terrified.

"We have no choice. This car won't go any faster. They're getting too close," I explained as we were jerked forward with a heart wrenching bang. They were trying to push us off the road.

Giovanni grabbed the wheel and nodded, his focus straight ahead, as I rolled the window down further and gripped the roof with both hands. "I'm going for it…just keep driving and get them out of here!"

Sitting on the window ledge, the wind blew my hair in my face, blinding me almost completely. I took a deep breath and pictured Christian's face before pulling myself up onto the roof. Even on my hands and knees, the wind from the speed of the little car rocked my body and threatened to throw me wherever it wished. I concentrated on keeping myself, hair around my eyes and in my mouth, steady.

Giovanni, warn me if you're going to turn…

Pretty straight for a while…be careful…

I had to act before the humans started shooting. Fighting the wind to keep my balance, I bent my knees and pulled the hair off my face with one hand while keeping the other out to my side. I threw my hair behind me, letting the wind take over while I freed my hand, stretching my arm out in front of me. Would this work? I had no idea. Flying was something completely different from what I was about to do now.

Lily, the road curves in less than a mile…hurry!

My fangs protruded without intent as a fierce growl escaped my throat. With my knees bent and my head forward, I pushed off the roof of the speeding car. The wind pushed me back as my arms flailed in front of me to counteract it. I pictured Christian's blue eyes before I slammed into their hood with a deafening crunch.

EIGHTEEN

W hat the hell are you doing?" a woman's voice screamed as the wind hummed in my ears. "Get her off us!"

My body jerked to the right, but I grabbed the window frame, keeping myself on the hood. It was taking all my might to keep my flying legs from pulling me off the hood of the car.

"This damn window won't go up! Do something to get her off!" She yelled at her passenger.

"I don't know what to do. There's nowhere to go. Where's your gun?" he yelled as he looked over at me and his eyes grew wide. The car swerved dangerously close to the edge of the road before the driver recovered and looked straight ahead again. I reached in and grabbed her arm, making her jerk the wheel to the right, one front tire dangling on the edge of the hill for a moment. I took that opportunity to grab her and pull.

Hard, pointy things scraped my back, my bare arms, my legs, my face. The wad of hair in my mouth tasted like mud. My hands gripped something soft and warm, my left hand feeling something damp. The screams were hard to distinguish; which was mine, which was hers? Was the dizziness going to stop? A piercing boom in the distance made me open my eyes enough to realize we were tumbling tangled together down the side of the hill.

The searing pain in my back and the stillness of the trees made me realize we stopped. Still gripping her shirt, I jumped to my feet as she lay limp in front of me. Her wide eyes stared past me and down the hill where black smoke blurred out the scenery. She licked at the blood running from the side of her mouth.

"Please…don't kill me…" her voice came out in a gurgled whisper and she tried to get up.

"Why shouldn't I? You came to take an innocent woman and her children to their deaths," I spat at her as I let go of her shirt and pushed her against the ground. Her cries were immediate as she landed against a rock.

"I had to get them," she cried harder. "They would have killed me if I refused. Please, let me go." *She will believe me. She doesn't know who I am…*

who I am and what I can do…I can get out of this…come back for her later…

"Oh, really? Is that what you think?" I crouched in front of her, lifting her face with my fingers under her bruised and swollen chin. "You think you can hurt people and everything will be just fine. No problem at all for you, huh?"

"What are you saying? I didn't hurt anybody." Her tears stopped. Her eyes grew blank as the color drained from her face.

"You have and you will. The first chance you get, you'll kill me since you couldn't get to them. I don't think I like that idea," I put my hand to my temple as if I were thinking. "What to do with you now?"

"Please, *señora*. I am begging you. Let me go," she whispered, avoiding my eyes.

I leaned in close to her bloody lips, inhaling her scent. It was familiar though I wasn't sure where I knew it from. "I am going to give you what you deserve, eternal rest."

Pulling her to her feet, I put my face close to hers. A moan escaped her as she threw her head back, whether to scream or give me easy access, I wasn't sure, but I sank my fangs into her neck, letting the warm sweetness flood my mouth, warming my throat, filling my mind with images of her pathetic life. When her heart stopped as the last drop filled my mouth, I picked up her limp body and held it over my head. The black cloud, flames now visible, were right below us at the base of the mountain. I hoisted her toward the burning rubble. Straightening my shirt and wiping the hair away from my face, I turned and made my way back up the hill and toward the road.

Giovanni met me at the top and took my hand, pulling me the rest of the way.

"Are you ok?" he asked as he examined my face, lifting my chin softly with his fingertips.

"Yeah, I'm fine," I answered. "The woman isn't though."

"I know. I saw the insane stunt you pulled. The children haven't stopped talking about it. They think you're like Wonder Woman or something." He laughed and shook his head.

"What about the others?" I asked as we started walking toward the car parked on the side of the road.

"Did you happen to see all the smoke?" he asked. I nodded. "That was them. They lost control when you pulled the driver out and went off the embankment. I watched for a while, but no one escaped the wreck."

"Any witnesses?" I asked. I wanted to feel bad about killing the humans, but I couldn't make the feeling come.

"No. We seem to be the only ones crazy enough to use this road. It was more treacherous than I expected."

"Lily, that was incredible!" Paco screamed as I got into the car.

"Paco, please. She could have been killed," Lucia warned him.

"But I wasn't. And neither were any of you. I think we're safe to leave here now," I turned to Giovanni. "To the airport?"

THE FLIGHT BACK to Lima was uneventful, with the exception of the questions. Every time Paco and Alegría tried to ask about what I did, about what happened to the woman, and about what happened to the others in their car, Lucia changed the subject. After a while, they gave up and let their excitement over their first airplane ride take over. They smiled from ear to ear, though Paco looked a little nervous when the plane tilted as it made a turn over La Cordillera Blanca, part of the Andes Mountains.

Walking down the hall to the apartment, Lucia and the children looking around them with fascination as they followed, I tried to communicate my happiness to be back to Christian. When he did not respond, though I knew we were close enough to communicate that way, I stopped. Paco bumped into me and started laughing.

"Sorry about that," he said.

I could sense Fiore, Aloysius, and even Lucas inside the apartment. Margarita sat outside on her chair, her eyes shifting over everyone in our company, but no Christian.

"Maybe he went to feed," Giovanni whispered, reading my mind.

I shook my head. "He wouldn't go by himself. Besides, he just fed. Something's wrong." I signaled for Margarita to open the door before we even reached it.

"Oh, you're back," Aloysius stood from the sofa. "Welcome," he said to Lucia and her children.

The children inspected Aloysius from head to toe before moving their eyes to Lucas. When they reached Fiore, Alegría's face lit up. "You are so pretty, like a doll."

"Thank you, Alegría," Fiore said, plucking the girl's name from my head. "You are very pretty too, like an angel," she smiled at Paco before taking Alegría's hand. "Let me show you to your rooms. I'm sure you'd like to freshen up and rest before dinner."

She disappeared up the spiral stairs with Alegría and the others. I turned to Aloysius.

"Where is Christian?" I asked.

"After we returned from the television station, he said he needed to go for a walk, get some air," he explained.

"He should be back any minute," Lucas added. "He was anxious for you to get back."

"Will there be anything else, *Señor*?" Giovanni interrupted.

"No, Giovanni, and thank you. You did a wonderful job as usual. Go on home and take a break." Giovanni nodded, smiling at me before leaving the apartment.

"How long has he been gone?" I asked.

"Oh," Aloysius looked at his watch. "About two hours. He shouldn't be much longer."

"You let him go off by himself?" I crossed my arms across my chest.

"Lily, he's a grown man," Fiore said as she descended the stairs. "And a vampire. He can take care of himself." She wrapped an arm around Aloysius's waist.

"Does no one think this is the worst time for him to be wandering the city alone?" I threw a glance at Lucas, who stood by the window, anxiety in his eyes, and looked as if he'd jump out any moment.

"Lily, you're exaggerating. What were we supposed to do? Send him to his room so he wouldn't go anywhere without you?"

I rolled my eyes at Fiore. They were right. Christian was a grown man and, as a vampire, he had powers of his own. I couldn't blame them for having faith in him.

"You're right. I guess I worry too much. Anyway, you said something about dinner? I could…"

"No," Aloysius threw a hand up. "Carmela will be here soon to prepare dinner for the humans."

"I'm a little offended that you don't trust me in the kitchen," I turned my lips into a frown, pretending to pout. "I could make something just as well as Carmela."

"Actually, it's not that we don't trust you with the cooking. We just would like to keep the apartment fire free." Aloysius's smile grew wide.

Lucas laughed and finally walked away from the window, his soft features twisted. He sat on the edge of the sofa and looked at the floor.

"Lucas, what's wrong?" I asked, rushing to sit next to him.

He turned his face toward me, looking at me but not seeing. "Mariana didn't come home last night."

"Oh," I turned to Aloysius who nodded to confirm he already knew. "So, you haven't fed?"

"Not blood, just food," he finally focused on my face. "But I'll be ok. She will be back. I know she will. She wouldn't do that to me."

I wished I had as much faith in her as Lucas did.

Aloysius changed the subject before I could say anything else. "Do you want to watch the tape of Christian on the news before the others come down?" he asked me.

"Uh, sure," I replied and looked at Lucas. His lips smiled weakly though his eyes betrayed his worry. If Mariana didn't return before the night was over, Lucas would be in danger.

As we watched the tape of Christian pleading with the public about Jose Luis's disappearance, the others came down the stairs, the children running ahead of their mother. Aloysius clicked stop on the remote and stood to retrieve the cassette from the bulky old VCR he had instead of a DVD player. Alegría ran toward me, her rosy cheeks freshly washed and her hair in two neat braids.

"It's so pretty upstairs. I love our room," she settled herself on the sofa between Aloysius and me, pulling her little legs up and wrapping her arms around them. "I get the top bunk. I beat Paco at rock, paper, scissors," she whispered to me.

"Alegría, feet off the sofa," Lucia warned as she took a seat in the armchair. Paco walked to the window and pulled the curtain aside.

"Wow! I can see all of Lima from here. This is great!" He turned and smiled at us before returning to the scenery sprawled out below him. Just seeing him there made me dizzy.

About an hour later, as we sat and chatted in the living room, Carmela called us to the dining room. Aloysius tried to find out all he could about Lucia and her children, avoiding silence at all costs. I knew he was trying to keep my mind off Christian, who still had not returned. When I had gone upstairs to wash my face and comb my hair, I tried to call his cell but to no avail. It went right to voice mail, telling me that his phone was turned off. A lump claimed my throat at that moment and refused to go away. Now we sat around the table, Aloysius, Fiore, and I pretending we weren't hungry but sipping on coffee, while the others enjoyed their dinner. Piled on three plates was a mound of green rice they shoveled hungrily into their mouths. It didn't smell at all bad, but it looked as if it were moldy.

"It is cilantro," Aloysius leaned over and whispered to me. "And duck."

"Oh." I turned to face him. *Christian should be back by now. Something is definitely wrong.*

A little more time, then we worry. He thought as he smiled at me. Fiore nodded, agreeing with him.

If he's not back soon, we can go look for him. He might just be lost. He will find his way back. She squeezed my hand under the table.

That is a possibility and, with his limited Spanish, he may be having a hard time getting directions. For the sake of the three humans, I tried to put it out of my mind, at least while they were enjoying dinner.

As the hour ticked by at the pace of a snail, the conversation at the table continued. The children were both enjoying their second helping of dessert which was some kind of thick purple pudding with bits of fruit sticking out here and there. Alegría told us all about her friends, from school and from the neighborhood, as she revealed a purple tongue every time she shoveled another spoonful into her mouth.

I tried to listen to everyone and participate in the happy chatter, but I couldn't help but drift away. The feeling in my gut was a familiar one, one I thought I would never again have to experience. Dread filled my dead heart, seeping down from my mind. I shook my head to dismiss the thought, but it was useless. I no longer felt Christian's presence, not in the city, not in the apartment, not in my soul. He was gone.

NINETEEN

Fiore, Aloysius, and I sat in the living room, soft classical music playing on the stereo, coffee cups in our hands. It had taken a while to get the children to settle down enough to go to bed. Lucia had been yawning through most of dinner, but the children were too excited about their new surroundings to care about their mother's exhaustion. Thankfully, due to their excitement about being in the luxurious apartment, they had momentarily forgotten to ask questions about their father. That would probably come tomorrow.

"I know you're worried about Christian, and I am too. He's been gone too long. But I don't understand what you mean by he's gone. Gone as in…?" Fiore cut herself off.

"I'm not sure exactly how to explain it," I admitted.

"Please, try, Lily." Aloysius's eyes softened as he looked at me with concern, the same concern Aaron often showed.

My coffee cup clanked against the glass coffee table as I set it down, wrapping my arms around my knees.

"I feel like I did when Ian left me. Not at first, of course. It took a long time for me to stop feeling Ian at all. I think the feeling decreased as Ian got further and further away, geographically I mean." Did I even just make any sense?

Fiore looked at Aloysius and then back at me. "I'm not sure we follow you? What feeling exactly?"

"It's an emptiness, an emptiness so complete I feel like I was hollowed out. Even when Christian and I were not in the same room, or even in the same building or city, I always felt him. His mind or soul or whatever, felt like it was intertwined with mine. I felt him when we came back from Chiclayo, for a while, and then suddenly, he was gone." I looked away so they couldn't see the red spilling down my cheeks.

Aloysius stood and came to kneel in front of me. He unwrapped my arms and took both my hands in his. "Do you think he's…?" He turned to Fiore but she looked away. "Dead?"

"What? No!" I yanked my hands free. "How could you say that?"

"We're just trying to figure out what you're feeling."

"I don't really know how to explain it. You know the connection between a maker and a vampire. When Ian died, even though it was at my hands, it was as if part of my soul had just been yanked out of my body, however momentary that had been," I explained, hoping that made more sense.

"I know what you mean," Aloysius stood and went back to his seat next to Fiore.

"What?" I asked, pulling a tissue out of the box on the end table.

Aloysius's eyes widened and I could swear I saw his pupils dilate. He looked away before continuing. "I mean, I understand what you're saying." He reached for Fiore's hand, cradling it on his lap.

"I don't know what happened to Christian, but I know he's alive." At least I hoped with all my might that I was right.

"You know, Lily, I don't think this is likely, knowing how much Christian loves you and all but," She looked at Aloysius as if asking his permission to continue. He nodded. "It is possible for a vampire to mentally renounce his maker."

"What are you talking about?"

"Not that I believe he would do that, at least not by choice, but it is possible. A vampire can renounce the connection, the feelings, and the loyalty he feels to his maker. As long as it's what he truly wants and he truly believes in it, it can be done." She bit her bottom lip, most likely nervous I would lose my temper. Instead, I sat quiet for a moment, letting the information sink in.

Aloysius sat as if he were a statue, barely blinking, his chest and shoulders still. Fiore fidgeted, playing with the flaring sleeves of her sweater, crossing and uncrossing her legs.

"No," I said and stood, taking another tissue out of the box and rubbing my cheeks almost raw with it. "I don't believe that. He would never do that to me. I'm going to look for him." I turned and went to the door, slamming it behind me.

"Good evening, Miss Lily," Pepe greeted as he tried to run past me to open the front door before I could reach it. "Will you be needing a taxi?"

"No, Pepe, thank you," I smiled at him as he held the door open. There was no need to scare him. He was just doing his job. "Oh, by the way, did you see my husband leave?"

"Yes. I was already on duty both times," he answered.

"What do you mean, both times?"

"He left and did not want a taxi. He walked that way, I think," Pepe pointed up the street to the left. "He was gone for about…I don't know…a half of an hour and then he came back."

"Was he alone when he came back?"

"Yes, Miss Lily. I thought it was strange because he did not take the elevator. He went up the stairs instead. He was only up there for a few minutes and when he came back, he hailed a taxi himself, even though I could have done it for him."

"I see. Thank you, Pepe." I left him standing on the sidewalk as I crossed the street and walked to the left. No, I really didn't see. I didn't get it at all. Why would he leave, return and leave again so quickly, and then leave again in a taxi? And how did Fiore and Aloysius not know he had come home and then left again? I decided that didn't matter right now. Looking for Christian was all I wanted to do, whether or not I felt him anymore did not matter one bit.

My legs pumped as though they moved of their own free will. I had no idea where I was going or why. Christian didn't want to be found. He renounced me and I had no idea why. I had no idea what I was looking for. He'd been gone for hours, could be anywhere by now. Regardless, I kept running until I was in sight of the park. I slowed my pace so as not to scare anyone.

"Lily, wait up," someone yelled from behind me. My stomach did a somersault until I realized it was not Christian's voice. I stopped and spun on my heels.

"Lucas, what are you doing here?" He stopped just two feet in front of me, his sunken eyes focused on my face. His breathing came fast and ragged, as if he had run for miles.

"What are you doing here? Where is Christian?" He bent over slightly, his hand pinching his side.

"Christian is gone. I'm looking for him."

"What do you mean gone?" He straightened, catching his breath just a bit.

"I mean gone, as in disappeared, left, renounced me as his maker and wife, I guess." The bitterness in my voice surprised him and he took a sharp breath.

"That's impossible," he reached for my hand and led me to an empty bench. "Sorry, I need to sit for a minute. I've been running behind you since you left the apartment."

"It's not impossible, apparently. He must have done it because I don't feel him at all." I bit back the tears by clenching my lips. Anger was more useful to me than tears.

"That man loved you more than anything in this world. That was easy to see," he squeezed my hand. "Something must have happened."

"Something like what? He left. Just left. There was nothing we couldn't accomplish together. Why do this now?" I yanked my hand out of his and stood. Sitting here was just wasting precious time I didn't have.

Lucas stood with me but said nothing. He had no ideas, no answers. It wasn't until that moment that I noticed how bad he looked. My anger had consumed me so much that I had paid no attention to his appearance.

"Mariana hasn't returned, has she?" I turned to face him. He swayed in the breeze. If the wind gusted, he would be blown over.

"No. But that's not important right now. We have two people to find. Come on, I'll help you look for Christian." He nodded toward the road leading to the beach. I started walking that way with Lucas by my side.

"It is important. You look like you're going to fall over any minute. You won't be much help to anybody this way," I hoped that didn't sound like blame.

"I know I need to exchange blood soon, but I'm ok for now. I ate a huge dinner. That should hold me over for a while," he quickened his pace. "I know when I need to think I go down to the beach. It's such a solitary and tranquil place at night. Maybe he went there."

"Why were you following me, anyway?" I asked as we walked down the cobblestone street.

"I was on my way to your apartment and I saw you."

"Do you have something on Jose Luis?" It was the first time I thought about him since Christian disappeared. Guilt rose like a lump in my throat.

"We did receive a few calls since the segment aired on the news, but nothing promising. One guy said he has him and wants money for him, a million dollars, in fact," he laughed. "The guy sounded like he was in his nineties and lives in Puno, or so he says."

I had to laugh at that one too. "And the other calls?"

"One spoke a language we couldn't identify though we did record the call. The interpreters finally deduced it was nothing but made-up gibberish. The last caller hung up as soon as we started asking personal questions about him. We do know one thing for sure though," he stopped walking.

"What?" I swallowed the lump.

"There were no signs of a struggle at all in his room. The only prints there match his and the nurses taking care of him for the last day or so of his stay."

"So, he did leave on his own?"

"Lily, all the signs point in that direction but I'm still not one hundred percent convinced. The chief wants to halt the investigation." He searched my face.

"What? That's ridiculous. He'll die if we don't find him. What part of that do they not understand?" My fingernails dug into my palms.

"I didn't say *I* was giving up. I still want to help. We will keep looking for him. I promise. But..." He took a couple steps backward, away from me.

"But what? How can there possibly be a 'but' in this situation?" I yelled.

"To find Jose Luis, we are going to need to focus all our energy and resources on him. We can't do that if we're looking for Christian too."

I stepped toward him and grabbed a fistful of his tee shirt. His eyes widened with fear. "Have you lost your mind? Stop looking for my husband? Never!"

"Lily, please calm down and... Could you please put me down?" His eyes, though wide, looked somewhat amused. When I looked down, I realized his feet were about seven inches from the ground.

"Oh, sorry," I lowered my arms and he touched the ground, but I didn't let go of his shirt. "I can't stop looking for my husband. Something happened to him. He didn't do this on his own. I'm sure of it." My anger changed to despair and the tears let loose. His eyes widened even more and all the color in his face drained. I let go of his shirt and turned away, trying not to scare him. "I can't lose him too."

"I know how much you love him. Unfortunately, he doesn't want to be found right now. Jose Luis needs you. He's more urgent right now. He's sick, remember?"

I struggled to hear the question, his voice trailing off. I turned just in time to see him stagger backward and fall against a tree, holding his arm out to steady himself but missing the trunk. He fell flat on his back.

"Lucas!" I ran to his side and dropped onto my knees. "Lucas, are you okay?"

"I..." He tried to lift his head but couldn't. "The whole world is spinning. I need..." His eyes closed and his head rolled to the side.

✑ TWENTY ✑

loysius, Fiore, open the door. I thought as I entered the elevator with a limp Lucas in my arms. As the elevator climbed, I looked at his face. His face took on wrinkles around the eyes reminding me of spider legs, his hair grey at his temples. As we suspected, the aging process was speeded up. If he didn't exchange blood soon, who knew how long he would last?

The elevator doors opened, and I rushed down the hall. Margarita stood from her seat at the door and rushed to meet me. "What happened?"

"He needs blood. Hurry, open the door," was all I could say. I didn't know if Margarita knew Lucas was half vampire, but it was not important, not to her anyway.

"Here, give him to me, Lily," Aloysius said as he took Lucas from my arms and rushed toward the stairs. "I will put him in your room. Lucia and the children are asleep but no need to scare them."

Fiore rushed ahead of us and threw the bedroom door open. She ran to the bed and pulled the blankets down.

"Mariana has not made an appearance, I take it?" Aloysius asked as he set Lucas down, placing his head on Christian's pillow.

"No. What do we do now?" I stood at the foot of the bed looking at the awkward scene in front of me. Fiore pulled the blankets up over Lucas, who occupied the spot on the bed that belonged to my husband. My stomach knotted painfully.

"The only thing we can do," Aloysius answered.

"No," I gasped. "He isn't ours to claim."

"We have to do something or he'll die," Fiore moved Lucas's head from side to side with her fingers, examining his face. "He's aging already, and very fast."

"Mariana did this to him. He's her responsibility," I argued.

"So, we watch him die?" Aloysius came to my side and placed a gentle hand on my shoulder. "Can you live with that, Lily?"

I swallowed the lump in my throat and thought about Christian. What would he want to do?

"Lily, dear," Aloysius took my face in his hands and turned it toward him, his eyes intent yet comforting. "Christian is gone right now. He can't decide for you. You have to decide whether you can allow Lucas to die or save him."

"You can't possibly be asking me to turn him," Tears streaked down my cheeks before I could bite down and stop them. "He would be attached to me then. I can't do that, not to Christian."

Fiore came to stand beside him. "Maybe there's another way."

"What do you mean?" Aloysius looked at her, his hands stopping the tears from reaching my chin.

"What if there's just an exchange? That would get him back to normal for a while, I think, and then he can decide what he wants." She looked at Aloysius. His face brightened.

"You may be right. Maybe that would work and we don't have to do the extreme. I can do it if you want, Lily."

"No. He's Mariana's responsibility but I was with him when this happened. I'm the one he knows best. He's been trying to help us all along and it's the least I can do to repay him," I said. Aloysius dropped his hands from my face.

"Are you sure you feel up to it?" Fiore asked as she stroked my back.

I nodded. "But, will he have an attachment to me from that?"

"I think he will but it should be temporary. The attachment will be broken when he is turned completely or when Mariana exchanges blood with him again, whichever comes first," Aloysius explained.

"Just be careful not to take too much from him. He's weakened already," Fiore warned as she led Aloysius out of the room by the hand. "We'll be right outside if you need us."

Instead of sitting on Christian's side of the bed, I walked to my side and climbed up next to Lucas. He looked lifeless laying there, the covers tucked under his chin as Fiore left them. His heart beat weakly, barely audible, his eyes still tightly shut.

How could I do this to Christian? How could I allow another man to become attached to me, even if it was for the sole purpose of saving his life? Did Lucas even want to live without Mariana? It didn't matter. I had to do it, if not for him, then for me. He was the only connection I had to my past, a past where the sun rose and set around my loving parents. A past where my only care was what my next story would be about and what Elizabeth would think of it. A past Ian took from me when he brought me into his life of hell and somehow, in some crazy way, Ian keeps taking away my future too.

Christian, I'm sorry but I have to do this. I can't let Lucas die like this. The thought of Christian brought the lump back to my throat and I wanted more than anything to run out of the room and into the ocean. I wanted to drown out the nightmare my existence had become. Lucas stirred and brought me back to reality. His eyes still shut, he pushed the covers down a little and then his hands fell back down as if they were too heavy for him. I had no choice.

Cradling the top of his head in my hand, I turned his head just enough to bare his neck. Sweat beaded on his jawline but his skin felt cold under my fingers. I leaned down and inhaled his aroma, my eyes closed, my fangs lengthening on their own. I sank my teeth into his tender flesh and he moaned. I stopped just long enough to look at him, but he eyes remained closed. His sweet blood filled my mouth completely before I swallowed, heat coating my throat. Images of his past floated past my eyes, a dog running and jumping to catch a Frisbee, Elizabeth grinning at him from across the room, batting her eye lashes when he turned as he felt her stare. I walked down the street, my arms full of old musty books, turning into the corner drugstore. Mariana screaming at him, tears in his eyes, contempt in hers. When the drum of his heart slowed in my ears, I pulled away and wiped my mouth with my sleeve. His eyes were still closed, his breathing more shallow.

With my fangs still protruding, I brought my wrist to my lips and punctured it. I cradled the back of his head so he wouldn't be lying flat and brought my bloody wrist to his mouth.

"Drink, please, Lucas," I coaxed. I had no idea if he heard me or if the blood itself awakened something in him, but he clenched his mouth around the punctures. He brought one hand up to hold my wrist in place as his mouth eagerly slurped what I offered. I closed my eyes and pictured Christian, hoping his image would lessen the guilt I felt, if I could imagine it was him instead. The drum of his heart, stronger and faster with every sip, told me he'd had enough.

"That's enough now, Lucas."

His hand clamped tighter around my arm, keeping his mouth in place, his tongue working to get every possible drop.

"That is enough, Lucas," He did not stop. "Enough!"

He grabbed my arm with two strong hands, forcing me to pry them off. I jumped off the bed as his eyes opened.

"Mariana?" he whispered. "I knew you'd come back."

"It's not Mariana," I answered, keeping my distance. "It's Lily."

He sat up so fast his movement was a blur. Looking around the room, he tried to focus his eyes. Though his hair was cut close to his scalp, it still managed to stick up.

"How are you feeling?" I moved a few steps closer to the bed, not sure if he was going to attack or pass out.

"Ok, I think. What happened?" He looked around the room again. His eyes settled on the wedding picture on the dresser. "Why am I in your room?"

"You passed out on me when we were talking. I carried you back here." I let that sink in a moment. He turned back to me.

"I wouldn't have survived it, would I?" He ran his fingers through his hair. "No, don't answer that. I already know. She didn't come back."

"I'm sorry but no. I didn't know what else to do so I..."

"Please, come sit down. I won't bite, I promise." He patted the mattress.

I did as he asked, my feet still on the floor. "I gave you my blood."

"I know. I can feel it. I can feel you...in here." He brought a hand to his chest.

"It's only temporary, until she comes back. Then you will be hers again. I mean..." I froze.

"I know what you mean. You are not cheating on Christian, if that's what you're thinking," he moved closer to me. "You did it to save my life, though I wish you hadn't."

"What?" I jumped up as he was trying to push the blankets off his legs. "What the hell are you saying? That I did this for nothing?"

"In a way, I guess," He stood and came toward me. "Even though I don't feel her in here right now," He pounded his fist to his chest. "I love her. I don't want to be without her."

"You just may have to be. Get used to that idea."

"Really? Like you and Christian? He chose to renounce you or did you forget?" He tried to take my hands but I spun and walked away.

"How dare you compare Christian with Mariana? Christian is my husband. Christian—"

"Lily, please. That's not what I'm trying to do at all. I just want you to start thinking about the fact that Christian does not want to be found and he may never be coming back," he said almost in a whisper.

"I can't do that, Lucas. I refuse. His disappearance makes no sense. We fought so hard to be together, to stay together. Why would he walk away when we finally are together? Why would he leave Jose Luis and Leilani?" I backed toward the door.

He shook his head and his eyes softened. "I don't know, Lily."

"He told me he'd love me forever, spend eternity with me." My voice cracked.

"I don't know but Mariana said the same things to me. She made the same promises, and she didn't keep them either." He reached for my arm to keep me in the room. I batted his hand away, making him stagger a few steps.

"You know what, Lucas?" I barked through gritted teeth.

"What Lily?" The crack in his voice betrayed his amused look.

"I should have let you die!" I spun and walked out the door, slamming it behind me.

"Lily, what's wrong?" Fiore asked as I reached the bottom of the stairs. She and Aloysius walked toward me. I threw my hand up when I reached the front door.

"Please, don't," I warned, trying not to look at them, afraid I'd change my mind. "Let me go. I need to be alone for a couple days. Lucas is ok. Please tell Lucia and the children I'm sorry and I'll see them soon."

"What happened, Lily? Can't we talk about it?" Aloysius pleaded but respected my space. He kept his distance.

"What about looking for Christian and Jose Luis?" Fiore asked before I could answer Aloysius's question.

"The police are in charge, or Lucas, or whoever. Christian is not coming back," I turned the knob and pulled the door open, still keeping my back to them. "I have my cell if you need me, but only in case of an emergency. I don't want to be bothered otherwise." I closed the door behind me, half expecting it to open again and for them to try to stop me. They did not. Margarita only nodded a greeting as I passed.

Once on the street, I turned left, heading toward the busier part of town. At this late hour, and on a weeknight, there weren't as many people around but a few still walked the brightly lit sidewalks. Every time someone came my way, he or she crossed the street rather than share the sidewalk with me. I must look as angry as I feel. It was just as well. Blood did not appeal to me at the moment. All I wanted was to be alone.

The lobby of the hotel, the first one I came across, was brightly lit with crystal chandeliers. Plush chairs in dark colors scattered about the open space gave it an old feeling. Not surprisingly, an old gentleman in horn rimmed glasses and wearing a bow tie greeted me when I stepped up to the desk.

"May I help you, *señorita*?" he asked as he looked me over above his glasses.

"Yes, please. I would like a room."

"Ah, an American. What brings you to our lovely country?" He picked at the computer keyboard with one finger while he waited for my answer.

"Um, I… Do you have a room or not?" I regretted my tone as soon as the words came out of my mouth. It was none of his business though.

"I am sorry, Miss. I just get a little bored this late at night. It is hard for a man my age to stay awake these hours, you know. We have two rooms left," he eyed the monitor over his glasses again. Why did he even wear them? "A matrimonial and the penthouse."

"That's great," I said pulling out my wallet. "I will take the penthouse."

Twenty-One

My room turned out to be a lot more modern than the lobby. The king-sized bed had six enormous pillows on it, and I threw myself on them as soon as I shut the door. Rolling on my side, I spotted the cordless telephone on the nightstand. Kalia. Kalia would know what to do. She would help me deal with everything that was going on. She would know how to calm me, how to keep me grounded.

I reached for the receiver and started dialing the area code for Astoria. I slammed it back down. What was I thinking? Kalia wanted nothing to do with me. She didn't care how much that hurt. She didn't care how much it hurt to lose my husband and my son all in the same week. She didn't even know. I picked up a pillow and whipped it across the room. A lamp crashed to floor, the bulb popping before it shattered in bits all over the polished wood.

I lay back and rested my head on my arms. How had this all happened? One minute I had no one in my life, and I was happy about that. Well, maybe not happy but I was used to it. I was content alone. Then suddenly a neighbor asks me out on date and I freak. I freak so badly I leave the only place I'd called home for more than a mere few months. A woman walks up to me on the beach and bam, I'm surrounded by friends and love and all those warm fuzzy things just to have the rug yanked out from under me. Tears streaked down my cheeks, and I rubbed at them with my white sleeve, angry at their constant intrusion.

Pushing myself off the edge of the bed, I ran into the bathroom. The shelf above the toilet contained two rows, three high, of white towels. I grabbed two of these, and trying to avoid my image in the mirror, left the room and went back to bed. I pulled the top pillow out and wrapped it in a towel, giving myself permission to cry without ruining the hotel linen.

Why would Christian leave? He told me he loved me, that he wanted to spend eternity with me, long before I gave in to him. I was the one who fought it all along, the one who decided that it was wrong to fall in love with a human. My mind wandered back to that first kiss, the passion and the fire in our bodies when our lips met on that beach on a night that seemed like so long ago. I threw myself on top of him, giving in to the desire I had been fighting since the day I laid eyes on him. I felt his soul in that kiss, a soul I didn't dare possess though I wanted more than anything to do so.

It wasn't him who walked away then. It was me, with my conscience and my morals. I wanted to protect him from the monster I became the night Ian took my life and replaced it with what became my hell. It was Christian who insisted. Christian who insisted on talking to me, on getting to know me better, on seeing me again and ignoring the signs that should have kept him far away from me.

And I did leave him. I was the one who ran the afternoon he noticed my heart didn't beat. My mind wandered back to that afternoon and the pleasure and the pain we shared. We lay on his bed supposedly watching a movie when we let our passion get the best of us. Our lips met and the fire ignited, a fire that burned hotter than any fire I had ever had the pleasure of warming myself to. My desire became something different than his and my fangs made their appearance, threatening to control my mind and my body. I hurt him physically that day when I banged his head off the headboard trying to stop him from taking control of my body. Worst of all, I hurt him emotionally when he laid his head on my chest and realized it was silent. Without explanation, I ran from him, swearing to myself that it would be forever.

The stickiness of my blood tears woke me out of the memories only long enough to change the towel on the pillow. I wanted to grieve and cry and scream until I didn't feel anything at all anymore. I wouldn't have been able to do that at the apartment. The children would have been terrified. Aloysius and Fiore would have done anything in their power to lessen my pain, to cheer me up, and I didn't want that. I welcomed the pain and let it engulf me, feeling its comfort and emptiness and hurt.

The tears became a constant stream as I pictured his face, the blue eyes that looked at me as if I were the only thing that existed in his world. The look of total love and desire, of total commitment and devotion the night he asked me to marry him and I threw myself on top of him, knocking him over on the sand and showering him with kisses when I accepted.

The pain engulfing me the night he died in the cabin, the night the last drop of his blood was taken by Ian, took control of me again as my sobs became louder and less concealed. I didn't even try to stop the pained sounds escaping my mouth. What was the point? No one heard me. No one cared.

I sat up and looked around the room again, trying to focus through red-stained eyes. The emptiness and quiet of the room felt so familiar, so welcoming. Could I do it again? Could I continue on alone, always alone, as I had lived for almost ninety years? I didn't want to, but what choice did I have?

Christian, can you hear me at all? If you can, please think about this. Please really think about what you're doing to yourself, to me, to us. I looked at the door as if Christian would walk through it any moment and tell me it was all some sick joke. His way of getting back at me for all the trouble I'd put him through. *I don't understand what is happening to you. Why did you change your mind about us? Why did you stop loving me? How did you even know you could sever the connection between us?*

That last part gave me a little sliver of hope. Someone had to have told him it was possible. He couldn't have known on his own that he could renounce his maker and cut all ties. Which meant someone was with him. Someone taught him how to do this. With frustration and exhaustion, I threw myself back onto the pillow, closing my eyes to shut the world out.

The sun set, shading the room in greys which turned to black and eventually turned to yellows and oranges as it rose again. The hours ticked without my knowledge until the sun set again and the pattern was repeated. I'm not really sure how long I lay there, three, maybe four days. The pain never stopped, never lessened. The burning in my throat increased, taking my breath away, and still, I didn't move. I wasn't sure how long I could go without feeding, but I was about to find out. Luckily, the hotel staff heeded the do not disturb sign hanging on the door; otherwise, I may have done something rash to quench my growing thirst.

I rolled over into the fetal position, wrapping my arms around myself as if I could make all the pain disappear, as if I could protect myself. And I could, I'd done it before, after Ian left me and I was forced to fend for myself, to learn about my new existence as a vampire, one I really knew nothing about. The problem now was that I didn't want to. I had love, true love, and I wanted it back. I wanted all of it, all of them. I wanted Christian, Aaron, Kalia, and Jose Luis. I wanted the laughs, the warmth, the talks, everything that came with the territory, even the arguments. None of them wanted me, though. And that hurt more than my human death, more than losing Ian ever had.

Sitting on the edge of the bed and wiping my face with the tissues I found in the nightstand drawer, I looked around the room again. The balcony doors stood across from this side of the bed, the lights of the city distinguishable through the venetian blinds. I walked over to the chain and pulled them open. The sight took my breath away. Two lounge chairs sat on either side of a round glass table, at the end of that, just below the wall, was a round metal fire pit. This balcony was meant to be enjoyed. That wasn't going to happen. But what took my breath away was how high I was. It had to be at least twenty stories, maybe more. I hadn't paid attention to the elevator dial as it climbed.

I sank onto one of the lounge chairs as I lost my balance. What made me, afraid of heights, decide to rent the penthouse? Rolling off the side of the chair, I crawled back inside on my hands and knees like a total coward. An indestructible vampire afraid of heights, who ever heard of such a thing? I've chopped heads off, drained killers and rapists, fought my way out of all sorts of things, and I couldn't handle heights? That would have to change.

With my legs shaking and my breathing coming at a ridiculous speed, I turned, stood, and made my way closer to the wall. Every step took coaxing from my mind, my brain trying to remember exactly how to pick up my foot and make it move, then pick up the other and do the same. It seemed like an eternity, but I finally made it there, grasping the cement wall with white knuckles. Pushing off my legs, I managed to hoist myself up on the wall to a squatting position. My body shook and I almost fell back off a few times but regained my balance. Once I steadied my legs, I slowly rose to a standing position, my knees locked to keep me still.

Christian, I just want to tell you one last time that I love you more than anything or anyone in this world. I wanted to spend eternity with you. I wanted to be yours, mind, body, and soul until the end of time. You didn't want that, though I thought you did. And I'm sorry. I'm sorry for all the things I said when I was angry and confused. I'm sorry for all the things that happened to you because of me. I'm sorry I brought you into my miserable world. Even in death I will never be able to tell you just how much I truly love you and how sorry I really am.

I took a deep breath and closed my eyes. Pushing off my legs I brought my arms to my sides and kept them there, as tightly as I could manage. The wind whistled in my ears and blew my hair as I plummeted toward the ground. *I'm sorry.*

❧ TWNETY-TWO ❧

I don't know what made me think jumping off the top of a skyscraper was a good idea. Obviously, it did nothing to take away my pain and anguish. Whatever made me think a vampire with the ability to fly could actually die from a fall I will never know. The one thing I do know is that, regardless of whether or not I may have caused any damage to myself, I wasn't ready to die. Something in my mind, and possibly my body, took over and prevented my fall. I also realized I had taken flight seconds before hitting the ground, something I didn't think I could do. So far, I was only able to take to the air by diving off some height and coasting on the wind. This was a whole new thing, a power I had never felt before, to be so close to hitting the ground but controlling my body to fly upward again.

Walking down the almost empty street, I made sure the few passersby didn't look at me in any strange way. I had made myself invisible as I fell, just to be sure I didn't scare anyone, but I wasn't sure if it was effective. Apparently, it was. People passed by and only looked at me to nod or to avoid hitting me. One gentleman even said hello as I skirted around him, his smile showing obvious admiration.

I still wasn't sure if I wanted to check out of the hotel or stay a while longer. The truth was, I wasn't sure I had any tears left in me. I had cried for about three days without a break and, though the pain was as real after that as the first day, I knew I had other things to do. Two children depended on me to save them, whether or not one of them knew it. Just as I neared the entrance to the hotel, resolved to check out and get back to reality, my phone vibrated in my pocket.

"Fiore, what is it?"

"You have to come home now, Lily," she said in a stern voice, one that demanded no argument. "Something's happened. We need you."

"Ok. I will be there as soon as possible, just let me—"

"No. Now, Lily."

The desperation in her voice shocked me so I turned toward the street and hailed a taxi, mumbling a goodbye and slamming my phone closed.

"What is going on?" I asked as Giovanni led me into the apartment, leaving Margarita at his post at the door.

Aloysius approached from the kitchen. "Tell me how you're feeling, first."

"I've been better, but that doesn't matter right now. Why did you call me back here in such a hurry? Have you heard from Christian?"

"I am very sorry but that is not the reason," He took my hand and led me to the sofa, motioning for me to take a seat. "Jose Luis called."

"When? How? Is he coming home?"

"Slow down, Lily," Fiore sat next to me and took my hand. "He called about a half hour before you got here. Apparently, one of his captors forgot to take his cell phone with him when he left the room they're keeping Jose Luis in. He took advantage and called us."

"So, he's ok?" I asked and looked at Aloysius. He nodded. "What do we do now?"

"We go get him," Aloysius said. "He is not sure exactly where he is, but he thinks he is somewhere on the mountain."

"Which mountain?" I was starting to lose my patience.

"He thinks it's the one he lived on. He said he hears traffic and a lot of voices, especially during the day. They've been keeping him blindfolded so he can't describe his surroundings. He did, however, recognize some of the voices he'd heard. He even thinks he may have heard his sister, but we can't be sure. There are a lot of children living up there."

"It must be the same place I was held. Let's go get him!" I demanded as I pulled my hand out of Fiore's and stood, already rushing to the door.

"Wait, Lily," Giovanni placed a hand on my shoulder and stopped my progress. "We need a plan. We can't just go rushing up there without knowing what we're doing."

I spun on my heels and glared at him. "Why not? We know he's up there. We just find him and take him."

"It's not that simple," Aloysius approached with caution. "If we show up there searching house after house, they will know. They will alert whoever has him and they might move him, or worse."

"Don't say it, please," I put my hand up to stop the words from escaping his lips. "You are right. Did you ask him how he's feeling?"

"He said his headaches have been getting worse, more frequent and acute, but he is otherwise unharmed. They've even been feeding him."

"Speaking of feeding, where is Lucas?" I had forgotten all about him in the last few days, so wrapped up in my own loss I'd forgotten his.

"He decided it would be best if he stayed away. He didn't want to cause you more problems," Fiore explained.

"Did Mariana return?"

"No. He still hasn't heard anything from her."

"How is he surviving this?" I tried to hide my worry but doubted it worked as Aloysius's eyes met mine.

"Fiore has been taking care of him. They meet once a day," he explained. "He's not upset with you, if that's what you're thinking. He said he understood how you feel and he's there for you if and when you need him."

"I feel so bad for what I said to him. He lost someone too and I belittled his feelings and got caught up in my own pain, completely ignoring his." I dropped back down on the sofa.

"Well, he didn't see it that way. Anyway, he is on his way here. We will need all the help we can get. Everyone is on their way in to help us," Aloysius explained.

Giovanni's cell rang and he walked out to the hall to take the call. That left just the three of us, the apartment quieter than I would have expected. "Where are Lucia and the children?"

"We set them up in another apartment in the building. They too have a bodyguard with them. We didn't want to alarm them anymore than they already are. Their father still hasn't shown up or called. Jose Luis will be back here, and we don't know what condition he will be in. We thought quiet and rest would be best for him."

They seemed pretty certain that Jose Luis would be coming back. I wished I had as much faith in our rescue attempt as they did, but regardless, I knew we had to try.

"We will be bringing him home, Lily," Fiore said as she read my mind. "Why don't you go up and take a shower, change your clothes before everyone else gets here?"

"I guess I should," I turned toward the spiral staircase. "It doesn't feel right to be doing this without Christian."

"I know. It doesn't feel right to us either," Aloysius put an arm around Fiore to include her. "He will turn up too. I'm sure of it."

I turned without answering him. I had no idea what was going through Christian's mind, no idea what made him turn his back on me and on our marriage.

"Wait up," Fiore said behind me. "I'll walk with you."

When we reached the room Christian and I shared since our arrival in

Lima, I hesitated at the door. All his things would still be inside. My anxiety grew as I talked myself into opening the door.

"If you want, I'll get your clothes for you. Just tell me what you want. You can trade rooms with me if that helps," Fiore laid a hand on the small of my back, her touch reassuring and comforting.

"No, I have to get a grip on this. He left me. He regrets me, us, what he is, all of it. I have to keep going for Jose Luis's sake." I gripped the doorknob and forced my wrist to turn.

"I admire your strength, Lily. I don't know if I could be as strong in this situation. If Aloysius suddenly disa—I 'm sorry, I didn't mean…"

"No, it's ok. You really are in love, aren't you?" I walked over to my dresser and pulled a drawer open, grabbing the first shirt I saw.

Fiore smiled though her eyes didn't. "I guess I am. It's been a long time since someone loved me back, too. It's just that…" Her gaze dropped to the floor.

"What is it?" I hoped I had nothing to do with her confusion. She raised her head and smiled.

"Don't worry, Lily. I still love you, but in a different way now. I consider you more like a sister. There's a bond between us that will never be broken."

"Then what is it?" I grabbed a pair of jeans from the closet shelf, along with a towel.

"I don't know how to say it exactly," She patted the mattress for me to sit. "I'm not really sure if Aloysius feels the same way. He treats me great. He's loving and caring in all the right circumstances, if you know what I mean?" She winked.

"Then what's the problem? He looks at you with admiration in his eyes, like he worships the ground you walk on," I insisted.

"That may be, but he pulls away sometimes. He gets this look in his eyes like he's seeing something other than me, even when he's looking right at me. I ask him what he's thinking about and he always insists it's nothing."

"Has he told you he loves you?" That may have been prying a bit too much, but it may also help her, so I waited for her response.

She looked at the floor again. "No, but I haven't told him either."

"What are you waiting for?" I lifted her face with the tips of my fingers.

"I can't do that!" Her eyes widened. "It may be totally acceptable nowadays, but I come from a different time, a time where I would have been ousted because of my feelings for you. I just can't." She stood and went to my dresser, pulling a drawer open. "I think you'll need these, too." She handed me underwear and a pair of socks. It was her way of dismissing the subject, something she must have learned from Aloysius.

"Oh, right," I said and stood, intending to head for the bathroom.

"Hold on a minute," Fiore grabbed my wrist. "That's not what I brought you up here to discuss."

"Oh?"

"Yesterday, sometime in the morning, Aaron called."

My body froze. "Did he ask for me?"

She shook her head. "He wanted to talk to Aloysius. I'm not sure what they were talking about at first, but I think it was about you toward the end. I heard Aloysius telling him what is going on here. He agreed to keep Aaron informed so he must have asked."

"Probably just a formality," I said and walked out of the room, closing and locking the bathroom door behind me. Just a formality, that's all.

~ TWENTY-THREE ~

Tears flowed freely again as the warm water washed over me, rinsing all the dirt away but none of the pain. Did Aaron ask about me or did he only listen and pretend to be interested in what Aloysius was saying? Did Kalia ask Aaron to ask Aloysius how I was doing? Memories of them fell hard upon me like the drops from the shower head.

I'm not sure how long I stayed in the shower, but by the time I was dressed and ready to go downstairs, I heard voices coming from the dining room. "Sorry I kept you waiting," I said as I walked into the room and toward the only empty chair which happened to be beside Lucas. I sat and looked away, but out of the corner of my eye, I saw him stiffen in his seat.

Fiore sat on my other side, Giovanni at one end of the table and Aloysius at the other. Across from Fiore, Lucas, and me were Margarita, and Carlos. Vicente and Mauricio sat behind them on stools taken from the kitchen. They all nodded a greeting when they met my eyes.

"Lily, we started without you so let me bring you up to speed," Giovanni said. As head bodyguard, he must be in charge of the rescue effort. I nodded for him to continue. "Having been on the mountain before, I know the basic layout. Not everyone living up there is a hunter or witch. In fact, most of the inhabitants are innocents, which is why we need to keep this as simple and fast as possible."

"I understand but how are we going to find Jose Luis without searching every house? That could take hours and by that time they will know we're there," I said as I met Giovanni's eyes. I felt Lucas's eyes on me but avoided turning my face. I knew I overreacted to what Lucas had said the day I exchanged blood with him but now wasn't the time to make amends. That would have to wait until later.

"That's what we were discussing while you were upstairs," Aloysius replied. "Giovanni knows Arturo personally."

"What?" I looked at Giovanni and stood. "How is that possible? Have you worked with him?" My hands clenched under the table.

"Please calm down," Fiore whispered and took my hand. "Let him explain."

"Years ago, when Melinda first started making trouble for everyone, Arturo and I made a pact to protect the city. He was always against vampires, but we had an understanding. The vampires who lived here previously knew how and where to hunt and knew making other vampires, especially when not warranted, was not allowed. Arturo and I worked together to prevent Melinda from creating vampires to serve her."

"Then why are they working together now?" I asked, trying to stay calm.

"We don't know," Aloysius answered instead of Giovanni. "The only reason we can think of is that Melinda brainwashed him somehow, probably promised him something."

"Knowing where Arturo lives is helpful because I'm assuming he is keeping Jose Luis with him. He has the most protection up there and he will be using that to his advantage," Giovanni explained.

"So, what's the plan then?" I patted Fiore's hand under the table to let her know I was calm enough to continue.

"You and Aloysius will transport to Arturo's place, grab Jose Luis and, hopefully Leilani, and get out. The rest of us will be right below so they can't get past us," Giovanni said looking at the rest of the guards to make sure they understood.

"Sounds logical and all but, what makes you think Leilani will be with them?" I countered.

"You're right to doubt they'd be together, but we have to prepare for that possibility. And if she is with them, the possibility also exists that she may not want to come with us. Who knows what they've told her. We also have to consider…" Giovanni looked at Aloysius.

Aloysius turned to me. "We may also find Christian up there. The rest will not only keep the others away from us, but they will also search for him," he explained. I shook my head and everyone looked at me.

"Christian is not up there. He wasn't taken. He walked out on me."

Lucas turned to me. "But Lily—"

"No, Lucas. You may not believe Christian capable of leaving but I think I do. Maybe he had enough. Maybe he wants to be free and happy and that's not possible as long as he stays by my side. There are way too many problems that I seem to cause. I don't like that possibility, but I understand it," I choked back tears. Vicente pulled a tissue from the box on the counter and handed it to me. "I have to let him go. You need to do the same with Mariana."

Lucas looked at his lap, his hands wrapped tightly into fists. Instead of answering me, he just nodded. Aloysius cleared his throat and took our attention from Lucas, leaving him to fight his own tears.

"We will do whatever possible to get out of there without a fight. We do nothing but search and grab, if you know what I mean, unless of course they engage us," Aloysius turned to me. "No matter what, Lily and I will be grabbing who ever we can rescue up there and coming right back here. If there is a fight, the rest of you will take care of it. There is no need to put the children in harm's way. Understood?"

"Yes, sir," everyone uttered in unison.

"We wait until sundown then, less chance of tourists getting in the way." Aloysius stood and motioned for Giovanni to follow him into the other room, probably to talk over the specifics.

"Lily, are you ok?" Fiore wrapped an arm around my shoulders when I stood, her voice low since the others were still talking as they exited the room.

"Yes, or I will be, anyway," I pushed my chair under the table with more force than I intended, making Fiore take a step away. "This isn't the first time this happened to me, but I'll be damned if it's not the last."

"What do you mean by that?" she asked as she positioned herself in the doorway.

"I mean, this is the second time I gave my heart away only to have it trampled on. I will not make that mistake again. If there is one positive thing about me it's that I learn from my mistakes."

"Do you honestly think Christian up and left you? That just doesn't seem possible to me. Not with the way he loves you."

"Fiore, I know you mean well. You're as much a romantic as I am—or was, anyway. If he were taken, I would still feel the connection to him. I would still feel like he was a part of me, a part of my soul," I paused and took a step back, placing a hand on the edge of the table to steady myself. I shook my head to stop the tears. I didn't think I had any left, yet they threatened to show my weakness. "I fell in love with Christian the first time I set eyes on him. I should've known to stay away, fought the urge harder than I did. But no. I was selfish. I wanted him and I got him. I took him away from everything he knew, from his friends, from a promising career, from a normal life. Instead, I condemned him to death, to an existence as lonely and eternal as mine. As much as I want to search for him, beg him to come back to me, I know I don't deserve the happily ever after I know was possible by his side."

"You are being way too hard on yourself, Lily." She stepped away from the doorway and came to take my hand in hers, looking into my eyes. "He loved you. He was willing to do anything to be with you, including die for you. I wouldn't give that up without a fight."

"But he did, Fiore. Don't you see? He left without as much as an explanation or a goodbye. And even if he was taken, he still renounced me, and my love. He's gone. I am trying to accept that. Why can't everyone else do the same?" I pulled my hand out of hers and rushed out of the room.

"Where are you going?" Fiore yelled after me.

"Just need to get some air," I yelled back. Had anyone else asked, I would've just kept going, but Fiore didn't deserve that. She had defied the others in Ireland, turned her back on them, to fight by my side. She had saved my life on more than one occasion. Fiore deserved my respect more than anyone.

"Lily, wait up," Lucas's voice rang above the constant beeping of car horns. People rushed past me on their way to work, school, and whatever other normality their day consisted of. I quickened my pace as much as I could without running. I wanted to be alone, to think, to forget, at least for a little while, all the losses I'd suffered in the past year.

"Leave me alone," I yelled back as he approached despite my speed. "I want to be alone. Go bother somebody else, will you?"

"You always were stubborn," he panted, trying to catch his breath.

"Look, Lucas, just because you knew me before, when I was human, doesn't mean you can meddle in my life now."

"Ouch," he said and turned his lips into a pout. "I'm not trying to meddle in your life. If you remember correctly, it was Aloysius who brought me into your life when he asked for my help in finding the boy."

"Exactly," I stopped walking so I could turn to face him, glaring at him. "You were brought in to find Jose Luis, nothing more, nothing less."

"I understand that. It's just that, well; I thought we could be friends. After all, I knew you when you were a child."

"I don't need any more friends." I spun on my heels and started walking. He followed close on my heels.

"Everyone can use more friends. What makes you any different?"

"In case you hadn't noticed, I'm a vampire. I need to feed and survive, that is all."

He laughed, stopping me dead in my tracks and filling me with anger from head to toes. "What is so funny?" I screamed making passersby jump and hasten their step.

"You think that makes you so different than anyone else? Just because you suck blood for survival?" He said quietly and crossed his arms over his chest.

"You still feel. You still love and hate and cry. The only things that make you different are that you don't eat and drink like a human. You don't sleep and you don't die. Well, not dying isn't quite true but you know what I mean. Just because you're a predator doesn't mean you don't need anything else."

He looked at me, but I was too furious to open my mouth, not here in front of all these humans. Instead, I looked at the ground, my hands balled into fists ready to slam into his face if he said anything else.

His soft touch on my chin startled me out of my fury as he lifted my face to meet his eyes. "Look, Lily, I know you're hurting. I know you think you have to be tough and powerful. I know you think you have to take care of everyone but what about you, huh? Who's going to take care of you?"

Though I wanted to scream at him, my voice came out a broken whisper. "I don't need anyone to take care of me. I can do it myself. I always have."

His lips softened into a smile. "That's what I mean. You're not taking very good care of yourself lately. I can tell by your color that you haven't fed. I can tell by the blank look in your eyes and the coldness in your tone that you're trying to push everyone away who isn't Christian."

I swallowed hard and pushed his hand off my chin. "You think you know me so well." There was no conviction in my voice. I knew what he was saying was true, but I wasn't ready to let him know it.

"No. I'm not saying that at all. I'm hurting too, believe me, Lily. I love Mariana, despite what everyone else thinks of her. I know her in a way that no one else does. I know how loving and tender she can be. Believe me, I felt like pushing everyone away at first but, as you well know, I don't have time to do that. I have a job to do and that's to find Jose Luis. It's because of you and this case that I have made new friends. I feel less alone with you, Fiore, and Aloysius in my life. I think you would feel the same if you only allowed yourself to embrace them instead of pushing them away."

He was right, I knew, but for some reason it felt better to hang on to my anger and hurt. I didn't feel like arguing with him at the moment, not in the middle of the sidewalk anyway. "There's a coffee shop about two blocks that way," I pointed. "Want to go get some?"

"You're changing the subject," he said with a smile. "But sure."

The outside tables were all taken so we settled for one inside. A small shelf in the corner contained a television, set to a soccer game, the volume so low I doubted anyone besides us could hear it. We ordered two lattes and sat back in silence. Everything Lucas had said outside was true. I was pushing everyone away like I did when I didn't want to get hurt. It was a habit I formed after Ian left me all those years ago, a habit I wasn't sure I wanted to break, especially now. Christian was the last person I expected to hurt me, but I was wrong. He hurt more than Ian ever did because I loved him more.

"Lily, do you plan to feed anytime soon?" Lucas interrupted my thoughts.

"I don't know, maybe…"

"Look," he pointed at the television where they cut away from the game and an announcer stood with a microphone in his hands. He stood on a narrow street, a bare mountain visible in the background, a group of people in typical Peruvian dress standing off to the side. The words "Breaking news" flashed at the bottom of the screen in Spanish.

"We are standing on a street in the northern town of Chulacanas to bring you breaking news," the announcer said holding his earpiece tight against his ear. "In the early hours of the morning, farmer Tito Ayala walked to his chicken coop to collect his eggs. He noticed his barn door open and went to investigate, assuming his cows had gotten out. Instead, he found two of his three cows still in the barn, both dead. When he noticed the third was missing, he walked around to the back of the barn, finding a man there instead of his cow." The announcer paused and looked at the old man who appeared next to him. "*Señor* Ayala, what did you see?" He held the microphone to the man's mouth.

"A man lay on the ground, next to a barrel of water I keep there for the cows. His eyes were open so I thought he was alive. No, he was dead." The man opened his eyes wide and stuck his tongue out to the side. "Like this."

The announcer tried not to laugh. "There you have it. The unidentified body of a man in his mid-thirties to early forties was found this morning along with the two bodies of the cows. There were no visible signs of a struggle."

A woman jumped into view of the camera, attracting the attention of the announcer and making him turn. "*Vampiros*," the woman said, making fang marks with her fingers at her neck. "*Fueron vampiros.*"

The announcer stepped away and said, "The town's people are speculating that it was vampires who caused the deaths, however, police are investigating, and the coroner is examining the body of the man for the true cause of death. If you have any information on the identity of the man, please call the number on your screen. He is described as…"

Lucas looked at me, his eyes full of amusement until he saw the worry in my eyes. "Are you thinking…? No."

Christian.

TWENTY-FOUR

D o you really think Christian is responsible for those deaths?" Lucas asked as we walked out of the café and headed toward the park.

"I don't know what to think." I admitted, though something nagged at me. "He knows how to do it. He knows to cover his tracks, cover the wounds, and hide the bodies. And, I don't know that Christian would go after cows. That part really doesn't make sense."

"And what happened to the other cow?" Lucas asked as we reached a bench and took a seat, our paper coffee cups in our hands.

"No idea, unless it ran away. But still, why cows when he had a man there?"

"I don't know. He is still a newborn. Maybe he was just that hungry. What I really want to know is, if it was him, what the hell is he doing up there?"

How did he get there and where is he headed were also questions I wanted answered but didn't voice. Every fiber in my being told me to get on a plane and go look for him in that area, however, my mind reminded me that he didn't want to be found.

"Where do you think he's going?" Lucas asked anyway.

"Back to the US I'm assuming. He did take his passport, but I know he has no money. That doesn't make sense either," I ran my hand through my hair, as if that would wipe away the thought of Christian wandering the Andes alone. He was a vampire, but could he take care of himself, this early on? Would he make it to the United States on foot with hunters possibly tracking him along the way? My stomach turned at the thought of him being found by them, especially if they'd been alerted by the recent killings.

"After we get Jose Luis and his sister back, I think we need to follow Christian's trail," Lucas said.

"We don't even know if it was him," I turned to him. "It could've been anybody. It's possible it wasn't even a vampire, possible that the villagers' just have overactive imaginations." At least, that's what I wanted to believe.

Lucas looked at me with concern. "Yeah, maybe you're right." He was dropping it for my sake, but I didn't mind.

"He obviously doesn't want to be found so we are not going to look for him. He won't answer his phone or return any of my calls, and believe me, I left many messages. It is obvious, at least to me that he wants out. That's exactly what I'm going to give him," I stood and picked my empty cup up off the ground. "We better get back before Fiore and Aloysius send a search team after us."

Lucas laughed as he took my cup to deposit in a trash can we passed. "So, am I forgiven?"

I looked at his pouty face and couldn't contain my laughter. "Forgiven, for now." I took his proffered arm and we walked in silence the rest of the way to the apartment.

"Everything ok?" Fiore asked as she met me on the way to my bedroom.

"Yes," I answered and walked into the room, motioning for Fiore to follow me. "Have you heard anything else?"

She shook her head. "No. We're set to go around nine or ten tonight. We want to make sure all tourists have cleared out. It will keep them out of harm's way and make our search easier, if Jose Luis isn't where we think he is."

"Sounds good," I sat on the bed next to her. "Where is Aloysius?"

"He took Lucia and the children out for lunch. Margarita and Carlos went with them. He's taking them shopping for more clothes afterward, so he won't be home for a while."

"I think I should pack up Christian's things, get them out of the room," I said, my voice barely audible.

Fiore took my hand and squeezed it. "I don't think that's a good idea, especially before what we have to do tonight. I think it's best to keep your mind clear and your spirits as high as you can."

"Yeah, maybe you're right, but I'm going to have to do it sometime."

"And I promise I will help you when you're ready. I won't let you get all sad all by yourself." Fiore wrapped an arm around me and squeezed me to her side.

"So, what do we do until then?" I asked.

"I have an idea. Let's go to the beach. It's a nice day, not sunny but not too cold," she suggested.

"Aren't we going to stand out as the only two on the beach at this time of year?"

"Who cares?" Fiore laughed. "We don't know any of those people. Get your bikini and I'll meet you downstairs." She stood and left the room giving me no chance to protest.

Leave it to Fiore to want to go to the beach right before a battle. Sometimes I wished I could be as carefree as her. I knew she was having some difficulties in her relationship with Aloysius. She felt unsure as to where they were heading since he never told her he loved her. I could understand her concern, but I also saw the way Aloysius looked at her, hung on her every word when she spoke, and worried about her, even if she didn't know it. I saw his face light up every time she entered a room, just the way Christian's did.

"Stop it!" I muttered to myself. I grabbed my bikini out of my drawer and slipped out of my clothes. Christian wasn't here to help me with the tie at my neck, so I struggled to do it myself. I slipped my jeans and shirt back on, grabbed my towel and a book, and stuffed them into a bag. Looking at myself in the mirror, hair in a messy bun, I decided I was ready.

Fiore and I found a quiet spot to lay our towels on the beach. Since neither of us had thought to cover our skin with some colored foundation, we figured it was best to stay away from curious eyes. Lying on my stomach facing the water, I propped my head on my arms and took in the sight. A sea duck sat on top of the water, its wings tucked at its sides, letting the soft roll of the waves carry him back and forth to the shore.

"That would be a peaceful life, don't you think?" Fiore turned to me, laying her head on her arm.

"Oh, I don't know. I'm sure there's some predator out there he has to fear and run from."

"Yeah. That would be Melinda the Condor."

That comment made me laugh. Fiore's amused eyes told me she pictured what I pictured, Melinda with the body of a condor, but with her human head, swooping over the water to catch the duck with her nail-polished talons. We both laughed so hard I forgot about everything for a few precious moments.

"Lily, did anyone ever tell you how hot you are?"

"What?" I lifted my head to get a better look at her face, to see if she was joking.

"I am being serious. I would kill to look like you."

"Are you crazy?" I jumped up and sat back on my knees.

"Really," Her eyes stayed focused on mine. "You have the most gorgeous brown eyes. Actually, I think they're black. They're so deep I could get lost in them and never find my way out."

The conversation she and Christian had while I was healing from being staked came rushing back to me. I looked away and focused on the waves, the duck now gone. "And I would kill to look like you," I said hoping she wasn't hearing my thoughts.

"Yeah, about that…"

She'd heard. I busied my hands by digging in my bag for the book I'd packed, not even remembering what it was. "You don't have anything to explain. That conversation wasn't meant for me to hear."

"I know but I knew then you could hear. I also know how hard you tried not to look at me after that," she sat up facing me. "Christian wanted to know what my problem with him was. I felt I owed him an explanation since I knew I wasn't treating him well."

I held a hand up in front of me. "Seriously, Fiore, you don't owe me any kind of explanation. I did hear your whole conversation and I understand why you two acted the way you did with each other, all the bickering and nitpicking, the constant wise ass remarks."

She inched closer to me. I backed away as best I could while sitting on my legs.

"Lily, I don't want you to think I was imagining the whole thing or making it up or anything. I did think I was in love with you. I was jealous of Christian and the love you showed for him." She paused to look at my face, noticing the tears welling in my eyes. "I'm sorry. I didn't mean to bring him up right now. I'm trying to cheer you up and I'm making it worse instead."

"Don't worry about it," I wiped my eyes with the back of my hand. "I can't help it I'm so lovable." I laughed to ease her worry.

"You said it," she smiled. "Can I ask you something?" Her tone turned serious again.

I raised my eyebrows.

"It's more a favor than a question," She bit her bottom lip. I nodded. "I'm curious… Did you ever think of me…you know?"

"What? I don't think I do know." I moved back and crossed my legs in front of me, sitting Indian style to get some distance.

"I'm sorry," she looked at my eyes again. "I should just come right out and ask."

I gulped. "What already?"

"Can I kiss you? I always wondered what it would feel like," she said, her face sure and unafraid.

My head spun and my muscles tensed. I had a feeling that's what was coming but hearing it from her lips was totally different. I couldn't get my mouth to cooperate and form words, so I just nodded, suddenly starting to shake. She gave me no time to think as she leaned toward me, her face inching closer, her lips moist in anticipation. I held my breath and closed my eyes as her hand found the back of my head, pulling me closer, her fingers twining in my hair.

Her lips touched mine with such softness that I wasn't sure I didn't imagine it, at least at first. As my stomach fluttered, her kiss got harder, her tongue pushing my lips apart and finding mine, dancing with it. Her other hand pushed against my lower back as she pushed my body against hers. I tried to lose myself in the new experience, tried to picture this beautiful, sexy Italian woman holding and kissing me so passionately but all I saw were Christian's blue eyes. I felt his perfect mouth against mine, his strong manly hands against my body. I reached and put my hand against the back of Fiore's head, feeling her long, thick hair, but I still pictured Christian. My stomach sank with guilt.

"I'm sorry, Fiore," I whispered when we parted. I looked down at the sand, afraid to meet her eyes. "I can't do this."

"It's ok, Lily. I understand. Thank you for letting me satisfy my curiosity," she answered as she crawled back onto her towel.

"So?" I asked trying to lighten the mood. "How was I?"

She smiled, her eyes sparkling. "You were great. You have very soft lips, did you know?"

"I guess but..." I wasn't sure how to say it.

"How did I feel about it?" she asked for me. "I liked it. You are gorgeous and sexy, smart, sophisticated, but..."

"But I'm not Aloysius?" I smiled, catching her eyes.

"Yeah, I guess you're right. You're not Aloysius."

"You are so in love," I teased as I shook my towel out, swatting her with it before folding it and shoving it back in my bag. "He loves you too."

"I hope so," she said as we made our way back to the street and home to prepare for the rescue. "I just wish he'd tell me how he feels."

"He will. He's a bit slow. He's a man, remember? He'll tell you when you least expect it."

Changed and ready to go, I met the others where they were gathered in the living room. Aloysius gave me the once over with his eyes and then turned to Fiore and did the same. Fiore glanced at me as if nothing had happened. Aloysius smiled but said nothing to either of us. Could he possibly know? Maybe, and maybe it would help Fiore get what she most deserved. Before I could pull her aside and question her, Aloysius called us to attention.

"Lucas, Fiore, Lily, and I will be leaving from here as soon as we have the ok from Giovanni. The rest of you know what to do and where to do it. I will give the ok to retreat as soon as we have the hostages we are attempting to rescue. Understood?" He looked at everyone and they nodded. "Very well then, to your vehicles. We will await your call, Giovanni."

The whole group filed out the door on their way to the vehicles waiting in the parking garage under the building. They were to position themselves on the mountain, scope out the area, and then call Aloysius so the rest of us could disappear from here and reappear at Arturo's house. My confidence diminished when I instinctively looked for Christian who would normally have been standing next to me. Taking his hand, I would have felt safer and surer of myself. I no longer had that luxury.

Aloysius leaned into me. "We will talk about him later. I saw something today that makes me wonder."

"Yes, I know. I saw it too."

"Innocents and animals? That could become a problem, for him, for all of us," Aloysius whispered in my ear and then straightened. He walked to take Fiore's hand but not before his eyes met mine with a coldness I'd never seen in him. A chill ran down my spine.

ॐ TWENTY-FIVE ॐ

W e're on," Aloysius announced after handing Fiore her cell phone. He motioned for us to form a circle, all of us holding hands. We did as he asked, and I automatically shut my eyes.

"I will never get used to that," I said as I struggled to keep my balanced when the spinning from the transport subsided. The look on Lucas's face was priceless, wide eyes and a bit of a greenish hue to his skin. "You ok?" I whispered to him.

"Yup," was all he managed to say as he fought not to get sick. "That was something."

"Tell me about it. Don't think I'll ever get used to it," I whispered to him, finally letting go of his hand. The room was dark and musty, but at least it was steady.

I hear his heart. It's weak, very slow. I thought, hoping my companions heard me.

"Lily is that you?" Jose Luis asked in a raspy voice. "Who's there?"

"Shh," I walked to the bed once my eyes adjusted and dropped to my knees next to him. His face was damp with sweat, his eyes heavy with lack of sleep. "Are you ok? Did they hurt you?"

"No. I'm just so tired, hungry," he whispered.

"Where is Leilani? Is she here?" Aloysius stood behind me.

"I have not seen her at all. I don't know if she's here, but they say she is not. They keep telling me she is dead. I do not believe them." Jose Luis struggled to sit up. I placed a hand on his chest to stop him.

"It's ok. We will come back for her. Right now, we have to get you out of here," I said as I placed an arm behind his neck and the other under his knees, ready to pick him up.

"Please, let me, Lily," Lucas whispered behind me. I dropped him, knowing Jose Luis would be more comfortable in Lucas's larger arms.

"Not so fast," Melinda said as the room flooded with light. "Why in such a hurry?"

"Stay away from him, you…you bitch!" I jumped to my feet, spreading my feet apart, ready to lunge at her. It wasn't until my eyes adjusted to the light that I noticed Arturo standing behind her, a wooden stake in his hand.

"I would but I can't," Melinda walked to a chair in the corner of the room and pulled it toward me. She motioned for Arturo to get the chair on the other side. She turned her gaze on Lucas, Aloysius, and Fiore. "Leave us please. We are going to have a little chat."

"There is no way we would allow that. We are here to get the boy and get out. We do not want a fight, not tonight," Aloysius said in a calm voice, his eyes glued to Melinda's.

"It's just conversation, dear Aloysius, that's all," she said as she motioned for me to sit. I didn't move.

"I don't think so, Melinda. Let the boy go. He's sick and he needs treatment," Aloysius, still calm, took a step toward her. "Now if you'll excuse us—"

"Arturo, please escort these people outside." She turned to Aloysius. "We are just going to talk, that's all. You have my word. To prove that to you, I will even leave the door open."

Aloysius looked at me. I nodded, willing to do anything to hurry this along. Jose Luis looked paler and weaker than ever, his face twisting with pain every few minutes. "We'll be ok."

Aloysius nodded and led the others out of the room. As Melinda promised, the door stayed open. She took a seat and crossed her legs as if she were about to chat with a long-lost friend. I pulled my chair back a few inches, closer to the bed, and sat.

"Why such interest in this kid?" she asked, her voice low and even. I felt like I would jump out of my skin, and she was calm and controlled. She tossed her hair, black this time, behind her shoulder and waited for my answer.

"He is sick and needs our help. He has no one else."

"That is not so. He has Arturo who has been taking care of him for years. Arturo is his family," she explained.

I balled my hands at my sides. "Arturo is not his family. He doesn't love him," I said, trying to keep my voice down for Jose Luis's sake. I glanced back at him, and he looked terrified, his eyes glued to Melinda's stoic face. "Why are you so interested in him, anyway?"

Melinda looked at Jose Luis as if thinking about her words. "Why not? He's a sweet kid, smart, kind, funny, a perfect child. We just want what is best for him. Same as you."

"I don't believe you!" Jose Luis jumped at my tone, and I regretted it instantly.

"There are many reasons why he is an asset to Arturo, to us," She stood and moved to stand behind her chair, placing both hands on the back. "He is very useful."

"What asset exactly? Help me understand what you all want from him."

"I owe you no explanation. He is not your child, never was and never will be. Look at you, you're what? Two, maybe three years older than him?" Her smile made me cringe.

I jumped to my feet but did not move away. "What good is he to you like this?"

"I can train him, help him improve his powers," Melinda explained as if that were all it would take.

"What powers? His mindreading? There are many others who can do that. Why him?" I yelled, no longer caring if I scared anybody.

"No, my dear. You are so naïve, so young," She took a seat again and motioned for me to do the same. I refused, anger rippling in waves through my body. When I didn't move, she continued. "Haven't you ever noticed that your powers are stronger in his presence, more accurate, more controlled?"

"What are you talking about?" I asked in disbelief. We had only used our powers in emergency situations around Jose Luis.

"Yes, it's true. He can read minds, but his stronger more interesting power is what he can do to others with powers. If we can use him when training others, it would be most beneficial."

"Training who?" I asked and then a lump rose to my throat. "Leilani?" I whispered.

"Yes, Leilani, for starters."

"I thought she was dead. That is what you told him, remember?"

"I don't have to explain that to you either. All you need to know is she is not on this mountain so do not bother looking for her. You will be wasting your time."

So, Leilani was still alive, somewhere. "I need to take him back to the hospital."

"I don't think that will be possible," She stood again and I did the same, ready to lunge at her and rip her head off if need be. "Calm down, please. You're making me laugh."

"What good is he to you like this?" I yelled.

"I can use him. I can train his powers. Make him better and stronger than he already is," she said.

"What good will it do you when he's dead?" I spat glaring at her. "Look at him! Go ahead, take a look!" Melinda looked past me at the skinny, weak boy on the bed. "Can't you see he is dying as we speak, you idiot?"

Melinda shrugged, actually shrugged her shoulders. "I guess," she said as she stepped to the side, leaving me a clear shot to the door. "Fine. Take him."

My jaw dropped. "What? Just like that?"

"Yes, just like that. There will not be a fight tonight. I promised. I keep my word."

"What do you mean you promised? Who did you promise?" I tried to remember if she had promised Aloysius but could not remember hearing those actual words out of her mouth.

"That is my business. Be glad I am a woman of my word. Be thankful that someone out there is looking out for you. I'm not really sure why but, so be it. Take him and get him the help he needs." She motioned toward Jose Luis who looked just as shocked as I felt.

I turned and picked him up off the bed, cradled him in my arms as his head rested against my chest. As I prepared to carry him to the door, Melinda walked toward us. I knew it was too good to be true. We were not getting out of here without a fight. She leaned toward me, her hands behind her back.

"Oh, one word of advice," she whispered. "I'd be careful with Aloysius. He is not all you think he is." She turned and walked out the door, Arturo following close on her heels.

"What's going on?" Fiore asked when I stepped out of the house with Jose Luis in my arms.

"I have no idea. She told me to take him and leave, that there would be no fight tonight. I'm not questioning it, let's just go," I said looking at Aloysius.

He stretched a hand out to Fiore. She pulled her cell out and handed it to him. After contacting Giovanni and telling him to get the others and go to the apartment, he grabbed Fiore's hand. Lucas took Jose Luis from me and I took Fiore's hand. That left one hand each to hold Lucas's, no one to hold Jose Luis's.

"Will it work like this?" I asked, worried that there needed to be more physical contact. I had no idea what would happen if one of us let go, no idea where that person would end up.

"It should. Lucas, keep him tight against your chest and whatever you do," he turned to Fiore and me. "Do not let go of Lucas's hands under any circumstances," Aloysius explained as he looked from Fiore to me. We nodded and I closed my eyes. No matter how many times Aloysius transported us like this, I would never get used to the ground falling from beneath my feet and the world spinning in circles. All I could do was hold on, shut my eyes, and wait for the landing.

As the rest landed on their feet in the living room, I landed on my butt. It just so happened that the sofa broke my fall. As soon as I got my bearings again, I ran to Lucas. He stood looking totally unfazed with Jose Luis still securely in his arms.

"What the hell just happened?" I asked as I motioned for Lucas to place Jose Luis on the sofa.

"That was totally awesome," Lucas answered. Jose Luis smiled and nodded.

"That is not what I am referring to. I meant, what the hell just happened with Melinda? Why were we not attacked? Why did they just let us walk out of there with Jose Luis?" I took Jose Luis's hand in mine and kept my voice at a normal volume though I really wanted to scream.

"That was strange. I figured she wanted you in there alone so she could take advantage. Trust me, we listened to every word from outside," Aloysius came to kneel by Jose Luis, looking at his face with concern. Jose Luis looked weak and exhausted. I wasn't sure if it was his cancer or what he had just been through. "I tried to get into her head, but she was completely focused on what she was saying to you."

"What did she mean by *she promised*? Who did she promise?" I asked.

"Is that what she said her reason was for not fighting?" Fiore asked as she took a seat in one of the chairs.

"Yes. But she refused to say who she made a promise to," I stood, preparing to have Jose Luis taken to his room where he could be more comfortable. "Unless…"

"Unless what, Lily?" Aloysius picked Jose Luis up and walked around the coffee table with him in his arms.

"Christian. Could she have made some kind of deal with Christian?"

⤝ TWENTY-SIX ⤞

"D o you need anything besides a drink?" I asked as I helped Jose Luis into bed. He had taken a quick shower but had needed my help getting into his flannel pants. His head hurt worse when he bent over. Though he tried to hide his pain, he could never fool me.

"This is good," he said as he sipped from his glass of juice and placed it back on the nightstand. "I think I will watch television for a while."

"You should probably try to get some sleep," I requested looking into his bloodshot eyes.

"I am really not that tired. I did a lot of sleeping lately. There was nothing else to do." He grabbed the remote and turned on the set.

I kissed his forehead and turned to leave the room.

"Lily?" he called just as I reached the door. I turned to face him. "Um, I wanted to say thank you."

"Thank you?" I went to sit by his side. He scooted over to give me some room, his face suddenly scrunched in pain. "Does it hurt that much? Maybe we should get you back to the hospital before—"

"No, please. I don't want to go back there. There is nothing they can do for me anymore. I would rather just stay here." His face grew more serious. "I was trying to say thank you for coming to get me. That was very brave."

"You don't need to thank me, or any of us. We did what needed to be done. You are part of this family now. I'm just glad they let you go without a fight."

"Yes. That could have been really bad. I know you were totally outnumbered since they have so many of them up there," He looked down at his lap. "I wanted to ask you something."

"What is it?" I placed my fingers under his chin and lifted his face. "You don't have to be afraid to ask me anything."

"Where is Christian?"

Anything but that. I should have expected it though since he had never seen us apart. He had never known us to not work together. I had no choice but to answer honestly. If I didn't, Jose Luis would see right through it. "I truly don't know."

"Did you have a fight? Is he angry because I'm—"

"No! Don't ever think that. None of this is your fault. And no, we did not have a fight. He just…" How did I say it so he would understand when I didn't even understand what could have made Christian turn his back on me, on us? Jose Luis wanted to stay with us, both of us, not just me. I looked into his face as he waited for an answer, his eyes glued to mine, full of hope and wonder. "He had to go away for a little while but, he'll be back."

"Ok. I hope he returns soon. I want to see him before I—"

"He will be back soon. I promise. Now just watch a movie and relax. I will be up in a little while to check on you. Maybe by then you'll be hungry." I kissed his forehead again and rushed out of the room.

I lied to him, flat out lied. Christian wasn't coming back, ever. I felt it in every fiber of my being, yet Jose Luis believed me. I knew what he was about to say. He wanted to see Christian before he died. I was going to lose him too if I didn't do what needed to be done yet I didn't know whether or not Jose Luis was even willing. We hadn't talked about his alternatives and now it was all up to me and me alone. Making that decision alone didn't hurt as much as it angered me. Christian could not have picked a worse time to turn selfish.

As I headed toward the stairs, Fiore caught up to me. "So, how is he?" she asked.

"He tries to say he's ok, but I can see how much pain he's in. He couldn't even dress himself. I wish I knew how much longer." I tried to swallow through the constant knot in my throat.

"Did you talk to him about his options yet?"

I shook my head. "I want to talk to Aloysius first. I'm not really sure what to say to Jose Luis and," I sat on a step and looked up at Fiore's concerned face. "I can't believe I have to do this by myself now. It wasn't supposed to be this way."

She kneeled behind me and rubbed my back with one hand. "I know it wasn't, but it isn't your fault. You are Jose Luis's mother now. He needs you."

I laughed. "I know. It's kind of hard thinking of myself as his mother when I'm technically only four years older than him."

"I guess I can see your point. But you have to remember that in experience you're almost a full century older than him."

"Yeah, I guess you're right," I stood and gave her a quick hug. "Let's go talk to Aloysius. I need a little advice on what to say to Jose Luis. Oh, by the way, does Aloysius know what we did at the beach?"

"Not one bit and I think we should keep it that way. Don't ask don't tell, right?" She winked.

"Right." It was probably for the best considering the time period Aloysius came from and how formal he always acted. I couldn't imagine his reaction to something like what Fiore and I did.

Aloysius was just hanging up the phone as we approached the kitchen. The expression on his face automatically turned to concern when he saw us enter. "How is our boy feeling?"

"He says he's ok but I know better. He can't even bend down because his head hurts worse. He even needed help getting dressed and getting into bed. He has no appetite either. He's watching TV now," I explained as I pulled a chair from the small table in the corner of the kitchen and sat.

"Any new injuries from his captivity?" he asked as he sat across from me, motioning for Fiore to take the last chair.

"No. According to him no one hurt him or made him do anything. He says he did nothing but sleep while he was there."

"That's good. At least they didn't add to his pain. What is your plan now that he's back?" He reached across the table for Fiore's hand.

Fiore's face lit up as she gave it to him and my stomach sank. She looked at me with guilt on her face and tried to pull away from his grip. "Please, don't, Fiore. It's ok. I just really miss him is all," I explained.

"I know. I wish there were something we could do. Shouldn't we be going to where the news report came from to see if he is there?" she asked looking at Aloysius.

"I thought so at first, but I think it might be useless. If my guess is correct, he's been traveling north and heading toward the United States."

"Then we need to track him," I insisted.

"Who knows how far he got or where he is planning to cross the US border. It could take us weeks to find his trail, even with an experienced tracker," he paused to take my hand too. "Jose Luis and the other children need us more right now."

"I understand but Christian is out there all alone. He's a newborn for Christ's sake."

"I understand what you're feeling right now. As his maker you feel responsible for him," his eyes softened. "But you have to remember he is an adult, and he made his choice."

"You seem to forget I'm not only his maker. I'm also his wife," I pulled my hand away from him and stood. "He walked out on me without so much as a *go to hell*. He owes me an explanation."

Aloysius stood and came to stand in front of me. "Lily, believe me, I understand your pain. I know what it is like to lose someone you love. But you can't let it consume you, especially when there are others who love you and depend on you."

"I know Jose Luis is depending on me and I will be there for him," I felt calm enough to sit back down. I needed his advice and the last thing I wanted was to be angry with him. It wasn't his fault Christian left. "I don't know what to do now. I feel he doesn't have much time left. He doesn't want to go back to the hospital either. He said..." Tears filled my eyes. Aloysius and Fiore reached for my hands at the same time, bringing a smile to my face despite the grief eating away at me.

"What did he say?" Aloysius asked in a mere whisper, pain obvious in his eyes.

"He didn't actually finish the sentence, but he was about to say that he wants to see Christian before he dies. I wish I could give him that."

"That is, unfortunately, not in your hands. Have you spoken with him yet about what his options are?"

"No," I swallowed the tears fighting for release. I had no time to feel sorry for myself. "That's what I wanted to talk to you about. I'm not sure what to say to him."

"How about I make a pot of coffee?" Fiore jumped to her feet as if she needed something to do. Aloysius and I both nodded. She went to the cabinet to begin her task.

"Let your heart do the talking, Lily. That is what you're best at," Aloysius said as he turned his attention from Fiore to me. It was obvious it was hard for him to keep his eyes off her. As much as I envied the fact that they could be close with each other, I also felt happy for her. Aloysius snapped me out of my head with a squeeze of my hand. "Tell him what you want and then let him weigh his options. Make sure he thinks about what becoming a vampire will mean to him and to his sister. I am sure we will get her back and she will have to deal with whatever changes may take place, whether that is him leaving us for good or him becoming one of us."

"I hadn't really thought about what his decision would mean to Leilani. That changes things," I took the steaming cup Fiore offered me and smiled at the comfort of it. My soul ached more for Christian's comfort, but I pushed the thought out of my mind.

"Not necessarily," Fiore started handing Aloysius his cup and placing hers in front of her as she sat. "You have to remember Leilani was raised in a paranormal world. Things that would seem like complete fantasy to others are everyday occurrences to her. Remember, she herself is a witch. She may be too young yet to understand what it all means but she still knows it's there."

"I somehow keep forgetting the fact that Leilani is a witch. She just seems too young to me to have such strong powers," I admitted.

"She was born that way, just like her mother. I'm sure she knows her brother has acquired some powers too, even if they are not as extravagant as starting fires. She's also been around vampires since Melinda imposed herself on the hunters," Fiore said as she stirred her coffee. She tapped the spoon on the side of the cup and placed it on the saucer.

"It is true that she's been around vampires but that's just what I mean. She's being used by them. She's being forced to offer her blood as nourishment for vampires. I wouldn't be surprised if she fears us, or even hates us because of it." I put my cup down and fell back against my chair, stretching my legs out in front of me. "It's very possible she won't even want to be near us let alone live with us."

"That may be so," Aloysius said. "But I doubt she would want to stay away from her brother once she's reunited with him. Besides, if she sees Jose Luis loves you and trusts you, she will too."

"I hope you're right," I sat back up and looked to both their faces. "How do you feel about Jose Luis becoming a vampire at fifteen?" That is what my biggest issue was with the whole thing. He was so young.

Fiore and Aloysius looked at each other before looking back at me. Fiore nodded for Aloysius to answer me. He held my eyes with his. "A lot better than I do about him dying at fifteen."

TWENTY-SEVEN

Fiore decided to stay by my side while I talked to Jose Luis, so we made him a sandwich and walked to his room together. As we opened the door, panic hit me like a slap in the face. The smell in the room had changed since I left him less than an hour ago. Sniffing the air as I walked in, I couldn't quite place it. It was a mix between smoke and wet dog, or something like it.

"What is that smell?" I whispered to Fiore.

"I'm not sure," she answered as she turned his light on. The television still flickered in the darkness. "Oh no!"

Jose Luis leaned over the side of his bed, his head over a garbage can on the floor. At some point, he had managed to get up, walk across the room, and bring the can to the side of his bed. He looked up at us as we approached, his hair plastered to his head with sweat. His skin had turned from pale to something of a bluish-gray hue.

"What's wrong?" I asked running to his side. My fingers brushed the wet hair off his forehead. Fiore placed the plate with the sandwich on top of his dresser across the room.

"I feel sick," he panted and turned his face back to the trash can. "But nothing is happening."

"Fiore, can you please get some crackers and ginger ale?" I turned to her and motioned toward the dresser with my head. "And can you please get that out of here?" I didn't think the smell of the sandwich would help him any.

"Yeah, sure. I'll be right back." She grabbed the plate and left the room.

"Do you think you can sit up?" I asked as I propped his two pillows against the headboard. "Sitting might make your stomach feel better than lying flat."

"Why now?" he asked, tears running down his cheeks. By the look on his face, he was not talking about his nausea.

"I don't know why God does what he does," I took his clammy hand in mine. "I know one thing though. You do not have to go if you don't want to."

His eyes widened and then narrowed with suspicion. "What do you mean? Are you saying what I think you are saying?"

I stood to fetch a washcloth from his drawer. "Let me wet this and then we can talk."

Before he could respond, I rushed from the room and into the bathroom. As my head spun, I leaned against the sink to steady myself. How could I possibly be thinking of taking his blood, of draining his body until his heartbeat almost completely faded? Of taking the life of a fifteen-year-old boy and replacing it with this absolute hell called vampirism? He would never have children, grandchildren. He would never grow old with someone and then move on to wherever it is we go when we die, a normal human death, the way it was supposed to be. How could I even begin to explain that to him, let alone wish it for him? I had been so certain it was what I wanted if only for the selfish reason of not losing yet another person I love. And now? I didn't think I could go through with it, even if it turned out he wanted it.

"Lily, are you ok? He's not… that close, is he?" Fiore poked her head into the bathroom. She couldn't bring herself to say the word. Death, absolute and constant death. What my existence was made up of.

"No…I don't know," I said as I wiped my eyes and turned the faucet on. "I want to wipe his neck and head down, maybe cool him off a little. Did you get what I asked for?"

"Of course. He's nibbling on the crackers now. He asked me to see what was keeping you."

"Thank you," I said as I rung the washcloth out. As I tried to take a step away from the sink, I faltered and fell back against it. Fiore came running to steady me. "What's wrong, Lily?"

"I'm…I'm just sick of it!" I suddenly felt strong enough to stand on my own and stepped away from her, spinning on my heels to face her. "I'm sick of all this shit, the deaths, the heartbreaks, the constant drama, and the threats. I'm sick of all the pain. I'm nineteen years old!" I threw the washcloth into the sink and slammed the bathroom door shut so Aloysius and Jose Luis couldn't hear. Fiore backed herself against the sink. Her expression changed from amusement to worry.

"I understand what you're saying, believe me—"

"No, Fiore, you don't truly understand. You were turned as an adult. You can go to a bar without a fake ID. People don't look at you funny when you're out late at night by yourself. I on the other hand, died a teenager. I never got to be an adult, not really. I was never given that choice."

"Let me tell you one thing, Lily." The set of her eyes told me to shut up and listen, though I wanted to continue my rant. "Most of us were not given a choice. Most of us, including me, were turned by force, with lies and empty promises. So yes, you are a mother and a wife now. Your husband is presently AWOL, I understand that, but you still have responsibilities. That poor me thing doesn't really work for you. I know you better than that. I know how strong and determined you are. You want to be a teenager, fine, go ahead. But not until after you take care of what you need to take care of. The husband and the child, they were your choice. You chose Christian and you chose Jose Luis."

"What? I know I chose Christian but—"

"You could have found Jose Luis a home, any home, but instead you chose to keep him because you chose to love him," She reached out to touch me and I backed away. "Fine. Feel sorry for yourself if that's what you really want, but do it after you take care of the boy you love. He needs you now; the strong, nurturing, and caring woman we all love, not the child you'd rather be because you feel you are owed that. Nineteen is just a number."

My jaw dropped at the firmness of her words. Though I wanted to fight her, I couldn't. She was right. Jose Luis didn't have to stay with us. We could have turned him over to child services or whatever agency was like it in Lima, but we didn't, I didn't. I chose to love him. I chose to open my home and heart to him and, hopefully, his sister. She was right. I couldn't be a coward now.

"Ok, you're right. I did choose to be his mother and I know I need to act like it. I'm going to talk to him," I said as I went to wet the washcloth again.

"Good," she placed her hand on my shoulder and squeezed. "That's more like it. Do you still want me in there?"

I turned to her and smiled. "No, thank you anyway. I need to handle this one."

Jose Luis sipped warm ginger ale while I sat and held his hand. Looking into his eyes, his warmth radiated and touched my face, my hands, and comforted me though it was him who needed comforting. The goodness and love in him shone like a light surrounding him, a light I felt I could touch but didn't dare; afraid I might tarnish it with what I am.

"How are you feeling now?" I asked, taking the glass he handed me and placing it on his nightstand.

"My stomach feels a little better, thanks. I did eat some crackers." He looked at the plate.

"Good. Maybe you'll feel good enough to eat some soup later. Carmela is coming to cook for you and Lucas. He's going to be staying with us too, at least until Mariana comes back," I told him. I knew he liked having Lucas around. "I think it's time we talked."

"I am ready," he sat up straighter. "Please do not be afraid to say anything to me."

I nodded. "You say you don't have much time left. I know you're right. I can feel it, sense it, and even smell it."

"What do you mean smell it? Is that possible?"

"Apparently it is. I never knew that before, but I also never knew anyone who was sick and going to die. The deaths I've witnessed were sudden, usually by accident and sometimes caused by me," His eyes widened as I expected. "I sense you are close. Maybe not today, maybe not tomorrow, but close nonetheless. I want to know what you want to happen now." I held my breath and waited as he thought about my words.

"Do you mean if I want to die, like God wants me to, or if I want to be like you?"

He understood more than I had given him credit for. "Yes. If it were up to me, I would turn you right this minute, but it's not up to me. It is completely up to you to decide what you want, and I will respect your decision." He looked confused. "I am not saying I would like it if you died, not at all. I love you and it would be a great loss. I'd miss you, we all would, but it is your choice."

He pulled his hand out of mine and grabbed his head. "I do not know how much longer I can stand this pain. I am scared to die. I am scared to leave you and Christian, Fiore, Lucas, and Aloysius, too, but…"

"But you need to know more. That is why I wanted to talk. I want to explain to you what becoming a vampire is like, especially at your age. I want you to have all the facts, and also to consider your sister, before you make any decisions."

He nodded. For an hour we sat and talked. I explained everything I had experienced, everything I had missed by being this way, and everything that had become an obstacle because of it. He silently listened and allowed me to talk, nodding and sometimes cringing in pain. When I paused in case he had questions, he said nothing. I continued and told him of all the events that led up to meeting him. I explained what the attachment between a maker and a vampire was like, how overwhelming it sometimes felt, and how eternal it really was. I told him that once he chose, and if he did choose to become a vampire, there would be no turning back. I explained the things that were a danger to us, and the only ways we could die. I saved the worst for last. Taking a deep breath and trying to control my tears, I explained how Christian had left and how he had renounced his attachment to me, his maker, so completely that I could not even feel him anymore, letting him know that was also an option if he chose it later.

"Until this actually happened, I did not know it was even possible," I explained. "But he did it. He chose to let me go, mind, body, and soul. I can no longer feel him just as I am sure he can no longer feel me."

"So, what are you saying? That I could do the same thing to you if I wanted to?" His hand squeezed mine and I jumped, thinking he was in pain. He smiled and looked me in the eyes. "I would not do that to you. If I picked what you are offering, I would love you just as much as I do now. I know you are not much older than me, but I trust you. You know a lot more than me. You lived almost a hundred years. You know more than my mother did." He laughed at what I assumed were memories of his mother and her struggle to contain Leilani's powers and hide her own from the world.

"I know you love me. I can feel it. That's not even a question in my mind. I just want you to be sure, absolutely sure. You would stay forever fifteen, never aging, never dying. You'd live the loss of your sister. I want you to make sure you could live with that."

"As long as she was happy in her life I wouldn't care. I just have one question," he said as he held my eyes again.

"What is it?" I said, expecting something complicated.

"Will it hurt?"

"Like hell," I answered and laughed. That was likely not the answer he expected. A knock on the door made us both jump. "Yes?"

Fiore opened the door a crack and peeked inside. "I'm sorry to interrupt but there's someone here to see you, Lily."

"What? Who?" I asked, my stomach already turning with anticipation. Could it be Christian?

"Just come down, please," she answered and left, giving me no chance to question her further.

Jose Luis looked at me with a smile on his face. "Go ahead downstairs. I will think about it while you are gone."

"Do you know something I don't know?"

"No, but go ahead. I will see you soon. I promise."

❧ TWENTY-EIGHT ❧

Lucas stood at the bottom of the spiral staircase as I approached, a smile spread across his lips. "What's going on?" I asked stopping on the bottom step. I heard no voices coming from the common area of the apartment.

"Someone is here to see you," was all he said.

"I know that much. Who is it?"

"Go see for yourself," he said and held his arm out. "In the dining room."

"Thanks. You're a lot of help," I barked as I walked past him. He laughed as he followed close behind me.

My legs shook and my hands trembled at my sides as I walked through the living room and toward the dining room door. I stopped a moment to listen but heard nothing. The scent coming through the closed door was familiar, but I couldn't quite place it. My hope was diminished when I realized it wasn't Christian's scent. Regardless, they were being awfully secretive. I placed both hands on the door and took a deep breath before pushing it open. Aloysius sat at the head on the table and Fiore stood just to his side.

"What's going on?" I asked as I stepped into the room. "Fiore and Lucas said—" I froze as my eyes rested on the pale blond head to the right of where I stood. Crystalline blue eyes met mine and I swayed as I lost my balance, steadying myself by gripping the back of the chair in front of me.

"Lily," Aaron greeted. Next to him, sitting with her back straight, legs crossed like the lady she is, sat Kalia. She smiled at me with the same warmth I always knew. My jaw dropped.

Lucas came to stand behind me, placing his hands lightly on my shoulders for support.

"Aren't you going to say something?" Aloysius asked with a smile on his face. Fiore's smile was just as big.

"I—I'm—I don't know," was what came out. Lucas pulled out the empty chair across from Aaron and pushed me down onto it before sitting next to me.

"Lily, dear, it's good to see you again," Kalia said. I turned toward her with my mouth still open. "You're looking well."

"I don't understand," I turned toward Aaron. Warmth spread through my body, and I shook it off. "What are you doing here? Did you come to finish me off?"

Everyone in the room laughed. I fisted my hands on my lap. "Is this some kind of sick joke?"

Aloysius stood and took Fiore's hand. "Let's leave them alone for a bit, shall we? I'm sure they have a lot to talk about."

I looked at Lucas for help, but he just smiled and followed them out, nodding at me before closing the door behind him. Turning to my unexpected guests, I narrowed my eyes as I looked at Aaron. "What do you want?"

"We came to talk to you. Please allow us to explain," he pleaded with his usual fatherly voice.

"There is nothing to explain. I tried to kill Maia, in self-defense, I might add. You took her side. That is all there is to it," I stood to leave. Kalia stood, red tears streaming down her porcelain cheeks.

"That is what we need to talk to you about. We need to make things right. We were wrong," she said as she looked into my eyes.

My jaw dropped again, and I made no attempt to close my mouth, unable to hide my shock. "What? Are you really admitting you were wrong?"

"Ladies, please sit down," Aaron asked as he took Kalia's hand and guided her back to her seat. I did as he asked only because I was curious as to where their little charade was going. "We know the truth. We now know Maia used us and lied to us. We loved her so we believed everything she told us. I don't know, maybe not entirely. We know she wasn't perfect, not by any means. I think sometimes we just turned a blind eye to the things she did. Anyway, we are sorry we doubted you. Sorry we said the things we said to you. We came to tell you that."

Tears came to my eyes, and I wiped them away with the back of my hands. I refused to let them see me cry for them. "What happened? How did your little angel finally reveal her true colors to you?" I didn't care how bitter I sounded or if my words stung them.

Kalia bit her lip and looked at Aaron. "It wasn't really her. Christian came to us a couple of days ago. He told us everything."

I jumped out of my seat so fast my chair fell onto its back. "Christian was with you? Is he still there?"

Aaron came to my side and picked up the chair. He pushed me onto it again and then sat next to me, turning my face so I could look at him. "No, he's not. He said he wanted to make things right for you, wanted to tell us the truth about what happened with Maia. He told us all the things she said and did that day on the mountain. He helped us search her room while she was away on another vacation. We tore her room apart looking for anything that might confirm what he was saying. It was Christian who found the loose floorboards under her bed, within them her birth certificate and other documents confirming what he said. He left right after that."

"And you let him?" I asked. "You should've made him stay."

"It wasn't up to us, Lily," Kalia explained. "He asked us not to ask him anything, asked us to promise him that. He only wanted to make things right for you. All he said is that he was doing what he needed to do for you."

My head dropped to the table and Aaron's hand stroked my hair as I finally released the tears I was fighting, my body shaking with my sobs. How could he think leaving me was what I needed? How could he decide something like that for me?

"Lily, please don't cry," Aaron coaxed as he leaned over me. "We will figure out what is happening to Christian. I have a feeling he is not going to stay away forever. I sensed his love for you, even as he walked out the door."

Kalia's hand now rested on my back as I felt her lean over me too. "Can you please forgive us for what we did? Life is not the same without you in it."

I raised my head and looked at them through the redness of my tears. My body tingled from the warmth climbing from my toes all the way up to my head. My stomach fluttered and my lips pulled into a smile without my permission. I wrapped my arms around both their shoulders and pulled them closer. "Yes, of course I can. I love you both and I've missed you so much," I cried as they squeezed me back.

"Oh, God, Lily we are so sorry. You have no idea how many times we—" Kalia cried.

"Please, don't Kalia. It's over. We're here now, together," I said as I kissed her cheek and then turned to kiss Aaron's though he beat me to it. "That's all that matters."

"Isn't this great?" Fiore asked as she and Aloysius stood in the doorway, Lucas peeking in from behind them. "I love happy endings."

The three of us laughed as we stood, Kalia and I looking like something from a horror movie with tears smeared on our faces. Fiore rushed in with tissues in her hand. She handed one to each of us before wrapping her arms around me. "I knew all about it," she whispered in my ear before she stepped back.

"You little sneak," I said and punched her arm playfully. "That's who you were on the phone with?" I looked at Aloysius and he smiled.

"Thank you," I said as I wrapped my arms around him. He returned my hug.

"No need." He kissed the top of my head before breaking free. "I knew my great grandson couldn't truly be that stubborn."

We all laughed at that as Aaron wrapped his arms around Aloysius and patted his back. He whispered something into his ear and Aloysius smiled. He motioned for us to sit down.

Aaron's face suddenly turned serious, his expression changing from happy to worry. He raised an eyebrow. "What is happening here? Why do I smell death?"

Aloysius explained, "Jose Luis has brain cancer, inoperable at this point. Melinda had taken him from the hospital, and we just got him back. He is not doing very well, I'm afraid."

"That reminds me, I need to go check on him. I will be right back," I stood and turned to leave. I heard Aaron shift in his seat as his eyes bore into my departing back. I ignored it and ran up the stairs.

Jose Luis was still sitting up when I entered his room. His face lit up when he looked at me and a smile pulled at the corner of his lips. "Is Christian here?"

"I'm sorry but no," I sat next to him and took his hand. He looked as disappointed as I felt that it was not Christian. "It's Kalia and Aaron. They came to talk to me."

"That is good, isn't it?" He raised his eyebrows but scrunched them in pain.

"Yes, it's very good. I missed them so much and I'm glad they're here," I admitted.

"But something else is wrong, I can sense you are hiding something from me," he squeezed my hand though he did not have much strength. "Please tell me."

"Christian went to them a couple days ago, told them the truth about Maia. That is why they are here. They wanted my forgiveness," I explained.

"So Christian is in Oregon, right?" He looked excited in spite of the pain.

"I'm afraid I don't know the answer to that. He left their house after telling them the truth, but he didn't say where he was going."

"Oh," he said as a single tear rolled down his cheek. "I just thought…"

"I know. Me too," I wiped the tear away and ran my hand through his hair. "Have you decided, about what we discussed?" I held my breath.

"Yes," he backed away to look into my eyes. "I have. I want what you are offering. I want to become a vampire."

My stomach fluttered in happiness and fear mixed together. My happiness was extinguished in seconds when I heard a voice call from downstairs.

"Lily, a word please," Aaron called from the bottom of the stairs.

As I approached him, his back tensed and his face grew serious, almost angry. My hands started to shake but I balled them up to hide it. "What's wrong?" I asked though I knew exactly what it was. Aaron was against making new vampires.

"You know very well what is wrong," he snapped and turned from me. "Follow me, please."

Here we go. Because of this, I'd lose him and Kalia just as suddenly as I'd gotten them back, again.

TWENTY-NINE

Jose Luis managed to hang on for another month. Though he was weak and tired most of the time and his vision mostly blurry, he wanted to remain human until he could no longer fight. None of us actually thought he would fight as long as he did but he surprised us with his determination. He fought through the headaches on a daily basis and assured us he could handle it when we begged him to stop. He thought we might be able to get his sister back in time, so he could see her while he was still human and explain to her what the decision he made meant.

Aaron, though he was not entirely happy about the situation, understood my feelings for Jose Luis and also the fact that not only could I not bear to lose him, but neither could his sister. They had become orphans at such a young age that all they knew was the love and trust they had for each other. When Aaron argued with me, I reminded him of how he had allowed Kalia to turn Maia into a vampire, all to spare her life because she was so young. They believed Maia was ill, though her illness was only a ploy to get what she wanted. After comparing my situation with his own, he finally relented as long as I promised not to ever abandon Jose Luis. I also had to promise to make sure I trained him to hunt only criminals and to never shed innocent blood. Jose Luis and I had already discussed the conditions and rules he had to abide by once he was turned and he was in total agreement.

Kalia and Aaron remained with us. They called home from time to time but got no answer. They wanted Maia to be there so they could return to Oregon and confront her, but she stayed away. She had changed her cell phone number, which led us all to suspect she knew Christian had been there to talk to Kalia and Aaron and confirm she'd lied about everything. She was purposely avoiding returning and none of us had any idea of her whereabouts.

In the meantime, Lucia, Alegría, and Paco remained in the apartment upstairs though their father had been found alive. Giovanni and Lucas found Tomas roaming the beach one night, shirtless and shoeless. He was pale, thin, and pretty banged up. When they approached to speak with him, he panicked and tried to run before stumbling and falling to his knees. He was too weak to get away. Whether his memory had been wiped on purpose or whether he lost it because of his traumatic experiences remained to be discovered. He was currently in the hospital, receiving blood transfusions and extra iron, until he regained his strength. His tests showed no medical reason for his loss of blood, or memory, and when he was stabilized physically, he would be transferred to a psychiatric hospital so they could begin to deal with his mental status.

Because Tomas had no recollection of his kidnapping or anything that occurred up until he was found on the beach, it was decided that the children should be kept away from him, at least until he could begin to deal with what happened to him. Lucia went to the hospital every day to sit with him, leaving Alegría and Paco with us. The children spent most of their time in Jose Luis's bedroom, watching movies, playing games or looking at comic books with him. Paco was especially attached to him, wanting to spend every moment he possibly could by his side. There were nights when Lucia came to get them and ended up taking only Alegría with her, as Paco would refuse to leave and sleep on a cot next to Jose Luis's bed.

There had still been no sign of Mariana. Lucas went to work most days and then returned to the apartment to stay with us. Since he was still half human, he joined Lucia and the children for dinner upstairs every night. On the days he needed blood, Fiore, Kalia, and even Aaron took turns giving him what he needed. Though Lucas still loved Mariana, he was losing hope that she would return and give him what she'd promised: immortality. It was decided, with Aloysius's consent, that if she did not return soon, Fiore would be the one to change him. He would develop an attachment to her, his maker, and that was discussed at length. Lucas affirmed he had no romantic feelings for her but would always cherish the friendship that had grown between them. His attachment would be purely maker and offspring and nothing more.

Many nights were spent in my room with Fiore and Kalia. They always offered a shoulder for me to cry on when the pressures of what was happening to Jose Luis and my loss of Christian got to be too much. Though I still suspected Melinda had something to do with his departure, I stopped voicing it after a while. None of us could figure out why he would've done such a thing, so it didn't make sense to keep talking about it. The hole I felt in my soul because of his absence was closing a little bit every day with their help. I never wanted to forget him, but I knew I had to let him go. They were all right. I had others who loved me and depended on me and that's what I tried to focus on most days. I admitted that when I was alone, my mind filled with memories of him, and I felt as if I would burst. Which is why I barely spent time alone anymore.

"I SEE PACO is sleeping over again," Aloysius said as we all sat around the dining room table.

"That is one strong little guy," Giovanni said with a laugh. "He knows Jose Luis is dying and yet he acts like nothing is happening. I don't know if could have done that at his age. I would have been full of questions."

"Sir, do you need us anymore more tonight?" Margarita asked looking at Aloysius. "We'd like to go see a movie if you do not."

As I looked around the room, everyone smiled except Giovanni. He tried to act as if they were not an item, though the rest of us knew better.

"No, Margarita. You filled your post at the front door. You and Giovanni are free to go."

Margarita smiled and nodded at Aloysius before bidding the rest of us goodnight. Giovanni followed her out the door without a word. We all laughed.

"That's nice to see. They make a nice couple," Fiore said as she took Aloysius's hand. "If you'll all excuse us, we have tickets for a play tonight. If we don't leave now, we'll miss the opening."

As they stood Aloysius looked at me. "Will you be ok? Will Jose Luis…?"

"He's resting peacefully. You two go ahead. Lucas, Kalia, and Aaron are here just in case." I had left Jose Luis asleep after tucking him and Paco in for the night. Paco claimed he wasn't tired, but I knew better. Regardless, I turned the TV on for him before I left the room.

When they left the room, I turned to the others. "Things have been just a little too quiet lately, don't you think?"

"I think we should take it as a blessing, especially now. Jose Luis is fading. I can feel it," Aaron said. "I am glad we have been able to concentrate on him with no interruptions. Whatever Melinda and her clan might be brewing up, at least they are being slow about it."

"That is true. Is it possible that she did make a promise to Christian, and she is actually going to keep her word?" We could at least hope.

He shook his head. "I highly doubt it. She and her sister, Ryanne, are too vengeful for that, but we will take what we can get right now."

"Aaron, do you think…?" I started to ask when I was interrupted by screaming at the top of the stairs. We all pushed from the table and ran to the living room.

Paco ran down, stumbled, and fell down the last few steps, landing on his rear with a look of panic on his face. I ran to pick him up and saw tears streaming down his face.

"Paco, what is it?" I asked as I scooped him into my arms and stood with him. "Is it...?"

"Jose Luis. He get up to go to bathroom. He say he did not need me help and then he fall down. He not gets up," he explained the best he could with his limited English.

"Ok, honey. Thank you for telling us," I said to him and kissed him on his wet cheek. "Lucas, please take him home to his own apartment, make sure he didn't hurt himself from the fall."

Lucas nodded and took him from my arms, walking out the door with Paco's eyes glued on us.

"Oh, my God, Kalia! What do I do? Is it time?" I asked as the three of us ran up the stairs.

"Try not to panic, Lily," Aaron advised as he approached the open door to Jose Luis's room. "If it is time, we are right here with you." He squeezed my shoulder, and I took a deep breath.

"We will not leave your side, Lily, no matter what," Kalia said. She turned the light on and stepped aside. I nodded and entered.

Jose Luis lay face down on the floor at the foot of the bed. As I kneeled next to him, his heart beat faintly in my ear. His breath was also faint, and I sensed his life force dwindling away by the second. I laid a hand on his shoulder and rolled him over, careful not to shake him up too much in case he was nauseated. The color on his face was almost completely drained, his lips cracked and dry. Aaron rushed to our side and lifted him off the floor and Kalia pulled the blankets down on the bed before Aaron laid him down.

"Lily?" Jose Luis whispered, opening his eyes slightly and blinking against the light. "Is it you?"

"Yes, my love," I whispered back, tears already rolling down my cheeks. "It is me. I'm right here by your side." I squeezed his hand in mine, noting his warmth already leaving his exhausted body.

"Is Christian here?" he asked. "I want to say something to him."

I looked at Aaron. His face looked pained, his lips tight. He nodded for me to continue.

"I'm sorry, love. He's not here, but Kalia and Aaron are here with you, too. How are you feeling?" I'm not sure why I asked. I knew. I knew this was the end for him, at least of his human life.

He scrunched his face and tried to scream. Though no sound came out of his mouth, I felt his scream and pain in my soul. How could this happen to someone so young and innocent? How could God possibly allow a child to suffer in this way? It wasn't fair.

"Lily, don't do that to yourself," Kalia whispered in my ear. "He needs you now. It's time."

Oh, God. It wasn't supposed to be like this. It was supposed to be up to Christian and me, together, to bring him over to our world. My stomach ached all over again with his absence.

Lily, it won't do Jose Luis any good for you to choke up now. Kalia sat by my side. I nodded and wiped the blood tears off my face with the back of my arm. She was right. It was time to end his pain.

"Jose Luis, are you ready?" I asked as I leaned over him and whispered it in his ear. The smell radiating from his body was unmistakable. Death was ready to claim him now.

He arched his back as pain shot through him. His eyes opened wide as he stared at the ceiling and bit his lip to keep from screaming. Aaron rushed to kneel at the other side of the bed. The room suddenly grew cold, goosebumps visible on Jose Luis's arms.

"He is here, Lily," Jose Luis whispered as his eyes grew even wider. I looked around the room to see if someone had entered. No one had.

"Who is here?" I asked.

"He is here to take me with him. I don't want to go with him. I want to stay with you," he said as his heart beat even slower. "Please, Lily. Do it now, before he reaches me," he forced through clenched teeth.

✑ THIRTY ✑

I turned to Kalia, not sure what Jose Luis was talking about. She shrugged. "Now is the time, Lily." She pulled his pajama shirt off and tossed it aside. Turning his face to face her, she nodded to his neck. "If you want to save him, it's now or never. Once his heart stops beating on its own, it may not work."

Taking a deep breath and willing my body to stop shaking, I gathered what strength I had left and leaned over his neck. The vein there was still visible, though it pulsed irregularly. Kalia's tender touch on my back encouraged me. I allowed my mind to call upon my thirst hoping my fangs would emerge. When they did, I took another deep breath. Picturing Christian's face brought me the courage I needed at the moment. My fangs grazed Jose Luis's neck before sinking through the tender flesh.

As his life force filled my mouth and ran down my throat, images of his life flashed before my eyes. His loving parents doted on him and his sister, leaving them all too soon to be ripped from their home and from each other. Bits and pieces of his life with the hunters flashed in my mind, out of sequence and making no sense. The longing for his little sister, whom he was told was missing and then possibly dead, kept him going on a daily basis. He never gave up hope that she would return to him. His love for me and Christian ran through my body, warming my limbs and giving me the strength I needed to continue the process of turning him. As images of his days with us in the apartment filled my mind, his heart beat faintly in my ears until the thumps grew farther and farther apart.

"Lily, that's enough now," Aaron said as he stood from kneeling at his bedside. "His heart is almost completely stopped. You need to release him."

Reluctantly, I backed away from his neck, licking the blood at the corner of my mouth as I sat up. Kalia nodded when I held my wrist out to her, questioning with a raise of my eyebrows. Holding my wrist at my mouth, I bit down until blood flowed into my mouth. I placed my bleeding wrist over Jose Luis's partially open mouth. "Nothing's happening. Is he dead?" I asked when panic ran through me.

"Not entirely," Aaron answered. "Just let the blood flow into his mouth. If you start to clot, bite again."

"Try squeezing your arm a bit, make it flow faster," Kalia coached at my side.

I squeezed my wrist with my fingers at both sides, the open wound burning as I tried to ignore it. As I turned my head to tell Kalia it wasn't working, Jose Luis's hand pushed my hand away. He wrapped both his hands around my wrist and held on while he gulped at my flowing blood, filling his mouth as if starved. "That's it, my love. You're doing great," I said. I wasn't sure if this was exactly what was supposed to happen, but my instincts told me I was on the right path.

"Just a little more and you have to pull away, Lily. He will fight you, but you must," Kalia said and stood as if ready for his fight. "He will think he cannot stop, but he can, and he must."

It was my life flashing in front of my eyes as I listened to Kalia, as if he were pulling those memories from my mind. Ninety years' worth of memories, good and bad, ran through my mind until Aaron pulled me away from him, the flesh on my wrist burning as it tore out of Jose Luis's teeth.

"That's it," Aaron said and wrapped his arm around my waist, holding me tight against his body. I hadn't even realized until he squeezed me that I was trying to fight his grasp, trying desperately to give Jose Luis my wrist back. "The process is done. All we have left to do it wait."

"Why don't you come with me and wash your arm off before it heals," Kalia said as she took my other hand and walked me out of Aaron's arms and toward the door.

"No. He wants more. He needs more. I can't leave him," I yelled though she continued dragging me out of the room.

At the bathroom sink, Kalia ran the water and wet a washcloth. She leaned me over the basin and let the water from the cloth run over my neck. "Splash some water on your face."

"I thought we were washing my wrist," I said in a huff.

"It's already healing. I just wanted you out of there so you could catch your breath and calm down," she said and continued soaking the back of my neck. My shirt was now also wet.

"What did I do?" I said as I stood and grabbed a towel from the rack, drying my face. "I just drank from an innocent child."

"Lily, listen to me," Kalia replied. She led me to sit on the closed toilet while she sat on the edge of the tub, taking my hand in hers. "You did what you had to do to help him."

"Yeah, but," I lifted my head to look at her. The softness in her eyes calmed me more than the cold water had. "I just turned a child into a vampire. I condemned him to exist forever, never aging, never changing."

"Yes, you did do that, but," She leaned in closer so she could whisper. "It was what you both wanted. He knew the consequences he would have to live with. You were kinder than most when you gave him the choice and explained it all to him. It was ultimately his decision, and this is what he chose."

"But he's so young," I argued, still feeling guilty for what I'd done but relaxing more as her compassion and understanding radiated from her hand and into me.

She laughed. "That's only his body. His mind will continue to age the way it is meant to do. He will be an adult at the same age as anyone else. Besides, don't you think he will enjoy staying young and handsome forever?"

I couldn't help but laugh at her comment, picturing the smug look on his face when he told me about the girl he met at the movie theater and the fact that it was not his first date. "Great. So, I will forever be fighting the girls off him. That's just what we—I mean—I needed." The thought of Christian not being here for this important step in our lives saddened me. Kalia squeezed my hand, pulling me out of my runaway thoughts.

"Are you ok now?" she asked as she stood and took the towel from my hands, folding it and hanging it back on the rack.

"Yes, thank you. I know this is what we both wanted. It's just that this was my first time, knowingly anyway." I thought of the time I had turned Christian into a vampire and how different it had been. That had been totally unintentional. My blood tears had flooded into his mouth as I cried over him when Ian took his life and I had taken Ian's.

"Lily, back to the present, please," Kalia said as she heard my thoughts. "Jose Luis needs you here and now as he goes through the process of death and rebirth."

"Right," I said jumping to my feet. "I'm ok. Let's go."

Entering his bedroom was bit disconcerting as I did not hear his usual melodic heartbeat. Aaron had pulled up and chair and sat next to the bed, Jose Luis's hand in his. He stood and motioned for me to take his place and I did so gladly. This child, my son, would be feeling the same horrible pain I felt when I was turned, and ninety years later still remembered as if it had been yesterday. I would not let him suffer through it alone as I had. The slam of the front door snapped me from my thoughts again. Footsteps running up the spiral staircase followed.

"May we?" Aloysius asked as he poked his head in the doorway.

"Of course," Aaron said and ushered him and Fiore in.

"What happened?" Fiore asked as she looked down and mimicked Jose Luis's scrunched brows.

"Not long after you all left, Paco came running down to get us. Jose Luis got up to use the bathroom and collapsed. The time had come. Even he knew it. So, it's done," I explained and looked at his pained face. "Kalia, can you please get me a washcloth and basin with cold water?"

She nodded and rushed out of the room. Aloysius looked at Jose Luis and nodded before taking his place next to Fiore. "He looks good," he said.

"Are you kidding? Look at his face. He's in severe pain," I snapped.

"That is what is supposed to happen. Everything is progressing as it should," he explained.

Though I knew what the actual process involved, I couldn't stand to see him in pain and not be able to do anything about it.

"You are such a mother, Lily," Lucas said as he entered the room and came to the side of the bed. "Just remember, this pain is only temporary. It will pass soon enough and then he can be pain-free forever. He suffered more from his illness."

"You're right," I said and went to work wiping the sweat of his head and neck. "How was Paco when you left him?"

"Sound asleep," Lucas assured me. "I stayed with him until then. Lucia went back to bed since she plans on going to the hospital early. We get Alegría in the morning. I plan on taking the children to the zoo for the day, keep them away, if that's ok with you."

"That is probably best," I looked up at him and saw the distress on his face. "I guess this will be you soon, huh?"

He swallowed hard. "Guess so."

Everyone laughed. Aloysius looked at him with amused eyes. "Wimp," he said before leaving the room.

Lucas and I exchanged looks of surprise. Neither of us had ever heard a joke or a snide remark come out of Aloysius's mouth. It was nice to know he could be a smart ass if he wanted, instead of always so prim and formal.

Everyone left the room and gathered downstairs to await Jose Luis's re-awakening. I stayed by his side, wiping him down with cool water every few minutes and keeping him as comfortable as I could. As I sat by his side, I couldn't help but think about Christian. The pain of his leaving seemed as fresh now as it did the day I discovered him gone. Though I had tried my best to keep it under wraps for everyone else's sake, now that I was alone, I cried until I felt I could cry no more. Jose Luis died without him by his side and would awaken the same way. Whatever it was that Jose Luis and I, and hopefully Leilani, would do in the future, we would do it without Christian. Whatever decisions we made no longer affected him.

For the duration of Jose Luis's transformation, I decided to keep Christian out of my head. I needed to think about how we would get Leilani back and where we'd go after that. The three of us would be a family. We'd need a place to call home, especially since Leilani was so young. Leilani also needed to go to school. Jose Luis could go to school or choose to be homeschooled. That would be his choice to make, whether we stayed in Peru or settled somewhere else. We would have to make that decision together, as a family.

The next morning, Jose Luis started moving his legs and I jumped from my seat. Looking at his face, it was obvious his pain was not as severe as it had been last night. Everyone had checked on us throughout the night. Aaron and Kalia both commented on how quick his transformation was progressing and assured me that it was not that uncommon. Everyone was different and everyone took the amount of time their bodies needed. There really was no specific time frame for the transformation from human to vampire. Though Jose Luis was gravely ill and dying on his own, it seemed to be easier for him than it had been for me or Christian, for that matter.

The smell of smoke invaded my nostrils and I chuckled, wondering who was attempting to cook breakfast for the humans. I could just imagine Fiore at the stove wearing an apron, her sculptured fingernails dripping with egg as they punctured through the shells.

All hell suddenly broke loose as the sound of chaos trailed up the stairs, along with footsteps running up the stairs. I jumped from my seat as someone threw the door open, banging it against the wall.

"Fire!" Aloysius yelled, followed by a panic-stricken Aaron. "The building's on fire!"

THIRTY-ONE

"What do you mean the building is on fire?" I asked as I ran to the window and pulled the drapes aside. On the street below, people were filing out the doors, some coughing and gagging, some crying.

Aloysius grabbed Jose Luis from the bed and started out the door with him in his arms. Aaron grabbed my hand and pulled me from where I stood as if I were glued to the floor. "Where to?" he yelled to Aloysius as they ran down the hall.

"To the beach," Aloysius yelled back, already running down the stairs. "With Jose Luis in this condition, we can't risk contact with any of the other tenants. Everyone was told to meet there."

"Where are Lucia and the children?" I yelled to them. Sirens blared in the distance.

"Lucia was still home. They are with Lucas and the others. They should already be out of the building," Aloysius said as he touched the doorknob on the front door. "It's ok, not hot. I think the fire is below. We have to use the staircase."

"You should've let me jump from Jose Luis's room," I said as I fought to see through the dark smoke already making its way into the hall.

"And risk people seeing?" Aloysius said.

"Can't we teleport, or whatever it is you do?" I asked. There had to be an easier and quicker way.

"Again, we can't risk people seeing. It's a nice morning. People will most likely be on the beach. We can't just appear there." He grabbed the door to the stairwell and pulled it, running through. Aaron caught it before it closed and pulled me through it.

"When we get outside, slow down in front of the people gathered on the street. Once we're away from them, who cares, run like the wind," Aaron said as we rounded the landing and started down another flight.

As we reached the front doors of the building, the fire trucks were just pulling up. People gathered outside, their arms around each other, crying and looking up at the skyscraper they called home. A few people sat on the sidewalk, coughing into handkerchiefs or their arms. A little girl hugged her dog against her chest, her mom holding the back of her shirt to keep her close.

Paramedics exited their vehicles and looked around the crowd, taking a few of the coughing people and ushering them to waiting ambulances. The police worked to get the people to safety by holding traffic so they could cross the street. I looked through the chaos but saw none of our party save for Giovanni. He was the only one waiting for us.

"*Señor*, the child," a short, thin paramedic stopped next to Aloysius and looked over Jose Luis. I bit my lip but Aloysius remained calm.

"He is fine. He's just sick and his medication makes him tired. The smoke did not affect him," Aloysius explained in perfect Spanish before the man nodded and moved on to someone else.

As soon as we were away from the crowd, we ran full speed down the hill toward the beach. As we approached the spot Aloysius had designated as the meeting place, Jose Luis lifted his head.

"What is happening?" he asked with a raspy voice. I ran to his side.

"It's ok, my love," I assured him. "Everything will be ok. It was just a small fire in our building. We're on the beach."

Lucas approached as we neared the spot and took Jose Luis from Aloysius's arms, setting him down on a blanket spread on the sand. Jose Luis closed his eyes again.

"Where are Lucia and the children?" I asked. I dropped to my knees next to an unconscious Jose Luis.

"Margarita took them so they wouldn't see Jose Luis like this. She's getting them breakfast in town," he explained.

Kalia and Fiore sat down next to me and Kalia put her arm around my shoulders. "Why is he unconscious again? He was just awake and talking," I asked.

"It's nothing. It happens sometimes. His body just wasn't ready yet, but he probably woke up because of being jostled around. He'll awaken for good when he's ready."

That made sense and if Kalia was saying it, I believed it. As I looked around the surprisingly deserted beach, I noticed movement in the distance. Three figures approached, taking their time.

"Who are they?" I asked no one in particular as I pointed in the strangers' direction.

"Probably people out for an early morning stroll. They'll just pass, I'm sure," Aloysius explained but his eyes narrowed.

"Something's wrong," I whispered as a chill ran down my spine. I looked up to see how far the strangers had gotten and in what seemed like an instant, a beautiful, dark-haired woman appeared before us. Mariana. The supposed bodyguard we had previously used.

"What a beautiful day for the beach, don't you think so?" She smiled at us as if she were part of the family. "Lucas, my dear, aren't you going to kiss me hello? I've missed you so much."

Lucas stood stock still, his mouth open but no sound came out. Fiore and Kalia placed themselves in front of Jose Luis. Aaron took heed and did the same. Only Aloysius took a fight stance, his knees bent, his fangs out, and his pupils shining red.

"Oh, please, quit with the dramatics, will you?" Mariana looked at Aloysius and laughed, tucking her long black hair behind her ears, her dark eyes still glued on Lucas. "It just doesn't suit you."

"What do you want?" I asked and, for the first time since they approached, looked at her companions. Arturo stood next to Mariana and on her other side was their human servant, Maria. Both had blank looks on their faces.

"You know what we want," Mariana looked at me and motioned behind me. "We came for the boy."

"Absolutely not!" Aloysius yelled. "Melinda gave him back to us. Why would she suddenly take him back?"

"Personally, that is none of my business, so I didn't ask. I was given an order and I'm going to follow it. I'm just doing my job," she said with a seductive smile in Lucas's direction. "Baby, I think you should come work with us. It's much more fun than working for this dried up vampire and the benefits are definitely worth it."

"What the hell are you talking about? Work for whom?" Lucas finally got words out of his mouth.

"And who are you calling dried up?" Aloysius added.

"One question at a time, please," her voice was sickeningly sweet. "Melinda, of course. And you know I was referring to you, Aloysius. You've lost your power over this city. I suggest moving on. Lima has a new ruler now."

Lucas moved forward a few steps. His eyes softened when they reached her face. "Mariana, why are you doing this? I thought we loved each other."

"You loved me," she said without an ounce of compassion in her voice. "There's a difference."

"How can you say that? You didn't spend all those years with me and not love me," Lucas pleaded. I looked around and everyone stared at Mariana in disbelief at her cruelty.

"That's the difference between you and me. You are so trusting and gullible you believe anyone. You even believed me when I said I'd give you what you want," She laughed again and took a step backward, away from Lucas. "It was never my intention to give you immortality."

"You said it was. You promised!" Lucas yelled, finally losing his composure.

"No, sweet, sweet Lucas," she smiled again, and I saw red. "If you think back on our conversations, it was you doing all the talking. I just listened and nodded to whatever spewed out of your mouth. I never came right out and said I would turn you."

"So, why did you stay with me for so long?"

"Because I found you quite entertaining. You amused me, and…" She bit her lip like a shy schoolgirl. "You were great in bed. Like it or not, you are not my only one, right Arturo?" She gave him a flirty smile. We all looked at Arturo in time to see him stiffen. Mariana winked at him.

"Lucas, let her go," I said tearing my eyes away from Arturo. "She is not worth it. You will be turned by someone much better and much more powerful than her."

Mariana laughed and turned to me. "How sweet that you all took him in and made him one of your own. But tell me, just what kind of vampire do you honestly think our boy here will make?"

"A damned good and loyal one, unlike you, Mariana," Aloysius offered.

"Wrong. Just look at him," she waved her hand over Lucas's body as if he were nothing more than an exhibit. "He's a cop, for Christ's sake. What is he going to do, feed off animals or blood banks for the rest of his existence? Is he going to ask politely for blood instead of just taking it like a normal vampire? Now I have honestly had about enough of this. Just hand over the boy and we'll be on our way. You'll be free to return to your lovely apartment. The fire was only confined to the storage area and the garage."

"You started the fire?" Kalia asked.

"Maria was the star of that show. As a non-threatening human, no one questioned her when she entered the garage. Not even your beloved doorman. It was necessary to flush you all out without the humans interfering, not to mention Tomas's family."

I turned to look at Maria just as she turned and ran away down the beach. "Seriously?" Mariana rolled her eyes. "Useless human. Now, are you going to give me the kid or do I have to take him by force?"

"Malinda gave him back. She gave me her word that she wouldn't stop us from leaving that day. Why now?" I asked.

"She said you could take him from her then. She never said anything about her taking him from you later. She wanted you to turn him so that you would be his maker. The bond between you and him would be forever tight and it would hurt you more when she took him from you."

"No!" I screamed and jumped to my feet. "No one is going to take my child!"

"Then by force it is. One wave of Arturo's hand and your saviors here will be rendered immobile. Is that how you want to play it?" she asked as she smiled at Arturo. No one said a word. "Ok, Arturo. Work your magic and we get our prize just in time for breakfast."

Arturo raised his hands and closed his eyes. In a blur, Aloysius dove through the air and tackled him.

"No one takes our child." A familiar voice said. "Not without going through me."

As Aloysius rolled on the ground with Arturo, sand flying every which way, we turned back in the direction of the voice. The sand finally cleared enough to reveal a man standing with a gun in his hand and dark glasses on his face. His lips smiled toward me, and my stomach turned as familiar butterflies took over.

"Christian?" I dropped to my knees and stared at him. "Is it really you?"

THIRTY-TWO

He removed the sunglasses and smiled at me, taking my breath away as if it were the first time all over again. I started to move toward him and remembered the reason we were all here. Jose Luis. He needed our protection.

"What the hell are you doing here?" Mariana snapped looking at Christian. "You were supposed to stay away."

I suddenly remembered my anger with him. He had walked away from me, from our marriage, and from Jose Luis without a single word. Now Mariana was talking to him as if he were under her command. I raised my eyebrows and looked at him.

Christian stepped forward, dropping his sunglasses onto the sand and aimed a gun at Mariana. "It's very obvious to me that a promise was broken."

"You were supposed to be as far away as you could go. What are you doing on this beach?" Mariana snapped at him. She looked over to where Aloysius had tackled Arturo and noticed Aloysius had Arturo by the neck, holding him immobile, but was watching the exchange between Christian and Mariana.

"I had a feeling Melinda wasn't going to keep her word. Obviously, that feeling was correct," Christian answered her without taking his eyes from mine. I tried to look away, but it was as if a spell kept my eyes on his. I couldn't move, let alone breathe.

Mariana looked suddenly distressed as she noticed Arturo's helpless state. Maria had already disappeared from our view, not that she would have been of much use to her anyway. "Look, it's obvious that I'm outnumbered here, seeing as you even brought one of your goons," she looked at Giovanni who stood next to Kalia. "We can forget the whole thing. Just release Arturo and we'll be on our way."

Aloysius, Giovanni, and Christian all laughed in unison. "I don't think that is in our best interest," Aloysius replied. "What's to stop you from coming back with the whole clan? To tell you the truth, I'm kind of surprised Melinda sent you here practically alone."

Mariana started to back away but Lucas jumped behind her, wrapping his arms around her waist. "Let me go!" she screamed and elbowed him in the stomach. He lost his hold on her and she jumped forward, grabbing whoever was closest to her.

"Back off or she dies!" Mariana said with her arm across Fiore's neck. "I will break her neck."

I went toward her, but Lucas held his arm out and stopped my approach. "No, Lily. She's mine."

Mariana narrowed her eyes at him. She squeezed her arm around Fiore's neck tighter, causing Fiore's eyes to widen.

"So, it's her, is it?" she sneered at Lucas. "This is the one who's going to turn you. And I suppose you've already been drinking from her?"

"It is none of your business. You left, remember?" Lucas calmly answered, keeping his eyes on Fiore.

"But you are mine. You always were and you always will be," Mariana said with a smile that made all of us cringe with disgust. "She didn't even complete it yet and you're already crazed and ready to save her?"

"You lost your right to me the moment you walked away, the moment you lied to me. I feel no loyalty to you," Lucas said. He looked over at Christian. Christian nodded. "My loyalty lies with Fiore now so let her go."

"I don't think so. The Italian dies and then you leave with me. It's that simple."

Mariana released Fiore long enough to turn her around. At that moment, Lucas said, "Now!" and both he and Christian grabbed Mariana in one swift move, shoving Fiore to the side.

Christian aimed the gun at her temple.

"And what exactly do you think your pathetic bullets will do to someone like me?" she sneered though the panic was obvious in her wide eyes.

"Wooden bullets," Christian said as he prepared to pull the trigger.

Lucas released his hold on her and stepped in front of Christian, holding his hand out. "May I?" he asked.

Christian nodded and handed him the gun before walking to where we were hovering over Jose Luis. He looked at his face and the sadness in his eyes was obvious. He opened his mouth to speak when Mariana interrupted him.

"Please, are you serious?" Mariana looked at Christian. "You handed the gun to *him*, Mr. Compassion? He'll never do it. I can walk all over him for the rest of his life, and he'll never do anything about it. He never has. His new attachment to Fiore isn't going to change that."

"Mariana, don't underestimate me—" Lucas was interrupted by a sudden blur as Mariana dove at Fiore again. A loud pop exploded in our ears as her body dropped to the ground.

No one moved a muscle as Mariana rolled onto her back, the front of her shirt soaked in blood. "You make a great cop," she spit. "You missed my heart."

She then turned her head toward me. "By the way, dearest Lily, I would think twice about the company you keep, especially that one." She motioned with her eyes to Aloysius.

Christian ran over and dropped to his knees next to Mariana. Lucas jumped in front of him. "Please, allow me. This is something *I* must do," he said as he placed both hands on either side of Mariana's head. He looked her in the eyes and sadly but resolutely whispered, "I always loved you. You didn't deserve that," before turning her head and snapping her neck with a loud crunch.

The only thing that broke the silence following Lucas's courageous move was the sound of Arturo throwing up on the sand. "Go," Aloysius said as he pulled Arturo to his feet. "And let this be a warning to you and Melinda. We are a family and together we are stronger than any of you could ever be, no matter what your numbers."

Arturo wiped the vomit off his chin and looked at us before turning and running down the beach. As soon as he was out of sight, we turned to Lucas. He had dropped to his knees and held his face in his hands, his shoulders shaking from his sobs. I stood to go to him, but Kalia stopped me. "Fiore, please go to him. He did this to protect you, but no matter how he felt about Mariana right before he killed her, he loved her, and he'll be hurting because of it," She turned to me. "Lily, go take a walk with your husband. The rest of us will stay with Jose Luis. If he awakens while you're gone, we'll let you know."

I nodded and stood, wiping the sand off my knees. I took a deep breath and turned toward Christian. He held a hand out to me. I ignored it and walked past him, motioning for him to follow me. Aaron and Aloysius both looked as we passed them but said nothing.

About a mile down the beach, we reached a small pier. I walked onto it and Christian quietly followed behind me. Taking my shoes off, I set them aside and sat down, dangling my feet over the water. My legs were not long enough to touch the water, but the spray of the waves wet my feet and ankles with its coolness. Christian stood like a statue. I looked up at him, shielding my eyes with my open hand.

"May I?" he asked.

"You do what you want," I answered. I needed to hang on to my anger. I couldn't allow him to hurt me again.

"Lily, please, I never meant to hurt you," he said as he sat next to me, his bare toes just grazing the water below us.

"You could have fooled me," I blurted, the anger boiling to the surface. "You walked out on me, on us. You left without a word."

"I thought I was doing the right thing for you and Jose Luis. I thought you would be out of danger if I did as Melinda asked. I was wrong."

I turned and looked him in the eyes. "You did as Melinda asked? How could you? We took vows. We vowed to love and protect each other, no matter what!"

"That's just it," he said as he looked out onto the water. A pelican sat on a small wave and rode it to the end, taking to the air before finding another and doing it all over again. "She promised to leave you all alone if I left and never came back. She said your pain at losing me would be enough revenge for her. She said she would forget you ever existed. She lied to me."

"Of course, she lied. What else would she do? When did you even talk to her? I don't understand that."

"I did go for a walk that day. I ran into her in the park. That's when she taught me how to let you go, too. She was afraid that if we kept our connection, you would figure out the truth and find me. She said if you found me, it would make our deal null and void," he explained and turned to face me. As soon as his eyes met mine, my stomach did its usual flip.

"Then how did you get out of the country? How did you even get to Oregon?" I didn't understand how he got around so fast without money.

"Part of the deal, as long as I promised to stay away, was financial. I got back all the money Melinda and Maia stole from me, every penny."

I couldn't believe what I was hearing. After all that had happened between us, he was worried about money. "And you thought it was in my best interest to just walk out on me for money?"

"No, Lily. You're misunderstanding my words. I left because she promised they would all leave you alone, including Ryanne. That you and Jose Luis would be able to live a happy life, without their interference. The return of my money was just a plus. It's what enabled me to fly to Oregon and talk to Aaron and Kalia."

"That's another thing. What made you decide it was up to you to talk to them and fix things between us?" I was desperately trying to hang on to my anger, but it was disappearing with every syllable he uttered.

"I know you love them, and they love you. In the time we spent together, I grew to love them too and, like you, I couldn't just sit by and watch them be destroyed by Maia's lies and deceptions. I wanted to fix things so you could be happy again."

That did it. I jumped to my feet and started pacing the small wooden pier. He stood and grabbed my arm. I yanked it away from him. "How could you ever think that I would ever be happy without you? You made that decision for me though it wasn't yours to make. You left when I needed you most and for what? Melinda didn't keep her word. It was never her intention to do so! Why on earth would you believe her?"

"I realize that now, Lily. I know I hurt you but, though you may not believe it, I did it because I thought it would help. You've had nothing but grief ever since you met me." He looked down at me as I stood within inches of him. His breath blew the hair on my forehead. Instinctively, I wanted to reach out and touch him, wrap my arms around him, lose myself in his kiss. I fought the urge with all I had.

"But we needed you here. Jose Luis needed you. I had to do it alone. He asked to see you before he died. It killed me that I couldn't give him that," I explained. I was losing my resolve and I'm sure he knew it. He reached out and placed his fingers on my chin, lifting my face to meet his eyes.

"I am so sorry about what I did. If I didn't think it would help, I wouldn't have done it. I just wanted you to live in peace and you haven't been able to do that since we met."

"It was never about you," I insisted. "It was always Ian. It's still Ian. That's not going to change, regardless of whether or not you're with me. Don't you understand that?"

A single blood tear rolled down his face. I fought my body.

"Again, I'm sorry. I never wanted to hurt you. I love you so much that I would have stayed away forever if I knew it meant your happiness," he wiped the tear away with his free hand. "You did a great job with Jose Luis, by the way."

"But we were supposed to do it together."

"I know and I'm truly sorry. Please let me..." He stumbled over his words and took a deep breath.

"Let you what? Make it up to me? Is that what you think will fix this?" I hung on to my stubbornness while my anger subsided.

"I don't know what will fix this," he said into my hair as he rested his lips on the top of my head. My knees weakened and he wrapped his arms around me before I fell.

"How do we undo what Melinda taught you to do?" I asked in a whisper as his strong arms held me up. I leaned my head back to look at his face.

"Like this," he whispered back as his lips found mine. The only thing keeping me upright now was his grasp on me. I had no fight left as his tongue parted my lips. He kissed me hard and I returned every bit of it as I sighed and pressed my body against his. Warmth radiated from my toes to my head as his fingers tangled in my hair and I lost all sense of where we were and how we had gotten here. I wasn't even sure where his body ended and mine began, or even whose breath was whose, whose fingers touched whose skin, or whose sigh was whose. I lost complete control of my body and soul as they melded together with his, to be one as they were meant to be. All I cared about is that I had my Christian back—in mind, body, and soul.

We parted reluctantly when we heard a shout from further up the beach. Kalia ran toward us waving her arms in the air, kicking sand up as she went.

"He's awake! Jose Luis is awake!" she shouted.

Christian looked at me and smiled, grabbing my hand and pulling me toward the sand. "What are we waiting for? Our son is awake!"

THIRTY-THREE

"Jose Luis, how are you feeling?" I asked as we approached. He blinked against the increasing sunlight and then held his hand to his forehead to shield his eyes.

"I think I feel good. I'm not sure yet. I should get—"

His eyes widened and a smile grew in an instant when he spotted Christian behind Kalia. He got to his feet and dove at him so fast Christian didn't have a chance to react and was knocked to the sand on his back. With their arms around each other, they lay and laughed. The rest of us looked and each other and joined in the laughter. Kalia put her arm around my shoulder and smiled at me, her eyes full of love. I had my family back, everyone together again, but how long would it last this time?

Forget about all of it for now. We are all back together again, well, except... Her look became distant for a moment, and I knew she was thinking of Maia. She shook her head and looked back at me. *We must enjoy this reunion. This new beginning, of sorts.*

I nodded and, wrapping my arm around her back, squeezed her to my side. I had known how much I missed and needed her, but I guess I hadn't realized exactly how much I loved her until now. She beamed when she heard my thought. Aaron walked over to where Jose Luis and Christian were still on the ground and helped Jose Luis up before offering a hand to help Christian. Both of them wiped the sand off their clothes before joining the rest of the anxiously awaiting group.

"I guess I am a little stronger now, huh?" Jose Luis asked with a shrug of his shoulders. We all laughed.

"Let's go home," Aloysius said. He had already folded the blanket and carried it under his arm. At some point, though I had no idea when, he had also taken his shoes off and rolled his pants up. Fiore ran over to take his shoes from him, laughing at his bare feet.

"What? Do not tell me you have never seen a man walking barefoot on the sand?" he teased.

"A man, yes. A prim and proper, ancient vampire, no," she teased back. "This gives me an idea."

"Oh, no," I cut in. "I'm not sure any of us are ready for your ideas."

She smacked me in the back of the shoulder. Jose Luis came to my rescue.

"Hey, lady," he said in as tough a voice as he could manage. "Hands off my mother."

"Well, excuse me," she held her arms in the air in surrender, shoes and all. "No, seriously, just listen to me. We have all been through a lot lately. We need a breather and, since we are all vampires here and no one is affected by the cool weather, even Lucas, I propose we take a short vacation. Kind of like a celebration, a big, happy reunion."

My eyes automatically went to Christian; remembering the last trip we took together. He met my eyes, and I knew he saw what I was picturing—our moment in the hot springs. I looked away.

"But what about my sister?" Jose Luis asked. "We still have to get Leilani back."

"And we will, trust me," Aloysius interceded. "I think, under the circumstances, Fiore has a point. Lily and Christian just reunited, as did Kalia and Aaron with Lily. And you, my boy, will need a little time to adjust to your new state. A few days away might be just what we all need to rejuvenate us and prepare us for whatever it is we'll have to do to get Leilani back."

"But what about Lucia and the children?" I asked. "Tomas is still in the hospital."

"Margarita and I will take care of them," Giovanni offered. It was obvious by his firmness that he agreed with Fiore's idea.

"And I can help," Lucas added. In all the happiness of seeing Christian again, I had forgotten to even check on how Lucas was feeling after losing the woman he loved.

"Nonsense, Lucas," Aloysius said. He stopped at the bottom of the steps that would take us back to the street and turned to face us. "You are now part of this family, and you need this as much, or more so, than the rest of us." Aloysius turned and began climbing the stairs with the rest of us trailing behind.

"I guess the boss has spoken," Lucas whispered under his breath.

"I heard that," Aloysius said without a glance back. We all laughed.

Two police cars and one fire truck still remained outside the building. Upon inspection of the outside, we saw nothing wrong, and since the police were busy writing in their pads and didn't stop us when we approached the front door, we entered without hesitation. We were told to run to our rooms and pack and hurry back downstairs as soon as we were ready. Since Margarita was still out with the children, Giovanni said he would meet up with them and let them know what was happening. He promised to take the children to the zoo as was planned for today and to keep them entertained while we were gone.

"Lily, can you pause for just a minute, please?" Christian asked as I tossed things into my suitcase. I looked up at him and the butterflies started their usual fluttering. How did he manage to cause that after all this time?

"But Aloysius said to—"

He came to me and wrapped his arms around me, interrupting whatever was on my mind. "I know what he said but I need a moment," he stepped back enough to lift my chin with the tip of his fingers. "Do you think you can ever forgive me?"

Looking into his warm blue eyes made my whole world spin out of control. It was like a ride, but no matter how scary it was, I didn't want it to stop, and I certainly didn't want to get off.

"I don't know, Christian," I kept my voice low so no one else could hear. There were way too many mind-reading vampires in one place for my liking. "You really hurt me. I thought I'd never see you again. I thought you changed your mind and finally ran away, like I expected you to when you found out what I am."

"Of course not, Lily. I love you, vampire and all," he whispered, his voice soft and sexy, sending chills through my body. "I never stopped thinking about you or loving you, not even for a minute. Please forgive me."

I shook my head, "I don't know."

"Please tell me what I have to do to make things right between us. I don't ever want to lose you again, no matter what." Fear showed in his eyes, and I knew I had to stop what I was doing to him.

"You really want to make this right again?" He nodded. "Well, let's see… I want lots of romance, you know, flowers, carriage rides, moonlit walks on the beach," his frown changed to a smile and lit up his eyes. "Then I want lots of hand holding, touching, caressing, and of course, lots of kisses and whatever else that might lead up to."

My feet left the floor as he wrapped me in his arms and spun around, kissing me before setting me back on the floor. "I love you so much."

"I love you, Christian. I never stopped and I never will." I leaned in again and, as his lips met mine, a knock at the door interrupted us.

"What is it?" We both yelled at the same time.

"Let's go, you two. Everyone else is waiting downstairs. You can make out later," Fiore yelled from the other side of the door before disappearing down the stairs.

"She has not changed a bit," Christian said. He zipped our suitcases closed and hefted them off the bed. "Shall we?"

"I believe that has been decided for us." I closed our bedroom door and followed him down the stairs.

The limousine waited in front of the building for us and that took us to a nearby marina where we loaded our luggage onto a motorboat and settled in for the ride. Aloysius navigated the boat himself. The ride to the island where we would spend almost a week lasted only an hour and a half. Jose Luis kept busy enjoying all the newness he was experiencing from becoming a vampire. He stood in the back of the boat and held his arms out to his sides. When the boat bounced, he kept his balance and that made him laugh hysterically. Once he became bored with that activity, he checked out his enhanced senses of smell and sight. He marveled at the discovery that he could see further into the ocean than he could when he was human.

"I bet I can swim a lot faster," he stated as he leaned over the side. "I bet I can even swim faster than the boat."

"Is that a challenge?" Aloysius yelled from his place at the wheel.

Jose Luis turned to Christian and me with excitement on his face. "Can I, please, please, please?" He held his hands together and bounced up and down like a five-year-old begging for candy.

"I don't know..." I shook my head and looked up at Christian. His smile widened.

"I don't see any harm in it. Does anyone else?" he asked the rest who were gathered around us. Everyone shook their heads. I nodded and threw my arms up in defeat. I knew I had to let him explore what he can do as a vampire, but it didn't stop me from worrying about him and wanting to protect him.

"You felt the same way about me at first, remember?" Christian whispered into my ear. "He was a pretty strong human. He will be an even stronger vampire, I'm sure. Let him explore his new state."

"Ok," I held my hand out to help Jose Luis onto the side rail. "Make sure you jump as far from the boat as you can. Propellers, remember? I will let you go on the count of three."

His eyes lit up and his lips widened in an ear-to-ear grin. Everyone who was gathered behind us only a moment ago ran to stand at the rail. I looked toward Aloysius and he smiled mischievously, his hand on the throttle and ready. He seemed to be enjoying this as much as Jose Luis and, if he felt sure about it, I had no reason not to. I nodded to the rest, and they nodded back, excitement in their eyes as if they were watching their favorite sporting team take on a rival.

"One...two...three," I yelled and everyone chimed in. I let go of his shirt and backed away, watching as he pushed off with his feet and dove into the air higher than I would have expected. I stopped breathing.

As we all gripped the railing in anticipation, Jose Luis made a small splash as he made contact with the water. He took a breath, his dark hair visible just above the water and then disappeared from view again. The boat sped up, rocking the spectators. Christian wrapped an arm around me and smiled. "Isn't it great to have some fun and not worry about anything else for once?"

"Yeah, for once," I replied as I kept my eyes on the ripples in the water where I thought Jose Luis should be. "Something else is in the water." I pointed.

"What? Where?" Aaron held his hand above his eyes to shield them from the sun.

I searched the water again and saw a dark trail just behind where I expected Jose Luis. "Right there. Don't you see it?"

"Yes, I do. What is it?" Aaron asked as his eyes caught the spot I pointed to.

"I don't know," I said as I kicked off my shoes, hitting Fiore in the leg with one. "I'm going in after him."

"No, Lily, wait," Christian grabbed me around the waist as I tried to climb the railing. "I think he's ok." He stared at the dark spot with squinted eyes.

I held my breath as I squinted and focused on the dark spot that had grown longer behind him. I wasn't even sure which trail was his anymore. Again, I tried to climb the rail but this time both Aaron and Christian held me back. Laughter suddenly erupted from the group, and they started clapping their hands.

"Wow! Will you look at that?" Aloysius yelled as he slowed the boat again.

~ THIRTY-FOUR ~

That is by far the most amazing thing I have ever seen in my life," Fiore exclaimed, her hands to her mouth.

"Unbelievable," Kalia said under her breath.

It wasn't until that moment that I realized I had pressed my face into Christian's chest, shielding my eyes from whatever was happening. "Look, Lily," Christian coaxed me. "You really don't want to miss this."

My jaw dropped as my eyes met with what all the oohing and awing was about. With Jose Luis in the lead, jumping clear out of the water before diving back under, was a pod of four or five dolphins. They were all jumping out of the water and diving back in just as Jose Luis was doing. I couldn't stop the smile that spread across my face. "That is absolutely incredible," I said as I stared at the group showing off in front of us. "They're doing whatever he does."

"I'd say he made some new friends," Fiore said as she reached my side with my shoe in her hand. She bent down and picked up the other one, handing them to me.

"Aloysius, you know he's going to beat us there," I pointed to the land mass coming into view.

"I somehow think he forgot all about racing. He's a little preoccupied right now," he answered with a laugh. "Most people have to pay for an opportunity like this."

After a few more jumps, Jose Luis stopped and started treading water as we slowed the boat to a stop. The dolphins surrounded him and vied for his attention. Looking at us and waving his arm in the air, his smile grew wide as he stroked one dolphin on the head with his free hand. "Look at me," he yelled. Another dolphin pushed the lucky one out of the way and placed its head under Jose Luis's hand. "They're fighting over me."

I laughed and nodded, full of pride. "Yes, they are. They really like you."

"Are you swimming to land or would you like to join us?" Aloysius yelled to him.

"I'll meet you there," he said as he looked toward the land. "I can make it in a few minutes. I'm not even tired."

As the boat lurched forward again, Jose Luis made sure he stroked all the dolphins before diving back under the water and heading toward the island. Christian and I stood hand in hand, smiling with pride and happiness. If anyone deserved this moment of calm and peace, it was Jose Luis.

The chatting group dispersed to gather luggage and belongings as Aloysius tied the boat to the post at the dock and we prepared to step onto the island. From the small dock, a few thatched roof cabanas, raised on stilts, were visible spread out on the beach. "What is this place?" I asked as we followed Aloysius off the dock and onto the sand. Jose Luis climbed the rocks on the side to join us on the beach. Christian was there to meet him and pull him up onto the sand.

"It belongs to a business. They use it for their employees to vacation. I know the owner and, since no one had signed up for this week, I rented it from him," Aloysius explained as he pointed to the cabanas. "There is one for every couple. I hope you don't mind sharing with Jose Luis, Lucas."

"Not at all," Lucas answered. He carried his suitcase and took Jose Luis's from me as he headed toward the cabana he was claiming. Christian and Jose Luis approached as I climbed the wooden steps to one of the available cabanas, next to the one Kalia and Aaron had claimed.

"Wasn't that awesome?" Jose Luis yelled as he ran on the sand.

"It really was. I'm so glad you liked it. We all did," I wrapped an arm around him, not caring that he was getting my shirt wet. "How do you feel?"

"A little thirsty, I think, but it's not too bad," he waved back to Lucas who waited for him on the small front porch. "I'm going to go see our room."

"What is he supposed to eat while we're here?" I asked Aloysius before he entered his cabana with Fiore behind him. "He's a newborn. He can't go without hunting."

"Not to worry," Aloysius looked down at us from his porch. "I thought about that before we left Miraflores. The refrigerator on the boat is stocked with bags of blood just for that reason."

My jaw dropped. "Where in the world did you get it?" I wasn't sure I wanted to hear the answer, but I asked anyway.

"I know someone at the hospital, but don't worry, they have plenty more." He turned and entered his cabana.

"Who doesn't he know?" I muttered as Christian led me to ours.

"For someone who mostly keeps to himself, he does seem to know a lot of people," Christian said as he set our luggage on the floor next to a double bed. Mosquito netting hung around the bed, and I noticed it was because the windows were just open squares with no glass and certainly no screens. There would definitely be no privacy on this trip.

Despite how primitive our accommodations appeared, a ceiling fan with a light hung above the bed. On both sides of the bed sat thin wooden night-stands and at the bottom of the bed was a trunk. A folded flannel blanket sat on the lid.

"I guess there's no harm in leaving our stuff in the suitcases," I said when I lifted the lid to the trunk and its mustiness invaded my nostrils.

"Come on, you two," Kalia yelled from outside. "We're going for a swim."

The rest of the afternoon was spent playing in the water and having a good time. Even the most serious of our group, Aloysius and Aaron, surprised us by sneaking up behind their women, picking them up, and throwing them in the water. Of course, not to be left out, Christian did the same with me, throwing me well over his head. Unfortunately for me, I landed within Lucas's grasp. Lucas grabbed me and threw me back to Christian before my feet even touched the sandy bottom. Jose Luis laughed until he noticed me swimming toward him and tried to turn to get away from me. I jumped out of the water as high as I could, my feet barely skimming the top, and twisted my body to aim in his direction. He screamed just as I grabbed him and threw him over my head.

"That's what you get for laughing!" I yelled as I swam toward the shore. The sun was finally beginning to set, its colors vibrant above the horizon. Shore birds flew in all directions above us. I wrung my hair out even though it was full of sand and walked toward the towels we had spread out on the beach. The rest of the group made their way out of the water and toward their towels, laughing and joking as they went.

"It couldn't get any more perfect than this," Christian said as he ran a smaller towel through my hair. "Our whole family, all together."

"I know," I said as I took the towel from him and set it on the sand next to me. "I just keep waiting for that to change. We can't possibly be this happy for long." I turned to look at him when I noticed Fiore.

"Fiore, what the hell are you doing?" I asked. She sat on her towel with her back to Aloysius as he rubbed lotion onto her back. She was working on her front. "You realize the sun is setting, right? Besides, we don't tan or burn."

"Of course, I know that," she pouted my way. "I just love the smell. Want some?" She held the bottle out to me. I shook my head and rolled my eyes at her.

"While you are all relaxing, I'm going to go gather some firewood," Aloysius stated, wiping his hands on the edge of his towel. "A nice bonfire is just what tonight calls for."

"I'll help you," Christian, Aaron, and Lucas chimed in at the same time. They stood and followed before Aloysius could answer. Jose Luis looked at me expectantly.

"Go on," I motioned. "As soon as your hunger gets uncomfortable, you come and get me. Ok?"

"Sure," he said and ran off to catch up with them. Though he always ran fast, there was a new grace to his gait since he was reborn. It was hard to believe that had only been this morning.

"It has been quite a day," Kalia said as she dragged her towel to my side with Fiore joining her on my other side.

"Yes, it has," Fiore said as she plopped belly down on hers. "It started as a bad day, but it will have a happy ending."

"I hope so," I said.

"Have more faith, Lily," Kalia took my hand in hers. "We're all together and we are all in one piece. What more could we ask for?"

"I know," I turned onto my stomach, my head toward the ocean, and rested my head in my hands. "But we're still missing Leilani. Then there's still the matter of Melinda and Ryanne to deal with and you haven't really resolved anything with Maia."

"One step at a time," Kalia said as she laid the same way on her towel. "We will get Leilani back and, as far as Ryanne and Melinda, there should be no problem. We are much stronger as a family than any of them could ever be."

"Why do you say that?" I asked considering one of our group was a brand new vampire and one was only half.

"Just think about it, Lily," Kalia took my hand and held it in hers. "What exactly are they fighting for? Revenge? Power? Their claim on the city? None of those things matter and, in the end, they have nothing because they don't have love. All they have is anger."

"That's true," Fiore said. "We are fighting to keep those we love safe. They don't love anyone but themselves, if even that. It wouldn't surprise me if they end up turning on each other, especially if they are all after the same thing."

"I hope you're right. It would be funny if they all turned on each other and we could just sit back and watch them kill each other," I laughed at the image in my head of Ryanne and Melinda trying to tear each other's heads off. "Oh, there's something I have been meaning to ask but haven't had a chance yet."

Kalia turned on her side to look at me. I heard the voices of the men as they approached and missed my chance again. Jose Luis led the group, a bundle of wood in his arms. The rest followed, laughing and joking with each other as they carried their piles. From the looks of it, we could enjoy sitting by the fire until the sun came up.

Jose Luis dropped his pile a few feet away from our towels and came running over to us. "I'm hungry," he said and dropped to his knees in front of the three of us. He pulled his top lip up and muttered, "Shee," I couldn't help but laugh at his pronunciation of 'see' while trying to show his protruding fangs.

"Ok, let's go to the boat," I got up with the help of the hand he offered me and wrapped my towel around my waist. "Lucas, are you hungry?"

"I got him," Fiore said and got up from her towel, leading Lucas to her and Aloysius's cabana.

As Jose Luis and I boarded the boat, I thought about another issue that had been lingering in my mind. Why was I warned, multiple times, about Aloysius not being who I thought he was? Did I dare just come out and ask him? No matter how helpful and caring Aloysius was with us, I couldn't help but feel a bit intimidated by him, especially when I thought about his reaction the first time we met; the first time he touched my hand. He had frozen in place when his skin made contact with mine and stared into my eyes almost with fear. Why?

⤜ THIRTY-FIVE ⤝

Once we finished with Jose Luis's first feeding, who enjoyed a whole bag of blood by himself, we changed out of our suits and gathered on the beach. Christian and Aloysius had a fire roaring, and Aaron had gotten the beach chairs from the boat and set them up around the fire. The sun was almost completely down, and some orange hues still remained over the water. We settled in our seats, staying silent for a few moments while we looked around in awe at the beauty of the island. The view was gorgeous and, looking around at my loved ones, I couldn't help but feel like maybe there was hope for happiness. For the longest time, I didn't believe in happily ever after. When I finally thought I did, it was ripped from my hands. Now, with all of us here together again, and with our new additions, I was starting to feel like maybe it was possible after all.

"Won't we need jackets or something for when it gets really dark?" Jose Luis broke the silence. Fiore laughed from across the circle.

"What's so funny?" I asked, already feeling defensive toward my new son.

"Nothing at all," she answered leaning to the side so she could see me around the fire. "It's just been a long time since I've been around a new vampire, besides Christian, of course, especially one so young. Christian knew more or less what to expect. Jose Luis knows only what he's seen."

"You're right, of course. I apologize," I said to her and then turned to Jose Luis. "You won't notice the temperature difference. You won't ever feel cold, and you won't ever sweat when it's hot."

He thought about it for a moment. "Then why do you wear jackets when you go outside in Lima? I am thinking you probably wear shorts in the summer too, right?"

"We do. We dress according to what we know the season to be. If we wear shorts in the winter, when everyone else is wearing jackets and scarves, we stick out," I explained.

"Stick out?" he asked, confusion at the idiom obvious on his face.

"She means that we try to dress like everyone else. We try our best not to draw attention to ourselves if we can avoid it," Christian explained. "The last thing we want is for people to start noticing our differences. We want everyone to think we are human, just like them."

"Whatever powers or gifts we have, we keep them from the human world. It is best if none of them think we actually exist," Aloysius added.

"How do you hide that? Some people already know vampires are real," Jose Luis added, looking around the group.

"Just a few do, but most people are not really sure. They have no actual evidence. They believe what they read or what they see in movies. They believe all the myths associated with us, not the reality," Aaron explained.

"Do you mean people think we cannot be around garlic or crosses? Like we cannot go into a church?" Jose Luis asked.

"Yes, among other things," Aloysius sat back in his seat, stretching his long legs out on the sand. "Some believe we are night creatures and they are safe from us during the day. Some even believe we cannot enter a building without first being invited."

"That is just funny," Jose Luis laughed. "If we had to wait to be invited, we could never even go into a store."

The whole group laughed at his comment. I looked around the circle and noticed how relaxed everyone had gotten. Kalia sat on the sand in front of Aaron, leaning back against his chair between his legs, his arms securely around her, his chin resting on the top of her head. Fiore sat close to Aloysius, his hand wrapped around hers on his lap. Lucas was the only one who sat a little apart from the group. I hoped in time he would forgive himself for what he had done to Mariana and found the love he so deserved. Regardless, he was now part of our family, and I knew it would only be a matter of time until he truly became one of us.

Jose Luis interrupted my thoughts as his curiosity, and the group's willingness to share with him, grew. "How did you all meet?" he asked.

"I met Lily at school," Christian volunteered. "She was a student in my archaeology class. I was human then."

Jose Luis's eyes widened with surprise. "You were her teacher? Is that allowed?"

No one could stop the laughter that escaped their mouths. I huffed and they laughed even harder.

"She was an adult," Christian defended himself. "I thought she was actually older than nineteen because of how mature she is. Of course, in real life, she is ninety, so she was totally legal, if you like old women." I smacked his arm playfully.

Jose Luis thought about it for a moment and nodded, turning to Fiore next. "And how did you meet Lily? You are Italian, right?"

"Yes, I am, but I was living in Ireland at the time," Fiore started, turning to face Jose Luis. "See, Ian, Lily's maker, brought her to Ireland. I met her there." I noticed Aloysius sat up straight.

"When were you in Ireland?" Jose Luis turned to me.

"Not too long before we came here. Ian left me a long time ago and then he decided he wanted me back after I met Christian. He kidnapped me and took me there, telling me he would leave Christian alone if I went with him. Of course, he lied because he had Christian too, only I didn't know it at the time."

"To make a long story short," Fiore interrupted noticing my distress at retelling the story. "Lily found Christian and escaped with him, took him back to America. They were hiding in a cabin in the mountains of Oregon when I found them. Lily and I became friends in Ireland and I wanted to help her." She shook her head and her eyes glowed with the memory. "Anyway, I got to the cabin and Lily dove across the room and jumped on me. She fought me thinking I was there to take her back to Ian. You had to have been there. It was pretty funny. She looked like a crazy woman with her hair flying all over the place."

"You really did that?" he asked me.

"Yes, I did." I turned to Fiore. "She should not have snuck up on me like that. It's her fault I attacked her."

"Yeah," Fiore said with a sigh. "But it ended well anyway."

"Can I ask another question?" Jose Luis asked, eager to learn all he could about his new family. We all nodded.

"Who here has made other vampires, besides you, Lily?" He turned to Aaron. "Did you make your wife?"

"No, she was already a vampire when I met her. But she made Maia, our daughter," Aaron explained.

Jose Luis, satisfied with that answer, turned to Fiore. "What about you? Did you ever make one?" Aloysius stiffened in his seat, his back straight as a board.

"A long time ago," Fiore answered. This was a story I'd never heard. "It was maybe a couple years after I was made. My maker also left me, and I hated being alone. I met a man, a very wealthy man, and fell in love. He was injured while hunting and was not going to make it, so I turned him. I never asked him if it was what he wanted."

"So, what happened? Where is he?" I asked, now as curious as Jose Luis.

"He stayed with me for a while, about ten years or so, but he was miserable. He had lost his wife and daughter about a year before I met him. It turned out he didn't want to live forever. He wanted to be with them, so he killed himself." She bowed her head to hide the tears starting in her eyes.

"He killed himself? How?" Jose Luis asked. "Is that even possible?"

Fiore wiped her eyes with a tissue she pulled from her pocket and smiled at Aloysius, apologizing for her reaction. Aloysius assured her by squeezing her hand. "He went on a killing spree in the small town where we lived. When he was discovered, he shouted that he was a vampire, right in the middle of the town square, and that he was not done killing. He vowed to kill everyone in town before moving on to the next. The authorities took him and tied him to a pole. His choice was obvious to me when he didn't fight them. As they lit the fire at his feet, he looked at me and mouthed that he was sorry. As he burned, I could see his lips moving as if he were praying. He got what he wanted."

"That is really sad," Jose Luis whispered. "But you have him now and he loves you." He motioned at Aloysius with his head.

"That is true," Aloysius answered. Fiore looked at him with shock in her eyes. He had never said it before. "The boy is right. I do love you."

Fiore jumped out of her seat, her smile widening as she forgot all about the tale she recounted of her Italian love. She wrapped her arms around his neck and kissed him, the rest of us trying to look away but unable to ignore the tender moment. "It's about time," she said and kissed him again. "I love you too," she said before going back to her seat, wiping sand off her knees.

She looked at the rest of us as we sat with wide smiles on our faces. "Carry on," she said.

"Uhh, so, yeah…" Christian said. The rest of us laughed.

"I made Aaron, my great-grandson," Aloysius volunteered. "He was deathly ill. We were very close, and I did not want to live without him."

"That is so cool!" Jose Luis said. "Is he the only one you made?"

Aloysius dropped Fiore's hand and folded his hands on his lap. He grasped them tightly as he looked around the circle, from one face to the next before settling his eyes on mine. I stiffened in my seat and a chill ran down my back. Could this be it? Could this be what I had been warned about? Christian reached for my hand, but I pulled it away, unable to even look at him. The sound of the waves against the shore grew louder, almost deafening as everyone grew totally quiet. I sucked in a breath and held it.

"No, my dear boy, Aaron was not my only one," Aloysius said, still holding my eyes with his as he rose from his seat and went to stand behind it. He took a deep breath before he said, "I made one other."

THIRTY-SIX

"O h, God, no," I whispered. Christian reached for my hand again, but I denied him. I didn't want to be touched. I didn't want to be calmed.

Aloysius's eyes softened as he looked into my eyes. "I made Ian."

I jumped to my feet and clenched my hands at my sides. Though we had just explained to Jose Luis that we do not feel temperature changes, I suddenly felt cold, freezing, to the point that my teeth started chattering. No one said a word, no one moved, except for their heads looking between Aloysius and me, back and forth in the deafening silence.

"Lily, say something, please," Aloysius said, keeping his voice low and even.

I looked out onto the water, forcing my eyes from Aloysius's. "I... I can't," I whispered as I turned and walked away from my seat in the direction of the water.

I heard motion behind me but didn't know what it was until I heard Aloysius's voice. "No, Christian. Please, let me. This is my doing."

Though I walked as fast as I could without running, Aloysius easily caught up to me. "Lily, please stop. Let me explain," he said just behind me. I paid no attention to him and kept walking, kicking up sand with every step. His hand grasped my elbow. I pulled my arm away from him and spun to face him.

"Don't you dare touch me," I yelled. "You have no right. No right at all."

"Please let me explain," he pleaded.

I turned around and started walking again, though I had no idea where I was going. I could no longer hear the rest of our group and knew I had walked quite a distance.

"Lily, please stop. I can explain," he said again as he followed close behind me. I had never heard him plead for anything and the sound of it made me smile. He pushed ahead of me and turned just as I slammed into him. I jumped away before he could touch me.

"How could you?" I screamed at him not caring if anyone else heard. "How could you keep it from me?"

"I thought it was best," Aloysius said as he tried to make eye contact with me. I avoided it.

"What makes you, or anyone else for that matter, an authority on what is best for me?" I asked with a tone that sounded as icy as my body felt. "I wish people would stop doing that!"

"You are right," he said and sat down on the sand, patting the spot next to him in invitation. I remained on my feet. "I should not have kept it from you. I should have told you as soon as I realized it."

"And when was that?" I asked when suddenly, the memory of our first meeting came rushing to my mind. "When you shook my hand, at Aaron's... you saw everything, didn't you?"

"Yes, I did, and I am truly sorry. I should have told you," he said with sincerity in his voice.

I finally dropped to the sand beside him, circling my arms around my bent knees. "Why didn't you?"

"Because it was done and I didn't want you to resent me," he tried to reach for my hand, but I moved further to the side. He looked hurt. "I am sorry, Lily, I truly am. I realize I should not have kept it from you all this time because now you probably resent me more than you would have if I had told you sooner. Am I correct?"

Besides the anger still turning my stomach, I had no idea what else I felt. "I don't know that I can resent you. You have stuck by me, regardless of your own flesh and blood's feelings," I said referring to Aaron. "You have been there to help since day one. I just don't understand why?"

"Why I kept it from you?" he said. "I thought you would walk away from me, and Aaron and Kalia, if you knew. I didn't want that to happen. They love you. Maybe I also thought you would think I hated you or resented you for killing my offspring. I didn't want that to happen either."

"I had no choice but to kill Ian and you know that. He was destroying everyone I loved to get to me."

"I know, Lily. I know you did what you had to do to protect the ones you love. I would have done the same, had I been in your shoes," he explained.

"How did you even meet Ian and why did you turn him? That's what I really don't understand," I admitted. My anger for him was diminishing though I wanted to hang onto it.

Aloysius took a deep breath and stayed quiet for a moment, searching deep into his past. "I had been alone for many years, roaming the world as I always did. I met Ian on a ship bound from the United States, where he had been placed in yet another temporary home, to Ireland. He said he was going home, home to a place where no one knew him or loved him, but home, nonetheless. He talked to me whenever he saw me, sometimes following me around the ship, vying for my attention. After a while, I stopped trying to hide from him. I allowed him to talk, allowed him to confide in me. He told me about the death of his parents, his childhood in the orphanage in London where he was used and abused. I began feeling sorry for him, pitying him for all he'd had to endure at such a young age. It wasn't until we were close to reaching port that I realized I had grown to love the boy as if he were my own."

"So that's why you did it? Because he suckered you into giving him what he wanted?" I asked.

Instead of getting angry or defending himself, he laughed. "Yes, he certainly did sucker me. What can I say? I guess I have a soft heart after all."

"But why him? What happened? You obviously hadn't been a part of his life for very long."

"After roaming the world alone for so long, I wanted a companion," he started but I interrupted.

"But you had Aaron. Aaron is your family, literally."

"Yes, that is true, but Aaron had made his own life with Kalia. Aaron didn't need me any longer, but Ian did."

"Do Aaron and Kalia know? About Ian, I mean."

"I only confessed to them recently, because of Maia," he admitted.

I nodded. "So, what happened with Ian?"

"As I said, I wanted a companion, someone to spend my endless days with, but I realized soon after his transformation that I made a mistake. Ian was wild as a human, a savage as a newborn, and completely untamable as a vampire."

I couldn't help but laugh at his description of the vampire I had known and loved. If I had realized how he was when I was still human, my life would have been much different. "So, what ended it between you?"

"Believe me, I tried to tame him. I tried to teach him how to behave in society, how to respect humans, but he would have none of it. He did try, for a little while, for my sake. He started killing only those who deserved punishment, but his attempt didn't last long. It wasn't long before he killed for the sake of killing with total disregard for anyone he hurt in the process. His ways became the source of constant arguments and tension between us. It wore on both of us and, after only a few years, we parted ways."

"Just like that?" I asked, surprised that Ian would do anything so simply.

Aloysius nodded and stood, brushing the sand off the back of his jeans. He held a hand out to help me up. I took it without hesitation. How could I hold anything against him when Ian had done much the same with me?

"Just like that. He left and I never saw or heard from him again, until I met you that is." He stood in front of me and, placing his fingers on the bottom of my chin, raised my head up to him. "Can you forgive me for not telling you?"

I smiled. "Of course, I can. No one knows better than I do how manipulative Ian could be when he wanted his way. I fell for everything he told me, all the lies, all the stories. It wouldn't exactly be fair of me to hold a grudge, now would it?"

"It amazes me how much you have grown and matured since I first met you." He wrapped his arms around me and squeezed me to him, kissing the top of my head.

"Thank you," I said as I hugged him back. "For telling me the truth and for sticking by me."

"Tell me something, Lily," he pushed back enough to look at my face. "Did you somehow know already, about Ian?"

"I had a feeling something didn't add up. Melinda and Mariana both warned me about you not being who I thought you were. I knew something was up, I just didn't know what." We started walking back toward our family who no doubt was speculating as to what might have happened between Aloysius and me.

"I can just imagine what they are thinking," Aloysius laughed, catching my thought. "With your temper, they probably think I'm lying on the beach somewhere."

"Am I really that bad?" I teased.

"Let me put it this way, *I'm* surprised I'm not lying on the beach somewhere, birds pecking at my eyes." He laughed as we approached the rest, led by the flickering fire in the darkness.

Jose Luis ran toward us before we reached them. "I am so sorry. I didn't mean to—"

I threw my arm around his shoulders. "It's ok. We are fine," I assured him.

"Aloysius, it's good to see you back in one piece," Aaron said as we reached our seats. Everyone nodded.

"So, everyone is afraid of the smallest vampire here?" I huffed as I slumped into my seat.

"Let me put it this way, Lily," Fiore said. "If you were the enemy we were fighting instead of Melinda, I would have been on the next plane to anywhere already."

"That is so funny," I mocked. "You heard me laugh, right? Or did I only laugh in my head?"

"I love you more than life itself but…" Christian took my hand in his but kept his body distant. "You are pretty damn scary when you're pissed off. No doubt about it." Everyone laughed at his comment, including Jose Luis.

I threw my arms up in defeat. "Fine. Go ahead and gang up on me. Just wait." I stood and started toward our cabana. "Christian, are you coming?"

He jumped up in an exaggerated manner. "Yes, of course, whatever you say." Loud laughter followed us all the way into the dark cabana.

The next few days were spent in much the same way as the first. We sat on the beach and watched the sun rise, combed the shore for seashells, and even went fishing with some rods we found on the boat. In the afternoons, we hiked around the island, collecting bananas and mangos to take home for Lucia and the children. In the late afternoons, we swam and relaxed on the beach. It was obvious the trip Aloysius planned was exactly what we all needed. Everyone was in good spirits, teasing each other and laughing. Jose Luis was adapting well to his new life and was trying to figure out what he was capable of doing as a vampire. One afternoon, he wore us all out when he insisted he could run faster than any of us and challenged us to race after race until finally, after about the sixth race, he beat us all. I found out I could become airborne with a good running start and a jump, but he accused me of cheating and challenged me to a rematch.

Soon after we arrived back at the apartment building, Christian suggested we go shopping for some gifts for Lucia and the children. Since we had been on a private island, we did not have the opportunity to shop and thought we should get them something to ease the children's pain a bit while their father was still in the hospital.

"Can I stay here? I want to see Paco?" Jose Luis asked.

"I'm not sure that's a good idea, considering…" I started but Giovanni stepped in.

"You can leave him with me. He will do fine around the children. He looks like he fed recently so that shouldn't be a problem. Besides, I will be with them every moment. Paco hasn't stopped asking for him."

"Ok, just make sure you make an excuse and leave if you start feeling uncomfortable," I told Jose Luis. I knew how close he and Paco had gotten and knew the little boy would come down to see him if Jose Luis didn't go up to their apartment. It was unavoidable either way.

Christian and I walked toward the park where the vendors set up their stands in search for something to get Lucia. I had a necklace in mind, maybe something with shells, and found a stand with just that as soon as we stepped up onto the round platform.

"What do you think of this one?" I asked Christian, holding up a sand dollar on a red beaded cord.

"That is beautiful. I think she—" his eyes left me and I followed them to a group standing by a bench.

"What is it?" I asked recognizing none of the people standing there passing a soda between them.

"Isn't that...?" Christian pointed to a woman holding a little girl by the hand. My breath caught in my throat.

"Leilani," I managed to choke out. My eyes remained glued on her as I thought of what to do. I didn't recognize the woman she was with but sensed she was human. Leilani looked around at the people nearby. A little girl walking by with a bag of cotton candy in one hand and a balloon in the other caught her attention and she followed her with her eyes.

What do we do? Christian asked me.

I don't know. But we are not leaving without her, one way or another, she's coming with us tonight.

THIRTY-SEVEN

I grabbed Christian's hand and moved us closer into the crowd. As soon as we had hidden ourselves by chatting shoppers, I felt a tug on my arm. I turned to look, expecting one of Melinda's people, my defenses fully awakening, when a short, white-haired man squeezed my arm tighter.

"*Ladrona!*" he yelled loud enough to catch the attention of the people closest to us. "*Ladrona!*" he repeated as my jaw dropped.

"Oh, my God," I said raising my other hand. I still held the necklace in my fist.

Christian dropped my hand and pulled the man's hand off my arm. He raised a hand, his eyes scrunching as he made a fist and prepared to strike the man.

"No, Christian," I yelled to him, grabbing his moving fist before it could make contact with the terrified man's face. "He thinks I'm trying to steal this necklace." Christian looked from me to my hand wrapped around his clenched fist. He reached into his pocket and pulled out a bill, handing it to the man. I felt his hand relax so I dropped it.

I apologized to the man, telling him I had forgotten the necklace was in my hand. He looked down at the bill Christian placed in his hand and smiled. He nodded before placing the bill in his pocket, turning, and going back to his stand. With not another word said, the spectators turned, and went back to their shopping as if nothing had happened.

"Apparently, we're both thieves," Christian whispered in my ear. "I steal pants and you steal necklaces. We make a great team."

I couldn't help but laugh at his comment thinking back to when he walked out of Macy's with pants he was trying on. At the time, stopping him from hunting in the mall had been more important than going back and paying for the pants, even if they were too short for him.

"Can you see them from here?" I asked. My height, or lack of, was not helping me at the moment.

Christian stretched his neck a bit to look over the heads of the people in the circle. "Yes. They are all still there. Leilani is trying to get the woman's attention, but the woman is too involved in her conversation."

"Do you see anyone familiar?" I asked.

"No," he said and turned to look at their surroundings. "It doesn't make sense though. Why would Leilani be out with no real protection? Someone has to be concealed somewhere, watching over her."

"I agree, but we have to take a chance," I whispered to him as I pulled him toward the edge of the crowd, closer to where the group stood. "We can't risk losing her now that she's so close. I just don't know how to go about it. The woman has a pretty tight grasp on her hand."

"I have an idea," Christian said as he turned to look to our left. I followed his eyes. A brief part in the crowd let me see a cotton candy stand. He stared at the swirling cotton candy with concentration. At that moment, I knew what he was doing and I needed to help. I pushed the person in front of me aside. Though she gave me a frustrated look, she said nothing and continued to move toward another craft stand. Focusing my mind on the people standing behind the cotton candy stand and behind the vendor, I willed one of them to pay attention to me. As the middle-aged woman asked the vendor for directions, the vendor turned to give them to her and pointed to the route she should take. The woman looked confused. He tried again. While he was busy with that, cotton candy floated in the air in a messy bundle, pieces falling off and floating in the breeze.

As soon as the candy was away from the stand, I looked to my left. Spotting two people walking on the sidewalk with their dogs on leashes, I concentrated on the larger of the two dogs. Within moments, the larger dog raised his hackles and tried lunging toward the smaller dog, barking and baring his teeth. The owners, shocked looks on their faces, struggled to keep their dogs from reaching each other. Now both dogs were barking, and the commotion drew the attention of the shoppers. The group where Leilani stood was too far from the growling dogs to be distracted by it, but Christian's impromptu plan worked. Leilani watched the cotton candy floating in the air with a wide smile on her face.

She tried again to get the woman's attention but failed. The young woman was very obviously trying to impress the man she was talking to, flashing her smile and tossing her hair over her shoulder. As she kept her eyes on the young man, Leilani had had enough. She yanked her hand out of the woman's grasp and ran off to follow the candy she so badly wanted. The woman turned for a moment, but the man reached for her arm, turning her attention back to him. She hesitated, shrugged her shoulders, and returned to her flirting.

"Now, Lily," Christian said without looking at me. He still focused on the floating treat Leilani followed down the sidewalk. Though everyone who saw pointed and crossed the street with fear, no one bothered to chase after it.

I ripped my hand out of Christian's and ran to Leilani. Turning my attention away from the dogs caused the larger dog to forget about his newfound enemy. The growling stopped, replaced by clapping, and tails wagged. The people who stood watching the impending dog fight cheered. At least their attention was still focused there. Leilani jumped to reach the cotton candy just as my arm circled around her little waist. She let out a scream, catching the woman's attention.

"Arturo!" she screamed. "Arturo! They have Leilani!"

I tightened my grip around Leilani's waist as I continued running with her, not bothering to look back. I was sure I could outrun a human. Through Leilani's screams, I did not hear Arturo pursuing us. Remembering his power, I realized his pursuit wasn't good. "Oh, crap!" I said as the wind picked up and pushed our bodies forward. He was starting a storm as an attempt to stop me.

Aloysius, can you hear me? We need help... I listened as I pushed my legs harder, but no response came. I tried Christian, hoping he would call Aloysius and get him to take us away. No response came from him either. The wind continued to pick up and we heard screams all around us as people ran for cover. Something hit the back of my leg as I ran with Leilani in my arms. Whatever it was, it was light enough to just bounce off me. The wind continued to push at my back as I ran toward the cliffs.

"Oh no!" Leilani screamed as a deafening sound echoed in my ears. Afraid to look back, I listened closer to the sound following us. It scraped the sidewalk and left it before hitting hard and continuing to come our way. "It's going to hit us!" Leilani screamed as she looked over my shoulder. I pushed my legs even harder as the sound got closer.

"What is it?" I yelled over the roar to Leilani. She was calming down now that she realized who I was.

"A big garbage can! It's coming, jump!"

I pushed off my legs. Shocked, I looked down at the ground I expected to have hit by now. My body was about ten feet from the sidewalk, my legs still running. I stopped my legs and started falling, screaming along with Leilani. I pumped my legs again and went back up, the wind pushing us along. I tightened my grip around Leilani as my legs pumped, our distance from the ground increasing.

"We are flying!" Leilani screamed as she tucked her face in my chest. The wind Arturo created worked against him instead of for him. It pushed me along as we climbed higher and higher until it no longer felt like it was controlling me but rather just a breeze blowing Leilani's loose hair in my face. I took a deep breath and turned my body to the left, aiming toward the outermost part of the park and toward the apartment building. As soon as I was comfortable with our direction, I leveled out my body, keeping Leilani tightly against me. Afraid that we had an audience, I looked down, dizziness taking me as soon as my eyes hit the ground. I shook my head to try to refocus. When I looked down again, I saw that the park had mostly cleared out. The few people still left were holding onto each other and fighting to walk against the wind Arturo created. Though the coast was usually windy, it was never this forceful. People screamed as a tree was lifted from the ground.

From where we were, I could no longer see where I'd left Christian. As much as I wanted to go back and land, to find him and make sure he was ok, I knew my first priority was Leilani. Christian was strong enough to take care of himself. He'd proven that more than once and I had to trust him. Arturo was his only challenge, and he was still busy with his windstorm, the storm that helped me instead of hindering me. Melinda would be furious to hear that.

Leilani and I landed on the roof of the apartment building with enough force to take me down with her in my arms. After regaining our composure, Leilani pushed the hair out of her face and turned her wide brown eyes toward me. Her little mouth hung open. We both started laughing as we sat and stared at each other. I brushed the rest of her hair away from her face and wrapped my arms around her, giving her a squeeze.

"I'm Lily," I said as I took her hand to help her up.

"I know. I remember you," she answered, wiping the dirt from her clothes.

"Who's here?" A man's voice yelled. We both stiffened and looked around. I put my index finger in front of my lips. "Answer me or I will shoot!"

"Aloysius, it's Lily," I shouted back. Leilani looked up at me as I led her toward Aloysius. "It's ok, Leilani. He's with me. He just can't see us yet."

"Lily, what in the world are you doing…?" He came to a dead stop in front of us and his jaw dropped. I smiled up at him, reassuring him I was ok. "Is this Leilani?" he finally asked.

"Yes. Leilani, this is Aloysius, my grandfather. Aloysius meet Leilani," I smiled as they looked each other over.

"What in the world are you both doing up here?" he asked as he turned to walk toward the stairs.

"This is where we landed. Why are you up here?" I asked as Leilani and I followed still holding hands.

"I heard you call to me and then we heard a commotion up here," he turned back to look at us. "That must have been some landing."

Leilani and I both laughed as we followed him into the building and toward the elevator. Once inside, I stepped to the back with Leilani in front of me, my arms circled around her shoulders as she leaned against me. *Did Christian get here? Have you heard from him?*

He just came in a minute before you landed. He was in the middle of explaining what happened when we heard the noise and I came up to check. Aloysius explained. No need to worry Leilani.

Where is Jose Luis? I asked.

He's still up in Lucia's apartment entertaining the children while she gets a shower. She just came back from the hospital. He will be coming back soon since it's getting late. The children will be going to bed. The chime went off and the elevator doors opened.

We need to prepare Leilani before he gets here. Before Aloysius could answer me, the apartment door flew open and Christian rushed out.

"Thank God you are both ok," he said as he took me in his arms, Leilani still holding on to my hand. He stepped away to look us over. "You took off flying from the ground."

"Yes, I guess I did. Arturo's wind was very helpful," I explained. "Had he started the storm in the other direction, this may have had a bad ending."

He nodded and smiled down at Leilani. He dropped to one knee to take her hand just as the elevator chimed. The doors opened again. There was no time to react as Jose Luis reached us and grabbed Leilani away from me, picking her up off the floor and spinning with her in a tight hug.

What should have been a happy reunion, turned into a nightmare as Leilani's eyes widened and she began screaming at the top of her lungs. Jose Luis placed her gently back on the floor and she backed away, still screaming. Christian dove through the air, knocking Jose Luis to the ground as something orange landed in the spot where Jose Luis had been standing just a second ago. Aloysius and I stared in shock as the small table with the flower vase that sat in the hallway was engulfed by flames.

THIRTY-EIGHT

Get her into the apartment," Aloysius ordered. It took me a moment to realize he was talking to me, as we were closer to the apartment than Christian and Jose Luis. I grabbed Leilani around the waist, picking her up off the floor and carrying her through the open door. I slammed it shut with my foot before running toward the kitchen with her in my arms. Getting her a glass of water and calming her down was my first priority, however, I didn't get that far.

"Leilani, what is wrong with you?" Jose Luis asked his sister in Spanish. Christian and Aloysius ran in right behind him, obviously having been unable to stop him from coming after us.

Leilani jumped off the counter where I had put her and hid behind my legs. "Stay away from me!"

"Leilani, it's me. Jose Luis, your *Cachi*," Jose Luis explained with a gentle voice, pain obvious in his eyes though he tried to hide it for his sister's sake.

"Lily!" Christian yelled as Leilani tried to run out from behind me. I grabbed her just as she launched herself toward her brother.

"NO! NO! NO!" she screamed as she kicked her legs. I fought to keep her in my arms while trying not to squeeze too tightly. When I didn't drop her, she began flailing her arms. I dodged her little fists but just barely. "You are not my brother!"

"Leilani, please calm down. You're hurting Lily," Christian said in as soothing of a voice as he could muster. He raised his eyebrows at me. I shook my head. I had a hold of her, and I would be able to maintain it. She would most likely panic worse if Christian took her from me.

"Not my brother!" She kicked, this time making contact with my shin. I sucked in a breath as pain radiated up my leg. For such a small girl, she had a powerful kick. "Not my brother! Not my brother!"

Jose Luis took a few steps closer. "May I?" he asked. I nodded holding Leilani a bit tighter. "Leilani, please listen to me."

"No! You are not my brother. I want my brother, not you!" Leilani screamed. Her kicking slowed down just a bit as did her breathing. Hopeful that she may be getting tired, I took a step closer to Jose Luis and nodded for him to continue.

"Leilani, do you remember when we used to sit in the garden and make kites? I used to let you make the tails and put them on yourself," he paused to wait for a reaction. Leilani continued kicking. Christian and Aloysius stepped up to either side of Jose Luis, preparing for another fireball. "*Mamá* used to let us get the eggs from the chickens and the chickens always tried to peck at you. It used to scare you, so you made me get the eggs while you wiped them off with your shirt and put them in the basket." He paused again, waiting for some kind of recognition from his terrified sister.

Leilani kicked again but without as much enthusiasm. Either she was exhausted or Jose Luis was reaching her.

"Remember when we were supposed to be sleeping but we snuck out and climbed the ladder up to the roof, when *mamá* and *papá* went to sleep? We would watch the sky, sometimes all night, looking for UFO's. And then one night, we finally saw one?"

"It was blue and green, just like my favorite shoes," Leilani said so softly that it hardly sounded like she spoke at all. She wiped the hair off her face and stared at her brother. His smile grew and his eyes lit up. He dropped to his knees and held out his arms.

I looked at Christian and Aloysius. They nodded but stayed on guard by Jose Luis. I took a deep breath and lowered Leilani until her feet touched the floor. She ran to Jose Luis taking me with her. It wasn't until then that I noticed I still grasped the back of her shirt in my fist. Christian smiled at me. I let go of her and let her brother embrace her.

"Oh, Leilani," Jose Luis cried into his sister's hair. "I can't believe you are finally here."

Leilani buried her face in the crook between his shoulder and neck and cried, wrapping her tan arms around her brother's neck. He held her just as tightly as she held him and closed his eyes, trying to fight back his own tears. Seeing blood all over his face would scare his sister more and he wanted to be strong for her. After a few moments, Aloysius and Christian relaxed, taking steps away from the embracing siblings. Christian came to my side and wrapped an arm around my waist. All three of us kept our eyes on the emotional reunion. The living room door opened with a bang against the wall and the three of us tensed again.

"What's happening? What was all the screaming?" Giovanni asked as he walked into the kitchen, Lucas on his heels.

"We got Leilani back," I answered him, smiling toward the two who loosened their grip and stared into each other's eyes. Jose Luis wiped Leilani's tears away with the bottom of his tee-shirt.

"What happened to you?" Leilani asked and sniffled. I grabbed a napkin from the counter and handed it to her. She wiped her nose and thanked me with a smile.

Jose Luis looked at Christian before answering. "Tell her the truth," Christian told him. "She will understand."

"Come on," Jose Luis took his sister's hand. "Let's go sit in the living room. I will tell you everything."

While Jose Luis led Leilani to the living room, the rest of us stayed behind, allowing them some time alone. Though Jose Luis was only fifteen years old, we all felt he was mature enough to handle talking to her and convincing her to accept his choice.

"The police called while you were gone," Giovanni said as he took a seat at the counter.

"What did they want?" I asked.

"They wanted to know if we knew anything else about Jose Luis or if we heard from him. I told him we thought he was back with the people he was living with before he came to us. I didn't know what else to say."

"That should do for now. If they still want to talk to him, they will have to look there. It's best they don't know he is here with us. They may want to come here and question him and that would create more problems. They don't need to see him this way. He looks too healthy," Lucas explained. "As long as they know he's safe and sound, they should stop searching for him."

"We will need to leave Peru soon. We can't risk anyone noticing the changes in Jose Luis. He's a regular in this area and knows too many people," I said. I turned to Lucas who was pouring himself a glass of juice. "What about you? What are your plans?"

He set the glass on the counter and looked at Fiore who had entered so quietly I hadn't noticed her leaning against the wall. "Fiore is going to finish the process tonight. I want to make sure I am strong enough to fight if it turns to that."

"Trust me, you are already strong. I'm turning you because it's what you want," Fiore explained and turned to me. "Jose Luis and Leilani are sitting on the sofa talking. I overheard a little when I walked in. She's asking what is going to happen to her."

"What happens to her will be totally her choice," I answered. Surprised eyes turned my way. I held up my hand. "No, wait. I said it will be her choice, but not until she is at least eighteen. I will not turn a child unless absolutely necessary." That was a decision I hoped Aaron could respect.

"So, what do we do now that we have Leilani?" Fiore asked.

"Yeah, I want to know. Do we leave with them and go back to the States, or do we wait and see what happens?" Lucas asked.

Aloysius stepped into the middle of the group. "I think our outcome will be the same either way. If we leave, they will come after us. If we stay, they will come after us even sooner. They want your children, and they will do whatever is necessary to get them. Besides, I don't think they are done with their revenge against you, Lily."

"So, what are you saying? That we stay and wait for them to attack? We can't let them attack us here. Too many innocent people would get hurt." I said. Either option suggested the same ending, death and losses for both sides.

"What if we go somewhere completely new, somewhere we've never been before, minimizing their chances of finding us?" Christian asked.

"Is that how you want to spend the rest of your existence, running and hiding? The children need more than that. They need somewhat normal lives, an education, friends, and whatever you can offer. Leilani will need it more than anyone since she's going to remain human." Aloysius folded his arms across his chest.

"You're right, but that means we fight them all while still trying to protect the humans," I said. The thought of fighting while three innocent human children were in our care infuriated me.

"We won't have much of a choice. They will not stop until they get what they want. It will not matter how far away we go. They will find us. I am very sure of that," Aloysius asserted, pausing to look at Giovanni. "Maybe we can send the humans away for a bit, keep them out of the way."

"That is a good idea, but they will still need protection. Some of us will have to go with them and that leaves lower numbers for those who stay to fight," Giovanni explained.

"That is not necessarily true," Aaron said as he and Kalia walked into the kitchen.

I shook my head in disbelief. "No, Aaron. I can't let your friends fight for us again. This doesn't even concern them."

"Lily, honey," Kalia said walking toward me. "Do you honestly think that matters to them? They are family, just like you, Christian, and your children. We protect family. Besides, do you really think they will ever let us live it down if they find out about this and know we didn't include them?"

We all laughed at that comment and the tension in the room eased a bit. "I guess that's that then. We also need to get documents for everyone who will be traveling once we figure out where they are going. Regardless, Jose Luis and Leilani will need passports and visas to travel to the United States," I said thinking about all we needed to do before we sent the humans away.

"Let me handle the travel documents for the children. I know a guy," Aloysius said as Christian and I laughed.

"I think it would be best if we sent Margarita and Giovanni with them since they've spent the most time with them. They seem comfortable with them," Christian suggested.

"Agreed," Aloysius said and looked at me. "Any ideas where we can send them for safety?"

"What about the cabin?" I suggested.

Everyone except Giovanni and Lucas shook their heads.

"They know all about the cabin. Besides, so does Maia and the less she knows the better right now," Kalia said.

Kalia's answer shocked me. She was finally realizing Maia was on the wrong side and had been all along. I never thought that day would come but instead of making me feel relief like I expected it to, I felt sadness. Kalia and Aaron loved her, vowed to protect her and take care of her for the rest of eternity. Maia had changed all that. She had given them no choice though they had tried to hang onto their love and trust for her. I couldn't imagine losing Jose Luis that way. Seeing Kalia's disappointed eyes broke all of our hearts. It was obvious by the silence in the room and by the eyes averting hers. Aaron went to her side and wrapped an arm around her.

"I'm ok, Aaron. I should have seen the signs way before any of this happened. I was blind to her lies and deceit because I love her. I will not allow her to hurt anyone else." Kalia looked up at Aaron and he leaned down and kissed her forehead. He understood exactly how she felt, and she knew it. "Well, I guess I'm going to go make some phone calls," she said and took Aaron's hand to lead him out of the room.

"We're going to go talk to Jose Luis and Leilani," I said taking Christian's hand. "Aloysius, since you know the globe better than any of us, maybe you can figure out where to send them?" I said with a smile. He smiled back and shrugged.

As Christian and I walked out the kitchen door, one of the guards came our way and stopped us. "This came for Kalia and Aaron Benjamin. It was left down in the lobby," he said and handed me a brown wrapped package about the size of a shoe box.

"Thank you." I turned to Christian. He shrugged.

Kalia stood in the corner of the living room and was ending her first call when she spotted the box in my hands. Jose Luis and Leilani stared at us with curiosity.

"What is it?" Kalia asked as Aaron also hung up his cell phone and came to stand in front of us.

"I don't know. It just arrived and it's addressed to you and Aaron." I handed her the box.

She looked at Aaron. "Besides Beth and Pierce, who else knows we're here?"

"No one that I know of," Aaron said and held his hand out to receive the package. "There is no return address on it. Actually…" He turned the box around in his hands. "There's no postage. This box wasn't mailed, it was personally delivered."

"Open it, please," I said trying not to sound as anxious as I felt as my stomach did a few turns.

Aaron set the package on the end table and ripped the brown paper off to reveal a plain white box. Taking the lid off the box with trembling hands, he pushed the crumpled paper used for padding aside and pulled out a small black object.

"What is it?" Kalia asked trying to get a better look at the object as Aaron flipped it in his hand.

"It's Maia's cell phone," he said and handed it to Kalia.

"How do you know it's hers? It could be anybody's," I suggested.

"This is her sticker," Aaron pointed to the sticker of a butterfly she had placed in the top corner of the back of the phone. He reached into the box and pulled out all the paper. A flat red object fell to the floor. Kalia reached for it before we could stop her. Her face turned whiter than her usual pale complexion and her knees gave out as Christian grabbed her under her arms and stopped her from hitting the floor.

"It's Maia's wallet, her ID." She gripped the wallet in her clenched hand and turned to Aaron. "What does this mean? Is she…?"

Regardless of what Maia did to us in the past, regardless of how much pain she'd caused, nobody, including me, wanted Maia dead. I realized then that, somehow, I had hope for her, hope that she would come to her senses, realize what she was doing was wrong. But now, that would never happen.

THIRTY-NINE

"Christian, why don't you take Leilani on a tour of the apartment?" I suggested as Leilani stared up at us with wide eyes.

"Good idea," Christian said and went to stand next to her, offering her his hand. Relief washed over me when she only hesitated a moment, jumping to her feet and grabbing Jose Luis's hand with her free one. Now that they were together again, she wasn't letting him out of her sight even for a moment. They disappeared up the spiral stairs.

"Let's not jump to conclusions, Kalia," Aaron said as he led his wife to the sofa and pulled her down with him.

"Yeah, Aaron is right," I said following them and sitting on the coffee table across from them. "It's not the first time they've set some kind of trap for us. I'm almost positive they're just baiting us."

"But they have her things," Kalia sniffled. "How else would they have gotten them? They are either holding her or they already killed her."

I pulled a tissue from the box next to me and handed it to her. "Or, and I hate to say this but, she is with them willingly. She has worked with them before."

"I know that. Don't you think I know what she's been up to by now?" Kalia's anger surprised both of us. Aaron placed his hand on hers in an attempt to calm her but it didn't faze her. "I know she's on the wrong side. I know how much hate she has in her heart and it's all because of her jealousy. She's jealous of everyone. She doesn't seem to realize that everyone worked for what they have, even their relationships. For some reason, she thinks everything should just be handed to her."

"I know, Kalia. But, despite everything she's done, I still care about her. She's young. She has a lot to learn yet. We will get to the bottom of this. That's a promise," I told her, not sure if she believed me or even if I believed myself.

She looked at me with wet eyes and a smile pulled at the corner of her lips. "I know, Lily. No matter what, I can't stop caring about her either. We've been through so much together."

"I totally understand. After everything Ian did to me and to everyone I love, I couldn't make myself stop caring about him either," I explained. "After his death, it still took me a while to accept him for the monster he truly was."

"I know what you mean. Maia broke our hearts, quite a few times, yet we still love her," she said looking at Aaron. She wiped her tears away again as Aloysius, Lucas, Giovanni, and Fiore walked out of the kitchen.

"I am going upstairs to take photographs of Tomas's family. Fiore is taking pictures of Jose Luis and Leilani. They all need passports. Are they upstairs?" Giovanni asked.

"Yes. Christian is showing Leilani around. Where are they going?" I asked but Giovanni was already at the front door and Fiore was halfway up the stairs. I turned to Aloysius.

"We are sending Tomas and his family to Ecuador with Margarita. That should be far enough away for them. Jose Luis and Leilani are going to Argentina with Giovanni."

"Is Tomas able to travel?" I asked. He had just gotten out of the hospital, and I knew he was still weak and tired.

"The doctors told Lucia he is medically out of danger. He just needs rest, and he can get that in Ecuador. His memory is returning slowly, and he is pretty traumatized. We are setting them up in a nice hotel," Aloysius explained before looking at Kalia and Aaron. "Any word on your friends?"

"Yes. Beth and Pierce will be arriving tomorrow afternoon and Riley and Raul in the evening. Riley is closing her club for a bit and her bouncers, the three vampires, are coming with them," Aaron explained.

"That's great. We need all the help we can get. It's time to end this once and for all," I said feeling some relief for the first time in a while. I turned to Lucas. "What about you, Lucas? When are you completing the change?"

"First of all, you can call me Luke, like when we were kids. Lucas just doesn't sound right coming out of your mouth," he said with a laugh.

"Okay then, Luke. When is it happening?"

"We are leaving in a few minutes. Aloysius rented a room for us across town," He looked at Fiore as she walked back into the room, camera in hand, and she smiled at him. "We thought it would be best if Leilani wasn't around while it happens. She needs some time to rest and heal."

"That is probably true. I haven't even had a chance to talk to her yet, but she seems to be doing better. She seems to have accepted her brother's choice, I hope. How long do you think this will take?" I asked looking at Fiore.

"Considering he's halfway there already, it shouldn't take as long as usual. We should be back by the time Beth and Pierce arrive tomorrow afternoon," she explained. She kissed Aloysius and wrapped her arms around his neck while she looked into his eyes in silence. He smiled and nodded at her, kissing her forehead before she stepped away. Whatever passed between them, the rest of us did not hear it.

Fiore and Luke walked out the door without another word just as Christian, Jose Luis, and Leilani reached the bottom of the staircase. "Everything okay?" Christian asked.

"Everything is fine," I answered and looked at Leilani who still held her brother's hand. "Are you hungry?"

She looked at Jose Luis. He nodded and smiled at her, reassuring her. "Yes," she answered in English.

I reached a hand out to her and, to my surprise, she dropped her brother's hand and took it. "You are learning English. That is great."

"*Cachi* says you not cook good," she said as I led her to the kitchen. Jose Luis, Christian, and Aloysius burst into laughter behind us.

"Thanks, guys," I said to them and as I entered the kitchen with Leilani. "I can use a microwave with no problem. Carmela, the housekeeper, left some food in the freezer. I can heat something up for you."

Opening the freezer while Leilani stood at my side, I pulled a few containers out. "What looks good to you?"

Leilani took a container out of my hands, lifting the corner of the cover to inspect its contents. She did the same with the other two containers before handing one back to me. "This is my favorite."

"That one it is then," I placed the others back in the freezer and put her choice into the microwave, setting the timer for four minutes. "Let's sit down."

She pulled a chair from the table and sat down, her feet dangling just above the floor. Her sneakers looked too small and were ripped and stained at the heels and toes. Upon closer inspection, her clothing didn't look much better.

"We need to take you shopping," I suggested as the microwave hummed behind us.

"Why?" she asked.

"Because you need some things. Your sneakers look a little worn, and too small. Is that Scotch tape? Never mind... You need shirts, pants, pajamas, things like that," I explained. The microwave beeped and I got up to check the temperature. Half of the container was still cold, so I stirred the contents and put it back in, setting the timer again, before sitting back at the table.

"No," she said. "I mean, why do you care about me? Why are you doing this for my brother and me? We don't live with you."

So, Jose Luis had not gotten that far in his explanation to his sister. She had no idea Jose Luis was with us permanently. Stalling a bit, I stopped the microwave and took her meal out. I grabbed a fork from the drawer and handed her the container. I then pulled a bottle of milk out of the refrigerator and poured her a glass. She sat and stared at me, not touching her food, and waiting for an answer.

"I know your mother and father passed away years ago. I also know you have been living with those...people...since you and Jose Luis were separated. Jose Luis does not want to go back with them. He was not happy there, and I think you feel the same," I stopped to give her a chance to answer. Instead, she took a forkful and blew it before placing it in her mouth. "Jose Luis wants to stay with us, and we want the same thing. He is family now and we would like you to be family, too."

She put her fork down and looked up at me with curiosity. "But you are vampires. Jose Luis is a vampire. I am not."

"That's okay. We can still be a family," I assured her.

"I know but, why can't I be one too?"

And there it was, the question I was dreading. All I could do was explain my reasons the way I wished it were explained to me. "You are only nine years old. At eighteen, you would legally be an adult. Don't you want to be an adult first?"

She thought about it a moment, tilting her head to the side and biting her bottom lip, the same way I did when confronted with a dilemma. "But Cachi is not an adult."

"I know he is not, but he at least looks like a young adult. He was dying from cancer. We couldn't wait. We had to save him now," I paused while she took a sip of her milk. "You might want to wait until you look like an adult since that's how you will look forever."

"But I do not want to be an adult," she said setting her fork down and wiping the corner of her mouth with her napkin, though she had only eaten half the bowl.

"Why not?"

"Because all the adults do is fight. They are always fighting and hurting each other. I don't like it." Her big brown eyes showed her conviction.

"It doesn't have to be that way," I started, though I had no idea where I was going with it. She saw my hesitation and continued.

"Why does Melinda want to hurt you? Did you do something to her?"

If I had actually done something to Melinda, or even knew her before all this started, it would be so much easier to understand. But I had done nothing to her. In fact, I had done nothing to her sister, who she was so protective of and hellbent on getting revenge for. Fergus was killed in self-defense, in a battle that had nothing to do with them. The thing was, Fergus had not even died by my hand. Regardless of that fact, Melinda was determined to hurt anyone in my life, and she was willing to use anyone she could against me, including Maia.

"No, I didn't. She is doing this for her sister. It's a long story and now is not the time to tell it. I promise I will tell you everything as soon as we are all safe." I reached for her bowl and raised my eyebrows. She nodded and pushed it toward me. No wonder she was so tiny. She barely ate.

"They are going to come for me," she said as turned in her seat to look at me. I placed her bowl on the counter and went back to my chair.

"I know they wanted you because of your power over fire," I explained. "But I also know they were tired of trying to train you. Melinda said you had no control over it."

"Yes. I know about that, but they still need me," she said.

"For what?" I asked though I was afraid to hear what they told her.

"They will die without me. They don't want to die. I don't want them to die. I don't want anybody to die," her voice faltered as if she were fighting tears.

I stretched my arm across the table and offered her my hand. She looked at it a moment before placing hers in it. She jumped when I closed my hand against her warm one but did not pull away. "Why would they die without you?"

"Because I am the only one with blood they can drink. They need my blood to live," she wiped the corner of her eye and took a deep breath before continuing. "I have special blood. They will die without it."

"Oh, honey," I stood and went to her side of the table, dropping to my knees, and taking both her hands. "They lied to you."

"Why would they do that?"

"Because they wanted to make sure you did not escape. It is not true that they will die without your blood. Nobody has special blood. They can drink any blood," I explained. "How often did they feed from you?"

"One or two times a week. They took turns," she explained as if it were normal. "They each drank a little and then I got to eat whatever I wanted after. One time, I ate a whole tub of *lucuma* ice cream all by myself."

"Sweetie, they lied. They were feeding from others, too. They were only saying that to you because they wanted to keep you there and use you for your fire."

Tears finally streamed down her cheeks, and she didn't bother to try to wipe them.

"I know it hurts when people lie. I am sorry that happened to you, but you are safe now," I hesitated for a moment but then took her in my arms. Instead of pulling away, she buried her face in my chest. "I promise we won't let them take you."

"I know, but…" she sniffled against my shirt.

"But what, honey?"

"I lied, too."

❧ FORTY ❧

"What did you lie about?" I asked trying to sound calm. I couldn't imagine what she would have lied about, but I prepared for a whopper. Before she could answer though, we were interrupted as Christian and Jose Luis walked into the kitchen.

"What are you ladies up to?" Christian looked from me to Leilani with a suspicious look in his eyes.

"I was eating but I am finished," Leilani said, and only then did I notice she had a slight Irish accent.

She must have picked it up from Melinda, who, come to think of it, had been speaking English with all her minions. She no doubt thought it below her to learn the language of the country she planned to control, just like Ian. Thinking about how much alike the two were made me clench my fists, bringing Christian to my side at once. I looked at him and smiled, reassuring him that I was fine. I needed to concentrate on Leilani. As I turned to her, she jumped up from her chair and rushed to the sink.

"What are you doing?" Jose Luis asked as he stepped behind his diminutive sister and looked over her shoulder.

"I'm washing the plate," she looked at him and rolled her eyes in a 'what else would I be doing' way. Christian and I started laughing. It didn't take her long to get back to her usual with her brother, despite his new state and how long she had been away from him.

"You should get some sleep, Leilani," Christian said, taking the clean dish from her and drying it before putting it back in the cupboard. "Tomorrow is going to be a big day."

"But I am not tired," she protested as she turned to face her brother, folding her arms across her chest.

"You look tired. And Christian is right," Jose Luis explained. "Tomorrow will be very busy. There will be a lot of vampires here and we have a lot to do."

Leilani turned to me. "They will want me?"

"What do you…?" I gasped when I realized what she meant. I walked over to her and kneeled so I could look her in the eyes. "Honey, no one will ever use you for food again. The vampires who are coming are our friends. They are coming here to help us stop what is happening with Melinda and her sister, so no one has to ever get hurt again."

"I can help," she said with a determined look on her face.

I turned to Christian. He smiled with pride. "That would be great but," he kneeled next to me and looked up at her. "Just this once, I think we should let all the grown-ups take care of it."

"But I…" Leilani protested, her bottom lip sticking out in a pout.

"Leilani, I know you are strong and smart, but…" Jose Luis intervened. "I need you to go with me. Who will take care of me if something happens to you?"

Leilani thought about it a moment. "Ok, I will take care of you. Like *mamá* did."

"Good, thank you," Jose Luis said and took his sister's hand. "Now let's get you to bed."

"Good night," Leilani said and surprised me by wrapping her arms around me. As soon as she released me, she did the same with Christian.

Jose Luis led her out of the kitchen and they disappeared up the stairs.

"That is one intelligent and mature little girl," I said turning to Christian as we sat on the sofa. "It breaks my heart, though."

"Why do you say that?" Christian reached for my hand.

"She hasn't had much of a chance to be a child."

"You're right," he looked at me with sadness in his eyes. "She's spent the last few years as a slave and feeder to those monsters."

"I can't imagine living like that every day. Did you know they told her they would all die without her blood?" My voice was a little louder than I wanted and I bit my lip.

"Why doesn't that surprise me?" He shook his head in disgust. "She will get to be a child again, with us. I hope that's what she wants."

I nodded and turned to face him. "She will do whatever her brother wants. She will not want to be separated from him again." Just then, the door opened and Aloysius, Kalia, and Aaron walked in.

"Where were you?" I asked as they came to stand closer to the sofa.

"We went to feed. I suggest the three of you do the same. We need to be ready," Aloysius said, taking a seat in a chair while Aaron took the other chair and Kalia sat next to me.

"Do you have the passports?" Christian asked.

"They will be ready in the morning. Giovanni is picking them up along with the plane tickets. They must be ready to leave tomorrow night," Aloysius explained.

Kalia turned to Christian and me. "Where is Leilani?"

"Jose Luis took her up to bed," I answered. "She says she's not tired but it's obvious she is. I doubt he'll be up there long."

"Well, if she lets me, I will take over for Jose Luis; sit with her until she falls asleep. You three need to go feed."

"Now?" I asked feeling unsure about leaving Leilani on her first night with us.

"We'll be too busy tomorrow with everyone coming and the planning we still have to do," Aloysius said, his expression softening. "She'll be fine, Lily. We are not going anywhere."

I looked at Christian. "He's right. We need to feed so we can be at our strongest. Leilani will be just fine. I know I wouldn't try anything with these four here," Christian said looking at the others in the room. They all laughed.

"It's settled then," Kalia said and rose, kissing Aaron on the head. "I'm going to go sit with Leilani, maybe tell her a story."

THE NEXT MORNING dawned cloudy and damp. An uneasy feeling settled over me and though I tried to hide it, Christian noticed

"What's wrong?" he asked as we dressed and got ready to take Leilani for some of the things she needed. "Are you nervous about the fight?"

"Of course, I am, but that's to be expected," I turned to him while buttoning my shirt. "I'm not really sure what it is but something else is bothering me. I can't quite put my finger on it." The impending battle did bother me, as well as the safety of the children and the humans, but there was something else, some kind of shadow hanging in the air.

"It will all work out. You'll see," Christian said and wrapped his arms around me, squeezing me to him. "Evil doesn't have a chance against us."

I hugged him back and leaned my face against his chest. "You're right. I will be fine," We had way too much to do today and standing here and analyzing my feelings wasn't going to accomplish anything on our list. "Let's go see if Leilani is up yet. Shopping with her will be a nice distraction."

When we walked into the kitchen, Kalia and Leilani both sat at the table. Leilani sat with a plate in front of her while she dipped her buttered roll in her coffee and milk. It was nice to see her smiling and looking so comfortable with Kalia.

"Oh, good morning," Kalia said when she noticed us. Leilani turned her head and smiled, unwilling to greet us with her mouth full.

"Good morning," I said to both. "How was your first night, Leilani? Did you sleep well?"

She swallowed her mouthful and wiped her mouth with her napkin. "Yes, thank you. I sleep all night," she turned to look at Kalia. "Miss Kalia tell me a good story."

"How do you know it was good?" Kalia laughed. "You fell asleep five minutes after I started."

Leilani giggled and shrugged her shoulders. "It start good. I see more when I sleep."

The three of us couldn't help but laugh. Leilani must have finished Kalia's story in her dreams.

"When you're finished with your breakfast, we are going shopping," I told her and pulled a chair out for myself.

"I like shopping," she said and then put the last piece of bread in her mouth, standing before she finished chewing. She grabbed her cup and swallowed the last of coffee and milk.

"I will wash your dishes," Kalia said with a smile. "Go wash up and put your shoes on."

"Okay," Leilani said. She wiped her mouth and balled her napkin up in her hand, placing it on top of her plate. "I hurry." She ran out of the room.

Kalia picked up Leilani's dishes and set them in the sink, turning back to us. "That little girl is very special." She leaned against the sink and crossed her arms over her chest.

"She is, isn't she?" Christian said with pride in his eyes. "It doesn't surprise me that they took her."

"What are your plans for her and Jose Luis?" she asked looking back and forth between us.

"We plan to keep them with us. No matter where we end up," I said. I didn't think that was even a question and wasn't sure why Kalia asked so I raised an eyebrow.

"Are you planning to stay in Peru? Because you know, there is more than enough room at our house in Oregon for all of you."

I turned to Christian. He said nothing but his smile gave me my answer. Though he had adapted to living in Peru, I knew his home was in the United States. I also knew the children would be safest there. Taking care of Melinda didn't necessarily erase the fact that the hunters and witches had taken Leilani before Melinda had started with her vengeance.

"That would be great. Thank you, Kalia." Before I could even stop myself, I walked to where she stood and wrapped my arms around her. I had missed her more than I even imagined. She and Aaron had given me a new chance at a semi-normal life and had, in the process, become a huge part of that life and I wasn't willing to lose that again.

"Of course, honey. You and Christian are family," she backed out of my arms to look into my eyes, holding them with the tenderness in her face. "I guess this means Aaron and I are grandparents, huh?"

"I guess it does," I said and wrapped my arms around her again. Christian stroked my back as Kalia held me. A knot in my stomach formed and I took a deep breath, determination taking over the worries in my head, filling me with hope for the first time since I'd fallen in love with the human that now shared eternity with me.

⋘ᗡ FORTY-ONE ᓷ⋙

We returned from shopping, our arms full of bags, trailed by Mauricio and Vicente, to find Beth and Pierce waiting for us.

"It's so good to see you," I said as I set the bags on the hallway floor. As soon as I was in front of them again, I turned to introduce Leilani. She stood behind my legs, peeking out of the right side, her eyes wide and glued to Pierce. I reached to move her out from behind me, but she stiffened and struggled against me. "Leilani, what's the matter, honey?" I smiled apologetically to both of them.

Beth approached taking her time and smiling warmly. "Hello, Leilani. It is very nice to meet you." Leilani stayed behind me, her eyes still glued on Pierce, ignoring Beth.

"Leilani, it's okay. They are friends of ours. They will not hurt you," I coached as I pulled from her grasp and dropped to my knees in front of her.

She leaned to whisper in my ear. "What is that man?"

Though she had whispered it so only I could hear it, Pierce laughed. He smiled and never took his eyes off Leilani as he approached, dropping to his knees next to me. "Hello. I am Pierce," He extended his hand. Leilani looked at me and I nodded. She looked back at Pierce and, hesitating only a moment, placed her hand in his. "I am a vampire, but I am also just like you."

"Like me?" she asked, finally looking a bit more relaxed as her curiosity piqued.

"Yes, like you. I am also a witch."

"Wow! You are lucky," Leilani said with a huge smile. "Maybe one day I be both. Then I can fight the bad people, too."

"Yes, my dear," Pierce said as he rose from the floor still holding Leilani's hand. "One day."

"I show you the apartment?" Leilani asked, her smile unwavering as she spoke.

"That would be lovely," Pierce said and shrugged toward me. "I am getting the grand tour from this lovely lady." They disappeared up the steps before any of us could comment.

"I guess Pierce has a new friend," Beth said as she took me in her arms.

"She has something in common with him," I said as I hugged her back and then stepped back to look at her. "I didn't expect Pierce to act so…"

"Warm and friendly?" she said with a laugh.

"I didn't mean anything by it but yeah, I guess that's it. He always seems so serious."

"Pierce never had children of his own, but he did have nieces and nephews he was very close to. From the stories he tells me, he spoiled them rotten."

"Where is everybody?" Christian asked.

"Kalia and Aaron are in the kitchen making dinner for the humans. She wants them to eat before they leave for the airport. Jose Luis is upstairs with Paco and his family helping them pack, and Aloysius went to the hotel to check on Fiore and Luke, possibly bring them back with him if they're ready," she explained. It wasn't until then that the smell of food cooking hit me.

"Right, food for the humans," I said and started walking toward the kitchen. Beth grabbed my arm.

"You're going to be a great mother, Lily," she said as she looked into my eyes. "There's no doubt in my mind, or any of our minds, about that."

"But I'm such a horrible cook."

"You'll learn," she said putting her arm across my shoulders and leading me toward the kitchen. "Besides, you have Kalia to help you. Trust me, that woman will be quite the doting grandmother."

ALEGRÍA, PACO, AND Leilani sat in the kitchen and ate the dinner Kalia prepared for them. Alegría and Leilani had hit it off from the second they saw each other, making the rest of us wish they were traveling together. Aloysius was right, however; they would be safer if they were in different places. The rest of us sat in the living room discussing plans with the newly arrived Raul and Riley. A few minutes into our discussion, the apartment door opened and Aloysius walked in, followed by Fiore and Luke. I jumped out of my seat and went to them, taking Luke's hands in mine.

"How are you feeling?" He looked like his usual self, but I knew looks could be deceiving when it came to vampires.

"I feel great, actually." He smiled and dropped my hands, which I noticed were the same temperature as mine. I no longer heard his irregular heartbeat either. "Where are the children?"

"Umm, well…"

"Lily, please," He shook his head and laughed. "I'm not asking because I'm hungry. I already ate. I just want to make sure they didn't leave before I could say goodbye."

Everyone in the room laughed except me. I dropped my head in shame and bit my lip before looking back up at him. The smile on his face told me he wasn't offended. "I'm sorry, Luke. It's just that, well, you know."

"No problem. I totally understand your concern, but you have to remember that I was already part vampire. Trust me, I learned self-control a long time ago," he explained as he crossed the room to introduce himself to the others.

The sound of plates clanking and water running interrupted the conversation that had resumed. I walked toward the kitchen and cracked the door enough to peek inside. "They are doing the dishes. Leilani is washing, Paco is drying, and Alegría is putting away."

Kalia smiled. "They are such great children. Don't you wish…?" She stopped talking and turned toward the window. Through the closed sheer drapes, the sun was making its descent into the horizon, painting the sky a deep orange. "What in the world?"

"What is it?" Aloysius said as he pulled the curtain aside, joined by Kalia, Fiore, and me.

"What do you see?" I asked. Leilani rushed out of the kitchen, Paco and Alegría close at her heels. Their faces had all gone white.

"All the dogs are… They are…" Leilani said as she tiptoed to the window to stand next to Aloysius.

"Barking, Leilani. The dogs are barking," I explained filling in for the word she did not know in English. She held onto me tighter, as if her life depended on it.

"The dogs are barking," Pierce repeated. "Is that a problem?"

"That usually precedes an earthquake. Hopefully it will just be a minor tremor," Aloysius explained. He looked at Leilani with concern in his eyes. "It will be ok, Leilani. We are all here. Nothing to worry about."

Just as they stepped away from the window and back toward the seating area, a rumble passed through the room. No one said a word as we looked at each other. For the next few seconds, an eerie quiet filled the room as no one moved a muscle except for their heads. I turned to Christian and went to reach for him as the room went into total and complete chaos.

The rumbling sound was replaced by screaming as the children ran to hold onto an adult, zigzagging to avoid falling objects. The apartment door flew open and Giovanni ran inside, followed by Vicente and Mauricio. "Everybody ok?" Giovanni yelled over the screaming children. I wasn't even positive I wasn't screaming myself as I struggled to hold onto Leilani and reach Christian at the same time. The chandelier over the coffee table crashed onto the glass sending shards every which way. Beth screamed and covered her left eye. Pierce dodged the chair making its way across the floor and reached her, pulling her hand away to check her eye.

"We have to get out of here!" Aloysius yelled over everyone else.

"The electricity is out," Giovanni yelled back. "No lights in the hallway. The elevator won't work, and the stairs are too unsteady." Just to remind us how unstable the electricity supply could be during an earthquake, a transformer blew up somewhere close by, a light briefly flashing in front of the window.

"Ok, listen up everyone," Mauricio's booming voice sounded above all the commotion. "Everyone go stand in a doorway, preferably on this floor. If there is not enough room, get under the dining room table. Now, hurry!"

People scattered every which way, dodging falling knickknacks, pictures, and lamps. Noticing we were out of doorways, Leilani, Christian, and I dived under the table, huddling close together as if that would stop the possible collapse of the skyscraper we inhabited.

"Why is this lasting so long?" I whispered to Christian.

His terrified eyes settled on my face before he looked at Leilani. "It's a big one. I love you."

His words twisted my stomach into knots. We had been through so much together, survived so much, only to die because of an earthquake. I don't think so. Not today. I held both of them tighter and did the only thing I could. For the first time in almost a century, I prayed.

"I want my Cachi," Leilani cried against my chest.

"He is ok. He's upstairs. He will come down as soon as it stops. I promise," I said back to her, hoping they were not trying to leave the building. Swaying staircases would not be the easiest things to maneuver, especially with Tomas still recovering.

"Is everybody alright?" Aloysius yelled from somewhere down the hallway. It wasn't until then that I noticed the movement had stopped. I pushed away from Leilani a bit and noticed she was shaking and tears rolled down her cheeks. I hugged her against me again.

"It's ok, honey. We're all ok. It stopped now," I explained and crawled out from under the table with her close beside me. Christian stood and took our hands to help us up. I turned toward the living room and yelled, "Somebody please call upstairs, see if they're ok."

The three of us walked into the living room as they were picking things up off the floor. Some things looked salvageable and some, like the glass coffee table were beyond hope. The sound of car alarms and barking dogs, both in the building and outside, filled the apartment. I tried to help but Leilani gripped my hand and wouldn't let go.

"The telephone lines are down," Giovanni announced as he came out of the kitchen. Just then, Jose Luis ran in.

"Oh, thank God," I yelled. Leilani released my hand and ran into her brother's arms. "Are Lucia and Tomas ok?"

"They are fine, a little scared but fine," he answered and kissed his sister's head. "They are all packed and ready to go."

"Giovanni, please use your cell and call the airport, make sure the flights are still on schedule," The room was losing light pretty fast as the sun made its final descent. It wouldn't be a problem for the vampires, but it would be for the humans. "Aloysius, do you have any candles?"

He hurried toward me with a smile on his face. "Actually, Carmela made sure to keep emergency supplies here. I thought she was nuts, but I have since changed my mind." He went into the kitchen and came back with candles, flashlights, and even an oil lamp.

"What would we do without her?" I said with a laugh.

"No flights today," Giovanni came back into the room and everyone else gathered there, dropping whatever cleanup they were doing.

FORTY-TWO

N ow what do we do?" Christian asked. We all looked at Aloysius.
"No need to panic. We will keep Tomas, Lucia, and all the children upstairs. They will be guarded. We are going to find Melinda and her gang but, if for any reason they should come looking for us, they only know about this apartment."

Christian and I took the supplies from him, but before we could get all the children together, the building began shaking again. Leilani screamed and ran to me, wrapping her arms around my legs.

"It's just an aftershock. It'll pass soon," Aloysius said and looked at Leilani. "See? It stopped already."

Everyone stood still for a moment, trying to determine if there was any more movement. There was none so everyone returned to what they were doing. Christian, Jose Luis, and I took Leilani upstairs by way of the darkened stairway. We managed not to scare anyone who might have been on the stairs as we walked in the darkness with Christian carrying Leilani. When we arrived at the other apartment, suitcases lined the side of the entryway.

"I guess we are not flying anywhere tonight," Tomas said as he maneuvered his crutches around the fallen chair someone had not yet picked up. Jose Luis grabbed the chair and moved it out of the way. Alegría and Lucia knelt on the floor picking up the pieces of a broken flowerpot.

"The electricity is out all over the city. You will all have to stay here. You will have two guards at all times, one inside, and one outside the door," I told him. Lucia paused to look at me, her face pale with fear.

Christian took Leilani to the sofa and set her down before taking the candles out of the bag and lighting them, setting them on any flat surface he found. He reached into the bag again and pulled out three flashlights, passing them out to Jose Luis, Tomas, and Lucia.

"Jose Luis, can you come with me for a moment?" I asked and stepped toward the open door so he would follow me.

"What is it?" he asked as soon as he shut the door behind him.

"I want you to stay with the humans. Having a third vampire with them will be best," I whispered the rest so no one inside could hear me. "Will you be ok, I mean, you know?"

His eyes widened in shock. "I do know and yes, of course I will be ok."

"Please don't be offended. You are a brand new vampire. Sometimes your hunger can feel overwhelming and, being new, you do need to feed more often."

"I know I am new, but I am fine."

"Are you sure?"

"Yes. I love these people, especially my sister. They are not on the menu," he said in a sarcastic tone.

I laughed and wrapped my arm around him, causing him to relax in spite of his anger. "I always knew you were strong. We are going to go find Melinda and her gang and put an end to this chaos. I am leaving you in charge of the humans. Two guards will be here in a few minutes to help you."

"Please do not worry about us. Just go do what you need to do and hurry back to us. I want to leave here as soon as possible. I want to go to the United States and really start my new life."

Just as we finished talking, two guards came walking up the hall. I hugged Jose Luis before walking him back through the door. Leilani sat on the floor, a flashlight in her hand, looking at both of us as we entered.

"You have to go," she said, her facial expression blank.

"I know. I just wanted to make sure everybody here is situated before I go downstairs to make plans," I assured her as I took a step toward her.

She shook her head, stopping me in my tracks. "No," she said, her eyes remaining locked on mine. "It is too late for plans. They are here."

"Go, Lily," Mauricio commanded as he pulled me out of the apartment by the arm and then positioned himself in front of the door. "Get downstairs!"

Without hesitation, I ran down the hall and to the stairway. Instead of wasting time by running down the steps, I jumped the whole flight, rounded the corner, and jumped the rest of the way. Giovanni stood outside our apartment.

"What's wrong?" he asked as I ran toward him.

"Leilani says they are here, in the building."

"We need to block the stairs," he said and opened the door to the apartment, going right to the other guards converged inside, awaiting the meeting.

"Lily," Christian ran in after me. "You took off without me."

"They are here," I yelled loud enough for everyone to hear. "They came to us. We're not ready for them. We still have to—"

Aloysius appeared at my side without me even noticing he moved. "Lily, it will be fine. We are all here. We can do this."

"But we don't even have a strategy yet," I protested.

"We don't need a strategy. Our only objective is to destroy them. All of them," he said, his eyes firm.

"Oh, God," Kalia cried as Aaron wrapped an arm around her shoulders. "Please think about it first. What if Maia is with them?"

"Then we try to do whatever we need to do to get Maia away from them safely," Aloysius said. "Then we destroy them."

"Just like that?" Christian asked.

"This will never end unless we do. They will always find a reason to pursue Lily and destroy any happiness she finds. We already know reasoning with Melinda is impossible."

"You have a point there," Christian answered. "I will get the box of weapons out of the closet. We will grab what we can and wait for them."

"Two of us are going upstairs to position ourselves at the doorway of the hall. The rest of us will stay with you," Giovanni announced as he and Margarita exited.

Christian returned with the box. "We don't have many wooden bullets left."

"I know. Carmela was supposed to bring more but she must have gotten held up because of the quake. We should have plenty of stakes, though, right?" Aloysius asked as he approached the box.

"Yes," Christian said and handed a stake to each of us as we stood around the weapons. "Grab a sword or knife, too. We stake and chop their heads off."

It was really strange to hear Christian talking like that, so brutal and lethal. But he was right; we didn't have time to waste. The quicker we ended this, the better.

"We ready?" Aloysius asked. Everyone replied that they were. "Out to the hall then. No reason to wait for them here."

As we filed into the hallway, a door opened down the hall. A man in his early thirties poked his out to investigate the noise, squinting his eyes in the darkness.

"Please go back inside and lock your door," Fiore yelled to him in Spanish. "Do not open it for anyone."

The man squinted harder trying to find the source of voice, but then gave up and went back inside. We heard his locks turning.

"Maybe we should go down to meet them," I whispered to Aloysius. "That would keep them as far away from the others as possible."

Aloysius opened his mouth to speak but was interrupted by a bang against the wall as the stairway door was thrown open. All of us automatically assumed fighting stances, our knees bent and our hands grasping our stakes.

"Lovely security you have in this building," Melinda's voice mocked from down the hall. "He will fit quite nicely in my collection." She shoved Giovanni ahead of her. Arturo walked on one side of her, and two vampires I'd never seen before on the other. Giovanni was gagged and his hands were tied behind him.

I am sorry...I tried to...

"Oh, zip it! No one wants to hear how cowardly you really are," Melinda taunted interrupting Giovanni's mental apology. "I will add the other one... the woman, to my collection, too."

I wanted to lunge at her, scratch her eyes out and feed them to her, but Fiore grabbed my arm. "They have the humans," she whispered.

My whole body stiffened at that realization. The children were no longer safe. They had been our first priority and their first target.

"Where is Maia?" Kalia asked before I could say what I wanted.

Melinda and the rest stopped about twenty feet in front of us. "Don't you worry about her. She is keeping the humans entertained. We wouldn't want them to get bored while we're having all the fun here now, would we?"

"You keep your hands off them!" I screamed and tried to run toward her. Fiore and Christian held my arms to stop me.

"You all seem like rational adults to me," Melinda said. She kept Giovanni in front of her, shielding herself from us.

Giovanni locked his eyes on mine. Though he didn't think of what he wanted, I knew. He was pleading with me to save Margarita. His love for her was obvious. He cared more about her life than his own. I nodded, promising him that I would do whatever it took to get her back.

"Lily, pay attention. I am talking," Melinda shook her head. "Always letting your emotions get the best of you. See all the damage you cause?"

"I didn't do this! You and Ian did this!"

"Hasn't anyone taught you not to speak ill of the dead? Ian is no more. May I remind you that it was at your hands that he died?" She looked at me for a moment and shook her head. "Anyway, I want to talk. I have a proposition for you all."

Aloysius stepped to the front of the group. "What is this proposition?"

"Give me Lily and no one else needs to die. It's that simple. You hand her over to me and all of you, the humans included, and Maia get to walk away, as will we." She tilted her head as she waited for an answer.

Hushed murmurs ran through our group and, before any of us noticed, Christian ran down the hall toward Melinda. He dove through the air, landing on top of her and Giovanni. I tried to run toward them, but Fiore and Aaron restrained me by wrapping their arms around my waist.

"Let's go get the children," Aaron said. "The rest can handle this."

He ran toward the stairway with Fiore, Kalia, and I following close at his heels. We ran up the stairs and reached the door, pulling it open. A scream caught us all off guard.

"*Dios mio!*" a woman yelled holding her hand to her chest. Her other hand held a leash with a small dog. The dog pulled at the leash, barking furiously, trying to get free of her hold.

"Ma'am, please go back to your apartment," Aaron said in Spanish.

"I will not. My dog has to go out," she said and reached down to pick up the furious fur ball.

"Then let him go on newspaper, but go back to your apartment, now! There is a man running around the building with a gun," Aaron said looking at us and shrugging without the woman seeing. "Go back inside and lock your door."

"Oh, thank you. Thank you, I will go," she said and turned, hugging her still barking ball of fur to her chest as she ran down the hall.

Reaching the door to the apartment where the humans were hiding, we found the door locked. Kalia stepped back and kicked it open. We ran inside and an eerie silence greeted us. We stood still and quiet, listening for the beating of their hearts.

"They're not here," Fiore said. "Where could they…?"

Laughter coming from somewhere down the hall froze us all in place and chilled my spine. I knew that laugh.

"Maia?" I yelled. A door slammed and the laughter disappeared.

"They took them upstairs," Aaron said.

"What makes you think up and not down?" I asked. The stake clutched in my hand almost felt like an extension of my arm.

"We would've passed them if they went down. How many more floors are there?" he asked.

"Just one more and then the roof," I answered already on my way to the door.

"Ok," Aaron said as we climbed up a flight. "We will check this floor first.

We can listen for their thoughts."

After a few moments of walking the hall, we agreed they weren't on this floor. Of course they were on the roof. Where else would they be? Determined not to let my fear of heights hinder our rescue attempt, I led the way up the last flight of stairs. I took a deep breath and pulled the heavy metal door open. Wind whipped my hair around my face hard enough to make it feel like a slap. The sound of hearts beating way too fast flooded my ears before I could look around.

"Oh, shit," Fiore said, her usual proper speech forgotten.

"What?" I asked holding my hair in my hand to keep it out of the way. "What is it?"

My stomach rose up to my throat and the ground felt like it was tilting. On a metal pole that was probably once one end of a clothesline, Jose Luis, Leilani, and Alegría stood gagged and tied. The other pole contained Lucia, Tomas, and Paco. Paco's head hung as if he were unconscious. Tears streamed down Lucia's cheeks and her bottom lip quivered silently.

"Jesus Christ," Aaron said behind me. "Look." He pointed toward the ground at the base of the pole.

Wood had been neatly piled around the base of both poles. Just then, as if awaiting her cue, Maia stepped out from behind a small cement structure used for storage. Her mouth held a fake smile, as if she were posing for a photograph. She tilted her head to the side and looked down, then back up at me.

"No!" I screamed and ran toward her, my focus only on the red gasoline container she gripped in her hand.

⟶ FORTY-THREE ⟶

Fiore grabbed me again and stopped me by wrapping her arms around my waist from behind. As I struggled against her, Kalia stepped forward.

"Maia, what are you doing?" Kalia asked and dropped to her knees. Aaron placed a comforting hand on her shoulder. "Please don't do this."

Maia smiled at the woman who thought of her as her daughter without an ounce of emotion. Regardless of the fact that it was already dead, it broke my heart.

"It was nice having you both as parents for a while, and I thank you for all you did for me. Of course, I liked the money and the traveling best, but that's beside the point," Maia explained with one hand on her hip while she swung the gas can back and forth with the other. "But to tell you the truth, the cozy, happy family thing just isn't for me. It was nice while it lasted but you have her now," she nodded toward me. "And her husband and children. You can all be a warm, loving family together. As for me, I like power. I like being a vampire, a killer. That's what I'm supposed to be, a killer. Not some avenging angel like your perfect Lily. Melinda lets me have that. She understands me and what I really want and is always so encouraging."

"But that's not really you, Maia," Kalia cried. "Aaron and I know you better than that."

"Oh, but that's not true. I put on a good show for you, that's all. What I really want is to be a feared and powerful vampire, the way we're supposed to be, not human-loving pansy asses like you. What good does it do to be superior to humans if we can't control them?"

Kalia forgot her pain and stood. "You ungrateful little brat!" she yelled.

"Little brat? You're that angry and you can't even curse? Wouldn't you rather have called me a little bitch?" Maia mocked with the smile still on her face.

"No," Kalia answered calmly. "When I think of 'bitch' I think of a grown woman. Brat fits you much better."

Maia's smile wavered and I wanted to laugh. I would have if I hadn't been trying to plan how to get to the poles and untie the humans and Jose Luis. Just as Maia started to answer, the door opened and the others stepped through. Melinda was led by the arms by Christian and Riley. The others followed behind them while Pierce helped Giovanni, who looked a little out of it but otherwise uninjured.

"Where is Margarita?" Giovanni asked in a weak voice.

Maia ignored him and addressed Christian instead. "What have you done to her?" she asked as she looked at Melinda.

"She's fine," Christian answered. "She just wasn't strong enough for all of us."

"Maia, make them a deal," Melinda said locking her eyes with Maia. Maia looked confused for a moment and then smiled again as she understood.

"Let go of Melinda and drop your weapons," she announced. The door to the storage building opened and Maria and Ryanne walked out. A vampire I'd never seen led Margarita. This one was small and thin and couldn't have been much older than sixteen.

"Margarita! Are you ok?" Giovanni perked up when he saw her. She nodded.

"Maria, take their weapons."

"Wait!" Aloysius said holding a hand up to stop Maria's approach. Maria's face drained of all color as she froze in place. "What's the rest of the deal?"

Melinda nodded to Maia. Maia cleared her throat and her eyes met Aaron's for a brief moment. The hesitation was apparent in her eyes, but it didn't last. "Release Melinda and hand us Lily. Then we walk away and you can untie them."

"That is out of the question!" Christian yelled. He walked to stand behind me and wrapped his arms protectively around me.

"Christian, it's fine. I will go with them," I said. The gasps heard from both sides were unmistakable.

"No, Lily. I can't let them take you. They will kill you," Christian pleaded. "That's all they want. To kill you to avenge that bastard, Ian."

"Listen to her, Christian. Isn't one meaningless vampire's death better than the deaths of all these innocent humans and children? How could you live with that?" Melinda chastised. Riley grabbed Melinda's hand with her free hand and yanked her head back.

"Oh, Melinda," Maia tried to get her attention though Melinda couldn't look at her. Riley had not released her hair. "I think I'd like to keep the cop for myself."

"Are you insane?" Luke balled his hand into a fist and growled. Maia looked a bit scared but hid it with a laugh.

"Oh, yeah. You're perfect for me," she said with a new smile just for him.

"You make me sick!" Luke growled out the words.

"Just me and Melinda. Luke is not part of the deal," I interrupted what was about to turn into a fight between Luke and Maia.

"Lily, no!" Aloysius intervened. "That is not even an option."

"It's my fight, Aloysius. It's always been my fight," I answered him with as much courage in my voice as I could muster. "Let me end this once and for all."

Christian stepped out from behind me. His eyes focused on the gas can in Maia's hand. His brows furled as he tried to focus his power on it.

"Stop him or he dies!" Maia yelled to me, her eyes wide. "His telekinesis bullshit isn't going to solve this. There's already a layer of fuel on the wood so I can still light them up and turn them into a bon fire. I even brought marshmallows." She laughed at her own joke.

"Christian, please look at me," I stepped directly in front of him, trying to get him to focus on me and not Maia. "Please let me do this."

"I can't, Lily. You're my wife, for Christ's sake. I love you."

"And I love you. I will always love you, no matter where I am. That will never change," I explained. "But these children need you. Jose Luis needs you to teach him what to do. Leilani needs you to help her grow up."

Red tears rolled down Christian's face as his head lowered and his lips met mine. His kiss was wet but it didn't matter. I grabbed the back of his head and pulled him closer to me, relishing in the taste and feel of him and his love, the love that would get me through wherever death took me. "Please take care of them. Please always remind them both of how much I loved them."

Aaron stepped behind Christian and gripped both his shoulders, pulling him away from me and toward the others in our group. I did not turn to look at any of them for fear that I would change my mind. Instead, I went to where Melinda was and took her arm, pulling her away from Riley. Riley only struggled for a moment before releasing her grip and lowering her eyes to the floor.

"I will go with you, Melinda, but they go first," I said. "If they do not leave here in one piece, there's no deal."

Melinda thought about it for a moment and then grabbed my arm, pulling me to the side. "Fine. Untie them and take them away from here."

Kalia, Beth, and Raul ran to untie the humans and Jose Luis. They picked Leilani and Alegría up, carrying them toward the door as the others followed with each other's help. Maia smiled at Kalia as she passed. Kalia didn't look at her. She walked to the doorway with the others and stood behind them as the humans and children made their way downstairs.

"Lily," Kalia said. "You have my permission."

"Huh?" Maia uttered. Before Kalia could say anything else, I pulled my arm back and punched Maia right in the nose. The loud cracking of her shattering bone caught the others' attention.

"Get them out of the building!" Aloysius yelled to the guards running down the stairs with the humans.

Jose Luis ran back in through the door and stopped next to Kalia.

"Leilani, no!" Giovanni yelled. Just then, Leilani ran in and grabbed her brother's hand, standing her ground.

"Go with the others, Giovanni," Aloysius said. "We can take care of her. Just get the others out of here."

"You lied," Melinda said as her face scrunched in anger. "You made a deal, and you didn't follow through."

"Let her go, Melinda," Aloysius said. "It's twelve against nine. You're outnumbered."

"No, that's not right," Leilani said from behind Jose Luis's legs. "It's thirteen against nine. Don't you know how to count?"

Melinda laughed at the authority in Leilani's voice. "And what are you going to do? Oh, I'm so afraid I can't stop shaking."

"I can—"

"Leilani, please be quiet," I said winking at her. "This is between the adults." Melinda's attention focused on Leilani gave me the opportunity I needed. I turned slightly in her grasp and elbowed her in the face forcing her to stumble back a few steps.

Ryanne took that as an invitation to go crazy, as only she could do, and dove through the air, landing on Raul. Her stake went up so fast and back down into Raul's chest that no one had a chance to react. The skinny vampire sliced Raul's head without much effort. Riley approached them, her teeth clenched, her hands in fists, and none of us could tear our eyes away. Even Melinda stood still watching. Riley wrapped her hands around Ryanne's forearms. Ryanne's eyes widened and the hair on her head started standing as if a balloon were being rubbed against it. We all watched with shocked fascination as Riley electrocuted Ryanne with her touch. After a few minutes of Ryanne staring into Riley's eyes with fear and silent pleading, Ryanne's skin started to burn. It turned brown and smoke came off her though there was no visible fire. The smell of burning flesh forced most of us to cover our noses with our hands. A few moments later, Ryanne was nothing but a pile of ashes blowing away in the wind. We ducked to avoid getting bits of her in our hair.

"Who's next?" Riley asked as she marched toward Melinda.

"Riley, no," I put my arm out to stop her approach. "This one's mine."

"And mine," Christian said from behind me.

I turned to see who else was ready to fight and spotted their human, Maria. Her jaw dropped when I looked at her.

"Please, don't kill me. I will leave. I will not ever come back. Please," she pleaded, tears streaming down her face as her chin trembled.

"I told you they would never give you what you wanted," I told her reminding her of our previous conversation. "They were just going to use you and then throw you away. Just go. Go live a normal life that doesn't include serving power hungry vampires."

"I will. Thank you," she said as she ran past us and out the door, slamming it behind her.

Maia, who had stood quietly holding her nose and watching the exchange, ran toward Leilani and grabbed her hand, pulling her away from Jose Luis. Before I could do anything to stop her, Kalia ran to Maia and grabbed her arm. Maia kept walking, pulling Leilani and Kalia toward the ledge of the roof.

"Maia, please. Get a hold of yourself," Kalia begged. "What are you going to do? Throw an innocent child off the building and to her death? That's not you!"

"That's exactly what I am going to do, Mo-ther," she pronounced the word as if it were poison in her mouth. "It is me. It's always been me. You were just too blind to see it."

I ran toward them, but it was too late. Leilani was pushed aside, landing at Aaron's feet in a heap. Before I could even say anything, Kalia grabbed Maia's head and turned it fast and hard, breaking her neck with a loud crunch. Maia fell to the ground, her terrified eyes frozen wide forever.

"Jesus Christ!" I screamed as Kalia dropped to her knees. Her eyes blank as she stared at Maia's lifeless body. "You killed her."

As I dropped to my knees to attempt to comfort Kalia, the wind picked up and debris flew toward us from the open storage room. Looking around the roof, I spotted Arturo standing with his arms up and his face toward the sky he attempted to manipulate. His lips moved rapidly as he chanted his curse. Christian was busy fighting the skinny vampire and Aaron had Leilani in his arms. Beth and Pierce had Melinda by the arms. Melinda stood and stared at Maia, her shock and disbelief apparent. That gave me the opportunity I needed.

Focusing my mind on Arturo, I opened a path to his mind. I invaded his thoughts without him having to make eye contact. He was too busy trying to conjure up his storm to move his eyes. I scrunched my eyes, my head pounding with the effort. I heard a scream but couldn't look away from Arturo. When I was about to give up, Arturo finally made a move. He lowered his head and, with his arms still in the air, turned and walked toward the ledge behind him. Lowering only one arm, he grabbed on to the short cement wall and climbed on top. He stood balancing himself in the wind and slowly turned to face me, his eyes wide with terror. His mind fought against mine, increasing the pain in my head. I held on with all my might. I raised my hand and waved, smiling at him, before he stepped off the ledge like a marionette with the strings cut and plunged to his death without so much as a scream.

Refocusing on a scream I'd heard earlier, I turned to see Carlos, one of our guards struggling against one of their vampire's raised stake. I took over Christian's fight with the skinny vampire and motioned for him to help Carlos.

"I got that," Christian said as he focused his attention on the stake pointed at Carlos's heart. Within moments, the stake floated in the air above the vampire's head, and I took that opportunity to break the skinny kid's neck and tossed him aside.

"No!" Beth screamed as she grabbed Riley in her arms and stopped her from falling.

Everyone stopped again when we realized Riley was missing her head. Melinda stood with the bloody sword in her hand. The whole roof suddenly turned red and my ears hummed as if a thousand bumble bees had made my head their home. I walked toward Melinda in even, measured steps. She smiled like she didn't have a care in the world but by the feathers growing out of her ears, her transformation to a condor had already begun. She was about to make her escape. There was no way that was going to happen, not today!

As she flapped her dark wings and raised herself into the air, she held her eyes on mine. "Are you proud of yourself for the deaths you've caused? Are you happy now?"

"I won't be happy until I know you're rotting in hell!" I replied as she made her way higher into the sky. "And you're making that trip tonight!"

I bent my knees and extended my arms above my head. Flying from land was not an ability I'd worked on developing, until recently, anyway. With a scream that made even my blood curdle, I grabbed her talons. Her disgusting wrinkled skin in my hands made me want to gag and let go, but I held on as tight as I could, trying to push the feel of it out of my mind, and avoided looking down.

"Lily, can I help?" Leilani screamed from below. Though Leilani was a human child, Melinda had been her captor for some time. Arturo had been her first captor, but he never made her share her blood with hungry vampires like Melinda did. Leilani deserved her shot at Melinda just as much as I did.

"What is that useless child yelling about?" Melinda said. That's when I noticed her still-human head. The image made me queasy even though I had seen her this way once before. The only bird part she had from the neck up were the ridiculous feathers sticking out of her ears. "I should have done away with that useless little pest a long time ago!"

"Be my guest, Leilani," I yelled down to her. From this distance, she looked like a little animated doll, so precious and innocent. "Just aim high! Don't hit me!"

"Hit *you*? What are you—?"

Melinda's words were cut off as a fireball struck her on her left side, forcing her to deviate from her upward route.

"One more, Leilani!" I yelled down and prepared myself to jump.

"Ok, Mama!" Leilani yelled and held her arm in the air, her concentration focused on Melinda. Jose Luis stepped next to her and took her hand, trying to increase her power with his touch. This time, the fireball hit her in the head and her hair helped fuel the fire, igniting the rest of her feathered body. She tried to get away regardless, pumping her wings harder despite the fact that her right wing burned. She veered toward the left and neared the edge of the building. A few seconds more and we'd be over the street. I clenched my stomach muscles and pulled my legs up, kicking her in the face. She screamed and stopped flapping her wings as blood poured down her chin. I opened my hands and fell to the roof, landing in front of Christian who was quick enough to wrap me in his arms. Neither of us could take our eyes off Melinda as she burned and floated through the air, her ashes floating away on the wind, just like her sister's.

Beth still hugged Riley's body to her, rocking her back and forth and murmuring in her ear. Pierce kneeled next to her and rubbed her back. Riley had been her closest friend. She'd lost two friends in this battle.

Jose Luis grabbed his sister and wrapped her in his arms, squeezing her until she complained. "Ouch! I can't breathe."

"How in the world did you do that?" Jose Luis looked at Leilani in awe. "I thought you couldn't control it."

"I lied to them. I practiced when I was by myself."

"You are amazing." He ruffled her hair before wrapping her in his arms once again. This time, she didn't complain and squeezed him back.

Christian held me in his arms, kissing my neck lightly as he watched the two children celebrating the end of Melinda. Arturo's end was also to be celebrated since he had kept them apart for many years.

"Did you hear what she called me?" I whispered.

"Yup, I did," he whispered in my ear. "You are a wonderful mom."

"Thanks. I think I finally believe you."

Leilani ran over to us and wrapped her little arms around both of us. Jose Luis looked on for a moment, shrugged his shoulders, and came over to join in the group hug.

"It's all over," I said.

"It's all over," the other three answered. My stomach turned at the thought of what happened to Raul and Riley, but Christian squeezed us harder. He was right. The time to mourn would come soon enough. We deserved at least a moment to celebrate our victory, the end to the chaos Ian had caused in all our lives.

"Let's go home," Christian said and let us go, holding his hand out.

I put mine hand in his and smiled. "Let's go home."

❧ Epilogue ❧

Leilani stood at the kitchen table carefully placing her new notebooks and pencils into her backpack. Kalia took her empty cereal bowl and juice glass to the sink, stopping to greet me with a smile on her way.

"Good morning, Leilani," I said as I approached her. Her smile lit up her pretty face. "Where is your brother?"

"He started school on his computer before I went to sleep last night. He has been working on it all night," she replied, rolling her eyes. "I think he likes it."

"I guess so," I helped her put her arms through the straps of her backpack and then turned her to face me. Christian walked into the room, having gone up to check on Jose Luis as soon as we got back from feeding.

"I wish Alegría and Paco could come to my party," Leilani said with a sad smile.

"I know, me too. But that's a long trip just for one weekend. Since Aloysius bought them that apartment, they will be in the same building, and we can see them when we go to Lima for Christmas. Alegría could even sleep over if you want."

"I would like that," Leilani said as her smile reached her eyes.

"Did Lily give you lunch money? She seems to forget that humans need food sometimes," Christian said as he took the camera and aimed it at us. "Smile. Pretend you're happy to be starting school today," he teased.

"I am happy to start school. And, don't worry," Leilani smiled and straightened her skirt, wiping crumbs off with her hands. "I have everything I need for my first day of school in America, even my English."

Christian laughed. "Yes, your English is very good. I guess you're all set then. To the bus stop." He turned and walked out of the kitchen and toward the front door. Aaron walked out of his office as Leilani and I passed, Kalia following right behind us.

"Is our big girl ready to go to work?" Aaron teased and held his arms out. Leilani ran into them without hesitating. She wrapped her arms around his neck and giggled.

"I'm not going to work. I'm going to school, silly."

Christian snapped another picture. "Ok, let's get one of all of us at the front door," he said and turned toward the stairs. "Jose Luis, come on! She's leaving!" he called up the stairs. Within moments, Jose Luis, his hair a disheveled mess, ran down the stairs.

Christian arranged us on the front porch with Leilani in front, and then set the timer on the camera. "Ok, everybody. Stand still and smile," he instructed as he ran back to us and arranged himself next to me. The camera clicked a few seconds later.

"Can I go now?" Leilani asked.

"Are you sure you don't want us to go with you?" I asked and knelt down to kiss her cheek.

"I am sure. I can do this by myself," Leilani smiled and reassured us. "I just have to go down there by the mailbox."

"Ok. We will be right here until the bus leaves," I gave her another kiss and then took Christian's hand as Leilani started down the driveway.

A few steps later, she paused and turned. I let go of Christian and started down the stairs, hoping Leilani had changed her mind about us accompanying her.

"Don't forget about tonight," she said, and I froze. She was still determined to wait for the bus by herself. "You said you would take me flying if it's not raining."

"Don't worry. I won't forget," I assured her and watched as her face lit up. One of her favorite things to do since we had returned to Oregon was to fly over the city while snug in my arms. She loved the view from the air and tried to name the buildings in downtown Astoria as we flew over them. Since it was Friday, I promised her she could stay up late so we could go flying without anyone noticing us.

"If you don't mind," Jose Luis said. "I'm going to go back to school."

"No, you go right ahead," I said and ruffled his hair more than it already was. Since becoming a vampire, Jose Luis had made the choice not to attend a regular school but to instead finish his education in an online school. He seemed to be adapting to and enjoying his new life, easing my mind a bit about his becoming a vampire at such a young age.

We heard the squeaking brakes of the school bus and turned to look toward the end of the driveway. The bus doors opened, and then closed a moment later before rolling back down the road. With Leilani safely on her way to school, we turned and entered the house. As we entered the kitchen, the front door opened and closed.

"Good morning, everyone!" Luke called as he entered the kitchen with his hands full of shopping bags.

"Good morning," I said. "Coffee?"

"Sure, thanks," He placed the bags on the table and went to the cabinet to grab a mug. Then he turned to me. "You just sit. I'll get it."

"What's with the bags?" Kalia asked as she sat at the table with a cup of tea in her hands.

"It's stuff for the party. You know, decorations, balloons, candles... Oh, and her present. Do you have wrapping paper? That's the one thing I forgot," he said as he came to the table with his steaming mug.

Since settling in Oregon, Luke had become a most beloved uncle of the children.

"You do realize the party is tomorrow, right?" I asked. Leilani was turning ten. She wanted to spend her birthday with us at home, watching movies and eating popcorn, but Kalia had insisted on a proper party. Of course, she would still make movies and popcorn part of the celebration.

"Oh, I know. I just wanted to make sure we were ready. Did you order the cake?" he asked. He was busy looking through the contents of one of the bags.

"Of course, we did. We have it all under control," I assured him. "Aloysius and Fiore will be here tomorrow around noon. Beth and Pierce will be flying in with them."

Fiore, Aloysius, Beth, and Pierce had flown to New York the day after the funeral. Aloysius thought Beth, especially, could use the distraction. She had been depressed since we buried Riley and Raul in the small, private cemetery just outside the city, the same cemetery where Aaron's family was laid to rest over a century ago.

"Riley and Raul did so much for us.," Luke said as he heard my thoughts.

"They gave their lives for our family. None of us will ever forget that," Kalia said looking at Luke with concern in her eyes.

"Umm," Luke started and continued to keep his eyes on the contents of the bag.

"What is it?" I asked impatiently. He had been acting a bit secretive since moving out to his own apartment the week before. "What's going on?"

"Do you mind if I bring a guest to the party tomorrow?" He finally lifted his eyes and looked at me, trying hard to hide his impending smile.

"A guest, huh? Would this guest happen to be female?" I teased. Kalia, Aaron, and Christian all stared at Luke. He dropped his eyes back to the contents of the bag. "Ah ha! It is a female. Okay, spill."

"Well, it's nothing serious, yet," He continued digging in the bag, averting our eyes with discomfort at our curiosity. "Her name is Autumn."

"Is she a vampire?" Christian asked and patted him on the back.

"Of course, she is and she's a nurse," Luke answered pretending to be offended, but his smile deceived him. "She's anxious to meet all of you."

"That's my man," Christian said and patted his back before returning to his seat with a wide smile on his face.

Before anyone could question him further on this new development, Jose Luis walked into the room. "I know I said I wasn't hungry when you went to feed," he said looking at Christian and me. "I was too busy with school to stop, but..."

"What is it?" I asked.

"I am hungry. Can someone come with me?" he asked looking around the room.

Luke pushed his chair out and stood. "I could eat. I'll go with you."

Jose Luis smiled and followed Luke out of the room.

Aaron rose and excused himself to go back to his office. Kalia gathered the empty cups on the table and took them to the sink, humming to herself, and turning on the water to start washing them.

"I can help," I offered as I reached her side.

"No, I got it," she turned and smiled at me. That smile didn't reach her eyes. I knew she was still struggling with Maia's death, but I also knew she was hurt by Maia's deception.

"It will stop hurting, in time," I said and wrapped my arm around her shoulders. She leaned her head against mine.

"I know. I will be fine," she kissed my forehead and turned her attention back to the dishes. "Let me know when you're ready to go. We need to finish our shopping before Leilani gets home from school."

I nodded and left the room with Christian. When we reached our bedroom, I closed the door and headed toward my dresser to look for a better shirt. Christian walked up behind me and turned me to face him.

"What's wrong?" I asked as I looked up into his eyes, those eyes that still made butterflies dance in my stomach.

"Nothing at all is wrong. That's just it," he wrapped me in his arms, and I rested my face on his chest. "Since the day we met, it's been nothing but chaos. And now..."

"What? You miss the chaos?" I teased.

"Absolutely not! I love our life together. All the chaos was totally worth the end result."

"It really was, wasn't it?" I sighed against him.

"Completely. If it is at all possible, I am even more in love with you now than I was before. Does that make sense?" He stepped back a bit to look at my face.

"It makes total sense. I feel the same. I wonder if it has anything to do with us being parents now. Did you ever imagine that would happen for us?"

"Honestly, no. I accepted the fact that we couldn't have children together, but it happened, and I wouldn't trade it for anything in the world," he said and leaned his head toward mine. "I would marry you all over again."

"And I would—" My response was interrupted by his lips pressed against mine. I wrapped my hands around his neck and tangled my fingers in his hair. The fire in my body was fueled by his kiss as he picked me up in his arms and carried me toward our bed.

As he laid me gently against my pillow, his sparkling blue eyes looked into mine and into my soul. "Kalia won't mind waiting a bit to go shopping."

"What's the hurry when we have all the time in the world?" I asked as I pulled him down over me.

"That's right," he said and covered my lips with his again, his body a perfect fit against mine. "We have eternity together."

"Eternity," I sighed and pulled him to my lips again. An eternity full of love.

Acknowledgments

I would like to thank my husband, Neil, and my sons, Jason, Ryan, and Collin for their patience and understanding while I've been locked away in a room writing. I could not fulfill this dream without their support.

I would also like to thank my friends and family for listening to me rant about plots and characters, and for not getting angry with me when my mind wanders in the middle of a conversation.

Thanks also to Carla, Nadine, Chrissy, Kevin, and all my nieces and nephews for cheering me on.

Thank you, as always to my wonderful publisher and editor, Michelle Halket— and to her assistant, Beau—you are both a blessing.

A special thank you to the winner of the title contest, Patty Trala Nichols and to all who participated in the contest.

LM DeWalt is a Peruvian American who has been living in the US for 30 years. She works as a teacher of ESL, Spanish, French, and accent reduction and is also an interpreter and translator. She has written for several Spanish language newspapers but her passion was always to write novels. Her love of vampires, and all things paranormal, started when she was seven years old and saw Bela Lugosi's Dracula.

She currently resides in Northeastern Pennsylvania, where it's way too cold, with her husband, three teenage sons and two cats.

Printed in the United States
by Baker & Taylor Publisher Services

Printed in the United States
by Baker & Taylor Publisher Services